Under The Same Heaven

Under The
Same Heaven

MARJORIE BRADFORD

Black Belt Press
Montgomery

The Black Belt Press

P.O. Box 551

Montgomery, AL 36101

Printed in the United States of America

The Black Belt, defined by its dark, rich soil, stretches across central Alabama. It was the heart of the cotton belt. It was and is a place of great beauty, of extreme wealth and grinding poverty, of pain and joy. Here we take our stand, listening to the past, looking to the future.

To the memory of
DR. GEORGE T. BRADFORD
who made all my dreams come true

Under The Same Heaven

CHARACTERS

IN HAYLEY, GEORGIA

Price Townsend/County Pa .... Rich tyrant of the county, now dead

Laura Townsend .... His widow

Rudolph Townsend .... His elder son and heir

Carlton Townsend .... His younger son, a rascal

Elizabeth Cooper .... An outsider, from New York

Victoria Tanner (Tori) .... Her granddaughter, age eleven

Paul Tanner .... Tori's absent father

Jake Potter .... A poor farmer

Mabel Potter .... His wife

Jessie Potter .... Their daughter, Tori's friend

Bubba James .... Hayley's Chief of Police

Hedda James .... His wife

Dixie Lee James .... Their pretty daughter

Will Fable .... A hobo who came to Hayley

Ottis Washington .... A kind Negro man

Doreen Washington .... His wife

Mary Lee Brown .... Their daughter

Amos Brown .... Their son-in-law, serving time

Mary Bea Brown (Boozie) .... Their granddaughter, Tori's friend

Hurd Buford .... The funeral director

Young Mose .... Elusive Negro moonshiner

Daniel J. Smith .... A newcomer to Hayley

Brother Oliver Goodson .... The preacher

Moira Goodson .... His wife

Crawford Welch .... Owner of the General Store

Sam Gates .... Unscrupulous businessman

Viola Gates .... His wife

8

Marvin Gates .... Their son, age twelve
Veda Gates .... Their daughter, age nine
Reese Jones .... The bus driver
Cora Jane Oates .... The postmistress

IN ALBANY

Jock Morehouse .... Sheriff of Daugherty County
Jack Hamilton .... Golf pro at Radium Springs
Marie Hamilton .... His wife
Wendy Hamilton .... Their daughter, age eleven
Rebecca Rigsby .... Tori's schoolteacher
Woody Price .... A wealthy visitor
Judge Jacob G. Allen .... Old friend of County Pa
Billy Harper .... The barber

IN ATLANTA

Thomas Moore .... A brilliant lawyer
Baxter Brooks .... Federal prosecutor

IN NEW YORK

Forrest Neill .... A writer
Wes Yesterhouse .... Owner of a publishing house
Millie Rhodes .... Wes's secretary
Camilla Goodson .... Brother Goodson's daughter
John Price Daniel .... A Broadway actor

PROLOGUE

Price Townsend leaned his head into the small cockpit of the plane.

"Everything all right up here, son?" he asked as he surveyed the sky ahead, filled with Georgia sun.

"Yessir, Mr. Townsend," the young pilot replied with a smile. "We'll have you in Savannah in fifteen minutes or less."

"That's fine, son," said Price. "You just plan on meeting Mr. Richmond and myself back at the field about sundown." He reached for the roll of bills in his pocket, peeled off a few, and handed them to the young man. "Here, you go have yourself a little fun while you wait."

The pilot smiled as he took the bills. "Why, thank you, sir," he said. "But you don't have to do that. The state of Georgia's payin' me."

Price Townsend smiled wryly. "I *am* the state of Georgia, boy. I *am* the state of Georgia."

He ducked his head and straightened up to his full height of six two, and began to make his way back to his seat, next to his companion on the flight, state senator George Richmond.

"Say, Mr. Townsend," the young pilot yelled back. "How come you never ran for office? I sure would have voted for you."

Price looked at Richmond and arched his brows. "Boy's got a lot to learn, don't he, Rich?"

Richmond smiled and nodded.

Price turned his head back toward the cockpit and yelled, "Hell, son. I don't need to get elected. I've done been governor for three terms as it is."

The other men laughed, and Price did too, but his smile faded as he resumed his seat next to his friend. He didn't feel like laughing. It was so easy, so familiar to slip behind that veil of charm, even now.

"I still don't understand why you insisted on coming, Price," said

George Richmond. "I could have taken care of this."

Price did not look at him. He laid his head back, closed his eyes, and rubbed his temples. "Senator," he said pointedly, "you just concentrate on keepin' all your little ducks in a row. You let me worry about the important things."

"Bullshit," replied the senator. "You know I have only your best interests at heart."

"You are being paid very well to protect my interests, Rich."

Richmond contemplated the man beside him, the richest man in south Georgia, the most powerful man in the state, the great "County Pa."

"You've never had to pay for my friendship."

"Do I know that?" asked Price.

Richmond frowned. It was time to back off. He had long ago given up trying to fathom the mind of the man beside him. But even so, this turn of events was downright foolish. What was he planning? It wasn't like him to change his mind, or to question anything, especially himself.

The senator turned to his companion, who rested with his eyes still closed, although he was not sleeping.

"Price," he said, "what is wrong? Is there anything I can do?"

"No, Rich. Nobody can do anything. Except me. Maybe I can do something. Or maybe it's too late already."

"Too late for what?"

"Everything, you fool."

Suddenly the young pilot yelled out, "We got trouble! Something's wrong!"

Richmond jumped to his feet, just as the little plane lurched violently.

County Pa began to laugh.

1

The legend began the moment Price Townsend died. He was the richest man in south Georgia, powerful enough to control bankers and politicians, powerful enough to touch the life of every citizen of Dougherty County. He died as he had lived, colorfully, mysteriously, when the plane he chartered crashed seven hundred miles off course. A year had passed, but his presence was still felt in Dougherty County. The simple folk of the region feared him no less now than when he was alive, and for good reason. For now, it was said, the ghost of County Pa walked the Townsend game preserve by night.

During his lifetime, Price Townsend not only ran the county, he owned most of it; including the game preserve, a dense green forest a few miles from the Townsend plantation, in the little town of Hayley. Three miles of barbed wire guarded the boundaries of the preserve on each side of Southland Road, with No Trespassing signs posted every five hundred feet. Local residents took the signs seriously: trespassers were shot. Thirteen years ago, not a legal eyebrow was raised when County Pa shot and killed a poacher. In Hayley, County Pa interpreted the law as he wished.

It was rumored in Hayley that many such unfortunates who wandered innocently into the preserve never came out. Some doubted that the rumors were true, but Price Townsend never denied them. If anything, he encouraged the rumors, as a useful deterrent to keep people off his land. Inevitably, after his death, children believed that strangers who wandered onto the preserve met their deaths, horribly, at the hands of the ghost of County Pa.

Price Townsend's widow, Laura, and his two sons lived several miles away, north of Hayley on Albany Road. A long red-brick wall ran around the plantation, and beautiful horses could often be seen running free.

Carlton Townsend, the younger son, was an avid hunter, and frequently brought parties of his friends out to the game preserve. Carlton's reputation was scandalous, and no one doubted that he would deal with trespassers the same way his father did. No sane person ventured onto Townsend land.

Carlton was much like his father: reckless, flamboyant, selfish, and devious. But he lacked his father's cold heart and tenacious ambition— few people knew that part of the Townsend fortune had been secretly built on greed, graft, and cruelty. Carlton spent County Pa's money in an endless pursuit of fun, spawning an endless debt of trouble.

Carlton, with his wild ways, was nothing like his older brother, Rudolph, who preferred raising animals to hunting them. In truth, Rudolph could never bring himself to shoot a deer. His love of animals, music, and literature had evoked many cruel jibes from both his father and his younger brother over the years.

Rudolph never lived up to his father's expectations, but then, neither did Carlton. In different ways, both his sons disappointed him. But it was to the responsible Rudolph that County Pa passed the power and the purse strings, upon his death. Within months, Rudolph had risen to a position of respectability in the community that could not be bought with money; respectability that was never afforded to Price Townsend in his lifetime.

It was Rudolph's influence that kept Carlton out of trouble, but even so, the brothers fought constantly. It was not in Carlton's nature to honor his father's decision to leave Rudolph in control of the estate, and he resented his brother bitterly. Carlton's disappointment at his relatively small endowment had frozen what goodness he possessed, and he was determined to claim his father's power for himself.

Carlton had a plan. He knew things about his father that had always been hidden from his mother and brother. He knew, because he had discovered the real reason County Pa wanted no trespassers on the game preserve—the reason intruders were threatened with death, the reason he encouraged rumors of unlucky hobos who never returned. County Pa had had a secret, and he never knew that Carlton had uncovered it. And now that the secret was Carlton's, it would be the legend of the ghost of County Pa that would perpetuate fear in the minds of the people, and keep them away from the truth buried deep in the shadows of the game preserve. It was Carlton who frightened the children with stories, who encouraged the superstition among the Negroes, and who left drunken hunting pals alone in the darkness of the forest. It was Carlton who created the ghost of County Pa. In the beginning, the ghost was just a legend to the children of Hayley. It was the summer of 1938, and life was simple in rural Georgia, and ghosts and superstitions were part of the fun of growing up. The country was getting back on its feet, the Great Depression becoming an unpleasant memory. It was a time for forgetting, a time for growth and optimism. Like their children, the parents of south Georgia looked to the future with hope.

That summer, as for many summers past, Tori Tanner and Jessie Mae Potter were best friends. The difference in their backgrounds didn't matter to the eleven-year-olds, although many Hayley mothers would not have encouraged a child's friendship with Jessie, who was considered not much better than poor white trash.

Rudolph Townsend was very fond of Tori, the daughter of his boyhood friend, Paul Tanner, also a native of Hayley. Rudolph had done much to foster tolerance in the community of Tori's maternal grandmother, Mrs. Cooper from New York, when she moved to Hayley with her daughter and son-in-law. After Paul's wife died, and he left town looking for work, Rudolph's patronage of the elderly Mrs. Cooper said much for her position in the community, now that only she and her granddaughter remained.

Paul was ruined by the big city, folks said. Once he had seen the world, he was not content to return to his hometown. How a good Southern boy could end up playing baseball in New York City and marrying a northern heiress defied the imagination. At any rate, what Paul Tanner did, or what his motherless child was allowed to do, was less important now than it once had been.

IT WAS the last day of August when Tori and Jessie began the adventure that was to change forever the meaning of the legend of the ghost of County Pa. Perhaps if both of them had not lived on Southland Road, the events that would take place when summer came again would have been different. If they had never crossed paths with Carlton Townsend that day, perhaps the ghost of County Pa would have remained only a legend. But Tori Tanner was destined to learn County Pa's secret, and her fate would be bound to the ghost of County Pa forever.

It was a beautiful morning. It was still early, and the air was thin. By nine o'clock the sun would be high enough, and the air humid enough, to send yard dogs under the porches for shade. Tori and Jessie were on Southland Road, picking blackberries at their favorite patch, which was close to the edge of the forbidden game preserve.

Jessie believed that the ghost of County Pa inhabited the preserve, and she was nervous about being so close, even in the morning. Tori was much more sensible. It was daytime, after all. Still, neither had ever dared to trespass.

With their pails full, and their hands and clothes stained black with juice, the girls climbed to the road, when the quiet of the morning was broken by the roar of an automobile engine. Turning, the girls saw Carlton Townsend's little red Jaguar sports car racing toward them.

When Carlton saw the children, he slammed on the brakes and the car spun to a stop beside them. Frightened, Jessie cried out and jumped behind Tori. Tori yanked her arm.

"Stop it, you goose," she told Jessie. "He'll think you're scared."

"I *am* scared," said Jessie, coughing as the dust enveloped them.

Through the dust Carlton yelled, "Whatcha got there, girlies? Blackberries? How about givin' me some?"

Tori stared at Carlton. She was used to his taunts. As a Yankee in Georgia, Tori was no stranger to teasing or to prejudice.

Carlton laughed at the defiant child. "Tell you what," he said. "Y'all come on and get in my car and I'll give you both a ride. Would you like that?"

Jessie's eyes widened.

"I'll carry you all over the game preserve if you've got the nerve,"

Carlton continued. "Of course, you gotta watch out for the ghost of County Pa. He just loves to scare little girls like you."

It was too much for Jessie. She dropped her pail and scampered down the slope, straight through the blackberry bushes.

Carlton laughed heartily, and Tori stomped her foot in anger.

"You stop trying to scare us, Carlton Townsend! We're not on your crummy old land. You leave us alone or I'll tell Rudolph on you."

Carlton feigned dismay.

"Oooh! Tell big brother? Please don't do that."

But the mention of his brother quickly took the fun out of it for Carlton. "Go ahead and tell, little girl," he said. "Tell the great and mighty Rudolph whatever you want. There's nothing he can do about it. Just don't let me catch you or your little friend on my land."

He revved up the engine of the shiny car and screeched off, leaving a cloud of red dust in his wake to choke Tori. She watched as he turned onto the dirt trail leading off Southland Road into the game preserve.

Jessie, looking wounded, climbed back to her friend and stared after Carlton with a pout. She looked at Tori, who was staring intently at the entrance to the preserve.

"I wonder what he does in there?" Tori mused. "He goes in there alone all the time. Never stays that long, either."

"I don't care what he does," said Jessie. "That's one mean man, jus' like his Pa. You got no call to be wonderin' about him."

"He's mean, all right," Tori replied. "And bad, too. I'll just bet he's got a still hid back in those woods. I'll bet Rudolph doesn't know a thing about it, either."

"So what if he does?" said Jessie. "Let him have his old still. I don't care."

"I do," said Tori. "He'd never expect us to follow him. So that's just what I'm going to do. And you're going with me. Come on, it'll be fun!"

Tori took Jessie by the hand and began to pull her along.

"Fun?" wailed Jessie. "That's foolish talk." She jerked her hand away. "Let go of me. I'm not going anywhere."

"Okay, I'll go by myself," said Tori, who began to walk along the road. "Stay here," she called back as Jessie stared after her. "Be scared. Be a chicken. I don't care."

"What about the ghost?" Jessie protested.

"It's daytime, goose," said Tori. "He can't come out in the daytime."

"Don't leave me," yelled Jessie.

Tori stopped and waited for Jessie to catch up.

"Oh, come on, scaredy cat," she said. "We won't let him see us. Let's just see what he's up to. We won't get caught, I promise."

With great reluctance, Jessie followed Tori down the slope to the border of the preserve. They slipped through the rusty barbed-wire fence, and walked until they found the dirt road Carlton had taken. Staying under cover of the brush, they sneaked alongside the dirt road, moving carefully, silently, always listening for the sound of Carlton's car. About a mile down the road they ventured into the woods to peek over a high ridge. There they spotted the car, pulled over to the side of a clearing. In the clearing was an old, run-down cabin.

"Look," said Jessie, "there's his car."

"Shhhh! Get down."

The ridge was high above the cabin. They crouched down behind a thick clump of bushes and waited. Once they stopped moving, they became aware of a strange silence in the forest. The branches of the trees high overhead were thick and intertwined, and the sun broke through the canopy in dusty patches.

"It's spooky in here," whispered Jessie. "Where are all the birds and crickets and things?"

"Watching us probably."

"Tori, maybe we should get out of here. I'm scared."

Just then, the door of the cabin opened and Carlton emerged, carrying a rifle. He walked to the car and opened the trunk. Horrified at seeing the weapon in his hands, Jessie stood up and started inching back before Tori could stop her. Suddenly, there was a loud snap as a dry branch broke under Jessie's weight. Carlton jerked around, cocking the rifle. Tori grabbed Jessie and pulled her back down.

"Don't even breathe," whispered Tori.

Carlton searched the ridge quickly with his hard gaze, ready to shoot anything that moved. After a few moments, he lowered the rifle to his side, satisfied that what he had heard in the silent forest was only a squirrel or a possum. He threw the gun carelessly into the trunk of the car, closed the trunk, got into the Jaguar and screeched off down the dirt road.

When he was gone, Tori stood up and looked curiously at the cabin.

"If we don't get out of here," said Jessie, "I think I'm gonna die."

"He's gone," said Tori. "I told you he wouldn't catch us. That was close, though." She looked down at her friend, who was still crouching down behind the bushes. "Hey, are you just going to sit there, or are you coming with me? Come on, I want to see what's inside that cabin."

"You go on," said Jessie. "I'll wait here and be your lookout."

"Oh, all right. Be scared." What a chicken, she thought.

Tori descended the slope carefully until she stood in the clearing below. Jessie watched as Tori crossed the clearing and mounted the steps of the cabin. The door was held with only a wooden latch. There was no lock. Tori slid back the latch and opened the door.

When something suddenly touched her from behind, Tori screamed and jumped away, throwing her hand out defensively, and knocking Jessie to the floor.

"Jessie Potter!" yelled Tori. "You scared the life out of me. Don't you ever sneak up on me again, you hear?"

The necessity for whispering had, by this time, been forgotten.

"I'm sorry," whimpered Jessie. She got up, rubbing her bottom. "I got afraid to be up there on my own."

Tori turned back to the door and peered into the darkened room. She took a few steps inside and stopped, looking around.

"See anything?" asked Jessie.

"No," Tori answered, "it's okay. Come on."

The room was empty except for some old cartons along one wall. It was dusty and dark. The boards in the wooden floor were rotten, and creaked as the children walked across them. The windows were covered with dirt, letting little light in. Old yellowed papers and sticks of broken, rotting furniture littered the floor. It was a thoroughly deserted and unpleasant shack.

"There's nothing here," said Tori. "What in the world does he come here for?"

"It's awful," said Jessie. She sneezed. "There must be rats in here."

Tori walked through an archway into the next room and stopped, staring.

"What is it?" asked Jessie.

"Come and look," answered Tori.

Jessie came around the corner and gasped as she met the face on the wall. It was a faded portrait of County Pa. It was very old, thirty years or more, painted when Price Townsend was about Rudolph's age. Jessie's hands flew to her face and she covered her eyes in fright.

Tori pressed her lips together in practiced tolerance as she looked at her friend. She grabbed at Jessie's arm.

"It's only a picture, silly," she said.

"But it's him!" Jessie croaked.

"Oh, come on," said Tori. "You remind me of Boozie. You're worse than Boozie, and she's nine."

Jessie peeked through her fingers at the horrible image. She glanced at Tori, who didn't seem scared at all.

"There's another room in back," said Tori. "Maybe there's something in there."

The eyes of the dead man followed the girls as they went through another door into a kitchen. It was small, consisting only of a row of cabinets with a sink along one wall, and a pantry. The back door was opposite the sink, and another archway led beyond the kitchen to another room. Tori walked into the kitchen and opened the pantry door. It was empty.

Before they had time to explore farther, they heard the unmistakable roar of an automobile engine coming down the dirt road.

"He's coming back!" screamed Jessie.

There was no time to run. Frantically, the girls tried to pry the back door open. It was no use. The car pulled up into the clearing and stopped.

"Quick!" said Tori. "Into the pantry!"

She pulled Jessie into the moldy pantry, pushing her down on the rotting floor. Yanking the door shut, she sat down beside her terrified friend.

The front door swung open with a bang and Carlton walked in. Tori knew at once that he suspected nothing; he was happily humming his favorite tune, a tune that, Tori had been told, had naughty words. She grabbed Jessie and clapped her hand over Jessie's mouth.

Carlton heard nothing as he walked straight through the kitchen and into the little back room. From their hiding place, the girls heard the sound of a door opening, and the sound of his footsteps on a stair. They huddled together in the darkness afraid to move.

There was a period of silence, save for a few muffled sounds the girls could not make out. After many long minutes, Carlton's steps could be heard again. The door closed and he dragged something across the room. Tori held Jessie tighter as Carlton walked back through the kitchen and out into the front room. He never hesitated, and as he went out the door he began to sing, "I'm gonna get me a dolly tonight, and I'm gonna love her till the broad daylight."

"Don't listen," whispered Tori. "Put your hands over your ears."

"Why?"

"Just do it."

The door slammed shut, and the voice faded away. Soon the car started, and Carlton roared off down the road.

When the sound of the engine died away, the girls jumped up and raced out of the cabin. They ran headlong across the clearing and up the slope, stumbling and falling through the brush, all the way to the barbed-wire fence. They found their pails where they had left them on the other side of the fence. Grabbing up the heavy pails, they ran back to the road and headed back towards Hayley. They gave out when they reached the Potter place, a mile outside of town. Exhausted and panting for breath, they sank down in the grass behind Jessie's house.

When she could breathe again, Tori began to laugh. Now that they were safe the girls talked of their forbidden adventure with glee. Tori could not know the significance of the little cabin, or that they had stumbled upon County Pa's secret lair. It was not to be her last encounter with Carlton, or with the ghost of County Pa.

2

About an hour later, Tori left her friend to walk the mile to her grandmother's house. After Tori disappeared over the hill, Jessie sat lazily in the grass where Tori had left her, shaded by a tall stand of bamboo beside the little brook that ran behind her house. The breeze came in from the pond in the hollow, and Jessie stretched out in the cool grass, relieved to be safe and unscathed after yet another of Tori's "adventures."

Jessie felt suddenly alone, aware of a strange silence in the sunny yard. She looked at the familiar tattered walls of her small wood frame house with its dog-trot hall, and saw no sign of activity. She felt a little guilty for neglecting her morning chores. But why did she feel such dread, such foreboding, as she looked at the silent house?

Was it just that she remembered again the drought, and the corn crop drying up on the bleached-out stalks in the field? Or the silent desperation she had seen of late in her father's eyes, the fatigue in her mother's glances? The door of the kitchen stood open and waiting. With a strange urgency, Jessie left her bed of grass and went to the door. The kitchen was empty and silent. Her mother was not there.

Quickly, she crossed the dog-trot to the door of her mother's bedroom. Mabel Potter lay still upon her bed, in the middle of the morning. Jessie went to her, reached out and touched her arm, calling her name softly.

Jessie jerked back her hand in fear when she felt her mother's skin. It was moist and very hot. Jessie knew her mother was sick, sick with a high fever, a killing fever.

"Mama!" she called again. "Mama, wake up!"

Mabel did not stir. She lay limp and damp upon the bed. Jessie took her hand and tugged at it to no avail. Dropping her mother's hand, Jessie backed away from the bed. She had to find her father.

"What's wrong, Jake?" asked Mrs. Cooper.

"Miz Cooper," said Jake Potter, "you have t' come, right away. It's Mabel, Ma'am, she's bad sick, burnin' with fever. I didn't know what t' do. All I could think was t' get you."

Mrs. Cooper took his rough hand.

"Don't worry, Jake," she said firmly. "She'll be all right. I'll come right now. Just let me call Tori."

She went to the kitchen and opened the screen door.

"Victoria! Come in. Quickly."

Tori dropped her ball. She could tell by the tone of her grandmother's voice that something was wrong. Bounding up the stairs, Tori opened the screen door to the back porch and ran into the kitchen.

"Meema?"

"In here, dear."

In the front room, Tori found her grandmother standing with Jake Potter. He held his hat in his hands, and there was a strange look on his face.

"Hey, Jake," said Tori hesitantly.

"Tori," said Mrs. Cooper, "run and get me my brown bag. In my closet."

"Is something wrong?" asked Tori.

"Mrs. Potter is sick, Tori. Hurry, now."

Without a word, Tori hurried off to get her grandmother's "medicine bag." Carefully, she carried it back to the front room and handed it to Jake. He took the bag and absently put his arm around Tori's shoulder. Tori had never known Jake to tremble before, and she felt a sudden catch in her chest.

"Don't worry, Jake," said Tori. "Meema will know what to do."

Jake looked down at Tori as if he only now saw her. He smiled. "I know," he said. "Your grandmama always knows what t' do."

From the door of the front porch, Tori watched as her grandmother's old LaSalle disappeared over the hill. She let the screen door fall shut and walked into the house. Sitting on the floor before the window, she clasped her knees, closed her eyes, and rocked herself.

Tori reached into the pocket of her skirt and withdrew a ragged envelope. She stared at the letter. It was from her father, Paul Tanner. Drawing out the folded paper inside, she read again the words she had underlined: "I expect to come for you very soon now."

The letter was dated June tenth, more than two months ago. Tori had not seen her father since May. He came less often now that he was married again, but this was the longest time he had ever been away. He had settled down from his work as a traveling salesman and established a business in his bride's hometown in Alabama.

A strange fate had brought Paul, a war hero whose athletic prowess landed him the job as star pitcher for the New York Yankees, together with Tori's mother, Mary Catherine Cooper, a New York debutante from an old, aristocratic family. When Tori was born in 1927, she was born into a life of privilege and refinement, of social position and power. But the Great Depression had changed everything. When the stock market crashed, so did the fortunes of the Coopers. But Tori lost more than a heritage she would never know. Before her fourth birthday she lost both her mother and grandfather Cooper.

Paul had gathered Tori and moved back to Hayley, his hometown. Tori's grandmother, Elizabeth Cooper, came along to look after Tori, intending to stay only a few months. But she found the change comforting and the climate pleasant, and decided to stay. There was nothing left for her in New York but memories of a way of life that was gone forever.

Tori was left in her grandmother's care, and Paul took to the road, earning a meager living as a traveling salesman, the only job he could find. Paul was dedicated and industrious, but few people had money to spend, and he was away for weeks at a time, visiting home as often as he could.

Mrs. Cooper had endured a great deal of tragedy, but somehow she managed to find within herself the strength and the faith to hold the family together. To help make ends meet, she began a small baking business, and also gave music lessons to the children of Hayley and Albany who could afford them. Little Tori was her greatest comfort during those first bitter months.

"Are we poor, Meema?" Tori would ask.

"No, dear," Mrs. Cooper would answer. "I would say we were comfortable."

"Comfortable poor?" Tori persisted.

Mrs. Cooper would smile and say, "Comfortable, honey. I'll never be poor as long as I have you."

With his absence from the community, and his fall from fame, Paul Tanner's star faded quickly in Hayley, leaving Tori and Mrs. Cooper to contend as outsiders in the community. It was Paul's childhood friend, Rudolph Townsend, who saw to it that they were given some measure of respect. For Rudolph attracted success to anyone he smiled upon, and he smiled on Tori and Mrs. Cooper.

What people said on the street and what they said in the privacy of their homes were two different things, unfortunately, and not even Rudolph's influence could bribe the tongues of the town children. It was the children who were bold enough to say the words in public that their parents said only in private, and they said them to Tori.

Tori folded the letter carefully and put it back into her pocket. She looked out the window in the direction her grandmother's car had gone, then went to her bedroom closet and pulled out the box that held her mother's scrapbooks and photographs. Sitting on the floor, she opened one of the albums and stared at the first photograph.

It was a picture of her mother on the day of her first piano recital. Mary Catherine was only sixteen years old then. She wore a beautiful white dress with a lace bodice, and a string of pearls. Her long brown hair was swept up in front, and fell in long ringlets below her shoulders. Tori reached up and absently fingered her own short, curly brown hair. She sighed as she replaced the album, then drew her mother's autograph book from the box. It was her favorite. The first few pages recorded the good wishes of guests at Mary Catherine's eleventh birthday party. As she turned the pages, Tori saw her mother growing up through the entries in the book. The last entries were on the occasion of her bridal shower.

Tori closed the book and replaced it in the box. As always, when she was troubled, Mary Catherine's treasures had comforted her, and she decided that someday she would again be rich. As the afternoon sun shone on, Tori lay on her bed daydreaming. She dreamed of growing up as her mother had, wearing beautiful clothes and going to elegant parties. It was not long before her daydreams led to a restless sleep.

JAKE POTTER walked hurriedly along the sidewalk of Hayley's town square to the General Store. He paused at the entrance of the store, then thrust the door open and headed toward the back counter, where the owner, Crawford Welch, was dusting his shelves.

He walked around the pot-bellied stove at the center of the store, the semicircle of empty chairs, and the three local men playing cards at a table. Snatches of conversation, a mixture of business and gossip, could be heard over the low drone of a paddle fan stirring the air above them. The men looked up when Jake walked in, but, seeing who it was, returned to their cards and their conversation without a word.

Most of the townspeople were not openly unkind to the Potters, they were just indifferent. It was an accepted fact: one had to tolerate Negroes and white trash, as long as they knew their place. In many ways the white trash, with their stubborn pride, presented more of a problem than the Negroes. Humble Negroes had their place, and were allowed to work in affluent homes. Nothing was expected of Negroes, but the white trash were somehow an embarrassment. Most folks felt they should try to make something of themselves.

Prejudice was not called by a name, it was simply a part of life, a natural and continuing attribute of personality that was not seen as wrong or sinful. The people of Hayley, Georgia, were good people, law-abiding, churchgoing, taxpaying citizens; evil is most complete when a man is unable to recognize it in himself. Prejudice is born of history, nurtured in adversity, and strengthened by human nature. Few escape its grasp completely.

To the men he passed, Jake Potter was a faceless nobody. For some reason, Jake was, today, more aware of his treatment than usual, and his head throbbed. He felt defeated, weary of life. If Mabel did not recover, he did not think he could face his grief, but he knew he had to think of

Jessie. He hesitated a moment longer before he summoned his courage and walked over to the counter.

"Afternoon, Potter," said Crawford Welch. "Come to put something down on your account?"

"No, sir, Mr. Welch," said Jake. "I hope to put somethin' down on it in 'bout a week."

It was a lie. Jake had exhausted every possible avenue. The crop had failed. No one needed painting, or carpentry, or firewood. He didn't know what he was going to do.

"Well, Potter," replied the storekeeper in a low voice, "I'm going to have to see quite a drop in your account before I can advance you any more credit. You know that, don't you?"

"Yessir, I r'member how you set that down for me, and I'll try my best t' pay you next week." He swallowed hard. "I came in t'day cause my wife is sick. It's bad, Mr. Welch. Miz Cooper said she'd rest easier if she had some of this."

He gave Welch the paper from Mrs. Cooper.

"Well, I'm sorry to hear that, Potter," said Mr. Welch. He turned to get the medicine from a shelf behind him. "What's ailing her?"

"Miz Cooper said she got bit by a spider," said Jake. "Poison's done give her a high fever."

"I see," said Mr. Welch. "Well, you're going to have a sick little woman on your hands for a few days, that's for sure. But this should fix her up." He put the bottle on the counter. "That'll be fifty cents."

"I can't pay you now," said Jake, "but I can drop off a load of firewood for the winter t'morrow. It's early, I know, but that's green wood, Mr. Welch, it needs a month or two t' dry out."

Welch sighed and took back the bottle. The temperature that day was in the nineties.

"Look over there, Potter," he said.

Jake didn't have to look. He knew firewood from last year was stacked to the ceiling.

"For your house, then? I could drop it by your house." His eyes pleaded with Mr. Welch. His voice was almost a whisper when he said,

"I hate t' ask you again, sir, but Mabel needs that medicine. Please."

Mr. Welch set his jaw, sighed, and looked away. He hesitated, then handed Jake the brown bottle.

"Okay, Potter," he said. "Bring it by the house tomorrow. I don't know where I'm going to put it, but I'll find a place somewhere."

Jake hung his head.

"Go on, go on," said Welch. "Get your woman well. Go on home, Potter, and I'll see you tomorrow."

"Thank you," Jake mumbled again as he turned and walked away. He heard Mr. Welch's soft mutter, "God, I'll never make any money in this town."

Beads of sweat clung to Jake's brow as he walked out into the sunshine. Drained and disoriented suddenly, he paused for a moment on the porch. The white sunlight was piercing, blinding; the heat seemed to sap the life from him. The street was a river flowing all around him. He felt himself begin to fall and he reached out and caught the railing of the porch. His heart pounding, he gasped for breath until the dizziness stopped.

When his legs could move again, he walked across the square to the train depot, went into the ticket office and sat down to rest. He was tired and hungry. The clerk looked up from behind his newspaper, grunted, and continued reading. He disapproved of Jake Potter coming to the depot twice a month, bothering the travelers, hawking the little wooden figures he carved.

A combination of fear, anger, and despair was building inside Jake, a dizzying hopelessness. The last of the supplies were gone. He could not bring himself to ask Mr. Welch for food as well as medicine. For two days he had not eaten, giving what was left to Mabel and Jessie. He would have to go to Mrs. Cooper—again. But he couldn't face her today. An overwhelming anxiety preyed on him like a huge devouring beast. Fatigue swept over him and he fell asleep.

About thirty minutes later, the four-forty from Montgomery chugged in, steam gushing and whistle blowing as it rumbled heavily to a stop. The noise startled Jake out of his sleep, and for a moment he did not know where he was. The whistle blew again and Jake sat up straight. He watched as passengers stepped down from the coach car, to stretch their legs while the locomotive took on water.

A well-dressed woman about Jake's age walked into the ticket office, to inquire about sending a telegram. With her was a small boy, dressed in short blue pants and a yellow shirt with a lace collar. His mother held him firmly by the hand. Jake stared at the boy, so clean and well-fed and beautiful he was. The little boy saw Jake staring at him, turned to his mother, and pulled at her skirt.

"Mommy, Mommy," he said, "that man is looking at me, Mommy."

The young woman turned and looked at Jake. A look of contempt came across her face. She pulled the child toward the door, jerking his arm. "You stay away from people like that," she said, "do you hear me? They're trash."

Deep in Jake Potter's tortured mind something snapped. Suddenly his mind was empty of sorrow, empty of everything except rage. His whole countenance changed; his face took on a look of confidence, his posture stiffened, his eyes went cold. In that moment, he knew what he had to do. He left the depot and headed home with the medicine for Mabel. On the sidewalk, he bumped the shoulder of Brad Crow, the barber. Mr. Crow turned and looked sharply at Jake. He was accustomed to having men such as Jake step aside for him on the street.

"Watch your step, boy," he protested.

Jake Potter kept walking.

3

The next day was the first day of September, the first day of school. Summer was over, but today Tori almost didn't mind going back to school in Albany. She would have so much fun tonight . . . at the ball.

On her way to catch the school bus that morning, Tori saw Mr. Buford heading her way. It was early for him to be about, and Tori wondered if somebody had died. Hurd Buford was the owner of the funeral parlor. Tori tried not to smile as she approached the dour man. She wondered if all morticians looked as funny as he did. He was tall and gaunt, and always wore black. He had a long thin nose, a straight thin mouth, and he never smiled. His eyes were sunken and had a faraway look about them. Children sometimes followed where he could not see then, imitating his stiff gait. He walked like he was measuring steps, marking off yards. His arms dangled.

"Hey, Mr. Buford," said Tori, her eyes on his black shoes.

"Miss Victoria," he mumbled absently.

Tori crinkled up her nose. Mr. Buford smelled of formaldehyde, even when he had no customers. If the wind was right, you could always smell him coming. The funeral parlor was near the depot, across from the warehouses. Mr. Buford's appearance, and the fact that he prepared corpses for burial, encouraged sinister tales of ghosts and ghouls among the children, who always gave him a wide berth. Tori was the only child in town bold enough to speak to him.

Tori saw the yellow school bus parked and humming next to the General Store. She quickened her pace, for she was anxious to ask Jessie about her mother. Many of the children were already on the bus, but not Marvin Gates. Marvin was a pest and a bully, the stocky son of Sam Gates, the greediest man in town. The bus driver, Reese Jones, was busy tallying heads. Marvin was tormenting Jessie as she tried to board the

31

bus. Tori fumed as she saw Marvin pull Jessie's braids, then kick dirt on her. Although she was late, Tori scurried into the General Store, ran to the back and put a nickel on the counter.

"One orange Nehi, please," she said to Crawford Welch.

"It's mighty early in the morning for a soft drink, isn't it, Victoria?"

"No, sir. I'm mighty thirsty this morning."

Tori took the bottle he handed her and rushed back to the bus, just in time. Reese Jones was closing the door.

"You're late, Miss Tanner," said Reese. "You almost got yourself left. Not a good way to start the new year, is it?"

"No, sir," said Tori, spotting Marvin's place on the bus as she entered. "I'm sorry."

Jessie waved to her, motioning that she had saved her a seat. Marvin was on the aisle, two rows in front of Jessie. It was perfect. She made her way back to Jessie. As she neared Marvin's seat, he stuck out his foot in the aisle to trip her, just as she knew he would. Tori smiled as she fell, and the Nehi tumbled right into Marvin's lap, soaking his white shirt a ghastly orange.

The children giggled as Marvin jumped up, sputtering, "Mr. Jones! Look what that Yankee trash did to me, Mr. Jones! Stop the bus, I have to go home!"

Tori was on her feet and flashing.

"You owe me five cents, Marvin Gates," she said angrily. "You *made* me spill my drink. You tripped me. I'm going to tell your mother on you!"

"You leave me alone, you Yankee, or I'll pop you one," said Marvin, now close to tears, anticipating his mother Viola's wrath at ruining his new clothes.

"I'll have no name-calling or fighting on my bus," said Reese Jones as he brought the bus to a halt. "Marvin, things like this wouldn't happen if you kept your hands and feet to yourself. Now go on home and change your clothes. This better not happen again or I'll speak to your mother myself. Do I make myself clear?"

Marvin ran from the bus, fooled again by Tori. He was too big to confront openly any more. The Lord had not seen fit to complement Marvin's size with a quick mind, so Tori found it easy to outwit him. Tori sat down next to Jessie and the bus rumbled slowly down the road.

"Did you hurt yourself?" asked Jessie.

"Of course not."

"Terrible waste of a good Nehi," said Jessie, smiling.

"You think so?" Tori pulled the sandwiches out of the bag. "Here, Meema sent your breakfast."

Jessie took the sandwich gratefully and removed it from its wax paper. "Thanks."

"How's your mama?"

Jessie stared at the sandwich. "I never seen her so sick. I'm scared, Tori."

"Don't worry," said Tori. "Meema said she'd be all right, remember?"

At the corner of the town square, the bus turned onto Albany Road. As Reese Jones passed the depot, he waved to a solitary figure standing solidly on the sidewalk. It was Police Chief Bubba James.

Bubba was the only police officer in Hayley, but he was enough. He thought a lot of himself, and so did everyone else. He had been appointed police chief twelve years earlier, and he was the perfect choice. Nobody argued with him. Even mongrel dogs scattered when he approached.

Bubba tipped his hat to Reese Jones as the yellow bus rumbled past. The children stared at him, and, without further encouragement, settled down for the ride to Townsend Elementary and Junior High School in Albany. The expected detours, starts and stops to pick up all the rural schoolchildren, lengthened the ten-mile ride to over an hour.

About halfway to Albany, the bus stopped at a country club development called Radium Springs to pick up Wendy Hamilton. The icy water of the natural springs there had long been an attraction for bathers during hot Georgia summers. The country club and golf course around the springs was another innovation of County Pa. Built in the twenties, the ballroom and restaurant of Radium Springs Country Club was still the smart place to go for those in Albany whose fortunes had not been wiped out during the lean years of the Depression.

Wendy was the daughter of the golf pro, Jack Hamilton, and lived in a small housing area on the grounds for club employees. She was Tori's age, and painfully shy. She was not an unattractive child with her blonde hair, green eyes, and delicate features, but she was quiet in the extreme. Studious and thoughtful, Wendy was easily pushed around by more outgoing children. She attracted the eyes of the older boys, however, who knew instinctively that she was soon to blossom into a beauty. The only thing about Wendy that was not quiet was her clothes. She wore surprisingly bright colors and flirty styles usually reserved for older girls.

Wendy waved to Tori and Jessie as she boarded the bus, and took the seat two rows in front of them, which had been vacated by Marvin. Tori had befriended Wendy, and protected her from the other children's taunting.

At last the bus arrived. The low red-brick school building was new and modern, forming an L-shape, with the elementary school in one wing and the junior high school in the other.

The first day of school came and went uneventfully. Marvin never showed up. Tori, Jessie, Wendy, Marvin, Chester Welch, and Hurd Buford's son, Horace, all had a teacher named Rebecca Rigsby for the fifth grade. Miss Rigsby was a no-nonsense spinster of thirty-five, who had an odd habit of applying Jergens lotion to her soft hands whenever she was not using them. If things went as they had in years past, Tori Tanner would be her best student. But Tori was not thinking of Miss Rigsby, or of her homework, or of the summer that was lost. She was thinking of the ball . . . .

WHEN THE bell rang at the end of the school day, the children raced eagerly for the bus. In thirty minutes, the bus reached Radium Springs. Tori got up with Wendy, and gave a note to Reese Jones from Mrs. Cooper, allowing her to be let off with Wendy to spend the night. Tori was excited about her visit with Wendy, for there was to be a Labor Day dance at the country club that night, and Wendy had plans for them to slip out and watch.

Jessie's happy smile of goodbye faded as she watched her friends walk up the fancy driveway of the country club. The grounds were beautifully landscaped, and tall sculptured hedges bordered the driveway. Jessie looked down at her faded cotton dress, so clean and carefully pressed by her mother's loving hand. It seemed sometimes that her young life was so hard, and tears welled up in her eyes as she rode away from the beautiful grounds of the country club.

It was after four o'clock when Jessie walked to the top of the hill on Southland Road and saw her small wood-frame house. The chair on the front porch was empty, and Jessie felt a tug at her heart. Even in winter, her mother sat in that chair on the porch each day, waiting for her to come home from school. But not today. The house was quiet and still; no one was about. Where was Pa? Jessie sensed something new, something ominous, something more than her mother's illness, and her heart began to race. She broke into a run.

Jessie bounded up the steps of the porch and walked through the dog-run to her mother's bedroom door. It was closed, which was unusual in the summer heat. She opened the door and walked into the room. Mabel Potter's face was flushed and damp as she lay sleeping beneath a quilt. It was hot and humid in the room despite the opened windows, but her mother trembled in her sleep, as if she were cold. Jessie was frightened, for she had hoped to find her mother better.

She ran through the house and looked out back, but there was no sign of Jake. Why isn't he here, she wondered as she went back to her mother's bed. She reached out her hand and shyly touched her mother's shoulder.

"Mama?" she said softly. "Mama, I'm home."

Mabel Potter opened her eyes. Seeing the concern in her daughter's eyes she smiled weakly and said, "Jessie, honey, are you home already? Goodness, I must be getting up." She stirred before Jessie could stop her, wincing in pain as she swallowed, for the spider's venom had caused her throat to swell nearly to closing.

"No, Mama, no," protested Jessie. "You must stay in bed and rest. Miz Cooper said so. Don't worry about supper, Pa and I will get it."

She pressed her mother back down on the bed with little effort, and felt the fever that was still raging through her body.

"Yes," said her mother, "I should rest."

Jessie glanced at the table next to the bed and saw a note. Jessie reached for the note and read, in her father's small jagged handwriting, "Jessie, give Mama one teaspoon of the medicine when you get home. I have a job in Albany. Take care of Mama for me. I mite be late. Be home soon as I can. Pa."

There was a glass and a pitcher of water, a spoon, and the bottle of medicine he had brought home the day before. She reached over and poured a little water in the glass.

"Here, Mama," she said. "It's time for your medicine."

She poured out a teaspoon of the brown liquid and offered it to her mother. She saw that it was hard for Mabel to swallow it, and quickly offered her the water. The water went down no easier, but her mother seemed grateful for it.

Suddenly calm now with purpose, Jessie said, "Now you go back to sleep, Mama. I will get the chores done. You have to rest so you can feel better. Maybe you can get up later, but now you have to rest."

"All right, honey," said Mabel. Almost immediately, she fell back to sleep.

Jessie went out of the room, leaving the door open. She walked to the back porch and sat down on the top step. The chickens ran to greet her, but she knew they were out of feed. There would be few eggs to gather. She sighed and walked to the shed. At least she could turn out the mule and water the cow. There was no hay either. A little later, Jessie went to the kitchen. She gathered up a few dirty dishes and put them in the sink. Grabbing the broom, she swept the floor before she went to the cupboard to find something to eat. She did not know it, but the cupboard was empty.

She was still tidying up when she heard the familiar rattle of Mrs. Cooper's old LaSalle. Suddenly, all her brave resolve vanished, and tears flooded her eyes as she ran to the porch and saw Elizabeth Cooper getting out of the car. She wiped away her tears, and ran to meet her.

"Hello, dear," said Mrs. Cooper, handing Jessie a paper bag. "Here, carry this for me. How is your mother today?" She took a steaming pot from the seat and smiled at Jessie.

"Oh, Miz Cooper," said Jessie, "I'm so glad you came. Mama seems worse than before. Pa's not here, and I'm afraid for Mama. She's so sick."

"Now, don't you worry, child," said Mrs. Cooper. "Let's put this up, then we'll go in and see her."

MARIE HAMILTON, Wendy's mother, was the social director of the country club. When Wendy and Tori arrived at the cottage behind the club where the Hamiltons lived, she had barely a word of welcome for them before she dashed off to see to last-minute preparations for the dance.

"She doesn't mean to let things get so messy," said Wendy, as the girls plopped down on Wendy's bed. "She's always busy with the club. She's the party director you know. Anyway, Hattie comes tomorrow, and she takes care of everything."

"I guess your mom has a big job getting everything ready for such a big party," said Tori.

"Oh, yes," said Wendy. "It seems like she has to do everything herself. She says you can't depend on the niggers to do anything right the first time. You have to be on them every minute."

A slight frown appeared on Tori's face. "Mary Lee works at the club, doesn't she?"

"Who?"

"Mary Lee Brown. I know Mary Lee. I don't believe your mother would talk like that about her."

"Oh, yes, Mary Lee. I do know her. She cleans up sometimes. Now, I *do* like her. She's nice."

"She's Boozie's mama," said Tori.

"Boozie?"

"Boozie. She's nine. We play together sometimes, and I don't care if she's colored or not."

"Really?" said Wendy. Her eyes widened. "My Mommy would

never let me play with a nigger girl."

"Why not?" asked Tori.

"I don't know," answered Wendy. "You just don't do that. They're not like us."

"Well, I do it," said Tori. "Meema never told me not to."

"That's because she's a Yankee," said Wendy. "Yankees do that, Mommy says. But we don't do it around here. People will call you a nigger-lover." A silent moment passed, and she looked up and met Tori's furious eyes. "What's the matter?" she asked apprehensively.

"Don't you call my grandmother a Yankee," fumed Tori, "and don't you call me a nigger-lover, either!"

"But I didn't."

"You did, too. That's a name, a wicked name. I'll play with whoever I want to."

"I'm sorry," said Wendy. "Don't be mad at me. It's just that if Mommy found out—"

"What? She'd call me names?" asked Tori. "But, Wendy, that's stupid! She'll have to call you the same thing."

"But I don't play with—"

"What about Hattie? Do you call her a nigger, too?"

Wendy was surprised by Tori's outburst. She had never really thought about it.

"I would never call Hattie such a thing," she answered. "I love Hattie. She has been working for us as long as I can remember. She's . . . my friend."

Tori looked at Wendy and said nothing. She arched her brows.

"So what?" asked Wendy.

"So, if I'm a nigger-lover, so are you. You said you love Hattie, didn't you?"

"But, it's not the same."

"It is! Tell me how it's different."

Wendy was at a loss to explain. "I can't," she said at last. "I don't understand, but I know I wouldn't hurt Hattie for the world."

"All right, then," said Tori.

"Why do people say things like that if they're not true?"

"Some people will say anything," answered Tori. "Especially people like Marvin Gates. He loves to hurt people's feelings."

"I heard him call you a Yankee, and a nigger-lover, too," said Wendy, "and I didn't like it one bit."

"Marvin is a loud-mouthed bully," said Tori. "Nobody cares what he says anyway. He's mean to everybody."

"Why?"

"He's just like his daddy, only dumber," said Tori. "His daddy has gotten rich lending money to people who couldn't pay him back. He takes their land. Meema says he preys on people like a hawk preys on chickens. He's been trying to run Jessie's father off his land for years."

The conversation between the two girls continued as darkness began to fall. Soon, the sound of music could be heard coming from the clubhouse. Wendy told Tori of a secret place she knew where they could hide and watch the dance. It was a small landing on the second floor, above the ballroom. It had a separate entrance, and led to a wing on the second floor which had been closed off to visitors. The spiral staircase at one end of the ballroom which led to the landing above had been barred by a gold chain. The rail of the staircase was hung with gay paper streamers and ropes of greenery. It would be a perfect place for the girls to watch the festivities without being seen.

4

Tori and Wendy quickly ate the sandwiches Mrs. Hamilton had left for them, and slipped out of the house. It was dark now, and they made their way across the golf course to the gardens surrounding the icy springs. They crossed the lovely white wooden bridge which spanned the springs and followed the bridle path through the woods. Tall pecan, oak, and dogwood trees stretched green limbs out to each other, forming a leafy archway above their heads. Long gray chains of Spanish moss hung like accusing fingers from the limbs of the trees as they walked silently through the woods. The path led to the back of the clubhouse, which was surrounded by a fence of rough-hewn timbers, the ends stacked at diagonal angles, one upon another.

The clubhouse was full of light and music, and they could see the lights of cars arriving in front of the building. The hum of conversation and laughter beckoned them, and the children crept closer. At last they came to the stairs which led to the second floor landing.

Tori had never been inside the clubhouse, and was too excited to worry about being caught. So far they had been lucky; no one had seen them.

They climbed the wooden stairs silently, and entered a dark hallway. At the end of the hall was a landing, where a single lamp atop a round ornate pedestal table gave the area a soft light. The spiral staircase was at the end of the landing. Opposite the table, the staircase rose to the third floor. The sound of the party was intoxicating, and Tori raced for the staircase.

"Wait a minute," whispered Wendy.

"What?"

"We have to stay out of sight and we have to be quiet."

"I know that," said Tori. "Come on."

Cautiously, the girls descended the stairs, with their heads tucked low. At the level of the sixth or seventh step down, the stair curved sufficiently to allow them to see the ballroom below. Wendy pulled Tori down and they crouched together on the wide stair, now able to peek between the streamers.

Tori gasped at the beauty of the scene below her. The ballroom was huge, the ceiling twenty feet high. The floor was made of shining squares of black and white marble. Three huge crystal chandeliers hung from the ornate ceiling, dimly lit so that they barely glowed with warm yellow light. The soft lighting of the room was enhanced by pink candles that sat on tables along the walls covered with fresh flower arrangements. Above the tables, alcoves were hollowed out of the walls, and in each alcove stood a marble statue of a beautiful maiden.

There was a huge fireplace on the wall opposite the girls. Above the fireplace was a large oil painting of a man sitting in a brown leather chair before a fireplace that blazed with light. The man was dressed in hunting clothes, and beside him on the floor were three hounds, sitting or lying at his feet. A well-stocked gun case was behind the man's chair, and on the wall above were the trophy heads of a wild boar and a twelve-point buck. The man in the portrait must have been very tall. His eyes were cool and penetrating, his strong square jaw set with authority. The sleeves of his shirt were rolled up to reveal well-muscled arms.

No stranger seeing the portrait for the first time would have guessed that County Pa had been sixty years old at the time the portrait was painted. The painting was huge, the frame heavy and ornate, but the casual nature of the portrait made it seem a bit out of place in that elegant room. Nevertheless, Price Townsend himself had ordered it placed here, and no one dared to move it.

Tori noticed the painting almost immediately. "Look," she said to Wendy. "It's County Pa."

"I know," said Wendy. She shivered. "I can't look at him when I come in here by myself. He's too scary. The maids are afraid to come in here to clean. They say the ghost of County Pa still walks these halls."

Just then, Tori caught sight of Rudolph Townsend. He looked very handsome in his tuxedo, and on his arm was Dixie Lee James. She was easily the loveliest girl in the room in her green silk strapless gown.

"There's Rudolph," said Tori.

"Where?"

"Over there in the corner." said Tori, pointing, "next to the girl in the green dress."

"Oh, that's Dixie Lee James," said Wendy. "They're engaged, I think."

"Not yet they're not," snapped Tori. "Rudolph will never marry her."

"Why not?" asked Wendy. "She's beautiful. I met her one day with Mommy and she was very nice to me."

"She fooled you then," said Tori, "just like she's fooling Rudolph. She's a big phoney. She was supposed to be taking singing lessons from Meema, but she never practiced. She only wanted to see Rudolph when he was at our house. She trapped him like a rabbit in a cage."

"You really think so?" asked Wendy. "I thought she was nice."

"She is nice when she wants something," said Tori. "You wait and see, Rudolph will never marry her."

Dixie Lee James was indeed the prettiest girl in the county, now that her only rival, Camilla Goodson, lived in New York City. Dixie Lee was a shapely size eight, and her fair skin was flawless. Even her feet were pretty. She had big blue eyes and long, light brown hair the color of warm honey. Dixie Lee was held in high regard by all the county's eligible bachelors, but few had the courage to call on her. Her father was none other than Chief of Police Bubba James, and Bubba had a gaze that could turn a suitor to stone.

The James family lived in a sunny little house in Hayley, near the General Store. Bubba's wife Hedda was an early riser. She began her furious, unrelenting cleaning each morning at seven. Hedda was a plain woman, but her house was spotless. Bubba liked it that way.

Their daughter, Dixie Lee, was a true Southern belle by design. Her manner was soft and gracious, as was expected of young ladies, but underneath was a cool, calculating woman. She was eighteen, in her senior year at Albany High School. She was, however, more interested in readying herself to marry well than she was in logarithms or eighteenth century poets.

Dixie Lee was fifteen the first time she saw the ballroom at Radium Springs Country Club. She had gone to a dance, where she had seen the fragile debutantes from Albany's upper-crust families. Dixie Lee knew herself to be lovelier than them all, and from that moment, she began learning how to emulate them.

She learned what gloves to wear and what fork to use. She practiced walking and talking. She made Bubba buy her an English saddle for her horse, Dandelion, which she renamed Highpocket. She sent to New York for catalogs of the latest fashions, and took them to Mrs. Cooper to copy for her. She always looked very chic, and was the first woman in Hayley to wear pants in public, jodhpurs.

Not a masculine eye in town failed to glance admiringly in her direction, but she set her sights on the most eligible bachelor around, Rudolph Townsend. To catch Rudolph would be no easy matter, for every belle in Albany had the same goal. Besides her beauty, Dixie Lee had something else in her favor, a cunning imagination. She knew that Rudolph, long accustomed to wealth and privilege, was put off by silly social butterflies. She knew the kind of woman he wanted, gracious and submissive, yet levelheaded and capable of handling a large staff.

For the past three years, Dixie Lee had molded herself into the perfect wife for Rudolph Townsend, and on her eighteenth birthday, she acted. She knew that Rudolph took music lessons from Elizabeth Cooper, so the Sunday after her birthday she joined the choir at the Good Shepherd Baptist Church. She told her father she needed singing lessons with Mrs. Cooper, and frequently dropped in when Rudolph was there, with a question about her assignment or to borrow some music.

Things moved along exactly as she had planned. She never chased Rudolph, only made herself available to him. Rudolph was enchanted by her beauty and her sweet, seemingly unpretentious manner. Luckily for Dixie Lee, Rudolph judged people on merit, not social prominence, and

Dixie Lee's lineage was not a factor. Rudolph knew and liked Bubba James. He was not a man of wealth, but he was a man of honor, and he had Rudolph's respect. In fact, Rudolph relied more and more on Chief James to save Carlton from the wrath of the county sheriff, Jock Morehouse.

Rudolph and Dixie Lee were soon a couple. Rudolph's mother, Laura, liked her as well. Even more important, Chief Bubba James also approved. Tori Tanner did not know it, but Rudolph, her protector and friend, was indeed now engaged to cool, calculating, Dixie Lee James.

Tori and Wendy watched with great excitement as the hall filled with elegant guests. Neither of the girls noticed that Chief Bubba James was also present, standing by the wall at the entrance to the ballroom, apart from the merrymakers. He had been invited to attend the ball as a guest by Laura Townsend, but Bubba preferred to come in an official capacity. He wore the same snappy uniform he wore every day, the same stiff crease in his trousers, the same deep polish on his boots, the same shine on his badge and gun.

Bubba James was not easily impressed. He had never been invited to Radium Springs as a guest before, but he walked in as if he belonged there. He stood aloof from the crowd, his feet planted firmly on the polished marble floor, his hands folded across his broad chest. Every now and then he caught sight of his daughter dancing or talking with other guests, but Bubba did not purposely try to spot Dixie Lee in the crowd. He was, as always, doing his job. Laura Townsend tried once or twice to entice him to leave his post with an offer of punch or an invitation to join the dancing, but Bubba respectfully declined.

He knew he had been invited only because of Dixie Lee, and he had no intention of being other than what he was, on this night or any other night. Bubba James demanded, and earned, respect from the Townsends on his own merits, not on those of his daughter. Never had a ball at Radium Springs been so well guarded, or proceeded in such a law-abiding manner as this one, with Chief James on the job.

It was orderly, that is, until Carlton Townsend made his late arrival at the ball. He breezed in, with a girl on each arm and liquor on his breath. The first person he saw was Chief James. Carlton released the girls, sending them with a playful pat on their sequined fannies toward the crowd.

"Well now, looka here," said Carlton with a squint at Bubba. "You're a little outta your league here, aren't ya, constable? You come to guard that little filly of yours?"

"You've been drinking, son," said Bubba calmly. "Why don't you go back to your lady friends and join the party before you get yourself into trouble?"

"Trouble?" Carlton feigned surprise. "Why, Mr. James, sir, you'll have no trouble from me. Come to think of it, that pretty little gal of yours will have no trouble from my fop of a brother, either. She couldn't be in safer hands, no sir! My illustrious brother is about as much of a threat to a woman as a little ol' flea. If I were you, Mr. Chief, sir, I'd go right on home and not worry about a thing. Why, if you like, I'll even be proud as punch to look after your little girl's welfare myself."

Carlton was not as drunk as he appeared to be. Far from it. But intoxication was a safe guise that allowed him to speak his mind. He would have loved nothing more than to get a rise out of the unflappable Chief James. Dixie Lee's impending entrance to the family Townsend gave him the best opportunity yet to chide Bubba, and Carlton's eyes twinkled with anticipation as he waited for Bubba's reply.

Bubba's cool, detached expression did not change. He put his powerful hands on his hips and stared at Carlton calmly. It was hard to get the better of Bubba, and Carlton, drunk or sober, was hardly the man to do it.

Carlton was disappointed that Bubba had failed to rise to the bait.

"Okay, okay," he said, "stay if you like. Hell, constable, sir, come on and join the party. How about a little drink? Or isn't that allowed?"

Rudolph appeared behind his younger brother, and put a hard hand on his shoulder.

"Please forgive my brother's little show, Bubba," he said with a mocking smile. "It's way past his bedtime, you see. He turns into a fool when the moon rises."

"Yes," said Bubba, never talking his stony eyes from Carlton, "and tonight I believe the moon is full."

Angrily, Carlton shook off his brother's hand. He stood for a moment surveying them both with a look of total contempt, saying nothing. Those two men, both of them, were thorns in his side. He was getting tired of their smart remarks and their superior smiles. He smiled falsely and turned away to find his dates.

They think they're both so high and mighty, Carlton thought, but ol' Carlton's got a surprise in store for them. He begin to laugh, and finding one of his partners, he launched onto the dance floor with all the grace of the water buffalo.

Rudolph and Bubba stood together silently and watched as Carlton's antics attracted a crowd of admirers. Carlton was, in his own way, irresistible to people. The women were fascinated by his good looks and wild ways, and the men admired his freedom and sense of daring and fun. His laugh was infectious. He was like a playful young stallion, kicking up his heels and running free, jumping any fence that hindered him. No one could deny it; the room seemed to come alive with laughter and conversation when Carlton took the floor. He danced with one girl after another, then paired off each girl with any unattached gentleman he could find. Soon the floor was filled with dancing couples.

"Always the life of the party," said Rudolph archly.

Bubba cleared his throat and nodded.

"Yes, he is that. Too bad somebody usually has to clean up the mess after the party's over."

Bubba looked knowingly at Rudolph.

"He's young, Bubba," said Rudolph. "He'll grow out of it."

Bubba looked across the room at Carlton.

"With all due respect to you, Rudolph," the Chief said, "I've seen his kind before. He's got just enough of the rebel in him to bring harm to your family sooner or later."

Rudolph frowned and shook his head in frustration. He was afraid Bubba was right.

"I understand your concern, Chief," said Rudolph, "but I have to believe you are wrong. He's got too much sense to mess up his life. You know what happened when Father died. All of this started after that. He resents the way things turned out, especially since he was my father's favorite. It was a terrible blow to him. I think that once he works out this resentment, he'll settle down."

"I hope you're right," replied Bubba, his eyes still fixed on Carlton.

"Good evening, gentlemen." The woman's voice behind them was soft and sultry.

The two men turned to see Marie Hamilton entering the ballroom. Wendy's mother usually turned men's heads, but especially so tonight. She wore a royal blue satin gown with a revealing low-cut bodice. Unlike most of the other ladies, who wore full, floor-length skirts, Marie's dress was short, just below the knee, and so tight it left little to the imagination.

"Good evening, Marie," said Rudolph with a slight bow of appreciation. "My, you look stunning tonight."

"Why, thank you, kind sir," Marie replied. She cocked her head and surveyed the two men openly.

"My goodness, Chief James," she said. "I've never seen such a sparkling uniform. You certainly cut a dashing figure." She smiled coyly and turned to Rudolph. "Rudolph, perhaps next year we should retire our tuxes and require that all the men wear dashing uniforms instead."

For the first and last time that evening, Bubba James smiled.

"Lovely party, Ma'am," he said.

"Indeed it is," agreed Rudolph. "You have outdone yourself this year, Marie. I know Father would have been proud."

A momentary frown passed over Marie's face, but she recovered quickly and said, "Yes. He was always so generous with his praise, always so good to Jack and me." She looked up at Rudolph. "Everyone misses Mr. Price so, especially tonight. The room seems empty without him."

Rudolph felt a sadness at her words he did not reveal, for his own memories of his father were very different from Marie Hamilton's. To other people, Price Townsend was gracious, even generous, but to Rudolph, he had always been distant and reproving. Despite his mother's explanations and excuses, Rudolph never felt his father loved him.

"You're very sweet, Marie," said Rudolph with the same confident voice as before. "We all miss him. But you've done a beautiful job here tonight and everyone is having a wonderful time."

He gave a courtly bow. "May I escort you in, Madam?"

"Charmed, kind sir," said Marie, with as low a curtsy as her dress would permit.

They joined the other dancers, and Rudolph swept her gracefully around the floor.

Across the room, a crowd of admirers stood surrounding Dixie Lee James. There was a momentary pause in the conversation of the men when they caught sight of Marie Hamilton's daring dress. Their fleeting lack of attention to her did not go unnoticed by Dixie Lee, who had seen Marie enter the room and flirt with both her fiancé and her father.

That hussy, she thought. Impatiently, she stood up from her chair, holding her perfect bust high. Immediately, she regained the attention of her circle of admirers.

Flirting was not a natural attribute of Marie Hamilton, it was something she had cultivated. Such was not the case with Dixie Lee James. Flirting was part of her nature, and she had perfected it to an art. It was a tool she used to control her admirers, and she was an expert at control. Compared with Dixie Lee, Marie Hamilton was a poor amateur with men.

All the men spoke at once, asking Dixie Lee for the next dance.

"Now, boys," said Dixie Lee with a luscious smile, "however in the world do you expect me to choose between you? You are all so hand-some."

She looked directly at Roger Downs, and her smile gave him courage.

"You need not choose, my dear," said Roger forcefully. "The next dance is mine."

Dixie Lee smiled and took his arm, as the other men sighed and winked at each other. Roger escorted her to the dance floor and proudly put his arms around her. They whirled around the floor.

As they passed Rudolph and Marie, Dixie Lee smiled invitingly at

Rudolph. Rudolph smiled back, and then began looking around the room for his friend, Alan Dunlap. He spotted Alan, and nodded to him. Alan understood the signal and nodded back, setting down his glass. He approached Rudolph and Marie and tapped Rudolph on the shoulder.

"May I cut in?" he asked politely.

Rudolph pretended to be disappointed to lose Marie.

"If you must," he said with a growl.

Alan smiled at Marie and took her in his arms.

"Sorry, old man," he called back to Rudolph as he swept Marie away.

Rudolph smiled at the little deception, then looked around the dance floor for Dixie Lee and Roger. His smile faded as he caught sight of Carlton cutting in on Roger. Roger stepped back, and Carlton caught Dixie Lee by the waist, pulling her close to him. As they began to dance, Rudolph's eyes were on his fiancée, for she was smiling at Carlton in a peculiar way that puzzled Rudolph.

The two had met many times, certainly, since Rudolph and Dixie Lee had started dating, and Carlton had always flirted with her, but she had always kept her distance. Now, she seemed to be enjoying Carlton's attention. She made no effort to free herself from his tight grasp.

Rudolph had no illusions about Carlton's intentions, for Carlton had taken girlfriends away from Rudolph before, several times. When they were younger, they had vied for the same women out of a sense of competition between brothers, squaring off against each other like prizefighters. Carlton, with his handsome boyish features often triumphed over the more rugged, but less classically handsome Rudolph.

Still, Rudolph had quite a few victories to his credit, especially Camilla Goodson, whom he had wanted to marry. He had lost Camilla not to Carlton, but to fame and fortune. She was a high-priced model in New York City now, and rarely came home to visit.

Dixie Lee was Rudolph's first real romance since he had broken up with Camilla, and he had no intentions of letting his younger brother interfere this time.

This romance was serious, and Carlton knew it. But things were different now, and Carlton was jealous and bitter against his brother as never before. Rudolph knew that Carlton was deliberately set on coming between him and Dixie Lee.

Carlton's interest was mounting with every step he took as he danced with his brother's fiancée. She was as soft as a kitten in his arms, and her full breasts rose to an exciting decolletage as he pressed her against his chest. Carlton was impressed with Dixie Lee, for she seemingly did not react to his charm. She was cool and aloof as she danced with him, but her eyes held a smothering challenge.

Carlton had watched her for weeks. With Rudolph, she was loving and protective. With other men, she was warm and witty. It was only to Carlton that she turned a cold shoulder. This was her mistake, for Carlton knew what she was doing. He knew women, and he knew Dixie Lee was not truly in love with Rudolph. But she thought she was, and she was determined to marry him. Her coolness toward him could only mean one thing, Carlton believed. It was defensive. It meant that he was a threat to her plans. It meant that despite what she thought she wanted, she was irresistibly attracted to her fiancé's brother.

Carlton was correct in most of his observations, although Dixie Lee's true feelings were either unknown to her, or she refused to admit them to herself. She had never been in love, and she did not know that the feelings she had for Rudolph were not love, but admiration and ambition. Dixie Lee knew instinctively that Carlton was a threat to her, but was blind to her own attraction to him. She knew he wanted her romance with Rudolph to end for his own satisfaction. She thought he was dangerous and wild, a man whose exploits with women were nothing short of scandalous. He was handsome, it was true, with his blond hair, his twinkling eyes, and his wonderful laughter. But any woman would be a fool to fall for him.

Dixie Lee was a lot like Carlton. She used other people to get what she wanted. She controlled them, and herself as well. At this point, the man she wanted to control was Rudolph Townsend. Nothing was to stand in the way of her marriage to Rudolph, especially not his brother.

Dixie Lee felt something she did not understand as she danced with Carlton and gazed into his laughing hazel eyes. She was dancing with a cobra, a deadly cobra who held her eyes fast to his. She was hypnotized and could not look away. Whatever his motives when he began to dance, Carlton had forgotten them. Something passed between them as they danced, something deep and shattering. It would be a long time before either one recognized the true meaning of the experience. For like Dixie Lee, Carlton, too, had never been in love.

Rudolph watched them dancing and felt a twinge of foreboding. He dismissed the feeling at once, refusing to allow himself to doubt Dixie Lee's loyalty and love. He smiled as he approached them to cut in, but at the back of his mind, a seed of doubt struggled for recognition. The way she looked at him . . . .

"May I?" Rudolph asked Carlton with calm authority.

"Of course, brother," replied Carlton with a chilling smile.

He released Dixie Lee reluctantly and walked away. Dixie Lee took a deep breath as she took Rudolph's hand.

"Thank you," she said. "He held me so tight I couldn't get my breath."

"Anytime," replied Rudolph.

As they glided effortlessly across the dance floor, Dixie Lee said, "You are the best dancer in the room, honey. I think Carlton must be the worst." She looked up at him and smiled, now warm and comfortable in the security of his arms.

"How can two brothers be so different?" she asked.

"I admit it," said Rudolph lightly. "The boy can't dance."

"I wasn't talking about dancing," said Dixie Lee.

"I know," Rudolph replied, looking away. "Let's skip it, shall we? He's my brother, after all. Eventually the two of you will have to learn to get along. Is that understood?"

"Understood," echoed Dixie Lee, but her eyes were on Carlton as he poured himself a drink at the bar, a few feet away.

Suddenly, Carlton looked up, right into Dixie Lee's eyes, as if he knew all along she was watching him. He smiled a wicked smile and raised his glass to her. His eyes were like a flame that burned into her, branding her. Dixie Lee caught her breath and looked away quickly.

Rudolph observed this exchange and looked up to see Carlton walking away. He saluted Chief James as he passed him at the door of the ballroom, and disappeared down the hall. Dixie Lee buried her head in Rudolph's chest and clung tightly to him. He said nothing as he looked down at her. A dull ache began to swell through his temples.

5

About thirty minutes after Carlton exited, a man dressed in black clothing stole to the window of Dr. Richard Waldrop's lovely colonial home on fashionable Branchway Road in Albany. Dr. Waldrop and his wife were enjoying the dance at Radium Springs. The doctor was a wealthy man, a third-generation physician, and he lived in the house his father had built in 1900. It was a three-story brick mansion, filled with valuable antiques. The man in black looked into a softly lit room. He listened for any sign of life within the house. Hearing nothing, he slipped quickly to the back door and let himself in. Few people locked their doors in those days. Silently, the man walked through the house, ignoring the treasures of three generations, silver, antiques, paintings, and priceless mementoes of three wars. The burglar was not interested in art or Civil War swords. He was after cash and jewelry. Things small enough to carry.

He crossed into the library and was pleased to find that the doctor was a coin collector. The coins were in a display case equipped with a latch and lock. He smiled as he saw that the lock hung open invitingly. His black-gloved hand left no fingerprints on the handsome glass case as he removed the coins. In their place he left a note bearing only the imprint of a cat's paw. He smiled as he closed and locked the case, for the note was absurd, but he knew it would not be received in the light vein in which it was intended.

Silently, he moved up the beautifully carved staircase to the second floor and located the master bedroom easily. Now for the jewelry. Only yesterday, Mrs. Waldrop's picture had appeared in the newspaper, wearing the emerald necklace handed down from Grandmother Waldrop. She may as well have put out an ad. When he found the jewel case, the heirloom necklace was the only thing he took.

At the country club, the ever-observant Bubba James had spotted Tori and Wendy in their hiding place at the top of the spiral staircase. He looked at his watch and saw that it was after eight o'clock. Casually, Bubba strode around the edge of the ballroom until he stood directly below the girls.

Seeing him coming, Tori and Wendy crouched down and stopped their excited whispers. The chief stood with his back to them, watching the party goers, saying nothing. They waited nervously. After about a minute, they looked at each other in relief. Satisfied that Bubba had not seen them after all, they returned their attention to the merriment below.

A full five minutes passed before they heard Bubba's low voice say, "Enjoy the party, girls, but get to bed in thirty minutes. It's already past your bedtime."

The girls froze. Bubba never turned to look at them and did not give their hiding place away. In a minute or two, he walked slowly back to his post at the entrance to the ballroom.

"Heck!" whispered Tori. "That darn Bubba James never misses anything."

"He said we could stay a little while longer," said Wendy. "How will we know when thirty minutes is up?"

"Oh, don't worry about that," answered Tori. "When he looks back over here, it will be time to go."

The minutes passed too quickly, especially since Carlton brought life back to the dance with his return close to nine o'clock. The girls were just about to make their escape, reluctantly, when there was a noise behind them on the landing.

"Shhhh," whispered Tori. "Someone's coming."

Tori and Wendy were sufficiently descended on the curve of the staircase to be hidden from the view of anyone on the landing. They sat still and listened.

Two people were coming down the spiral staircase above them from the darkened third floor. It was a man and a woman, speaking to each other in low tones.

"How do we get out of here?" asked the woman.

"That's easy, honeypie," replied the man. "There is a door down the hallway there, and stairs down to the back patio. We can slip back in to the party through the kitchen and nobody will be the wiser."

"We had better go down separately," whispered the woman.

"Smart girl," said the man. "And you told me you had never done this sort of thing before."

"Please, darling. Don't make fun of me. You know I'm not that kind of woman."

"You'll have to teach me to have better manners," said the man.

There was a long silence. Tori looked at Wendy, but she put her head down on her knees and closed her eyes tightly.

In a couple of minutes, the woman said, "When will I see you again?"

"You know where to find me. Come back tomorrow if you like. I'll work something out."

Again there was silence.

"Now scoot," said the man at last. "I'll see you downstairs."

The girls heard the door at the end of the hall open and close softly. They waited. The door opened and closed again. Tori relaxed.

"Whew," she said. "That was close."

Wendy did not raise her head. She was frightened. She had recognized the man's voice. It was her father, Jack Hamilton. The woman was not her mother.

"What's the matter with you?" whispered Tori.

"I feel sick all of a sudden." said Wendy. "Let's go now, okay?"

"Who were those people, do you know?"

"No," Wendy lied. "I just got scared. Now my tummy hurts."

"It was close, all right," said Tori. "That man would have probably skinned us alive if he caught us. He didn't want anyone to see him, I think. Come on, let's go. Bubba will be after us in a minute anyway."

They crawled back up the staircase to the landing, and crept down the hall to the door. Silently they opened the door and scanned the lawn and the patio below.

"Coast is clear," whispered Tori.

They scurried down the stairs and ran across the open lawn. They climbed over the fence and took the bridle path past the springs. Soon they reached Wendy's house, and slipped in the back door. Tori followed the still-silent Wendy to her room.

"Oh, Wendy," said Tori, "I've never had so much fun! You are so lucky to live here all the time. I wish I lived here, too."

Suddenly Wendy began to cry.

"What's the matter," asked Tori in surprise. "What is it, Wendy?"

"I . . . I do love it here," sobbed Wendy. "But we are going to move. I know we are going to move."

"What are you talking about?" asked Tori. "Of course you're not going to move. Where did you get that idea?"

"I just know it. I just know it. We're going to move and I'll never see you again."

"Did your daddy tell you that?"

"No."

"Your mom?"

"No."

"Then why do you think it?"

"I'm afraid, Tori. What am I going to do?"

"Don't worry," said Tori gently. "Everything will be all right. You'll see. But don't cry, please don't cry."

IT WAS almost eleven when the Waldrops returned home from the ball. The theft of the coins was discovered almost immediately. Dr. Waldrop called Chief Buck Taylor and Sheriff Jock Morehouse, while Mrs. Waldrop flew up the stairs to her bedroom.

Apprehensively, she turned on the light and saw her jewel case lying open on the bed. She almost fainted. Inching forward a few steps, she was surprised to see that most of her collection was still in the case. Suddenly, she was frightened, wondering if the burglar could still be in the house. Could he have been in the act of stealing her jewels when she returned home? Could he have dropped the case on the bed and hidden in the bathroom? Mrs. Waldrop cried for her husband and backed out of the room.

Dr. Waldrop grabbed a saber from the wall and cautiously searched each floor before the police arrived. When Mrs. Waldrop was assured of her safety, she walked to the bed and saw at once that her emerald necklace, the most valuable and most beloved piece of her collection, was the only thing missing.

Tears filled her eyes and she sat down heavily on the bed, upsetting a small glass ashtray which had been placed precariously near the edge of the bed. She jumped as the ashtray hit the floor. "What was that?" she asked tearfully as Dr. Waldrop reached down to examine the fallen object.

"The butt of a Lucky Strike cigarette," he said in disgust. It was not the doctor's brand.

Right in my own bedroom, he thought. The audacity of the man.

Dawn was breaking when Jake Potter entered his wife's bedroom. He found Jessie curled up in a chair beside her mother's bed. Mabel was sleeping comfortably, the chills gone and her fever broken. Jake did not disturb her. He went to Jessie and woke her gently.

"It's okay, baby," he whispered. "I'm home."

When Mabel Potter awoke Sunday morning, she felt as if she had awakened from a long restless dream. She remembered some of the last three days, the pain, the chills, the soothing presence of her husband and child, but much of the days she could not remember. Her head was clear and her temperature normal. Her empty stomach gnawed at her, and she knew she was better.

She sat up and saw Jake sleeping in a chair beside her bed. The lamp on the table was still burning. In his lap was an open book. His hands lay protectively about the cover of the book. Jake had only a fourth-grade education, but he had never stopped reading or stopped learning. He was determined to better himself, and he read any book he could beg or borrow. He spent many hours with Jessie, encouraging her to read. They would sit together with a book, and she would read aloud to him.

Mabel's heart went out to Jake, and tears filled her eyes. How she must have worried him. The bond between them was more than love, for they were also truly friends. Mabel was a natural nurturer, and her first thoughts were for his well-being, not for herself. She wiped away her tears and got out of bed, donning her homemade cotton robe. Quietly, she went to the front bedroom to check on Jessie, who was sleeping peacefully. Mabel stepped out into the warm morning air and crossed the open hall to the kitchen. She went to the pantry, hoping there would be flour and lard enough to make a pan of biscuits.

When she opened the door of the pantry, Mabel caught her breath in amazement. Her eyes widened and she stared dumbfounded at what she saw. The shelves were filled with food. There were sacks of flour and cornmeal, salt and sugar, tubs of potatoes and sweet potatoes, grits, oatmeal, salt pork, canned goods, even mason jars filled with fruits and jellies. Mabel had never seen her pantry stocked so well, even after the harvest.

Her joy and relief were tempered with caution. She wondered how Jake got the money to buy so much. Her mind strained to run in the direction of fear that Jake had come by the money dishonestly, but her belief in him held the thoughts at bay.

When she had recovered from the shock, she gave full rein to the relief and delight she felt, with no questions. Elated, she ran out to check the chicken coop. Perhaps the hens were laying again.

6

By Monday morning, everyone in Hayley knew as much about the sensational burglary of Dr. Waldrop's home as did his own neighbors in Albany. There was a lot of speculation, but most folks agreed that it must have been an outsider.

Sheriff Jock Morehouse, a crusty thirty-year veteran of law and order, was in charge of the case, as it was assumed the stolen goods would be spirited away from the city. Jock was no fool, and had released only the basic facts to the press. The exact items that were stolen were kept confidential, with only their estimated value, which was considerable, released to the public.

A reporter for the *Albany Journal* had seen the mysterious signature left by the burglar, the imprint of a cat's paw, but Jock managed to keep it out of the paper. He made a deal with Mr. James Ward, the editor of the *Journal*. If he would keep the note out of the papers, the sheriff would keep him abreast of the more confidential matters of the case, with the understanding that he would release only what Jock allowed. Mr. Ward kept his promise in his own way, but the headline of the next edition read "Cat Burglar Strikes."

Sheriff Morehouse was a good friend of Chief Bubba James and enlisted his help, along with Albany's Chief of Police, Buck Taylor. There were few clues, except those the burglar had purposely left.

It was a sensational case, but it was an age of sensationalism. Radio bulletins linked south Georgia with the world as never before. Everyone knew the names of the daredevils of the day, and followed closely the course of the war in Europe. Lord Chamberlain's voice was as familiar as that of President Roosevelt, and Howard Hughes's exploits were as well known as Charlie McCarthy. But cat burglars belonged in the serials, not in Georgia.

Chief James was on duty as usual Monday morning, buckle gleaming and gun shining, standing on the wooden platform of the depot as the early train pulled in, when he spotted a solitary figure, clad in black, making his way slowly across the grassy square. He limped and walked with a cane. It was Daniel J. Smith, a newcomer to Hayley. Smith was a loner, and never had much to say to anyone. Bubba was suspicious of strangers; it was part of his nature, or part of his job, one or the other. Now, with a dangerous criminal possibly still on the loose in Dougherty County, Bubba was more alert than ever.

Bubba watched as Daniel J. Smith hobbled toward him. The stranger had come to town about two months earlier, with no known ties of friends or relations, and had rented the old Bibb place out on Hemon Road. He had no visible means of support. He lived simply, and spent money sparingly in his new hometown.

Something about the man had always bothered Bubba. Smith was a character, certainly, with his thick white hair, white moustache, and his bent-over, awkward limping walk. He looked harmless enough to the average observer, but Bubba had noticed his cold, hard eyes. There was something behind those eyes, and Bubba wanted to find out what it was.

"Mornin', Chief," said Smith as he mounted the steps of the depot.

"Mr. Smith," said Bubba.

Smith did not seem to notice Bubba's probing stare.

"What's the story on this big robbery I've been hearin' about, Chief?" asked Smith in his high, scratchy voice. "Got any clues?"

"The story's all there in the morning paper," replied Bubba. "Read it for yourself."

"I have," said Smith with a half grin. "You know as well as I do they don't tell everything in the papers. What's the real story?"

Bubba put authoritative hands on his firm hips and said with a hint of reproof, "Mr. Smith, the case is in good hands. The culprit will be caught and put away before the month is out. Don't worry yourself about it."

The old man chuckled.

"Worry?" he said. "Hell, I ain't worried about it. More like interested, you see. It's the first excitement I've seen around here. And fascinatin' it is, too. See, I kind of get a kick out of solving mysteries. Read a lot of Sherlock Holmes stories, you know? It's great fun, solvin' mysteries, don't you think?"

"The days of Jesse James are long gone, Mr. Smith," said Bubba. "This so-called cat burglar won't be so hard to catch. He'll make a mistake, and when he does, we'll be there waiting."

"Oh, no doubt about that, no doubt about that," said Smith. "Good fun, though, watchin' the chase, eh?"

The old man tipped his hat to the chief and hobbled away, in the direction of the General Store. He had made it a practice to take up a position in one of the rocking chairs on the front porch of the store for several hours each day. He was becoming a familiar sight, sitting silently, smoking, keenly watching life pass him by, saying nothing to his neighbors. Bubba watched with faint irritation as the man walked away.

WEDNESDAY EVENING, Hayley held its annual turkey carnival to celebrate the harvest. Dixie Lee James was named queen, to no one's surprise. She rode down the main street and around the square wearing a blue gown and a rhinestone tiara, followed by the proud owners of the prizewinning turkeys, and also trailed by merrymakers who comprised virtually the entire population of Hayley.

They followed the queen's open car out Albany Road, laughing and buck dancing to the strains of Clarence Fisher's fiddle playing. Their destination this year was the Townsend plantation, two miles up the road, where a great barbecue was prepared for one and all.

While all of Hayley was praising the harvest, a solitary figure driving an old mule wagon drew up to Buford's Funeral Home on the far side of the depot. It was Young Mose, a local Negro. He was called Young Mose still, even though his hair was graying, and his father, Old Mose, had been dead for twenty years.

Young Mose came to Hayley about once a month for supplies, and was never known to cause trouble. Like his father before him, he knew well the behavior that was expected of him, and spoke little. No one knew exactly where he lived, and since he appeared to be a humble, peaceable man who knew his place, no one cared to find out. Old Mose had taught his only son well, and, for more than forty years, this quiet father and son made the best moonshine east of the Mississippi.

Young Mose muttered to himself as he climbed down from the battered wagon and began to unload wooden crates that were hidden beneath a blanket covered with hay.

"Man's downright crazy in de head," he grumbled, looking around the deserted yard. "Jus' plain crazy takin' dis kine o' chance. Tomorra ain't good enuf, no, gotta be tonight. Man's crazy."

He had pulled the wagon alongside Buford's long black hearse, opened the back door, and loaded the crates of illegal brew into an empty coffin as quickly as he could.

He breathed a sigh of relief as he locked the doors of the hearse and climbed back into the wagon. Buford had been right; there had been no one about to see him make his delivery. But nevertheless Young Mose determined that he would never be talked into such a foolish act again. Bubba James was not a man to be trifled with.

"Dat undertaker got ta learn ta have some respect fo' de law," muttered Young Mose as he turned his old mule around and headed home, to the hill country above the Townsend game preserve.

NOBODY CALLED Mary Bea Brown by her given name. Everyone called her "Boozie," because she was preoccupied with ghosts, spirits, hobgoblins, and the like. Anyplace she went, she could name the spirit that resided there. The forest was the dwelling of the Windigo, who walked with feet of fire. The hill country held the dreaded kitty-mow, the graveyard the Timekeeper, and, of course, the Townsend game preserve was haunted by the ghost of County Pa.

She was a prissy child, her knowledge of the netherworld giving her a superior air. In the summer months, Tori, Jessie, and Boozie were a trio, pulling pranks and creating fantasies from the limbs of the huge oak at the edge of the Cooper place. Boozie lived on the far side of Hayley from Tori, but she always accompanied her grandmother, Doreen

Washington, to Tori's house on wash days. Boozie and her mother, Mary Lee, had lived with Mary Lee's parents, Ottis and Doreen, ever since her father, Amos Brown, had been sent to the chain gang for running shine.

Ottis Washington was sixty-two years old, with kinky gray hair and a white, closely trimmed beard. He was a huge man, six feet five inches tall, with a round barrel chest and long thick legs. He had the biggest hands in three counties, and wore size fourteen shoes. He was so big that he never had much reason to fear man or beast, and as a result, he developed a protective nature early in life, especially with regard to all the children of the community. He was respected by all, and warmly greeted by the white folk when he met them on the street. At one time or another, he had rescued, doctored, or helped some family member of nearly all the residents.

Ottis never drank or smoked, and he was a tireless worker in spite of his age. He never missed a Sunday at his church, which he had helped organize and build years ago.

Ottis was known never to tell a lie. When Bubba James had come to look for Amos Brown, who had skedaddled from the mule-drawn wagon he drove for Young Mose, leaving its contents to the revenuers, Bubba had not searched the house when Ottis had said Amos was not there.

Amos was eventually caught and sentenced to five years on the chain gang in the marshes near Savannah. No one in town ever mentioned this wayward son-in-law to Ottis, and Ottis never blamed the white man's law for sending him up. At the trial, Ottis was called to testify, and he stated that he knew nothing about the boy's crime, but that the devil did.

All his life Ottis had butted heads with old Mose and his son about their moonshining, which to Ottis was a sin. "Don't look at me for help," he had told them, "when the devil catches up with you." It was not the law which had sent Amos away, Ottis believed, it was the devil, and you got to pay the devil his due. If Amos lived through his punishment, Ottis would welcome him back to the family with no condemnations, but he would beat him blind if he ever found he had not learned his lesson.

That Ottis was black never occurred to Tori when she was younger. He was her friend, carrying her on berry hunts in the woods and teaching her to fish. Tori loved all of Boozie's family, except for Doreen. Doreen was bossy and self-righteous, and possessed of a wild temperament the years had not dimmed. She was a curious mate for the gentle giant she had married, who overlooked her nature and saw her still as the willowy beauty he married forty-five years ago.

It was the children of the town who forced Tori to accept that Negroes were different—Marvin Gates and another classmate, George Desmond, and others who mimicked the beliefs of their parents. Again and again Tori was forced to defend her black friends against the brash ignorance which is childhood, and against the blind prejudice which hardens hearts and grows to mean maturity. It was the defense of her black neighbors and her impoverished friends which resulted in the blot which was placed on Tori and her grandmother. Some said that Tori's behavior was to be expected, as she didn't know any better, and her father was not around to teach her how to act in polite society.

Mrs. Cooper was aware of the attitude of the town towards herself, which was not expressed openly, but in subtle omissions. She did not try to fit in to their little society, and successfully fought the impulse to return dislike for dislike. She realized that the good folk of Hayley were the ones who didn't know any better. They had been raised in it, just as she had been raised in a more enlightened environment. Perhaps their journey through life had not yet brought them enough suffering to teach them life's true lessons. Mrs. Cooper did not condemn them. She commended them all to a higher power, and accepted her place among them with dignity and a charitable heart, which over the years did much to gain their begrudging respect, if not their affection.

Tori was young, and tolerance had not yet gained the place in her life that it had in her grandmother's. Ever the crusader, Tori had managed to blacken the eye or muss the clothes of every bully in town, until they outweighed her. The children respected Tori, for even children recognize courage and strength of conviction, but some of them continued their harassment because they knew nothing else.

7

The following Saturday morning, Ottis and Boozie appeared on the doorstep, fishing poles in hand, on their way to the pond called Froggy Bottom, which lay just beyond the game preserve, along the banks of the railroad tracks. Tori begged to go and was granted permission, and off they went, a lighthearted trio, kicking pebbles gaily aside.

They followed the tracks to Froggy Bottom, and Boozie became quiet and aloof as they passed along the southwest corner of the game preserve. This posture was not lost on Ottis, who was determined to rid his granddaughter of her fondness for spirits and legends, which the Bible called wicked.

"Git down offen yo' high horse, Miss Mary Bea," he said flatly. "You don' know nothin' bout what go on in that place. Ain't no spirit live there. Ain't never done it. You done fill up yo' mind wit more foolishness than I can rightly stan'."

Boozie said nothing, secure in her singular knowledge. The ghost of County Pa was there; she knew it. The place was not safe to set foot upon, and even the angels could not enter. Boozie lifted her chin defiantly and tolerated the ignorance of her grandfather.

Tori chuckled, but Ottis was determined to prove his point to the stubborn child. "You think he in there? You think he gonna reach out and grab me iffen I climb over that there fence? Where you git them ideas, chile? Come on, then. Let's see the ghost."

Ottis turned towards the fence and walked to the forbidden area. Boozie's brave wisdom melted from her face as she realized her grandfather was going to be foolish enough to trespass. He would be snatched away for sure, or eaten, or torn to shreds, or shot.

"No, Pap!" she cried. "Stop! You be kilt iffen you only breathe the air." She was frantic and threw down her pole, running after him. She grabbed his coattail and tried to hold him back, and was dragged along, hopping and skipping behind his long strides. She looked back at Tori, who was following good-naturedly, of the same mind as Ottis, since she herself had no fear of the ghost, at least not in the daytime, as she had come to no harm when she followed Carlton.

"Y'all crazy?" Boozie yelled at her. "Don't y'all got no sense? Help me stop him. He be kilt iffen you don't."

"Let him go, silly goose," said Tori. "Nothing will happen to him, I promise. It's about time you stopped being foolish." She caught up to them and grabbed Boozie away from Ottis, holding her back. Ottis closed his mind to Boozie's caterwauling and, reaching the barbed wire fence, held it down and hopped over.

Boozie's cries were silenced in horror when Ottis's feet touched the forbidden ground. She covered her eyes and sank to her knees, sure that he was gone forever. Ottis turned and looked at the pitiful child, leaning his big frame on his elbows at one of the fence posts.

"Mary Bea?" he said patiently. "Mary Bea?"

There was no response to the soft call.

"Boozie!" he thundered.

Boozie jolted upright, popeyed, confused that he could still be alive.

"Well," he said with a grin, "am I daid?"

"Come on, silly," said Tori, grabbing Boozie's arm and pulling her to the fence. Boozie was too shocked to protest and allowed herself to be pulled along.

As they approached, Ottis backed up farther into the dense overgrowth. When they got to the fence, Tori released Boozie and climbed through the fence herself. She ran to Ottis, yelling and jumping, her arms flying.

"County Pa, County Pa," she sang in a singsong, "Come and get me, County Pa!"

Ottis laughed at her antics, but rushed to her in a flash when she tripped over something and fell to the earth with a crash.

"Honeychile," he sputtered, "is you all right? You hurt, baby?"

He turned her over with gentle hands and winced at the condition of her right knee. It was skinned, but not too badly. Her right foot was tangled in a black strap of some kind, and he pulled the strap free as he sat her up.

"Lawd have mercy," he muttered to himself as he examined the knee. "It ain't too bad, honeychile," he said comfortingly. "No, that ain't too bad at all. You be fine. Come on now, stand up an put yo' pins under you."

"I'm fine, Ottis," said Tori as she rose. "You're not going to make me go home just for this, are you? See, I'm not limping. We can just wash it in the pond, can't we?"

Ottis scratched his head and stroked his whiskers as he tried to decide. The moonfaced Boozie stood at the fence, watching them silently. It was only her presence there with them that had saved them both from certain death, Boozie had decided, she who was now on such good terms with the spirit world. But the fact that Tori had gotten hurt was a sign, a warning to leave before something worse befell them.

Ottis, who remained on the ground where Tori had fallen, leaned back on his arms and said, "I don' guess there be any harm in . . ." He paused in his words as his left hand met the strap over which Tori had fallen. He glanced down at the leather as he continued, ". . . goin' on an' doin' some fishin'."

He forgot what he was saying as he turned to examine the strap. He saw at once that a black knapsack was hidden beneath a ridge of the large boulder against which he sat, covered with a pile of leaves. He pulled the sack free.

From outside the fence, Boozie began to feel the spirits flying. "Pap," she called, "don' touch that. It be evil. It belong to the ghost."

Ottis ignored Boozie's warning. Inside the bag he found a long rope, a flashlight, items of black clothing, a set of slender picks and other tools, and a pair of soft leather shoes such as he had never seen before. Ottis marveled at the ballet shoes.

"Who could all this belong to?" asked Tori, as Ottis was examining the items.

As if by magic, the sun went behind a cloud and an unnatural darkness invaded the dense forest. Tori never saw the expression that came over the face of the humble giant. He had never set foot on this land before, and the falling darkness at the mention of the dead man's name was not lost on him. A shiver ran down his spine, and his big eyes bulged. For a second he could swear he heard a fearful moaning above the trees. Ottis had never seen a ghost, but any God-fearing man has a healthy respect for the Devil.

"Why did he hide it there, in the leaves?" asked Tori.

Ottis shoved the items back in the sack. "Lawd know, chile. What that boy do nevah make no sense."

He replaced the sack and covered it over with a fresh layer of leaves, and stood up and brushed the dirt from his pants.

"Ain' none of our care. We trespassin' an we bes' leave this place. Come on, Miss Tori."

He grabbed her by the hand and walked back to the fence. Boozie's relief was practically tangible when Tori and Ottis were back on safe ground. The eeriness of the place had frightened all of them somewhat, Tori less than the others. The trio retrieved their fishing poles and walked the short distance to the pond in silence. At last Ottis spoke.

"Now, you listen to me," he said in a serious voice. "What we jus' done be foolish. The land posted, an' that the law. We done trespassed, an' that be a sin." He took both girls by the shoulder and faced them squarely. "Don' you nevah, needer one of you, nevah go back on that land again," he said, looking them straight in the eyes. "You hear?"

The girls nodded. Ottis looked at Tori.

"I don' worry about my chile," he said gravely, "she too scared to go. But you not scary enough, Miss Tori. You mighty free an easy in them woods. You been in there before?"

"I . . . ," she began, "I know better than to go in there, Ottis," she said, not wanting to lie to a man who never committed such a sin.

Ottis saw the thin line form between her eyebrows. He could see a lie on someone's face before they spoke it.

"I ask you a question, girl," he said, bending his face down to hers. "You been in there, or not?"

"Just once," she admitted. "Jessie and I—"

"Lawd God," he said. "Do you know what you done? Do you know what yo' daddy would do if he knew? He thrash the livin' daylight out o' you! And yo' granny. Why, yo' granny would nevah believe a good girl like you would do such as that."

Ottis walked away, shaking his head, muttering to himself. Tori heard part of it, and it stuck fear in her heart. "What else can I do?" he was saying. "These babies don' know no better. I have to tell Miz Cooper, tha's all."

Tori ran after Ottis and pleaded.

"I'm sorry, Ottis. I won't ever do it again, I promise. I know I'm not allowed on that land. Meema will be furious with me if she finds out. Please don't tell on me. I've learned my lesson, really I have. Ottis, please don't be mad at me."

Her eyes filled with tears, but she did not sob. Ottis heard the catch in her voice and turned around to look at her. The look of determination faded from his eyes when he saw her tears. He pursed and pouted as he looked at her, his great brown forehead wrinkling in resistance to the certainty that he would lose this battle. Ottis never could resist a tearful child. He gave in and walked to her.

He stooped down and took her hand. "Do you promise?" he asked softly, still towering above her although his weight was on one knee.

Tori looked up from lowered brows and nodded.

"All right, then," he said. "Let's go fishin'."

THAT NIGHT there was another burglary in Albany. This time it was old Meredith Jacob's home. The daring cat burglar looted the wealthy matriarch's home while she slept in her great mahogany bed on the second floor. Her silverware was taken, and the beautiful miniature jade collection left to her by her father.

The woman was wealthy and eccentric. In spite of her advanced age she insisted on living alone in her great house. Still spirited and feisty, although well into her seventies, the widow Jacobs still held the reins of her large family and her fortune.

Sheriff Morehouse was more infuriated by this burglary than he was by the first, for the burglar had even entered the bedroom of the sleeping woman and taken her jewel box from the night table, right under old Mrs. Jacob's aristocratic nose. He must have known that she was hard of hearing.

Once again, it was front-page news. Once again, the burglar had left his parting note, claiming the crime as his own. And once again, his name was on everyone's lips. Before the next turkey carnival, the cat burglar of Albany was to become a legend, a legend to rival the ghost of County Pa.

MABEL POTTER was sitting in her chair on the front porch, as was her custom, waiting for Jessie to come home from school. When Jessie appeared at the crest of the hill, she waved and ran the rest of the way home.

"Hey, honey," said Mabel, giving Jessie a hug. "How was school today?"

"Fine, Mama," replied Jessie. "But we had to write sentences again."

"For what?" asked Mabel.

"Wendy brought some licorice and Miss Rigsby found it on the floor."

"My heavens," said Mabel. Licorice was forbidden in Miss Rigsby's classroom.

"We were suppose to write 'I will not bring licorice to school' one hundred times," Jessie said. "But Miss Rigsby got mad and left because I asked how to spell 'licorice'."

Mabel chuckled and picked up the bowl of peas she had been shelling.

"Want me to help?" asked Jessie.

"No, honey. I'm near through, now."

"Where's Pa?"

"He's inside, sleeping. We mustn't wake him."

Mabel began shelling the remaining peas, and the two sat in silence. There had been plenty to eat for the last month, since Jake had gotten his job in Albany.

Jessie looked at the ground and pouted.

"He has to catch up on his sleep," said Mabel. "He works all night."

Jessie said nothing. There was a tense feeling, a strange awkwardness she sensed in her mother's words.

"He's lucky to have that job," said Mabel. "I don't know what we'd done if he didn't find that job."

"What does he do in Albany, Mama?" Jessie asked.

"He unloads freight," Mabel replied. "At the train station."

Jessie heard the little catch in her mother's voice as she answered. Mabel was worried about Jake. He had changed over the last month. He was distant, secretive, even hostile at times.

"But, Mama—"

"Don't you be questionin' anything your Pa does, Jessie," interrupted Mabel. "We got no idea what he goes through to put food on our table."

"But he never reads with me anymore," said Jessie. "Sometimes I feel like he's not here even when he sits across from me at the table."

Setting down her bowl, Mabel took Jessie by the shoulders.

"He'll be all right," said Mabel. Her eyes were determined. "Don't worry yourself. All of us will be all right. The Good Lord has always watched out for us, and He's watchin' out for us now. You just have to look over your Pa right now. He's got a sadness in him that we don't understand. But he loves us, jus' like he's always loved us, we know that. We got to help him if we can."

"How can we help him?"

"By lovin' him, like we always done," said Mabel. "That is all we can do. This will pass, honey. This will pass."

8

Carlton Townsend had been born lazy. It was no one's fault, really. He was just the kind of fellow who liked having other people do for him. As he was born a Townsend, there were always plenty of servants and hangers-on ready and willing to fit the bill. At the age of ten, Carlton was ordering the maids around behind his mother's back. He was his father's son.

Although he was raised in the same environment, Rudolph never acquired his brother's apparent lack of respect for others. Perhaps the ever-present specter of his father's disfavor softened Rudolph's heart to the same extent that it stiffened his backbone. Rudolph never lost the ability to empathize with the less fortunate, or to see the other person's point of view.

The two brothers had split up early, with Carlton running at the heels of his father like one of Price Townsend's beloved hounds, and Rudolph sitting at the feet of his mother, Laura, with a dozen books, or running in from the field with a rough bouquet of wildflowers he had picked for her. It was to Laura's credit that she always loved her husband, in spite of his faults, and that she loved her sons equally. It would have been natural for her to favor Rudolph, as her husband favored Carlton, for Rudolph was as tender of heart as Carlton was hard-hearted, and as hardworking as Carlton was lazy.

As long as Price Townsend was alive, he was able to keep the impetuous Carlton in line, and was not unknown to slap him down if the circumstances warranted it. Unfortunately, Carlton did not hold his brother in the same regard in which he had held County Pa. Now that his father was dead, no one could tell Carlton what he could or could not do. The reading of County Pa's will had been the spark which ignited bitter fires of resentment in the younger Townsend, for he had loved his father.

In his heart, Carlton had always known that Rudolph was a better man than he. At the last, even County Pa had betrayed him, deeming him an irresponsible child and turning his rightful inheritance over to Rudolph's control. The lion of Carlton Townsend's darker nature was thus unleashed.

September had passed into October, and on each Saturday night there had been a new burglary in Albany. The pattern of the cat had been established clearly, for he always robbed the wealthiest families and he always flaunted the authorities with clues. After the fourth burglary, the rich folk began to get nervous and started locking their doors. They clamored for action from the police. They began to stay home or leave their homes attended on Saturday evenings.

It didn't help. The cat burglar proved himself to be nothing short of a circus acrobat, scaling bare walls, reaching third-story windows with wires, or simply picking whatever locks barred his way. He entered occupied homes and managed to escape undetected. He came and went as he pleased, leaving glass unbroken and locks undamaged. Jock Morehouse and the local police were baffled.

The public outcry increased to a fever pitch, and Jock Morehouse called in an advisor from the Atlanta police department's detective division. He came up with nothing, but made a public statement that the local authorities were competent and were doing all they could.

Perhaps it was inevitable that the cat burglar's daring and skill began to evoke admiration from some segments of the population. Young ladies were heard to speak of him in whispers, wondering what he looked like, who he was. The young men seemed to admire him as well, and talked constantly of his courage and skill. Those with a grudge against the rich also smiled with each escape, thinking that the wealthy people he robbed somehow deserved it, just for being rich.

No one seemed to notice that the cat burglar left the richest family in the region untouched. The Townsends were without doubt the most enticing possible mark for a burglar, but the cat never struck them. Nor did he strike any business or warehouse owned by the Townsends. No one noticed, except Bubba James.

As often happens in mid-October, the days were still hot and humid. Autumn is a fleeting thing in Georgia; some years, the trees still hold green leaves on Christmas day. Only with an early frost are residents treated to the beautiful and brilliant autumn leaves that can rival those of the North. But there would be no early frost this year, and only the usual spattering of autumn color.

Carlton had enjoyed his morning, running his big Arabian mare unmercifully around the backwaters of the plantation. The horse was thoroughly lathered and heaving when Carlton returned to the barn. He had enough respect for the big gray to cool her down, before plopping down on a pile of hay in the half-light of the tack room for a nap. Carlton was pleasantly drowsy when he heard the inviting voice of Dixie Lee James calling his brother's name. He smiled expectantly and called out, "In here."

Dixie Lee was irritated with Rudolph. He was never where he was supposed to be, and never on time. There was always some pressing matter, some excuse. She would have to put her foot down. If he thought he was going to treat her this way after their marriage, he was in for a surprise. She had no intention of searching for him all over the grounds every time she came to call. He was still in the tack room, for heaven's sake. He hadn't even saddled his horse yet.

She opened the door of the tack room and saw him, reclining in the corner, as if he hadn't a thing to do in the world. The door swung shut behind her, sending the room again to a soft half-light. The manly smells of saddle soap, leather, and musky perspiration hung heavy in the room.

"Rudolph Townsend!" she exclaimed. "This is the third time you have been late for our ride this week. I want you to know—"

She stopped short as her eyes became accustomed to the light and she recognized the figure facing her. She felt herself stiffen. She felt vulnerable suddenly, as if he had made a fool of her. She had the impulse to turn and walk back to the house, but for some reason, she did not heed it. Her cheeks flamed.

"Oh," she said. "It's you."

Her heart began to pound.

Carlton did not stir from his place, but lay smiling up at her. It was a wicked smile, but an appreciative one. His eyes seemed to glow as he looked her over, touching her everywhere with his slow burning glance. She was a pretty thing, he thought. She wore brown jodhpurs and slim black riding boots, a close-fitting yellow shirt, and a tailored jacket which only seemed to emphasize her shapely bosom and tiny waistline.

"My, my," he drawled. "Are you really that disappointed, my sweet?"

His voice was deep and lazy, so rich it seemed to touch her, to hold her. She lifted her chin defiantly and looked down her nose at him. He must not know how he frightened her.

"Have you seen Rudolph?"

"Oh, he's around here somewhere, darlin'," replied Carlton, sitting up slowly. "I suspect he's got somethin' much more important than you to attend to. You know, like lickin' some politician's boots or pinchin' the scullery maid's behind."

Dixie Lee was shocked. Until now, she had been somewhat protected from Carlton's bitterness against his brother. Laura had always been there, or the servants. She had no idea Carlton hated Rudolph so much. She was afraid of him. He seemed different from anyone she had ever known. He was fascinating in a repulsive sort of way. Why didn't she just leave?

"You're not talking about Rudolph," she said. "You're talking about yourself."

Carlton laughed and pulled his knees to his chest.

"Oh, I get it," he said. "My illustrious brother is too good to be human, huh? I suppose you think he never even looks at another woman. Well, hell, honey. Maybe you're right. Maybe the two of you will get married and live happily ever after. Maybe he'll worship you like a damn goddess, till your looks are gone, at least. Maybe he'll lie at your feet like a little puppy, and lick your boots along with the politicians'. And maybe you two will never have a single day's excitement in your whole lives. Is that what you really want, Dixie Lee? I don't think so."

He was on his feet so fast she hardly knew what happened. He was kissing her, crushing her against him. Her arms were trapped against his chest. She pushed against him as hard as she could, but he was strong, and held her fast.

At first he hurt her, bruising her lips with his angry kiss, but then he slowed his attack, kissing her deeply, hungrily. Despite herself, despite her rage, Dixie Lee felt herself responding to him, going limp in his arms. This can't be happening, she thought desperately, but then she lost all reason, all ability to resist. It was wonderful. He was wonderful. Why didn't Rudolph kiss her like this?

The thought of Rudolph brought her back to her senses. Suddenly she began to fight again. She pushed him away with all her strength. It was less of an effort than she had managed before, however, and soon she felt herself melting again in his strong arms. He let her breathe at last.

"You're crazy," she gasped. "Rudolph's going to kill you, you know he will! He—" she did not have time to say more. He was kissing her again, warm, deep, slow kisses that sent fire raging through her body. For the first time in her life, Dixie Lee felt the hunger of desire, the abandonment of passion. She could not resist him. She kissed him back.

The door of the tack room opened noisily and Rudolph stood in the doorway in shocked silence, looking at them. Carlton released Dixie Lee and faced his brother, a slow smile of triumph spreading over his face. Rudolph did not see Carlton's smile; he did not have to. He was looking at Dixie Lee, and in his eyes was a mixture of hurt and anger at her betrayal.

She could say nothing, for she was filled with horror. She had not planned for this to happen; she could not possibly have imagined herself being put in this position. What could she do? All her plans, all her perfect, lovely plans gone in an instant. Her eyes pleaded with Rudolph. She tried to speak, but could not.

Without a word, Rudolph turned and left the tack room. Dixie Lee uttered a cry of despair and covered her face with her hands.

Suddenly, her dejection turned to rage and she turned on Carlton, who had resumed his place upon the hay.

"You beast!" she screamed. "You rotten, low-down scum! How

could you do this to me? I hate you, I hate you!"

She lunged at him, hand outstretched, to strike him in a guilty fury. Carlton caught her arm and twisted it easily behind her back, pulling her down beside him, her face close to his. Her breath was hot on his face, as he pinned her other arm behind her.

She was close to him again, her heart pounding, her emotions seething. She struggled to free herself, and pain shot through her arms and shoulders, draining her. She clenched her teeth and glared at him with eyes full of hatred.

He stared back at her with piercing hazel eyes and an anger that matched her own. He pulled her closer, crushing her chest against his. She felt a tingle in her spine, her legs, her arms.

Her panting slowed as her anger was replaced by something different and she realized he had trapped her again. Again he held her with his eyes. A warm, slow wave shuddered through her body and she felt again the ache of her desire. She suddenly became defensive, frightened again. Her large blue eyes opened wide in surprise at her response to him.

"He's not really the one you want," whispered Carlton, "is he?"

Tears flooded her eyes as he released her. She jumped up and ran, not so much back to Rudolph as away from Carlton. She paused at the entrance to the stable and saw Rudolph walking back to the house.

She couldn't talk to him now; she was too shattered. Oh, what must he be thinking? She had to explain, she had to make him see. It didn't mean anything, surely he must know that? Rudolph! He was good and kind and steady and wise. He was everything she wanted. She didn't want Carlton, she wanted Rudolph!

She must think! She had to get away. She would explain to Rudolph later, after he had a chance to cool down. He would listen to her then, she was sure of it.

She ran to Highpocket and mounted him. She turned the horse toward the drive and saw Carlton leaning against the door of the stable, watching her. She shuddered. But then, for a moment, she remembered the warmth of his mouth upon hers. She kicked the horse and galloped down the drive. Away from Carlton.

Rudolph couldn't believe what he had just seen. It was not that Carlton had tried to seduce Dixie Lee, it was that he apparently had succeeded. She had not been struggling, trying to get away from him; she was holding him, kissing him. And when he had found them, the guilty look on her face was undeniable.

Rudolph had thought she was different. And she seemed all along to actually dislike Carlton. It didn't make sense. For a moment he doubted his senses. Was it possible that he could have misinterpreted what he had seen? No, he thought, he was right. Damn it all! Damn them both to hell. He felt a piercing pain in his chest and the blood seemed ready to burst right through his throbbing temples. For the first time in years, Rudolph was in love again, and now his heart was breaking. He stopped and leaned against an old pecan tree near the wide red-brick walk in front of the house. His disillusionment faded as anger flooded him, stretching taut every fiber of muscle in his body, his fingernails digging into the palms of his hands. Carlton would pay for this! He looked back to the stable and saw his brother, mounting his big Arabian mare.

Rudolph covered the distance back to the stable in what seemed like an instant, and dragged Carlton down from the horse without a word. Carlton looked up at him from the ground where he had fallen, and saw that this would be no ordinary fight. The two brothers were not new to fighting, and Rudolph, being a full four inches taller and twenty pounds heavier than his brother, had often pitted his superior strength against the younger's fiercer nature, so that their fights were usually an equal match. But this time it would be different. Carlton knew he was in for the beating of his life the moment he looked at his brother's face, distorted with rage. Carlton's apprehension was tinged with a new, unwelcome respect for Rudolph, who had for once, Carlton realized, been pushed too far.

There was not time for Carlton to try to talk his way out of it. Rudolph dragged him to his feet and promptly flattened him with a blow to the left side of his jaw. When Carlton got back on his feet, he tackled Rudolph, and they tore at each other, blow for blow, with nothing held back, for the first time in their lives. For once, Carlton's go-for-the-jugular instinct was met equally by his brother, and he was thoroughly and soundly thrashed.

When it ended, Rudolph stood over him, his fury spent but unsatisfied, with no remorse at the sight of Carlton's swollen eyes, puffy face, and bleeding lips. He leaned down, jerked Carlton up by the lapels of his jacket, and said fiercely, "Next time I'll kill you." He dropped Carlton back to the ground and started to the house, unable to feel the pain of Carlton's blows, unable to feel regret for his lost love, unable to feel anything except his own anger.

CARLTON TOWNSEND had inherited something from his father which was not listed in his father's will. Carlton had the same supreme lust for power that made Price Townsend respected and feared. It would have never entered Carlton's mind that he could be the object of surveillance by anyone of importance. There was Bubba James, of course. He always kept an eye on Carlton, but he was, after all, small potatoes. And there was the Albany sheriff, Morehouse, but both these men represented little threat to the impetuous Carlton.

He was above the law, or at least, above the local yokels who tried to enforce it. Even if he did get into something his brother couldn't get him out of, the ultimate decision rested not with these elected buffoons, but with Judge Jacob G. Allen, Price Townsend's best hunting buddy and financial collaborator. No, Carlton did not have much to fear from Bubba James or Jock Morehouse, or from anyone else for that matter. He did what he liked, when he liked. County Pa was dead, but his place in that little society was not to be vacant for long, not if Carlton had anything to say about it.

Yet, Carlton was being watched. Watched by a man who was determined to cause the downfall of the entire Townsend family. He knew more about Carlton and his brother than either of them would have believed possible, and certainly more than either of them would have allowed, had they known of his existence. He knew, for example, that Carlton made frequent trips to the deserted cabin in the Townsend game preserve, and he knew why.

In the cabin was a secret room, a lushly furnished and carpeted cellar. The cellar was a carefully guarded sanctuary built many years ago by County Pa. It was in this room, sitting in a comfortable leather chair before a large rolltop desk he built from an unassembled kit, that County Pa recorded his secret deals, his kickbacks, his shady involvements. The records were all there, safe from the decent folk of the county and from the Internal Revenue Service. The money was there, too, or a good part of it. Price Townsend died while in the midst of transferring a huge chunk of his profits from Atlanta to Switzerland. Like his son Carlton, County Pa never suspected that anyone would have the gumption to interfere with his private business. He had, after all, encouraged such fear in Dougherty County that no one dared to even set foot on the game preserve, much less dare to enter the cabin.

County Pa believed that his secrets were perfectly safe from prying eyes. But Carlton knew. Carlton knew all. He had shadowed his father's every move when he came to realize that no one, not even his favorite son, could be admitted to the inner sanctuary that was his power. Carlton feared his father, but he did not trust him, and with good reason, as the reading of the will confirmed. Price knew his boy was clever, but he underestimated his resourcefulness. It had been easy, very easy, for Carlton to learn the secrets of the cabin, and to keep this knowledge from his father. Carlton told no one. He kept everything he learned from the papers in the desk to himself, all the deals, the crooked politicians, the evidence, and now that the old man was dead, the money. He knew where all the political bodies were buried, and that meant power. He would make his move one day soon, and then the ghost of County Pa would truly rule the forest again, resurrected in the son. But for now, while he waited for his chance to break into his father's position, Carlton bided his time, using the money to finance his gambling, his little extravagances, his women. Not even Rudolph suspected that Carlton was spending money quite so freely, for Carlton kept his excesses well hidden, or out of the state. Those he dealt with never questioned the money, for this was, after all, the son of the wealthy Price Townsend. Actually, few people knew the terms of the will, that Carlton was to be sustained on a generous, but conservative, trust, until his mother died.

There was a lot of money. Carlton had never even bothered to count it. He knew he was being careful enough in his spending to maintain his secret wealth, although he had begun to realize that so much money should not be allowed to lie fallow. The time was near for him to invest the money, or at least to put it in a bank where it could earn interest. How best to do this was the problem he was considering. Carlton should have counted the money. If he had, he would have realized that he was being slowly, and carefully, robbed.

9

To say that Dixie Lee was upset would not have been exactly true. She may have been upset at first, but within an hour after Rudolph had found her in Carlton's arms, her survival mechanisms had gone into effect, completely blocking out any troublesome feelings of remorse, guilt, or despair. All her energies now were centered on getting Rudolph back.

She didn't waste time seething at Carlton for what he had done. Whatever feelings she had for Carlton were buried deep, too deep for conscious awareness. He remained only a threat to her plans, a threat she was sure she could overcome.

The problem was Rudolph, not Carlton. He had seen them together, unfortunately just at the point where she had found herself kissing him back. Her mind wandered at this memory, but she immediately pushed her response to him out of her mind. It was no less than she would have expected from him, after all. And the fact that she kissed him back? Well, what girl would not? He was, after all, a very attractive man, wasn't he? Most any girl would liked to be kissed by him.

Despite herself, Dixie Lee found her thoughts returning again and again to Carlton. It wasn't just that he was handsome, Carlton possessed other qualities which were totally devastating to women. Dixie Lee could not put these qualities into words, but like all the eligible and not-so-eligible ladies of the area who had pursued Carlton, Dixie Lee sensed them. He exuded a sense of power, danger, animal magnetism. Women knew instinctively that nothing they could do, no feminine wile, could ever control or manipulate him. To put it simply, Carlton was masculinity itself, and that was exciting.

He was so different from Rudolph, she thought. Rudolph was another kind of man entirely. From the first time she saw him, Dixie Lee could look into Rudolph's gentle, idealistic soul. He was kind and courteous, a true gentleman. Dixie Lee knew he would make any lucky girl a wonderful, devoted, faithful, responsible husband. But he wasn't the kind who could be bossed around easily, either. Far from it. He was high-principled and high-spirited. The difference between Rudolph and his brother was that Rudolph could be manipulated, if it was done subtly, by the right woman. Dixie Lee considered herself to be the right woman. But perhaps for this very reason, Rudolph could never present the same challenge, the same ecstasy to Dixie Lee that his brother could offer her.

Dixie Lee was too much of a realist to choose chance over a sure thing. Her cool, logical mind told her that Rudolph would make her safe, secure, and happy. All her instincts told her to steer clear of Carlton, even though of the two brothers, it was, perhaps, Carlton that she could truly love. What Dixie Lee didn't realize was that she was the kind of woman who could only love a man who could outmanipulate her, who could take her out of herself. Only then could she respect him, and truly fall in love.

If it was to be a battle, she was ready for it. She would get Rudolph back, there was no question of that. It was just a matter of deciding the best way to go about it. Dixie Lee's manipulative talents were being put to a test, and she would not fail.

In her dreams, Dixie Lee was often pursued by a shrouded, demanding, powerful lover. A man she tried her best to escape from, but whom she desired to possess her. This conflict repeated itself over and over, but thus far, even in her dreams, Dixie Lee had never allowed herself to be mercifully sacrificed to her deepest desires. Again and again she escaped. But as time went by, she found that he came closer and closer to her soul. If Carlton Townsend could have observed her dreams, he would have smiled.

IT HAD been three days since Rudolph had caught Dixie Lee with Carlton. In that time, she had had no word from Rudolph, and she had stayed away, formulating her strategy. She had made the mistake of telling Bubba what happened, and he had become enraged at Carlton.

Only her desperate pleas had kept him from taking a whip to the young rascal. Don't interfere, she had begged her father. She was perfectly capable of straightening things out by herself. She must be avenged by Rudolph, she explained, not by her outraged father.

Bubba gave in to her, as he always did, but from that day, a hatred for Carlton began to fester within him. He had always disliked the young man, with his arrogant attitude, his sarcastic remarks, and his total disregard for decency and for the law. But Bubba James, being the man that he was, had not, until now, allowed his personal feelings to interfere with the equal dispensation of justice to all members of his jurisdiction. Bubba prided himself on treating the privileged and the powerful on even terms with the lowly and destitute. In his private views, he had the luxury of his own opinions, but in his public role, all men were created equal, and were to be treated equally under the law.

Bubba's hatred for Carlton simmered quietly, slowly, deep in the hidden labyrinths of his mind, to the extent that he gave it no thought after he had calmed down about Dixie Lee. It showed itself in other ways, subtle ways that were easier for Bubba to accept in himself. He found himself watching Carlton more closely, making discreet inquiries of people with whom Carlton did business. He asked trustworthy men he knew in Albany to keep him informed of Carlton's whereabouts and actions, and he wanted the names of the people with whom Carlton associated. He learned many things in this manner, most importantly the fact that Carlton was spending money with a vengeance. Bubba kept his knowledge about Carlton a secret, and bided his time, waiting for Carlton to trip himself up. One day the boy would learn that no one trifled with the affections of the chief's only child.

He need not have worried about Dixie Lee. If ever a woman was fit for a challenge, it was she. In the three days since the incident, she had waited for Rudolph to make the first move. She was not surprised at his silence, but it was essential to give him the opportunity. His failure to make any attempt at reconciliation would be the damning element she would use against him, if indeed he chose not to come to her.

On the morning of the third day, she acted. She wore her prettiest riding outfit, saddled Highpocket, and rode casually to the Townsend plantation. The sun was high when Dixie Lee reached the gates, and she thought with satisfaction that the sun would play fetchingly on her long brown hair. She saw Rudolph immediately upon rounding the curve of the drive, when she came in view of the neat, newly painted red barn to the left of the stable. He was there, leading a new thoroughbred colt to a tether pole in front of the barn. He looked up upon hearing the approach of her horse, and, seeing her, made no sign of welcome, but went back to his work, tying the colt to the pole and brushing him out in the sun.

Dixie Lee slowed her horse and walked him to the side of the barn, dismounted, and looped the reins over the white rail fence. She walked over to Rudolph with the dignity of a queen, and stroked the colt's flank. She said nothing until he looked at her at last, his eyes blank as he beheld her radiant beauty. She read a vague sadness in his glance. She had hurt him badly, needlessly, and there was an invisible wall between them now, which she sensed immediately. Her only hope of breaking down that barrier was to convince him that his eyes had deceived him, and that his interpretation of the event, not the event itself, was the sin.

In her softest, sweetest voice she said, "Hello, stranger."

"Hello, Dixie Lee," he replied dryly, as he continued to give the colt his attention, her presence beside him apparently of less importance than the grooming. His manner was cool, and Dixie Lee was a little surprised that her charms seemed to make no impression on him. She was wrong. Every fiber of Rudolph's body responded to her nearness. Only his mind could he control, holding his emotions leashed tightly, cruelly, with stubborn determination.

"I came because I want you to explain something to me," Dixie Lee said, and in her voice he heard a tremor of hurt. "Why haven't you come to me to straighten this out?"

"What is there to say?" he replied with apparent ease, which in truth was hard-bought. He kept his eyes on the horse, and she did not see the anger in his eyes.

"Is it so hard for you to say 'I'm sorry'?"

He turned to her abruptly, dropping the brush in its box.

"What are you talking about?" he asked harshly. Surely she wasn't implying that he owed her an apology instead of the other way around.

"I've waited three days for you to come," she replied, "and you haven't. I've cried myself to sleep over your stubborn meanness. How could you be so cruel? I wouldn't have thought you were capable of such a thing."

Rudolph listened intently to this unexpected speech. He tilted his head and observed her out of the corners of his eyes, trying to comprehend what she was saying. She couldn't be serious. The workings of the minds of women had always been an enchanting mystery to him, and he had never been able to figure them out.

Despite the barriers he had set between them, Rudolph's defenses were beginning to crumble. God, but she intrigued him.

"My dear," he said, "I'm afraid you are making no sense whatsoever. But please, continue. I would like to hear the rest of this."

"If you think I'm willing to let your stubborn pride come between us, you're wrong," she said. "I love you too much to give up without a fight. What you did the other day is just not that important. It's not worth being away from you, waiting for you to get up the courage to apologize. I've come to tell you now, I forgive you." She put a gentle hand on his arm and implored, "Don't torture yourself or me any longer. Let's forget what happened and learn something from it."

It was too much. Of all the things he could have possibly imagined her saying, this was not one of them. Rudolph threw back his head and laughed. And then, when he saw the shocked look on Dixie Lee's face, he laughed even harder. The more he laughed, the angrier she got, but he could not help himself. It's not funny, he tried to tell himself, but the laughter kept coming as if it had a will of its own. Despite his determination to break off the romance, he found himself feeling sympathy for Dixie Lee. Her expression was priceless.

When she could stand no more, Dixie Lee turned and walked away, then ran to the fence where she had tied Highpocket. At last, when he finally caught his breath, Rudolph started after her. He caught her before she could mount and grabbed her by the arm.

"Wait," he said. "I'm sorry. I was rude, I know. I don't know what came over me. Please stop."

She allowed herself to be caught, and turned to him with eyes that were moist with innocent, unbelieving tears. Dixie Lee was a fine actress, but this time the tears were real. Her plans were not working the way she had expected. Maybe he couldn't be swayed after all. Her tears were of frustration, and her anger was real. It was his fault after all, wasn't it? If he had just knocked Carlton's block off to begin with, none of this would have happened.

"What am I supposed to be apologizing to you for?" he asked. His voice was suddenly serious, and he searched her eyes for the truth. Unable to read her intent, he lapsed back into an attitude of amused patience. But his grip tightened on her arm when he said, "Try to make it good, Dixie Lee. The suspense is killing me."

Dixie Lee's eyes turned to fire and she wrenched her arm free. She stamped her foot and cried fiercely, "You unspeakable cad! How dare you say such a thing. You know exactly what I'm talking about, you beast! You left me there, you just turned your back and walked away and left me alone with that horrible, disgraceful wolf you have for a brother. He attacked me and you just walked away. I could have died right then and there. I always thought you cared about me, but you, you just ran like a frightened rabbit!"

Rudolph stared at her, his eyes cold with rage. "I run from no man, my dear," he hissed. "My brother least of all. It seems to me that the explaining for this matter is to be done to me, not the other way around."

It was as if she did not hear him, as she continued, her eyes flashing, "I would never have believed you could do such a thing. Why, he could have ruined me right there in the dirt, and you wouldn't have lifted a finger to stop him."

"How I deal with my brother is my own business," Rudolph snapped angrily. "He'll not interfere with me again. Nor with you, unless you prefer a casual roll in the hay to my ring on your finger."

Dixie Lee stared at him. The expression in her eyes faded to a look of hurt and bewilderment at this outburst. She looked away in despair.

"I've tried to be calm about this," she said finally, unable to meet his eyes. "I've tried to understand what you did because I love you so much, but you didn't even try to explain. I waited and I told myself there was some logical explanation for your behavior, that you would come to me and make me understand."

Rudolph's anger cooled as he saw the torment on her face. He was drawn to her against his will, bent as he was against forgiveness. His anger had raised his body to a fever, a fever which now burned more of passion than of rage.

"But you wouldn't come," Dixie Lee continued, now close to tears. "And then when I come here and try to talk to you, you laugh in my face. You insult my honor. You are worse than your brother! I was a fool to think you loved me, to think you were honorable and strong and brave. You're not! You never loved me! You—"

Dixie Lee's tirade was cut short when Rudolph grabbed her and crushed her lips with such a kiss of passion that she nearly fainted. Suddenly, he had lost the anger and disillusionment he had felt and nursed after finding her with Carlton. These feelings had been replaced by an overpowering passion for the angry, tempestuous, beautiful creature before him, and he kissed her as he had kissed no other woman in his life, his desire to possess her suddenly the only thing that mattered. The memory of her apparent surrender with his brother was rewritten forever in his memory. Love can overlook much, and somehow Rudolph forgot that the look he had seen on Dixie Lee's face was not that of a virtuous maiden for her rescuer, but that of a guilty sinner, horrified at being caught in the act.

The only thing which he could feel now, besides his love for Dixie Lee, was the determination that for once, his brother would not succeed in taking a woman away from him. The others had not mattered, for he had not been in love with any of them, but this time it was different. Dixie Lee belonged to him, and she would be his wife.

THE BEATING that Carlton Townsend had suffered at the hands of his older brother had done little to reform him or to dampen his spirits. His volatile nature and sharp tongue had gotten him in trouble many times, and black eyes were not new to him. Even his father had taken the strap to him long after he passed into the maturity of adulthood. Rudolph's thrashing had succeeded only in creating in Carlton a new respect for his older brother, not as a friend, but as an enemy.

He knew that Dixie Lee would come back sooner or later, to try to explain her way out of her seduction. She would have to, because Rudolph would be too proud to forgive her. Carlton chuckled as he watched the two of them from his upstairs bedroom window. She made it look so easy. He wondered what she had said to make Rudolph forget what he had seen and take her back. He watched as they stood there by the fence together, holding hands and talking, as if nothing had happened.

She had managed to blame the whole thing on him, of course, but how? Carlton knew women, knew them inside out, and he knew that Dixie Lee wanted him as he wanted her. The only trouble was, she didn't know it yet. He smiled as he remembered her soft body yielding in his arms, her lips melting into his. She was wonderful, fiery and passionate, headstrong and willful, binding her emotions and her desires beneath silken cords of determination. She needed a real man to break through those barriers. She needed a man who was just like her, only more so. Rudolph wasn't the one to do it. Carlton was.

His admiration for Dixie Lee grew immeasurably as he watched her win Rudolph back in only minutes, for, in the past three days, Carlton had been sure that the breakup would be permanent, and that he would have a free hand with her as soon as his bruises disappeared. Rudolph had been moody and silent, unresponsive to Carlton's good-natured greetings and lighthearted jibes since their fight. Carlton was too clever to let Rudolph glory in his victory by sulking. He had made it all seem like a lark, as if Dixie Lee were just like all the others they had vied for.

But she was different. Rudolph knew his brother too well to blame him completely. It was Dixie Lee he had been disappointed in, so much so that Carlton had assumed the romance was over for good. But he had obviously underestimated Dixie Lee. For there she stood, holding

Rudolph's hand, recapturing his heart.

It was at that moment that Carlton's feelings for Dixie Lee changed. He wasn't expecting it to happen, and certainly did not want it to be so, but for the first time in his life, Carlton Townsend was in love. He wanted her, wanted to own her, body and soul, wanted her more than he had ever wanted any woman. They were alike, he and Dixie Lee, an equal match, each a challenge to the other. She would never be happy with Rudolph, of that he was sure. And worse, Rudolph would never know her as Carlton could, never capture her spirit, or probe the depths of her passion. She would be wasted on him, Carlton decided, and ruined as well.

If he had not decided for certain before, he did so now. Dixie Lee would be his. To hell with the consequences. He would take her away from Rudolph one way or another, and make her his wife. Rudolph had been the ultimate winner with his father, but this time he would lose. He would lose the woman he loved, and for all the years to come, he would have to watch her in the arms of his younger brother. It would be a fitting retribution, and an honest victory, for she would be happy.

Yes, at last, Carlton would make Rudolph suffer, make him pay for treating him like a spoiled child, for trying to run his life, for holding himself above him like some lord of the manor. Carlton bristled at the thought of how his brother had managed to take over the reins of the county, setting himself up in the eyes of the community as some virtuous hero. What a joke. Rudolph was so stupid that he had no idea of the truth about County Pa's dealings or his money. He didn't even know how much there was or where it was. But Carlton did. He knew everything, facts and figures, names and dates. Rudolph was going to lose more than his girl; he was going to lose his empire, and soon.

10

On the night before Halloween, 1938, Orson Welles had plunged a goodly number of the Northeast population into a panic. His Mercury Theater presentation of H. G. Wells's "War of the Worlds" had sent thousands into the streets, seeking shelter from invading Martians. The panic was spared the residents of Georgia, however. The country folk had no radio to tune in, and the city folk apparently had the good sense to tune in the program from the beginning.

The hoopla made the morning edition of the *Albany Journal* on All Hallow's Eve. There was an editorial on page two which warned of the power of this newfangled means of communication and the dangers inherent therein, which was echoed in morning editions all across the country. As Georgia folks were sensible people, and enjoyed a good laugh as well as the next fellow, the serious nature of the issue was lost on many of them, and they spoke mostly of their glee at the fine joke played on those gullible Yankees.

Tori had never met Boozie's great aunt Colley, but when Halloween came, she often wondered about her. Colley Washington was the Delight Diviner. An elderly spinster, she lived alone in a cabin deep in the woods to the north. It was said she could see visions and tell the future. Nothing that happened in the county happened without Colley's knowledge. She could cure warts just by rubbing them. She knew the secrets of the forest and could mix a potion to cure the body or the soul. It was also said that the power skipped a generation. Many in the Negro community had no doubts as to Colley's successor. Little Boozie Brown had the gift.

ON THAT Halloween night, far across town, a man dressed in black emerged from a darkened house.

"Here, kitty, kitty," he said.

His voice was deep and rich, soothing. The old tomcat was suspicious, but hungry enough to saunter up to the man on the porch. He had found the man to be obliging in the past, and licked his chops in anticipation.

"Come, my little friend," said the man, picking up the ragged yellow cat and stroking his rough fur. "First a favor, then a feast."

He carried the old cat to a nearby chair on the porch. On a small table next to the chair was a partly opened tin of fish, a blank sheet of paper, a rag, and a bottle of ink. The cat purred, smelling the fish.

The man soaked the rag in the ink and pressed it to the front paw of the old tom. Then he removed the rag and lightly touched the cat's paw to the paper. The cat meowed as the man lifted him from the chair, away from the fish, and carried him into the house. "Quiet, little fellow," said the man in black. "You've earned your supper. First we must get you clean again."

The cat looked up at him and was met with cool eyes, much like his own.

"That's right," said the man. It's Saturday night."

"MY DADDY says he'll never come around here," said Marvin Gates, leaning forward in his seat on the bus behind Reese Jones. "My daddy says he only works in the city."

Reese Jones slowed the school bus as he approached the entrance of the country club at Radium Springs. He smiled to himself. If the cat burglar ever did hit Hayley, it would be Sam Gates's house he would hit first. Reese chuckled as he turned into the drive.

"Don't worry yourself, Marvin," he said over his shoulder. "And sit back in your seat. There ain't much in Hayley to tempt a high-class thief like him, not even your daddy's house."

"But my daddy's the richest man in Hayley," Marvin protested.

"Rudolph Townsend's the richest man in Hayley, Marvin."

"Oh, I wasn't countin' him," Marvin replied. "He don't really live in Hayley."

"Government says he does," said Reese.

All were talking about the cat burglar's latest caper on this Monday after Halloween, the second of November. He had managed to get through an unlocked second-story window of the Boswell home and make off with the banker's private cash. The amount was tactfully omitted from the news reports, but those in the know said banker Boswell, a somewhat unethical man himself, probably lost a lot more than he reported to the police.

Mr. and Mrs. Boswell, like most of the society crowd of Albany, had been away at the time of the burglary, at the Halloween Party at Radium Springs. A careful man, Boswell had hired a couple of off-duty sheriff's deputies to guard his home during the party, as it was on a Saturday night, and the cat always struck on Saturday.

He had thought it a fine joke to dress himself that evening as a pirate, but when he returned home and checked his money box, a shoe box in among his wife's hotboxes, and found he had been robbed, he showed his true colors by refusing to pay the deputies. The deputies swore they had not been drinking, nor left their posts. They had heard not a sound, they said, and questioned that any man could have got by them.

The school bus lumbered to a stop in front of the clubhouse and Wendy got on, making her way past Marvin, back to a seat held for her by Tori and Jessie Potter. She sat down heavily and propped her books beside her on the seat.

"Want some candy?" asked Wendy, reaching into the pocket of her brightly patterned skirt.

Tori brightened. "Sure," she said. "What do you have today?"

"Licorice."

Jessie looked at Tori and they both chuckled.

Wendy had begun bringing candy every morning for herself and her two friends. Tori and Jessie could not have known that Wendy was stealing the candy from the club snack bar in the golfer's lounge. It began in September, just after the Labor Day dance.

Wendy had been frightened by her father's behavior with the woman on the stairs, although she told no one. Wendy did not know what had happened, but since the dance, her parents had become cold to one another, and argued constantly. Every day, Wendy was afraid something terrible was going to happen, and she crouched in a closet and cried during her parent's violent arguments. Going to school had become her only escape, and she dreaded going home. Tori sensed that something was wrong, but Wendy would only say again that she might have to move.

The days flew by. Thanksgiving came and went quietly enough, coming as it did on Thursday, but the barriers went up as usual when Saturday came. It seemed that everyone expected the cat burglar to break his pattern soon. It was inconceivable that he would dare to continue his regular Saturday night visits. There were too many guards, too many eyes, too many waiting for him. But the burglaries continued. The cat's amazing skill astounded the public again and again. It was as if the mysterious looter delighted in taunting the authorities, daring them to catch him. The Sunday edition of the *Albany Journal* was sold out by nine o'clock each Sunday morning, in spite of the extra copies printed to meet the new demand. Legends were a staple of Georgia culture, and with the advent of the cat burglar, not even the ghost of County Pa commanded more respect.

A fortnight later, just before Christmas, there was a fire at the Townsend place. The big red barn burned to the ground, taking the stable with it. Rudolph had seen the flames from the window of the study and had called Chief James immediately, but the blaze fully engulfed the barn before the chief arrived. Rudolph and the Negro butler, Sam, had rushed out with buckets and tried to douse the flames, but their efforts were futile. When Chief James arrived, he and Rudolph managed to get all of the horses out of the stable safely before the flames spread, although the thick smoke nearly disabled them both in the process.

The intense heat forced the three back to the house, where they stood helplessly with Laura Townsend and the servants on the red brick patio and watched the flames devour the wooden structures. Carlton was nowhere to be found.

The fire burned unabated for more than two hours before settling into smoking, smoldering timbers. Several Hayley residents had come to offer their help, as Bubba had told Hedda to call Reese Jones before he left, but there was nothing anyone could do. The barn was far enough away from the house that the fire presented no danger to it.

The full moon lent an eerie light to the scene, creating bold black shadows beneath every tree and fence post under the cloudless sky. Laura Townsend, calm and unruffled by the disaster, had sent the cooks to the kitchen to prepare something to offer the men, and had instructed Sam to bring chairs out to the patio. The men sat on the patio eating sandwiches, drinking beer, and watching the embers die in the cool, humid night air. The house was in no danger, the fire was out, and the horses had been rescued and sheltered in the old barn in the far pasture. As the cost of replacing the barn and the stable presented no problem to the Townsends, the conversation turned from the tragedy to the clearing and rebuilding of the structures.

Bubba James was no expert on arson, but he suspected the fire had been deliberately set. He sat silently, listening to Rudolph and the men discuss the rebuilding of the barn and the stable. If Rudolph had no objection, Bubba had decided he would get an investigator to come down from Atlanta to go through the debris. Carlton's absence was significant to Bubba, in his present frame of mind. Dixie Lee had come home all smiles after her reconciliation with Rudolph, but Bubba James was not a man to forget such a trespass as the younger Townsend had committed with Dixie Lee. It appeared that Carlton had lost the battle for Dixie Lee, and that was probably quite a blow to his ego. And now the barn had burned down, with Rudolph's prize thoroughbred in the stable beside it. It was quite a coincidence.

11

It was also quite a coincidence that Carlton's gray mare was not in the stable when it burned. Rudolph had missed the animal and gone back into the smoke-filled stable to look for it, against Bubba's orders not to chance it. Bubba had followed Rudolph in with a wet towel tied over his mouth and nose, found him overcome with smoke inhalation, and dragged him out to safety. A few minutes of breathing fresh air had revived Rudolph, and no apparent harm was done, but Bubba spoke sharply to him for his folly.

It was after eleven o'clock when Carlton came home, riding up the drive on his big gray. Carlton had been a night rider as a youth, often conducting moonlight trail rides with his friends, but he had outgrown it long ago, and now usually preferred driving his sports car in the evening.

He took the mare out in the moonlight rarely now, and always in the summer months. The fact that he had taken the horse out on this particular evening was unexpected, but not surprising, and certainly not suspicious to Rudolph.

Bubba found it highly suspicious, for he had learned by discreet inquiry of Sam, the butler, of Carlton's usual riding habits, and he found this deviation from pattern significant. He kept his thoughts to himself, and watched with quiet intent as Carlton returned.

Carlton had not seen the smoldering ruins until he rounded the curve of the driveway. The mare had smelled the smoke more than a mile back, and had become more and more jittery as they approached home. When the ruins came into view, the horse reared and bolted, galloping up the drive toward the house, past the smoldering timbers which had been its home. Carlton nearly lost his mount, and regained control of the horse as it approached the patio.

He brought the mare to a halt and jumped off, turning to look at the ruins. He looked back to the house and saw the group of men assembled on the patio. He looked again at the smoking black timbers and swore.

At last he walked to the patio and said, "What the hell happened?"

Rudolph did not stir from his place, and with the shock of the fire long past, he answered calmly, "I would think that was obvious, little brother. We've had a fire. Don't upset yourself. No one was hurt and all the horses are safe."

"Well," Carlton replied, surprised by Rudolph's manner, "you're certainly very calm about this, aren't you? What the hell are you conducting here, a barn-burning party?"

"It seemed like a good idea at the time," replied Rudolph coolly. "Sam, get the boy a drink. One more won't do any harm."

Carlton spotted the chief, drinking lemonade, watching him from the edge of the gathering. He walked to the wrought iron table and sat down on its edge, ignoring Bubba.

"If it's not too much to ask, will somebody tell me what the hell happened here?"

Rudolph's eyes hardened. He leaned forward in his chair and replied, "The damn barn burnt down! What the hell do you think happened?"

No one present, especially Bubba James, missed the deadly undercurrent of conflict in the tone of voice of the brothers.

Carlton got some small satisfaction that he had managed to get a rise out of his brother, and said sarcastically, "I can see that it burned down, but what started it? Did you forget to put out your campfire? Did the cow kick over the lantern? What?"

Rudolph rose from his chair.

"I might ask you the same question," he hissed. "It's more likely that you dropped one of your blasted cigarette butts in the hay, don't you think? Just exactly when did you take the mare out? It wouldn't be around eight-thirty or nine, would it?"

Carlton glared at his brother and hopped down from the table. The two stood facing each other, faces distorted with rage, fists balled, when

Laura Townsend opened the double French doors and returned to the patio.

"Carlton, dear," she greeted him, walking out to him and putting out her hand. Carlton's face softened visibly at her appearance, and Rudolph's composure returned.

"Isn't it a shame, dear?" she continued. "Thank God, everyone is safe and none of the horses were harmed. We have a lot to be thankful for, haven't we?"

"Rudolph and these kind gentleman are already finalizing the plans for clearing away the mess and rebuilding the barn and the stable. I wanted to ask you, dear, don't you think we should relocate the stable this time? I suppose it was foolish to build them so close together, but your father insisted. I guess you never expect something like this will happen to you, though, do you?"

Rudolph took his seat again, and Carlton kissed his mother's hand and drew her closer.

"I'm sorry I wasn't here to help, Mother," he said gently. "I wanted to get out of the house and rode over to Radium Springs for the evening."

Bubba made mental note of this, as Laura replied, "But darling, there was nothing you could have done. It was an inferno in minutes. All any of us could do was sit and watch, and pray the fields didn't catch fire as well. Isn't that right, Rudolph?"

"Absolutely," replied Rudolph, his tranquil manner having returned.

"What do you think about the stable, dear?" Laura asked again.

"I think you're absolutely right, Mother," Carlton replied. "We can put the stable on the other side of the riding ring, or maybe behind the house at the far end of the lawn."

Bubba James rose from his seat and approached his hosts. "Mrs. Townsend, I'll be going now. I can't do anything else here tonight."

"Of course, Chief James," replied Laura. "You'll be needing to get back to Hayley. I just can't thank you enough for all your help. I hate to think what would have happened if you hadn't been here to get Rudolph out of that stable."

Carlton's ears pricked up at this strange statement.

"It was nothing, Ma'am," replied Bubba without emotion. "Sam would have taken care of it if I hadn't been here."

The butler's eyes widened at this statement as he stood silently by the French doors, and he swallowed hard. He was faithful and diligent, but such courage he did not possess.

"I'll be back tomorrow," the chief continued. "Maybe we can find out something about how the fire started."

"You're very kind, chief," said Laura. "We will look forward to seeing you."

"Goodnight, Ma'am." He nodded and looked toward Rudolph.

"Thank you again, Bubba," said Rudolph, and the look that passed between them was one of understanding, that a great debt was owed by one, but was not deemed binding by the other.

"Carlton."

Bubba nodded briefly to his prime suspect and turned to leave, not waiting for a reply.

He received none from Carlton, who was suddenly aware of a new coldness in the man. A puzzling feeling of being lured into a trap dawned in his mind. What was going on here? What was Bubba up to? No, it must be his imagination. He was getting paranoid. He dismissed the thoughts from his mind, but the sinking feeling remained in the pit of his stomach. Something was going on, but what?

Carlton had had a few drinks that night, but now he needed another one. The more he thought about it, the more he became convinced that Bubba James would try to pin the barn burning on him. Maybe more. It was ridiculous.

He guessed that Bubba had found out about his kissing Dixie Lee, because Bubba's attitude had changed toward him. This was not the tolerant lawman he had become used to, skeptical, expectant, condescending. This man was after his hide.

This surprised Carlton. He never imagined that his little tryst with the chief's daughter could have so eroded the dizzyingly high standards of Bubba James. It looked for sure like he had gone too far this time.

Carlton cursed himself and thought again of Dixie Lee. She was more trouble than he had bargained for, but he could not bring himself to curse her too. He loved Dixie Lee. It was a fierce, selfish, romantic love; a stubborn and possessive obsession. Carlton was capable of nothing more. The added factor of Dixie Lee's unattainability only made her more attractive to him. And the specter of her father's wrath only served to strengthen his determination and his anger. He had to have another drink.

Saying nothing to the others, he walked around the house and got in his car. The powerful engine roared to life and he sped down the driveway, past the party on the patio, past the smoldering ruins, heading back to the softly lit bar of Radium Springs.

The car was flying. The lights of the country club were in view when he hit a deer. The car sped out of control and went off the road, into a deep gully, flipping over twice and landing right-side up. Miraculously, Carlton had no broken bones. There was, however, a deep gash on his head, and a number of cuts and bruises. He was stunned, and sat with his hands on the wheel, not knowing where he was.

A young man appeared at the side of the car and wrestled with the door. It would not open.

"Hold on," he yelled, "I'll get you out of there."

He ran to the other side of the car and tried the door, but it too was smashed and would not open. He picked up a large rock from the ground, smashed away remnants of the already-broken window, reached in and grabbed Carlton, and pulled him out.

Carlton regained his senses and the two ran, stumbling, away from the car, through the gully, toward the entrance of Radium Springs. In seconds the car exploded, the force sending the two men reeling to the soft, damp clay.

The two men, tangled together on the ground, raised their heads and looked back at the flaming wreckage.

Hot beads of sweat covered Carlton's forehead, and his heart pounded. His head hurt terribly, as if a band of steel was compressing his skull, and the blood from his cut forehead ran slowly down his face.

But he was fully alert and aware of what had happened. He turned and looked at the face of his savior for the first time, and met the eyes of a young man he had never seen before. He was about Carlton's age, maybe a little older, and he was obviously a gentleman of means, for Carlton recognized the air of prestige and privilege which bonds all members of the upper class.

"Thanks," said Carlton, reaching for his handkerchief as he struggled to his feet. "I owe you one."

"It was nothing, sir, I assure you," responded the young stranger, also getting to his feet, and dusting the glass and dirt from his expensive suit.

"You must let me replace your clothes." said Carlton absently, immediately falling into practiced gentility.

"Nonsense, my friend," replied the man. "I won't hear of it. Come now, we must get you inside and see to that cut. Anything broken?"

"Don't think so," said Carlton, pressing his ribs. "What a hell of a thing. I've never had a smashup in my life."

"There's the carcass of a buck out on the road a ways back," replied the stranger. "Don't you remember hitting it?"

"Hell, no," said Carlton. "I don't remember a damn thing until I saw you."

"It was a hell of a crash," said the man. "You flipped that little car over two or three times. It's a miracle you weren't killed, my friend."

"I would have been, if it hadn't been for you," said Carlton.

He winced as he put his weight on his left leg.

"Ah," said the stranger, "so you're not as well as you supposed. Here, take my shoulder."

The two started toward the lights of the club, Carlton supporting himself on the strong hard shoulder of his rescuer.

"Who are you, anyway?" asked Carlton. "I pride myself on knowing everyone in this district. Are you new to Albany?"

"Yes," replied the man. "My name is Woodville Price. Woody to my friends. I've been here a month or two. I was invited here tonight by a friend, Alan Dunlap—"

"Alan?" interrupted Carlton. "I thought he was in Atlanta."

"You're absolutely right, he is," replied Woody. "He told me to come anytime and give his name."

"Damn lucky he did," said Carlton.

"And you, my friend. Who might you be?"

"Townsend. Carlton Townsend. Or what's left of him."

"Indeed?" said Woody. He waved his free hand as they approached the steps of the clubhouse, surveying the grounds. "Well, it seems I've rescued the owner of this fine resort himself."

"One of them," replied Carlton. "You like the place, huh?"

"It's perfectly charming. I intend to apply for membership at once. I've been busy since I've come, neglecting my social life. But I intend to make up for it shortly."

"Don't bother with the membership," said Carlton. "You've paid your dues in full. I'll speak to Marie tonight."

"How gracious of you," said Woody. "My thanks."

"Mine, too," said Carlton. He stopped and looked at his new friend. "Really, thank you for saving my life."

The two entered the club and were surrounded immediately by concerned members. Dr. Waldrop was present and attended to Carlton's injuries, while Marie Hamilton called Laura with the news of the accident.

Woody Price stood by calmly, quietly, making sure Carlton was comfortable and tended to. Carlton liked Woody immensely already, for his lofty manners seemed to rub off on everyone around him, and lift the atmosphere of the others into a higher plane.

He was about six feet tall, with longish dark brown hair and a neat, thick moustache and sideburns. His hazel eyes were startling in such a face, but were blurred behind thick horn-rimmed glasses. He walked with the grace of a prince, and charmed everyone he met, especially the ladies. His clothes were of the finest wool, and Carlton knew the cost of his Italian shoes. This guy was loaded, and apparently single. He was handsome in spite of the glasses, and the belles of Albany would be in for a treat, or so Carlton thought.

Laura Townsend and Rudolph arrived in minutes, and Dr. Waldrop told Mrs. Townsend that Carlton's head wound would require stitches. They would have to take him to the doctor's office in Albany. Rudolph had no harsh words for Carlton as he helped him to the car. He understood well that his brother would have died in the explosion had not Woodville Price been nearby. In spite of their differences, Rudolph loved his brother. Nothing made this plainer than a near-fatality.

BOOZIE HAD seen the ghost of County Pa. She had seen him not once, but three times, walking the grounds of the Townsend game preserve. To anyone who would listen, Boozie explained that it was only after dark that the ghost assumed his fearful shape. During the day, he appeared to look just like a regular human being.

Boozie had never met Price Townsend, but she had seen his portrait many times. She used to play in the big hall at Radium Springs when her mother, Mary Lee, cleaned and dusted. She had recognized the face of the apparition in the woods immediately. It was County Pa, all right.

Boozie claimed that the ghost had even spoken to her, warning her to stay off his land. He tried to catch her once, she said, but he couldn't, because she had been outside the fence. Apparently, the ghost couldn't step even one foot off the game preserve or he would evaporate.

Doreen was fascinated by the child's tales of the ghost, and told all her friends that Boozie was the chosen one, the next Delight Diviner. Word of the child's story spread quickly through the Negro community, and filtered back to the white folk of Hayley through their children. Ottis was convinced that Mary Bea was possessed by an evil spirit, and threatened to whip the tar out of her if he heard one more word about ghosts and spirits. But no one could shake Boozie's story. County Pa's ghost was real to her, whether anyone believed her or not. One person did, right from the start. Aunt Colley, the Delight Diviner, believed her, because Colley knew that every word Boozie said was true.

If others didn't believe, as some of the rural folk claimed not to, Boozie's story nevertheless resulted in the strongest taboo ever observed in the county. No one went within half a mile of the preserve if they could help it. Dogs were chained at night so they could not wander onto the preserve. The seriousness of the matter saw an end to even the calling of the name of the ghost of County Pa. To cross the fence was to die.

12

If anyone had seen the stranger walking alone along the railroad tracks that evening, they would have warned him of the mortal danger which awaited him. The solitary traveler who approached Hayley three days before Christmas wore a tattered leather jacket, and carried a pack on his back and a duffle bag under his arm. He was thin, rather tall, had a full black beard and covering his jet black hair was a weather-beaten hat with a faded green hatband.

During the Depression, hundreds of penniless wretches had come through Georgia. There were not as many now, and the residents of Hayley had gotten used to seeing them long ago. They were largely ignored. No one, for instance, would have taken the time to notice that there was something different about the man in the tattered leather jacket.

His walk was not that of an aimless wanderer, but the walk of a man with purpose and direction. His posture was erect, his face calm and determined. Nevertheless, he was what he appeared to be—a homeless wanderer, a hobo.

The man stopped to rest when he reached the eastern boundary of the forbidden Townsend game preserve. New to the country, he could not have known that the town of Hayley was just two miles down the tracks. He was tired, and the lush evergreen forest tempted him to ignore the trespass warnings. He pulled his jacket closer about his wiry body as the setting sun stole its warmth from the afternoon, and a cutting wind began to blow. He decided to make camp for the night, climbed the rusty barbed-wire fence, and entered the Townsend game preserve.

A carpet of crisp dead leaves and twigs snapped and crackled beneath his feet as he made his way to a clearing not far from the fence, the same clearing where Ottis had found the mysterious black knapsack three months earlier. The hobo set down his burdens and began to gather up wood for a fire.

When the fire was well established, the hobo sat back and warmed himself. The forest was dark now, and quiet. He noticed the stillness and listened for some sign of life. He heard nothing, not even the chirp of a cricket. The only sound was the low moaning of the wind through the trees. The hobo shivered and reached for a biscuit in his duffle bag. He listened to the wind as he ate, and wondered if a storm was coming.

When he finished the food, he got up and began to gather dry leaves into a bed for the night. He pulled a thin blanket from his pack and lay down next to the fire. He felt uneasy. The stillness was unnatural. The warm crackle of the fire seemed to emphasize the loneliness of the place; the thick towering pines seemed to make his presence seem tiny and insignificant. There was something sinister about this place. The man decided to leave it quickly, at first light.

He closed his eyes, but sleep eluded him. The wind became stronger, moaning low and steady through the pines, whipping the flame from the fire. The hobo shivered beneath his blanket and looked up to see thick black clouds racing past the new moon. He started defensively at the sound of a thunderclap. He rose quickly and kicked dirt into the fire. A storm was coming, a big one.

The hobo gathered his belongings and headed into the forest to find shelter, perhaps beneath an overhanging rock or under a large evergreen. He found a rutted trail and followed it, the wind whipping his face and chilling his bones. A flash of lightning lit the path before him, followed quickly by a crash of thunder. He saw, in the distance, another clearing, and in it, a rough cabin. It was the cabin of County Pa.

The hobo smiled when he saw this unexpected refuge, and broke into a run as the clouds broke, reaching the cabin just before the chilling rain soaked through to his skin. It was unlocked and he entered gratefully, closing the door against the cold wind. Inside, it was pitch black, the filthy windows barring even the glow of the night. The man groped his way to an inside corner and sat down, setting his burdens to the side.

Retrieving matches and a candle from his bag, he lit the candle and let the soft light spread across the room. The room was bare except for cardboard cartons stacked against the wall opposite him. Finding them empty, he picked up several and carried them back to his corner. He folded them out flat and arranged them into a pallet, a crude barrier against the cold wooden floor. He pulled out his blanket and swept it round his shoulders.

He carried the candle before him and walked through the cabin to the kitchen. He saw no evidence of humanity in the place, no forgotten tool or discarded bottle. He walked into the small room off the kitchen, and stood directly over the secret sanctuary of County Pa. He stooped down to take a closer look at the rotting rug which covered the hatch in the floor, and found it to be alive with worms and roaches. He dropped the edge of the thick rug in disgust and left the room.

The rotting debris crackled beneath his feet as he headed back to his corner, through the kitchen and into the dining room. When the gentle light of the candle fell on the wall facing him as he emerged from the kitchen, the pale ghastly face of a man seemed to jump out at him from the shadows, and he jumped back and cried out instinctively. Before the cry died away, he realized the apparition was only a faded portrait on the wall, but his body reacted with a surge of adrenalin before he could calm himself.

With a pounding heart and a damp brow, he took several deep breaths, then walked over to the portrait. He held the candle closer, and looked into the eyes of County Pa. The eyes of the dead man held him and he could not look away. A bolt of lightning struck a towering pine at the edge of the preserve, the thunder rocking the very foundations of the cabin. The face in the portrait seemed alive suddenly, seemed to welcome the violent power of the raging storm around them. As the hobo continued to stare at the face of the dead man, he was again aware of a menacing presence, a heavy oppressive force which clung to the place, as if the gravity there was able to suck and hold him, as if it wanted to swallow him up. He shivered. It was eerie, ghostly.

He fought the urge to run from the cabin, telling himself that his mind was playing tricks on him. He reached deep within himself for the common sense and levelheadedness that had allowed him to conquer his own dragons and bring him safely this far. His heart slowed its race and his breath came easier. He chuckled at his own folly. He looked County Pa dead in the eye and whispered, "Boo."

The hobo walked back to his cardboard pallet and lay down to sleep, as the wind howled and the rain swirled down upon the little cabin in sheets, battering the walls. He pulled his duffle bag under his head and closed his eyes. Something called to him from long ago as he lay there, comforting him. He was too tired to question the feeling, too weary to recognize it. In minutes, he was sound asleep.

As the stranger slept, the weather turned mean in south Georgia. A winter storm swept through from the north with forty-mile-an-hour winds and freezing rain that turned to snow. Snowflakes were a rare occurrence that delighted the children of Hayley, but they never seemed to stick, melting away when they met the wet earth, leaving only slick patches of ice here and there.

The children's dream of a white Christmas did not materialize, but they were treated to a fairy-tale-like scene the next morning nevertheless. The trees were transformed into glittering ice sculptures, long icicles covering bare limbs, bending them down to the frozen ground. Many of the limbs broke under the weight of the ice, and yards everywhere were cluttered with them. By noon, the heat of the winter sun had melted the unwilling sculptures and the icicles were gone, along with the north wind. Things were pretty much back to normal, save for the debris.

RUDOLPH TOWNSEND was on Southland Road early that morning, exercising his new thoroughbred stallion. He was pleased with the horse, finding him intelligent and easy to train. As he approached the game preserve, Rudolph noticed a slight change in the gait of the stallion, and he shortened the reins, putting a gentle, yet firm, pressure on the horse's bit. The stallion stopped and Rudolph dismounted.

Years of riding experience told Rudolph that the steed was slightly favoring his right leg. He inspected the right front hoof and found a large stone wedged there. As he looked around him on the frozen ground for a stick to remove the stone, he heard a sound behind him, and turned to see a man climbing over the fence at the edge of the game preserve.

The man was a stranger, and from the looks of him, a hobo. It struck Rudolph as funny that a man down on his luck would run smack into the man on whose land he had trespassed. Rudolph found a stick and bent to the stallion, raised up his leg and began digging at the stone. The horse whinnied as the stranger approached, and Rudolph spoke soothingly to the steed as the stick broke in his hand. Rudolph stood up as the man reached him.

"Howdy, friend," said the hobo.

"Morning, stranger," replied Rudolph.

Rudolph was dressed in a worn pair of Levis, a sheepskin jacket, and muddy boots. There was nothing about his dress or his manner which would have told the hobo that he was the richest man in the county.

Seeing Rudolph's friendly glance, the stranger paused.

"Fine animal you got there," he said. His face was drawn up in a grimace and his slouch made him look years older than he was.

"Sure is," Rudolph answered, patting the stallion's long neck. "Belongs to the squire up at the big house, yonder. Caught a stone in his hoof. You wouldn't happen to have a knife on you, would you?"

"Matter of fact, I do," said the hobo.

He set his bag down on the ground and fished for a knife, then handed it to Rudolph. Rudolph took the knife and turned back to the horse.

"I'm a stranger in these parts, friend," said the hobo as Rudolph worked to loosen the stone. "Would there be a town nearby?"

"Just over the ridge there," Rudolph replied, nodding in the direction of Hayley. "You plan on staying around these parts long?"

The stranger smiled.

"I don't stay around no parts long," he said. "Just lookin' for a little work and shelter for the night, is all."

"Got caught last night, did you?"

"Boy, howdy," said the hobo. "I thought you Southerners were supposed to have mild winters. I nearly drowned before I got lucky in them woods and found a little cabin to sleep in."

Rudolph chuckled and the stranger looked at him questioningly. "You'd been better off in the hands of Mother Nature than on that land, I think," he said with a twinkle of amusement in his eyes.

"How's that?" asked the hobo.

"The land's posted," replied Rudolph with a grin. "Belongs to the big mucky-mucks that own this horse. They shoot trespassers without a second thought, I'm told. Also say the whole place is haunted."

"That so?" said the hobo, rubbing his whiskers.

"I wouldn't go back there if I were you, friend," said Rudolph.

The hobo nodded thoughtfully and looked back to the forest.

"Haunted, huh? I might have to agree with you there. It was a strange feelin', a strange feelin' indeed I had in that there cabin last night. Even the forest critters seem to have deserted them woods. No, I have no wishin' to return to it. But I thank you for the warnin'. Mighty neighborly of you."

"Forget it," said Rudolph, as the stone popped free. Rudolph stood up and handed the hobo back his knife. "Thanks for the loan."

"Anytime," said the hobo. He extended a rough hand. "Good to meet up with you."

Rudolph shook his hand and said, "And good luck to you, sir."

Rudolph mounted the stallion and waved a hand in farewell. He turned the horse down the red clay road and galloped away, controlling the powerful animal with effortless grace.

Once Rudolph was gone, the stranger abandoned his slouch and stood up straight. His face relaxed, and the simple smile faded. He could be himself again. Without the pretense, he looked years younger.

"Decent chap," he said aloud.

It had become his habit to talk to himself when he was alone and lonely. Hearing his own words, he suddenly chuckled at his inappropriate choice of words.

"Or as Will Fable would say," he said with a grin, "nice feller."

The hobo shivered in the cold air and pulled his ragged coat closer to him. He looked back at the silent forest. He would not be back.

13

Tori was out in the yard gathering up the limbs from the ice storm when she saw a tall stranger coming down the railroad tracks behind her house, which was about five hundred feet from the back fence. He wore ragged clothes and an old hat with a faded green hatband. He carried a duffle bag under his arm and wore a pack on his back. Another hobo.

Tori paused in her work and stared as the man approached. Upon seeing her, the man smiled and tipped his hat. Tori smiled back and set down her burden of fallen limbs. She ran to the back fence to get a better look.

"Good day, missy," said the man. "Looks like you've got yourself quite a cleanup job there."

"Sure do," replied Tori. "It's sure a mess."

The man set his bag down on the top rail and propped one foot on the lower. Tori looked up and found the eyes of a friend. There was laughter in his eyes, and kindness.

"We had snow last night," said Tori, "but it didn't stick. The trees looked so pretty early this morning, just like castles. But look at all the nice limbs that got broken."

"Mother nature," replied the stranger. "You gotta respect her all right. She plays no favorites and she can turn on you in a minute." He looked at the scattered limbs. "That's the good thing about trees, though. No matter how many limbs they lose, they'll be back full and whole come spring."

"You're right," said Tori. "I never knew grown-ups cared much about trees."

"I'm well acquainted with trees, missy," said the man. "Been my shelter many a night, you see."

"That's my tree over there," said Tori. She pointed to a huge oak at the edge of the Cooper property. "Jessie and I climb up there every day in summer. We can see everything from there; General Store, the beauty shop, the square, everything. Well, except for the funeral parlor."

"It's a beauty, all right," said the man. "I had one like it once, a long time ago."

"Are you a hobo?" asked Tori.

The man laughed.

"I guess some people would say I was," he answered. "What do you think?"

Tori considered him closely.

"Well," she said, "you look like a hobo, but . . . . "

He compressed his lips and squinted his eyes, imitating the gestures of the child as she pondered the matter.

"But you don't talk like one," Tori said. "And you don't frown like one, either."

"Ah," replied the man. He seemed to agree with her, as if she were a detective correctly interpreting a string of clues.

"You don't walk like one, either," continued Tori. "You know, kind of bent over, like they're carrying a load of firewood or something."

"I see," said the stranger. "You're right, of course. I guess I better practice up a little more."

"You might better," agreed Tori, "because you're too tall, too."

The stranger stroked his beard in appreciation.

"Well," he said, "I can fix happy," he gave a mock scowl, "but I can't fix tall."

They both laughed, already friends. "What's your name?" asked Tori.

"Fable's the name, missy. Will Fable. And I travel all over this great country by the rails."

"But it's winter," said Tori. "Don't you get cold at night?"

"Cold? Why this ain't cold, missy. Cold is Montana and New York state. Michigan's cold. The Dakotas, now that's cold for you."

"Have you been all those places?"

"Why, of course I have. I come from the North. We have a lot colder weather than you ever get here in Georgia. I planned my travels to take me south for the winter months, you see. It has gotten colder down here than I expected, though."

"Meema says this is the coldest winter she's seen down here. At least since we've been here."

"And how many years is that?"

"Six or seven, I think," said Tori. "We're from New York."

"That so?" said Will.

"Well, Daddy's not," Tori corrected herself. "He's from here in Hayley. Mother and Meema were from New York. But Daddy played baseball in New York. For the Yankees. He was a pitcher."

"That so?"

Will Fable looked up and saw Elizabeth Cooper standing in the open back door of the house. She walked to the edge of the porch and stood watching them.

"Afternoon, Ma'am," said Will, tipping his worn hat.

Tori ran to meet her grandmother.

"Meema," she said excitedly, "come and meet Mr. Fable. He's a hobo. He travels all around the country on the trains. He's been everywhere."

Mrs. Cooper walked out to the fence with Tori. It was her custom to offer a night's shelter in the barn to any homeless travelers who passed her way, as well as a hot meal, if they proved they could be trusted.

"Good morning, young man," she said. "I am Elizabeth Cooper and this is my granddaughter, Tori."

"Will Fable, Ma'am," said the stranger. "I'm mighty pleased to make your acquaintance. That's a fine girl you have there."

"Yes," agreed Mrs. Cooper, "and she'll keep a fascinating fellow like yourself talking for hours if you let her. Especially if you mention trains. She dreams about them like they were living things. Her father says she should have been born a boy."

Will Fable saw at once that Elizabeth Cooper was tolerant and kind. "I noticed your granddaughter was clearing up the yard when I came up," said Will. "I'd be happy to lend a hand if you would allow it."

"We would both be very grateful for your help, I'm sure," said Mrs. Cooper. "Will you be staying long in Hayley?"

"Just passing through, Ma'am," replied Will. He looked down at the ground for a moment. "I don't take no handouts, Ma'am. I'm no beggar. I work for my keep. If you have any chores need doing, I'd be mighty grateful for the chance to earn a night's rest in your barn, yonder."

Although Mrs. Cooper was cautious with strangers, after speaking with Will Fable, she decided he was harmless. She had never found that kindness was repaid with evil. Only once had she turned a man away from her door, a man with liquor on his breath.

"You are welcome to pass the night in the barn, Mr. Fable," she said. "As to the chores, you may use your own judgment. Tori will bring you some supper at nightfall."

"Thank you, Ma'am. You're very kind. I'll just get started on the yard, then."

Tori was thrilled. "Come on, Mr. Fable," she said. "We can get this yard cleared up in no time."

The man set down his burdens as he came inside the fence, and the two got to work, side by side, with Tori asking question after question.

Mrs. Cooper walked back to the house and returned to her own chores. The man puzzled her. She had recognized the accent. He was from the North, New York or perhaps Pennsylvania. His use of colloquial terms did not disguise the fact that he was a man of intelligence and a man of some education. His bearing was proud and his manner courteous. She wondered if he, too, was a victim of the stock market crash who had found his way south. Yet most such men had by this time begun rebuilding their lives and their fortunes, for nine years had passed since the crash. He was a mystery, then. Will Fable's life history, she decided, was none of her business.

In about an hour, Tori and Will finished gathering up the fallen twigs and limbs from the yard. Tori sat down on the back steps to watch as Will used a hatchet to chop the larger limbs into kindling.

"I see the trains come through at night from my bedroom window," Tori said. "The eight-fifty stops at the depot, but the other two come late, and pass us by. Sometimes the whistle wakes me up, and I can see the lighted passenger cars from my window."

"Ever been on a train, missy?"

"We rode the train from New York, Meema says," Tori answered, "but I was too little to remember it. I'd love to go again. Meema says one day we'll ride to Atlanta."

"Maybe you will," said Will. "Hold on to your dreams. They keep you sweet."

They heard the sound of the back door opening and looked up to see Mrs. Cooper coming out on the porch, mixing bowl in her hands. Elizabeth surveyed the neat yard with a glance, and found herself impressed.

"Tori, you will have to come in now to help me. We have a lot of orders to get out." She looked at Will. "A fine job, Mr. Fable," she said. "And I appreciate the kindling."

"You're most welcome, Ma'am," replied Will.

"I'm afraid the barn is a bit of a mess, but it's dry. Tori will bring you some blankets after while."

"May I ask a favor of you, Ma'am?"

"Of course," she answered. "What is it?"

"If you don't mind," he said, "I'd like to build a small fire tonight. I find a fire good company. There will be no trace of it left when I move on tomorrow."

"That wood will be too wet to burn," she said. "You may use some from the stack here on the back porch."

Will nodded, and smiled his thanks.

THE WIND that whipped the area for days died out after the storm, and the night air was warmer. Will Fable sat comfortably by his little fire as darkness fell a little after four o'clock. From the house, he heard the sounds of a child playing carols on a perfectly tuned piano. He was content. He rose and went into the barn, opened his pack and took out a leather-bound pad and a pencil. Returning to his place before the fire, he opened the pad to a blank page and wrote the word "Hayley" at the top of the page. The light of the fire danced on the page as he wrote for the next hour. When the music from the house stopped, he put the pad away.

The screen door of the back porch opened and Tori descended the steps, carrying a blanket and a steaming plate covered with a napkin. Will stood up as she approached the fire.

"Here's your supper, Mr. Fable."

Will took the plate and set it down, then turned and took the blanket.

"Thank you, missy."

Tori sat down with him by the fire. He took up the plate and removed the napkin. The aroma of the food filled his nostrils and he sighed appreciatively.

"Meema said I could keep you company while you ate," Tori said.

"I'd like some company," said Will as he put the blanket around her. He looked down at the generous helpings of sweet potatoes, macaroni and cheese, and cornbread with butter.

"There's chocolate cake for dessert," Tori added. "But it was too much to carry all at once."

Tori talked easily as Will ate, answering his questions about Hayley, about Mrs. Cooper, and about Tori herself. It seemed he was more hungry for information than for food. Tori soon carried the empty plate back to the house, and returned with the cake.

"I wanted to ask you about all your adventures," said Tori, returning to her place beside him, "but all I've done is talk about us."

"Well, missy, it's hard for a man to eat and talk at the same time."

"I guess you're right," said Tori, "but after you finish that cake, it's your turn."

"Agreed," he said. When he finished the last of the cake he said, "Your grandmother sure can cook."

"You're finished now," said Tori. "Tell me all about your travels. You promised."

"There's not that much to tell," said Will. He leaned back on his elbows and looked up at the night sky, clear as glass and filled with brilliant stars. "You don't see a sky like this very often where I come from. It's a common sight in the desert, though, and down south."

"Don't they have stars where you come from?"

"Sure, but you can't see them like you can here. Up north there's a lot of factories and mills. The smoke gets in the air and blocks out the stars."

"Where?"

"Philadelphia, Pennsylvania."

"Ben Franklin," said Tori.

"That's right," smiled Will.

He looked back up to the stars. They had captured his imagination.

"Look there," he said, pointing south, "Orion has returned."

"What's Orion?"

"It's a constellation, like the Big Dipper."

"I know the Big Dipper," said Tori. "I'll find it for you." She searched the clear black sky in vain, and turned to Will in disappointment. "Where did it go?" she asked, mystified.

Will laughed. "It's winter, missy," he said. "You can't see the Big Dipper all year round. The sky changes with the seasons."

"How'd you know that, Mr. Fable?" asked Tori.

"My father knew all about the stars. He told me about them. We'd sit for hours and look at them. He's dead now. He died when I was eighteen, a long time ago."

"How old are you now?"

"Thirty-five."

"Wow," said Tori. "That's old."

Will smiled.

"Orion is easy to find, Tori. See that chain of three stars, real straight and close together?"

"I see it," said Tori happily.

"Now look. See those four stars there, that sort of form a long box around the chain of stars? See, just like four corners of a rectangle. That is Orion."

"Does 'Orion' mean box?"

"No," Will chuckled, "it means hunter. Orion the hunter. The three stars form his belt at the waist."

"Doesn't look like a man to me," said Tori. "Looks like a box."

"Here," said Will. "I'll show you."

He reached for his pad and turned to a blank page. He sketched in the stars, then drew the figure of a man to correspond to them.

"You have to see him in your imagination," said Will. "It's just a way the scientists have of naming the stars, you see."

"But the Big Dipper really looks like a dipper," protested Tori.

"Well," said Will, "they got lucky on that one, didn't they?" Tori laughed.

"But the constellations are important. They guided sailors for hundreds of years. They've had names since Bible times. One of the Psalms mentions the Seven Sisters and Orion."

Tori made a mental note of this; she would ask her grandmother to look it up for her. She looked at Will as he gazed heavenward, and wondered about him. He was like no hobo she had ever met. He knew about such wonderful things. He spent time with her and talked to her like she was all grown up. He made her feel safe and special. All formality between them was gone. It seemed natural for her to call him Will, for he seemed much a child himself to Tori.

"Tori, do you see the red star in one corner of the rectangle?"

"I see it, Will."

"That is Betelgeuse."

"Do all the stars in the sky have their own names?" asked Tori in amazement.

"All the ones in the constellations do."

"Gosh, Will! There must be hundreds."

"You're right," said Will. "Now, I'll give you a present that will last forever."

"What?"

"From now on, Betelgeuse will be your own special star. It will always be up there watching over you."

"Gosh," said Tori, her eyes wide with wonder. "My own star? Really, Will?"

"Well, you know its name, don't you? And you know how to find it?"

"I sure do!"

"Then it must be yours."

He tore from the pad the page he had used to sketch the constellation. He labeled the special star, and wrote its name and the name of the constellation for her.

"Here you are," he said. "The personal property of Miss Victoria Tanner."

Tori grabbed the paper and looked happily to her star, Betelgeuse. Will looked up, too, patting her on the shoulder. Just then, a falling star blazed across the sky.

"It's good luck," said Will. "The stars have sealed the bargain for you."

"Quick!" said Tori. "Make a wish."

Will watched as Tori closed her eyes tight. She wished with all her might that Will would stay forever.

"Will," said Tori, "Betelgeuse will never fall away, will it?"

"No" said Will. "None of the stars in the constellations ever fall."

"Why not?"

Will frowned. He never considered such a thing. Why didn't they, indeed? He did not know the answer. Then he smiled at the child.

"Now that's a question for the scientists if I ever heard one," he said. "I don't know."

Mrs. Cooper appeared at the door.

"Tori," she called, "say good night to Mr. Fable. It's time to come in."

Tori got to her feet.

"Thank you, Will," she said.

Impulsively, she hugged him. Then she turned and ran to the house, eager to tell her grandmother of the wonders of the universe.

14

It was Christmas Eve. There was to be a special communion service at the Good Shepherd Baptist Church at five-thirty that evening. The pastor, Brother Oliver Goodson, was assured of a full house, for his daughter Camilla had come in on the train from New York City two days earlier. The beautiful Camilla's presence at church never failed to elicit the attendance of every family in Hayley. Even the Presbyterians attended.

After breakfast, Tori took a plate of buttered biscuits and a bowl of oatmeal out to the barn for Will. It was a clear, cold morning, a little past seven o'clock. Tori saw that the fire was out and the barn door closed. With great delight, she remembered her visit with him the night before.

"Will," she called, "I brought you some breakfast."

She opened the door and walked into the shadowy barn, greeted only by the lowing of Bessie, the milk cow.

"Mornin', Bessie," she said, as she set down the plate. "Will?" she called again.

He was gone. She walked to the door and pulled it wide. She walked around the barn, calling for the hobo, but he did not answer. Surely, he would not have left without saying goodbye, would he?

"Heck!" said Tori with a pout.

She walked into the barn to get some hay for Bessie, and stopped in amazement, for the interior of the barn had been transformed. Nails had been placed at intervals on the wall, and various yard tools and implements were hung neatly out of the way, but within easy reach. The dirt floor had been swept of debris, and Bessie's stall cleaned. The cow was munching contentedly on a full trough of hay. Even the firewood had been stacked neatly, with a separate pile of small limbs and kindling off to one side.

Tori wondered how he had the time and the light to do it all. She walked over to a rough-hewn table next to the stall. The lamp was empty. Beside it was a note, one of the sheets of paper from the notebook Tori had seen last night. Quickly, she opened the note and read, in Will's beautiful handwriting: "Thanks for the roof, the vittles, and the company. I'll be back to say goodbye and clear the fire away before I leave."

Maybe he can stay another night, Tori thought, especially after Meema sees how nice he cleaned up the barn. Besides, it's Christmas!

Tori determined that she would stay close to the house all day so as not to miss Will's return. She retrieved the plate and ran back to the house, to tell her grandmother about the barn. Mrs. Cooper interrupted her last-minute baking to come out and see the great sight Tori described. She was delighted, and promised Tori the hobo could stay another night if he wished.

The morning was spent in the kitchen, with Tori helping her grandmother bake, package, and wrap the last of her Christmas orders. At noon they were ready to make their deliveries. They carried the boxes of cakes out to the old LaSalle sedan and put them in the back seat.

Will Fable waved as they passed him at the post office window. Mrs. Cooper stopped the car and said, "Mr. Fable, I want to thank you for cleaning up the barn. That was very kind of you. You are welcome to stay another night if you like. We have some special treats for Christmas dinner, and there will be plenty for three."

"I don't want to impose, Ma'am," said Will, "especially during this holiday."

"Nonsense," replied Mrs. Cooper. "Of course you'll stay. I insist."

"Why, thank you, Meema!" said Tori, with a secret look at Will.

"Tori and I have some deliveries to make," said Mrs. Cooper. "Then we'll be back."

"Yes, Ma'am," said Will, tipping his hat.

Later that afternoon, Mrs. Cooper carried a box to the barn. She found Will Fable sitting by his small fire, writing in a notebook. He put the notebook away as she approached, stood up, and took off his hat.

"Afternoon, Ma'am," he said. "May I help you with that?"

She handed him the box.

"Writing a letter?" she asked.

Will's eyes dropped to the ground.

"Yes, Ma'am," he answered.

"You have family in Pennsylvania?"

He hesitated. "Only my mother, Ma'am," he said. "I lost my wife and son in a fire about six years ago."

"I'm so sorry," said Mrs. Cooper. So this was the tragedy she had sensed in the man's past. "You loved them very much, didn't you?"

Will's eyes met those of Mrs. Cooper, and he read the kindness and sympathy they held. It gave him the strength to open his heart to her.

"I thought I would die myself of that misery," he said. "It has taken me a very long time to get over it."

"And have you?"

"Only after a long road alone, Ma'am," he said. "A journey that has taken me to the depths of my own soul. I believe I'm on the way back, now that my journey is ending."

"I can see that it is," said Mrs. Cooper gently. "I can see that you have suffered as few men have, but I also see a peace in your eyes. But you seem restless still."

"I have made peace with myself, and with life. But you are right, I still have a ways to go before my soul will not rage against what has befallen me." He put the box down and faced her again. "You remind me of another lady I met in my travels, a teacher. She was very kind to me. She showed me that I could amount to something."

"You have found a new reason for living?"

He smiled. "I have some people who have encouraged me."

"Encouraged you to write about your experiences? A book, perhaps?"

"Not much gets past you, does it, Ma'am?"

"I knew from the beginning that you were no ignorant vagabond," she said. "You give yourself away, son. Your manners."

Will smiled, remembering that even Tori had told him he made a poor hobo. He chuckled.

"I'm sure your book will be a great success, Mr. Fable," said Mrs. Cooper. "And that your life will be happy again, very happy."

"I hope you are a prophet, dear lady."

"You will send us a copy?"

"The very first one off the presses."

"Now, about that carton there," she said. "I have brought you some of my late husband's things. You are about the same size, I believe. See if there is anything you can use."

"Why, thank you, Ma'am," said Will.

He opened the carton and began to look through it. There were two suits, a pair of corduroy slacks, sweaters, shirts, even socks and underwear. All of it looked nearly new.

"They are, of course, not exactly fitting for a hobo," said Mrs. Cooper, smiling. "You may have to keep your shabby things over them until the new wears off."

"Mrs. Cooper," said Will, "you are an angel from heaven."

"One more thing," said Mrs. Cooper.

"Yes?" said Will, standing again.

"Tori and I will be going to Christmas Eve communion this evening at the Baptist Church. If you would like to go with us, we would be proud to have you as our guest. I can arrange something so that you can have a hot bath if you would like to go."

A look of caution came into Will's eyes. He stared at her for a long moment. Then he looked down at himself and rubbed his hand against his side, as if he were suddenly aware of his own poverty. When he looked at her again, there was great pain and sadness in his eyes.

"I haven't been inside a church in six years, Ma'am. Since the day of my family's funeral."

He put his hands in his pockets and turned his back to her. She waited silently.

"I cursed the Lord that day," he said. "I swore I'd never set foot inside a church again. I know now that it was grief and bitterness that spoke for me that day. It might be too late, but now I regret that I spoke so. Do you think He has forgiven me?"

Mrs. Cooper felt a tear spring to the corner of her eye. She blinked it away.

"He forgave you two thousand years ago, son," she said softly. "Don't you realize that?"

There was another long silence before the ragged man turned to face her.

"Mrs. Cooper," he said at last, "I would be honored to accompany you and Tori to church this evening."

Mrs. Cooper smiled. "I'll send Tori out with the washtub and put the water on to boil."

She turned to go back to the house.

"Mrs. Cooper?" called Will as she reached the steps.

"Yes?"

"You really are an angel from heaven."

"WHERE THE hell is Dixie Lee?" asked Bubba James as he looked at his watch. It was already five o'clock and the Christmas Eve communion service was to begin shortly.

"She's still out riding, dear," said Hedda James. "Don't worry. She'll be here any minute. I've laid out all her clothes for her. It will just take her a few minutes to change."

"It will take her an hour!" stormed Bubba. "She's going to miss the service, and that's all there is to it. That girl has gotten some mighty big ideas in her head the last few months, and she's gotten damn inconsiderate. She'll have to answer to me for this, though. This is the last straw."

Hedda knew that Bubba was incapable of true anger at his daughter, the darling of his heart. There would be no punishment, no recriminations, for all Bubba's thundering. Dixie Lee could manipulate her father with little more than a smile.

"Now settle down, Ellory dear," said Hedda. "After all, it's Christmas Eve, and we are going to the Lord's house for worship. Let's put our day-to-day problems aside and try to realize the importance of this Christian occasion."

"We'll just have to leave without her," said Bubba, now somewhat subdued. "Get your possibles together and come on."

"Yes, dear."

It was a short walk for the Jameses to the Good Shepherd Baptist Church, a small, white clapboard building at the corner of the town square. There was already a crowd gathered at the steps of the church when Bubba and Hedda arrived. The bell in the steeple was ringing through the brisk, chilly night air. A thousand stars twinkled above, as if to remind the people below of the starry night in Bethlehem long ago.

The spirit of the season was greatly in evidence, not just in the poinsettias in the alcoves of the tall, clear-paned church windows; it was in the hearts of the people as well. Bubba greeted those on the steps of the church and stopped to talk, as Hedda went on ahead to speak to Brother Goodson and his wife, Moira.

"Evening, Crawford," said Bubba to Mr. Welch. "Wilma and Chester gone in already, have they?"

"Yeah," replied Crawford. "Wilma's dying to see what Camilla's wearing this year, I guess."

"I see you finally gave in and closed the General Store early this year," said Bubba.

Bubba was not interested in Crawford's answer. He was watching the approach of Daniel J. Smith. The newcomer was alone, as always, limping across the grassy square. Bubba did not like him. He always had something derogatory to say, especially about the cat burglar. He seemed to imply that the thief was smarter than the law enforcement officials in the area, and that they would never catch him. He was beginning to get on Bubba's nerves.

"Hello, Chief," said Reese Jones, arriving with his family in tow. He turned to his wife. "Bobbie Joe, take Joe Bob and Bobbi Sue on in and get us a seat. Looks like Camilla has not lost her touch. I want to talk to Bubba a minute."

Mrs. Jones herded her children into the rapidly filling sanctuary, and Reese turned to the chief.

"Is it true, Bubba?" Reese asked. "Was there really no robbery last Saturday night?"

"Far as we can tell," answered Bubba. "Nothin' has been reported."

"But that's the first Saturday since Labor Day the cat burglar didn't make a strike. He's been regular as sunrise. What do you think happened?"

"Nothing lasts forever, Reese," said Bubba. "The net is so tight in Albany a spider couldn't get through it. Maybe he tried and saw he couldn't pull it off this time."

"You boys don't have him in custody, do you?" asked Reese. "Under wraps, you know?"

"No."

"Gonna catch him, Chief?"

"Oh, we'll get him all right. He's smart, but he's not that smart. We've got a profile on him. It's narrowed down the field of suspects, I can tell you that."

"Maybe he'll have to change his habits, Chief. Run on a Friday, or a Wednesday when everyone's at family night supper."

"Even if he does, he'll still walk right into a trap one day. We're close, Reese. Real close to nabbing him. Don't worry about it. The scoundrel's days are numbered."

A long yellow and black Packard town car turned off Albany Road at the square, and all heads turned to acknowledge the arrival of the Townsends. The whole town knew of Carlton's accident and of the loss of the barn and the stable a few days earlier. Carlton had not been seen since the wreck, and everyone was wondering about the extent of his injuries. Dr. Waldrop was not a man to ignore the rules. Not even his own wife knew how badly Carlton was hurt.

The car drew up to the church. Rudolph was driving with his mother beside him. Carlton was not with them. Rudolph emerged, and with a friendly wave to the men assembled on the steps, went to open the door for Laura Townsend. Laura took his arm and together they approached the crowd.

"Good evening, gentlemen," said Laura, "and a merry Christmas to you."

The men bowed slightly and cleared a path for the elegant woman, tipping their hats and mumbling their greetings. Rudolph smiled and shook a hand or two as he passed, putting everyone at ease with his gracious manner. They did not pause, but continued into the church.

The Townsends were greeted at the door by Brother Goodson, who was delighted by their attendance and their patronage. Brother Goodson had once fancied Rudolph as a son-in-law, but had long since resigned himself to his daughter's ambitions. The Townsends entered the church and took their customary place in the left front pew, in front of Sam Gates, his wife Viola, and Marvin and Veda.

Rudolph had seen Camilla, his old love, sitting in the right front pew with her mother and Hedda James as he passed. He felt a not-to-be-forgotten tug at his soul upon seeing her again, this woman who had broken his heart. It was tempered for once with satisfaction, however, for at last Rudolph had met a woman who had replaced Camilla in his affections, Dixie Lee James. Rudolph seated his mother, then excused himself and walked over to Camilla.

"Merry Christmas," he said.

"Rudolph," said Camilla, "how wonderful to see you. You look very handsome this evening." Camilla leaned forward and waved to Laura across the aisle. "I understand congratulations are in order," she continued. "Hedda has just been telling me all the news, and I'm very excited for you and Dixie Lee. I wish you both great happiness."

She was ravishing in her mink coat, and her words to Rudolph were sincere. Camilla was a rare beauty, at ease with herself and everyone around her. Everyone, young and old, male and female, prince and beggar, adored her. Rudolph was trying very hard not to.

"Thank you, my dear," he said. "The wedding is in March. We hope you'll be able to come."

"I know I will," Camilla answered. "I can't let my best friend in the world down. I'll be there."

"How are you tonight, Moira, Hedda?" Rudolph nodded to the preacher's wife and his future mother-in-law, "I was hoping Dixie Lee would be here. I planned to steal her away from you and make her sit with me. Where is she?"

"She's late," said Hedda with a chuckle. "Bubba was fit to be tied. I know she was planning on coming, but she went out riding and wasn't back before we left. I'm sure she'll be here shortly. Tell me, how is Carlton getting along?"

Camilla sat silently, listening to this exchange, smiling her lovely smile, looking from one to the other with her generous, unusual, blue-gray eyes. She felt something, too, as she sat so near to her old love. It was regret. But her life was too exciting to give up. For anybody.

Moira Goodson, Camilla's mother, tried to keep from fidgeting as she watched Camilla and Rudolph play out their chosen parts. It broke her heart. Even if it was truly over between them, Moria knew her daughter was still in love with Rudolph.

"Is that a mink coat she's wearing?" said Viola Gates. Her greedy eyes narrowed as she nudged her husband and nodded toward Camilla Goodson.

"Be quiet, woman," Sam Gates whispered as he stared at the preacher's daughter. "Humph," he grunted, turning his eyes from her at last, with great effort. "I could buy a hundred acres of land for what that fool coat cost. Don't be getting any ideas in your head," he said to Viola. "The answer is no."

Sam Gates turned his attention back to the tall windows of the little church. Dollar signs and balance sheets again filled his mind, as he mentally tallied the contributions made thus far for the purchase of stained-glass windows. Gates was a deacon, and the head of the budget committee.

Hurd Buford and his family were sitting discreetly on the back pew of the church. Mr. Buford's profession colored all his social activities, it seemed. He was never greeted by his fellow townspeople without some measure of reserve, except by Brother Goodson, who apparently understood and appreciated the necessity of his work.

Mr. Buford's plump little wife, Rosie, had a surprisingly sunny and warm disposition, and was not subjected to the same subtle rejection as her husband. It was she who convinced the mortician that his attendance at all the major social functions was essential, although she could never get him farther than the back row.

Buford liked sitting on the back pew. It afforded him a perfect point of observation of all potential customers. He found himself looking repeatedly at Mabel Potter, who sat with Jake and Jessie in the pew in front of him. She was wearing what appeared to be a new dress under her well-worn Sunday coat, and a new hat. Buford could tell that under the light rouge she wore, her cheeks were devoid of color. He had heard that Mabel was often ill, and he gazed at her with pursed lips and expectant eyes.

But Mabel was not the only member of the Potter family that interested Buford. Turning his ghoulish eyes to Jake, he stared at him long and hard, as if he were trying to decide if the color of satin lining for a new coffin should be blue or white.

Jake felt the cold eyes of the mortician on him, and shifted uneasily in his seat. Jake disliked Buford immensely, and wished he would look away. Just then, Chief Bubba James walked by on his way to his seat, and Jake's mouth went dry. He swallowed hard. He had been all right until he had walked into the church that night. Now, he was overcome with a sense of guilt and fear, and he wondered if he would have strength to harden his heart, and finish the terrible thing he had begun.

As Elizabeth Cooper began to play the organ softly, Jake felt hot tears sting his eyes as he considered what the consequences of his actions might eventually mean to his family. Quickly he feigned a yawn and lazily rubbed his eyes to hide the tears.

Mabel looked up at him then, with a loving smile. In the warmth of her glance, Jake forgot his fears and took her hand. It was worth it, he decided, it was all worth it to see her well again, getting stronger and healthier each day. His cold resolve returned, but there was a gnawing in his stomach he could not ignore. There was no other way . . . .

Tori Tanner was in seventh heaven. She sat with Will Fable on the aisle of the middle pew. Both she and Mrs. Cooper had been astounded at the transformation of the hobo after a bath and a shave. He was handsome, and his physique flawless. The late Mr. Cooper's suit was only a hair's breadth too small for him, and when he presented himself at the door to escort them to church, Tori thought he was almost as handsome as her father.

The handsome stranger did not go unnoticed by the townspeople. Mrs. Cooper had introduced him as an old friend of the family from up North, who had come to spend the holidays with them on his way to his winter home in Florida. No one questioned this story, for Will Fable, like Elizabeth Cooper, had been raised in wealth and educated at the finest schools. The good people of Hayley tended to be reserved with outsiders, especially Yankees, but all were clearly taken with this man's proud carriage and impeccable manners. All the young girls were fascinated by him. They huddled together, talking about him in hushed whispers. Even Camilla Goodson was impressed, and, because the Coopers had arrived early, Camilla had spoken to Will at length about her life in New York, finding, at last, someone as well-traveled as she to talk to.

Tori was thrilled by the fun and adventure of the masquerade, and busily whispered the names of all the townspeople as they arrived. They made a game of guessing occupations, and Tori nearly choked when Will guessed that Rudolph Townsend was a groom for a rich family. Will didn't mention his meeting Rudolph to Tori, but told her that he could tell just by looking that Rudolph was destined for greatness.

Will took the longest time guessing the occupation of Daniel J. Smith. Smith seemed to fascinate Will, and he observed the grizzled gentleman for nearly half an hour, whenever he could manage it discreetly. He decided at last, and reduced Tori to tears with the announcement that Daniel J. Smith was the football coach at the high school.

Mrs. Cooper's playing filled the little church with reverent music, and it seemed to Tori that there could be nothing better in the world than to be there, right then, on that special, wonderful night. Brother Goodson entered the room from a side door and stepped up to the pulpit. The congregation, and the visiting Presbyterians, settled in and waited expectantly.

"We will praise the Lord in song," announced the boyish, blue-eyed minister. "Please turn with me to page thirty-three in your hymnals as we sing 'O' Little Town of Bethlehem'."

Mrs. Cooper began the introduction to the hymn. The sound of books sliding from racks, and pages turning, mixed with the shuffling of feet, as the congregation stood up to sing. The door of the church opened noisily behind them and closed again as a latecomer arrived. Dixie Lee James walked up the center aisle to the front row, arriving just before the signal was given to begin singing.

She could not have timed her entrance more perfectly, and she seemed oblivious to the sensation she caused. The ladies of Hayley were shocked, and stared open-mouthed, as Dixie Lee strode down the aisle of the church—in pants. She was wearing her new riding outfit, the short, tailored, blue velvet jacket, snug brown jodhpurs, and high, shiny black boots. A matching brown bowler with a blue velvet bow and streamers covered her golden brown curls. In her black-gloved hand she carried a riding crop, and she tapped her boot smartly as she walked to her seat.

The menfolk of Hayley were not used to seeing a woman as shapely as Dixie Lee wearing pants in public, and they, too, were shocked, but delightedly so. Dixie Lee smiled sweetly at Camilla Goodson as she brushed past her, taking her usual seat on the front row next to her father. The cue for the singing was missed by many, and the hymn began in momentary confusion, but soon all voices were raised in somewhat distracted praise.

Bubba James was furious. He struggled to sing, but fell silent during the second and third verses. He refused to look at his daughter again during the rest of the service. Camilla Goodson was amused, for the girl's ploy to steal the show was so obvious, and, Camilla thought, so unnecessary. Laura Townsend, always gracious, pretended not to notice her future daughter-in-law's attire.

Rudolph could not suppress his disapproval, and frowned openly. When the grape juice was passed during communion, Rudolph looked over at his fiancée and was met with a bewitching twinkle in her eyes. He struggled to keep his anger intact, but found he could not resist her. By the end of the service he was licked, enchanted by Dixie Lee like the rest of the men present. Not even Bubba James was immune, and he took his daughter's hand when the last hymn was sung. When the worshipers

were dismissed with a final blessing, Chief James escorted Dixie Lee down the aisle, and no one, not even Viola Gates, had the nerve to publicly reprimand the chief's little girl.

IT WAS almost nine o'clock when Bubba James left his house to make his final rounds. He could not be too careful now, as the cat burglar apparently was breaking his pattern. Sooner or later, Bubba figured, the cat burglar would want to expand his territory, and Hayley just might be his home ground. Bubba found himself wanting to believe that somehow Carlton Townsend was responsible for the crimes. He fit the profile, even smoked Lucky Strike cigarettes. And Bubba didn't fail to realize that the first Saturday the clever criminal failed to strike was the same that Carlton Townsend was laid up in bed. But logically, it just didn't add up. What motive could the boy have? Hatred? Resentment? Revenge?

In spite of his private thoughts about Carlton, Bubba found that he was becoming overly suspicious of strangers and of newcomers to Hayley. He even felt a twinge of distrust about Daniel J. Smith. The man was crippled and elderly after all. What possible damage could such a man do? But he was such an oddball. And where did he get his money? He had no visible means of support, as far as Bubba could tell. It wouldn't hurt to keep an eye on Smith for a while, Bubba decided. His instincts for these things were hardly ever wrong. Or was he overcompensating, seeing boogey men around every corner?

Bubba checked the locks on all the places of business around the square, and returned to his car. He drove slowly past the train depot and the warehouse, coming finally to his last stop, Buford's Funeral Home. He had stopped checking Buford's lock because the mortician was meticulous about security. Besides, Bubba had never known anyone to enter the funeral home voluntarily. If any place in Hayley was less in need of locks, it was this place. Bubba could not help but smile as he remembered the latest ghoul story circulated by the town children about Mr. Buford.

As he rounded the curve of the road he saw a light at the back of the funeral home, and he pulled the patrol car up to the receiving porch. The chief saw Mr. Buford unloading some cardboard boxes from the back of the hearse. Buford looked up warily upon seeing the lights of the car, then relaxed as he recognized the vehicle when Bubba dimmed the lights.

"Evening, Chief," said Buford, returning to his work. "Oh yes, and Merry Christmas."

"Same to you," Bubba replied. He lit a cigarette as he walked up to the receiving porch of the mortuary. Bubba watched as Buford unloaded yet another carton from the back of the hearse. "Big Christmas this year?"

"Better than most," said Buford.

"Can I give you a hand?"

"No thanks, Chief," replied the mortician, "I can manage. Things all right in town, are they?"

"Locked up tight."

"Well, just to be safe," said Buford, "I put another lock on all my doors." He carried the last of the boxes to the back door. "I won't lie to you. All these robberies have got me a little spooked."

Bubba was amused by the man's choice of words. He tried to suppress a smile, but his eyes betrayed him.

"Something funny?" asked Buford calmly, walking back to the chief, under whose very nose he had just unloaded ten boxes of illegal whiskey.

"Not at all," replied Bubba, recovering his professional attitude. "I guess your boxes just reminded me of the coat I have boxed up for Dixie Lee at home. I can't wait till she sees that coat in the morning."

"I've got a happy morning in store for my little ones as well," said Buford, smiling.

Bubba stared at the dour man, realizing he had never before seen Hurd Buford smile. The man's sickly white skin wrinkled up into deep, ghastly creases as he smiled, revealing jagged, yellow teeth. Bubba showed no reaction, refusing to let his face reveal his disgust. He had trained himself to show no emotion. It was part of the job. Bubba flicked away the cigarette.

"Well, don't trouble yourself about the cat burglar, Hurd," said the chief, with all the authority of his office. "But I won't argue with taking a few extra precautions. If this criminal decides to add Hayley to his list, he'll find it's not as easy to operate in a close-knit community as it is in a big town like Albany. There's not as much leeway for secrecy in a place where everybody knows everybody else's business."

"You're right about that, chief," said Buford. "It's mighty hard to pull the wool over anyone's eyes around here, all right. I guess we all have you to thank for that."

"I appreciate the vote of confidence, Hurd," said Bubba. "I guess I'd better be going. I have my own Santa Claus playing to do."

"Good night, Chief."

"Good night."

For the second time that evening, Hurd Buford smiled his vampirelike smile, waving to Bubba as he drove away. The great Bubba James! What a joke, he thought. His snide opinionating of the chief was interrupted by the jangling of the telephone in the back room of the funeral parlor. Buford looked in the direction of the phone with annoyance. There was only one reason that telephone would be ringing this time of night. Rosie was under strict orders never to disturb him or tie up the business line, so it was only death that rang the bell.

"Hell's fire," muttered Buford. "On Christmas Eve, yet. Haven't I got enough to do tonight?"

Reluctantly, he entered the house and answered the phone. Sure enough, he learned that the elderly father of Viola Gates, visiting for Christmas from Albany, had the poor taste to die in his sleep on Christmas Eve. Buford scowled, hearing the wailing of Viola in the background, as Sam Gates explained the situation, asking him to locate Bubba and for both of them to come right over. Buford cursed his luck as he hung up the phone. He carried the last of the illegal moonshine into the back parlor and headed out to pick up Chief James.

15

When they returned home from the Christmas Eve communion service, Mrs. Cooper invited Will Fable to stay for Christmas dinner the next day. Will said repeatedly that he did not want to impose, that she had done enough for him already. Tori begged and Mrs. Cooper insisted. He agreed to stay.

He woke late Christmas morning, past nine o'clock, several hours later than his usual time of rising. It was perhaps a subconscious wish to sleep late, for early Christmas mornings held only sad visions of his little son racing to the tree and opening his presents. It was still hard for Will to believe that first his wealth, then his family, had been so easily and so quickly taken from him. He had learned not to look back in these last six years, except perhaps, on mornings like this.

As he lay beneath the warm blankets on his bed of straw, Will heard again the soft sounds of Tori's piano playing from the house. Like Elizabeth Cooper, his own childhood came to haunt him. He closed his eyes and saw his mother sitting beside him on the piano bench, patient and encouraging; his father stroking his gray beard, smoking his pipe, and listening to his only son's halting version of "Fur Elise." They were in their forties when they had become parents. Will was raised with the full benefit of the wisdom and patience afforded his parents during their childless years. He had not thought of his childhood in a long time. Funny what comes to your mind on Christmas. His father was dead now, his mother still living in Pennsylvania. She was much like Elizabeth Cooper, a survivor, a tower of inner strength. Will had known somehow that his absence from her life would be understood.

Mrs. Cooper had told him to come to the house when he awakened, to warm himself by the fire and have some breakfast. He was a little surprised that she managed to keep Tori from coming out to get him earlier. He smiled fondly at the thought of Elizabeth Cooper. Leave him alone, dear, he could hear her saying to Tori, he'll come in when he's ready. Will got up, stretched, brushed the dirt and straw from his new trousers, ran his fingers through his hair. He walked out into the daylight and crossed the yard to the house. He mounted the steps, opened the screen door, crossed the porch to the kitchen door, and knocked.

Mrs. Cooper gave him a warm smile when she opened the door. The man who stood at her door bore no resemblance to the ragged hobo she had first met. Before her stood a neat, prosperous-looking, handsome young man with perfect manners and perfect grammar. Only the eyes were the same. Will's green eyes were arresting, filled with tragedy and wisdom, kindness and humility, laughter and hope. They were the eyes of a sage, or a saint.

"Come in, Will," she said. "Merry Christmas."

"Thank you, Ma'am," said Will. "Merry Christmas to you."

"Tori," she called, "Mr. Fable is here."

Tori rushed in, wearing her new dress.

"Look what I got for Christmas, Will," she said, holding out the dress and posing left and right. "Isn't it dreamy?"

"Perfectly fetching," said Will.

"Would you like some breakfast?" asked Mrs. Cooper. "It's still on the stove. Tori and I ate hours ago."

Will was not hungry. He had long been out of the habit of eating breakfast, or of eating three square meals a day. He wanted only the companionship of his new friends.

"No, thank you, Ma'am," he said. "I'll wait for dinner."

"Then come on," said Tori, grabbing his hand. "You have to see the tree, and the other presents I got."

"Go ahead," said Mrs. Cooper.

Will was dragged from the kitchen. He looked back at his hostess and was struck again by the kindness in her eyes. Soon Will and Tori were sitting before the fire, talking of faraway places and things. The house was filled with the aroma of Christmas: Scotch pine, hickory wood, turkey and dressing. Something was happening to Will as he sat there, welcome and warm, listening to the happy child talk, something that had begun the day before when he and Elizabeth had talked, something that had touched him further as he sat with Tori in the pew of the church. It was a cleansing, and more than dirt had been washed away in yesterday's bath.

"Do you want to?" Tori tugged at his arm. "Will? Do you want to or not?"

Will realized he had not been listening to the child.

"I'm sorry, honey," he said. "Do I want to what?"

"See me play," said Tori. "On the piano."

I'd be honored," said Will. "Can I sit with you on the bench?"

"Sure. Come on."

Together they went to the piano. Tori began to play Christmas carols, one after another. They both sang along. Mrs. Cooper came to the door of the room and listened for a while, watching them fondly, then returned to her baking. When Tori hit a sour note a while later, Will said, without thinking, "E-flat, Tori."

Tori stopped playing and looked at him.

"You can play?"

"Well, yes," he answered. "I used to. But it's been a long time."

"Why didn't you say so?" asked Tori. "You play the next one. Please?"

Will laughed. "Okay, I'll give it a try."

Will began playing a slow, beautiful tune. Tori watched in amazement as his tough fingers glided gracefully over the keys. It was a song she knew, a song her mother used to play, a song she could never master. Mrs. Cooper came into the room and watched Will as he played. She saw the training, recognized the style. More and more of this mysterious stranger's past was becoming an open book. She had been right about him. Only an affluent family could have fostered such effortless skill. How beautifully he played "Clair de Lune." When he finished the song, no one spoke for a moment.

"That was beautiful, Will," said Mrs. Cooper at last. "Please play another one for Tori. She can learn from you."

"No," said Tori. "I want to learn to play that one. Show me, Will. Please?"

Will Fable looked into Tori's eager brown eyes. He had come to love this child, this wonder. From deep within him, a new desire was born, a need rekindled. He longed again for a family of his own, for roots, for stability. He had gathered enough material for several books, he had known that for a long time. But the will to go back, to try again to live a normal life, had eluded him. Maybe now he was ready. It could not have been an accident, for him to be led here, at this time of the year, to these extraordinary people. It was a higher power, an almost tangible presence he felt in this house. Will knew that it was not just the birthday of Jesus this day. It was his own.

"All right," promised Will, "I'll teach you after dinner. But now, you should go in and help your grandmother with that delicious dinner she's fixing. I'm sure she could use some help. Deal?"

Reluctantly, Tori agreed, and went about the business of carrying, stirring, and setting the table. Her mind raced. There must be a way to keep Will from leaving the next day. He just had to stay! Maybe he was tired of roaming around, especially in the winter. Surely, he would like a nice warm place to stay and good Cooper cooking for a month or two. It just made sense. He could stay with them and help around the house or do chores, something, anything, just so he wouldn't leave. Tori had learned so much from him already, and he was so much fun. She smiled, thinking of the grand joke they had played on the town the night before, and on all those swooning girls.

But what about Meema? She liked Will, Tori was sure of that. But she was funny about strangers, especially hobos. She let them stay overnight, fed them, but then expected them to be on their way. It was different this time, though, wasn't it? She had taken him to church, invited him into the house, invited him to dinner. If Tori could only think of the right way to ask, maybe she would agree to let him stay. Tori stewed about this matter so intently she hardly realized it when everything was done, and it was time to sit down at the table.

"Call Mr. Fable in to dinner, dear," said Mrs. Cooper.

Roused from her thoughts, Tori looked at the dining room table as if for the first time. It was beautiful, with a centerpiece of poinsettias and red candles, and glorious dishes of food all around. At the head of the table was a golden-brown turkey, seven pounds at least, brimming with stuffing. Next to a bowl of green peas and onions was a sweet-potato casserole, covered with sugar-glazed pecans, a plate of homemade buttered rolls, and at the other end of the table, Tori's favorite treat, blackberry pie.

It was a meal such as Tori would not see again for months, but Tori never realized she and her grandmother lived only a few steps above poverty. Mrs. Cooper could turn a plate of sweet potatoes into honey, and turnip greens into heaven. She could make muslin seem like silk, and turn cotton into velvet. Tori never felt she was poor. Mrs Cooper saw to that, with a lot of hard work, love, and sacrifice. Perhaps it is better for a child to be weaned on these things, for luxury and comfort can rob the soul.

"Will," said Tori excitedly, "everything is ready. Come to the table!"

They all took their places, with Will being given the seat at the head of the table, and the honor of carving the admirable bird.

"We shall now ask the Lord's blessing," said Mrs. Cooper.

She joined hands with Tori and offered her other hand to Will. He grasped her hand reverently as she and Tori bowed their heads.

"Mrs. Cooper?" said Will. They both raised their eyes to him. "I would be honored to ask the blessing today."

Mrs. Cooper smiled and nodded to him. Her heart was aglow, and she thanked heaven silently for the change she had seen in this man. With a glance at Tori, she lowered her eyes again, and Tori followed suit.

Will bowed his head. There was a long pause before he spoke. For the first time in six years, Will knew that a heavenly presence was there, that someone was listening, that someone could hear him. Mrs. Cooper waited patiently, knowingly, her head bowed, her hand in Will's. Tori squinted one eye open for a second, puzzled by the delay. Then he spoke, and Tori quickly closed her eyes again.

"Heavenly Father," he said, "another prodigal son has found his way home to you today." He paused again. Tori peeked at him again in response to this strange blessing. What did the story of the prodigal son have to do with Christmas? She glanced furtively at her grandmother and bowed her head again, lest she should be caught.

"This is a special day," Will continued, "for both of us. For all of us." He squeezed Mrs. Cooper's hand. "I ask your forgiveness for my folly, and seek humble entrance to your gate. I have learned my lesson and I will never go far from you again. Bless this lovely family, at whose table I sit, and thank you for letting me be here with them today." Again he paused. "I understand everything, now, Lord. You never deserted me at all. You've been with me every step of the way. For this, I thank you. Amen."

Mrs. Cooper lifted her head, and saw Tori staring at Will, her mouth open in amazement. Elizabeth quickly tugged at the child's hand and frowned a message: stop gaping. Tori saw her look and recovered, glancing sideways away from their guest, and trying to look dumb. When she looked back, her grandmother was smiling and did not let go of his hand for many moments.

Tori broke the heavy silence.

"Carve the turkey, Will," she said. "I'm starved!"

The two adults looked at her, then back at each other and began to chuckle together. Did they have some kind of secret between them? Tori was puzzled even further.

"Did I say something funny?" she asked.

"No, dear," laughed Mrs. Cooper. "You are absolutely right. Let's carve the turkey and enjoy the wonderful bounty the Lord had seen fit to provide for us." She glanced at Will. "All of us."

Never was a Christmas feast enjoyed so thoroughly as on that cold, sunny afternoon. During dessert, Will was persuaded by Tori to recant some of his travels and adventures. He told them of high mountains, deserts, palm trees, caves and rivers. He told of forests alive with strange creatures, the elk, the brown bear, the grizzly, the cougar. Waterfalls, geysers, trees a thousand years old, all these he had seen. He told of the great Pacific Ocean, straining and tearing against the rocky cliffs of the

California coast, where you could almost imagine what it was like at the beginning of the world.

Mrs. Cooper sat with Tori and Will at the table long after the last bite of pie was eaten, listening to the vivid descriptions of their wandering friend's travels, and of the people he had met along the way. She realized what a gift for tale-telling the man possessed, and was content in the knowledge that his writing would bring him a successful new career on which to build a new life for himself.

Will thrilled Tori with a frightening folk tale about the kitty-mow, a ghostly fable in which a bobcat was transformed into a creature of the night with unearthly powers. When at last Will seemed to run out of stories and adventures, Tori was completely captivated. There was a little silence before Tori asked a disturbing question.

"What makes a person become a hobo, Will?" she asked. "Why did you become one?"

It was the question of a dreamer. Will frowned slightly and glanced at Elizabeth. She lowered her eyes. Will realized he may have made all his travels seem tempting and exciting to the child. He needed to be sure he hadn't misled her, making his hard, lonely existence seem like a wonderful life to dream about.

"I want to tell you the rest of it now, little one," he said earnestly. His voice was different. "All these things I've told you about are true, and it's a wonderful thing to be able to travel and see this great country, but only if you can do it the right way. My way is the wrong way. The things I've seen haven't pleased me like they were meant to. I was not of a mind to appreciate them when I started out on the rails.

"I was doing what I suppose most people who become hobos do. I was running away, you see. I lost everything in life I had or cared about. I didn't tell you about that. I had a lot of money once, and a family. I lost my money and then my family died in a terrible fire. After that, I didn't want to live anymore. I couldn't see that what had happened to me was not some terrible injustice, some horrible punishment I did not deserve. I hated everything and everybody, everyone who had not had to suffer the way I did. I couldn't see that thousands of other people were suffering as badly as I was. I thought I was the only one who had been hurt.

"I left my mother to fare for herself, and ran away, Tori. I wanted to think of nothing, to care about nothing, not even my mother. Some wild instinct told me, I guess, that if I was thrust out in the world with no support, if I had to live by my wits, to struggle just to survive, then I wouldn't have the time or the energy to grieve.

"Believe me, I got my wish. I jumped on a boxcar with only the clothes on my back. The railroad carried me far away from all I was familiar with, all I cared about. I spent terrible, lonely days and nights in one boxcar after another, always heading west. I didn't eat. My insides gnawed at my stomach and my mind. I punished myself with guilt and suffering, as if I had been guilty of some terrible crime.

"Then I left the railroad car in a vast wilderness land. I walked and walked until my feet were blistered and my legs ached, always alone, always afraid, knowing that any day I might be bitten by a snake or eaten by one of those bears I told you about so casually. I was forced to eat things I would never admit to you, to survive. I wasn't cut out for the wilderness. I was just a sick, stupid boy trying to be a man, sorry I left, afraid to go on, afraid to go back.

"That hobo I told you about, Forest Bill, found me near-dead from heat and exhaustion and hunger, somewhere in northern Arizona. A greener fool he never laid eyes on, I'm sure. He took care of me, got me healthy again, and taught me how to survive. I traveled with him for nearly a year. We were always moving, throughout the Rockies, the desert, and on to California, Oregon, and Montana. When we parted company, I had learned a lot about myself, about other people, and about how to survive. But I was empty inside.

"I think I changed, then, when I got back on my own, and not for the better. I started to enjoy the challenge of surviving by my wits. I became an observer, a cold, detached student of human nature. It was like I wasn't a member of the human race anymore, I was separate from them. I learned how to manipulate people, to trick them, to master them as I had mastered Nature itself. They were to be watched, studied, like a bug mounted on a pin. I felt nothing then. No guilt, no despair, no hatred, not even loneliness. I had buried the past, and myself with it.

"You wouldn't have wanted to know me then. I was worth nothing to anyone, especially to myself. I stayed that way for a long time, I don't know how long. Then, gradually, I began to change again. I began to get myself back, to feel again. I can't put a time or a place to it. You see, everywhere I went, people were, for the most part, kind to me. To me, a stranger. I was using them to get a free meal or a place to stay, but still, they were kind. I began to lose my suspicion of them. One day, I heard myself say thank you, and I knew I meant it at last. I began to trust people again, and, I guess, to trust myself. I had lived through terrible hardships and managed to survive; I guess I realized that maybe I wasn't such a worthless nobody after all.

"I continued to wander, riding the rails, slowly getting back my ability to feel like a human instead of an animal. It was the kindness of strangers like you and your grandmother that brought me back to life. After I had been on the road and the rails for about four years, I decided to start writing about the people I met and the places I had been. That's what's in all those little notebooks you were so curious about. I started writing because I didn't want to forget. One day I read back over what I had written months before. I found myself enjoying the story, laughing at myself.

"One day I was chopping some firewood for a woman who had offered me a night's lodging in exchange for some chores. I dropped one of my notebooks in her yard and she found it. When I brought some wood up to the house, I found her reading it. Since I had dropped it, I couldn't fault her for looking at it. As it turned out, she was an English teacher and she wrote poetry—even had a book of it published once. She really surprised me by telling me she thought I was a gifted writer. She asked me if I was an author, traveling around the country disguised as a hobo, gathering information for a book. I can't tell you how funny that struck me. If only she knew what I had been through. But to save face, I told her I was. She insisted on reading the rest of my notebooks.

"To make a long story short, that sweet lady, Evelyn Mills was her name, turned my life around for me. She gave me the name of her publisher in New York, and wrote him a letter of introduction for me. I sent the letter to him, along with some pages of manuscript Miss Mills typed up for me, and he wired back a cash advance and a contract. That was a year ago. I've been working really hard on the book since then, using the money he sent when I had to, but mostly still traveling as before. I sent the publisher a chapter at a time, written out in longhand, when I had it finished. So far, he hasn't sent one back.

"I just couldn't go back home, though. I had changed so much from the miserable person I had become, but I found I couldn't take that last step. I was still afraid to face life, to face my mother and my friends in Pennsylvania. I was still searching for something I had lost, something buried deep. What it was, I did not know until yesterday."

Tori had listened intently, walking with her new friend every mile, seeing what he saw, feeling what he felt, throughout his long journey.

"Yesterday?" she asked. "What did you find yesterday? You were *here* yesterday, Will."

Will glanced over at Mrs. Cooper. She felt a tear spring to her eye, and looked away. Will turned back to Tori.

"Well," he said, "first I found two very special friends I will always treasure. But last night, when we went to church, I found another friend, one I must have been searching for all along."

A vision of Will giving the blessing, that strange blessing, flitted through Tori's mind, and she understood. She nodded.

Even when touched deeply by an encounter with things spiritual, the human animal finds it difficult to share such experiences. Perhaps such things are on a level that is so personal, so intimate, that they should not always be shared. It may be for this reason that Will was grateful for Mrs. Cooper's suggestion that they excuse themselves from the table. With a motherly glance, she asked Will to take Tori into the living room and "keep her occupied" with the piano while Mrs. Cooper cleared the table. It had been an emotional experience for all of them, this finding of the lost sheep. It would be a Christmas to remember always.

Later that afternoon, Mrs. Cooper and Tori left the house to make some visits to special friends. Mrs. Cooper insisted that Will remain by the warm fire in the living room while they were gone. Again, Will was amazed at the goodness and charity of this woman, who trusted him, a stranger, to come into her home. After they had gone, Will sat in the cozy, comfortable room thinking. He wished he could somehow remain here, unseen, to watch over this kind woman, to see this child grow up. He smiled at this thought, and wondered what they would think if they knew what he was thinking. A man they had known only three days wanting to become their protector, part of their family. How presumptuous. From hobo to guardian angel in three days.

Only three days, and his life would never be the same. Did they have any idea what a difference they had made in his life? He did not know. He sighed and poked the fire. No, he must be leaving shortly. He had a life of his own to build, or more correctly, to rebuild. He must leave, and he would never see his new friends again. No, that was too hard. But he must not intrude upon their lives. If the book was a success, he would have money again, maybe more than he imagined. Perhaps he could keep in touch, or maybe watch over them from afar, anonymously. They had become too important to him to leave behind forever. He would think of something. First, he must wait and see what would happen in his own life.

Maybe there was something he could do for them now. Something more than chores. He had, in the past three days, done most of the things that needed doing around the place. He had stocked them well with firewood, cleaned and organized the barn, and fixed the car and the fence. It wasn't enough, not for them. All at once, he remembered the lumber stacked in the barn. There were nails, too, and tools. He had an idea. Mrs. Cooper would have to go along with it, of course, but he knew she would. It would not take long, only a few hours, but Tori must not be there to see it. It must be a surprise. He would ask Mrs. Cooper to take Tori to visit one of her friends tomorrow afternoon. Then, after he had gone, she would find it. It was perfect. A happy excitement filled his chest and he laughed out loud. Oh, what a Christmas! He smiled and stretched out his legs before the fire. In a few minutes he was asleep, a deep, restful, dreamless sleep.

16

It was Sunday, December twenty-sixth, and for the second week in a row, there had been no burglary in Albany. Ten days after the accident, and Carlton could stay in the house no longer. Daily visits from his large circle of friends had made his recovery easier, but the one person he most wanted to see never came. She had visited the house once or twice that week, but she did not come to his room. She brought no cakes, pies, or cards, as the others did. She offered him no sympathy, no pleasantries, no gossip, no jokes. But she was more conspicuous by her absence than if she had.

Carlton saw her that night when he walked into the bar at Radium Springs with Woody Price. She was with Rudolph, sitting at a table with some of the regulars, playing cards. Carlton spotted her immediately, and the welcome cries of well-wishers who surrounded him as he entered, as well as his good-natured replies, seemed like a silent movie to him. He was aware of nothing but her presence.

Their eyes met across the room and she did not turn away. The air around the two of them was charged with a strange excitement noticed by no one else in the room, except Woody Price. Woody was a practiced and skillful observer of people, and he saw at once that there was something between them. Woody had read between the lines of his conversations with Carlton since the accident, and he knew that Carlton was in love with his brother's fiancée. And unless he missed his guess, this meeting seemed to indicate that Dixie Lee was engaged to the wrong man.

Rudolph rose at once and went to Carlton, putting a hand on his shoulder and asking if it was not too soon to be out of bed. He shook Woody's hand heartily, and accompanied them to Carlton's regular table. Rudolph had seemed to forget his animosity toward his brother in the days since the accident, and could not have been more concerned or protective of him. A brush with death has a way of putting things in perspective, and Rudolph was not the only one who saw a lot of things differently.

Carlton had done a lot of thinking while he lay flat on his back. The concussion had given him severe headaches for the first few days, and it was the first real pain he had ever had to deal with in his life. During this time he had been acutely aware of the kindness of others, when the feel of an ice pack on his forehead was worth more to him than all of County Pa's money. His mother sat with him for hours, saying nothing, working on her needlepoint. He was comforted by her presence, and appreciative of her silence.

Rudolph had been like the father he had always wanted, but never had, in County Pa. He kept the servants quiet, instructing them to enter the room only to bring food or to tidy up in silence, for even the sound of speech was painful to Carlton at first. He allowed visitors after a few days, when the headaches subsided, but stood by to be sure they kept their visits short. He had Dr. Waldrop in to see Carlton every day, and insisted that the doctor's instructions as to diet and medication be followed to the letter.

Carlton felt a new and, at first, a grudging respect for Rudolph, and as the days went by, he felt the bonds of their brotherhood more than ever before. He spent hours thinking back over the years, of things that had happened. More and more, he came to realize that his resentment of Rudolph had always been tied to his love-hate relationship with his father. County Pa had scoffed at Rudolph's refusal to hunt, and Carlton had done the same. Every time County Pa had thrashed Carlton, Carlton had resented the fact that Rudolph had never done a thing to result in the same treatment. Carlton had been his father's son, and his father's favorite, but he had also at one time or another been called every name under heaven by his father. Neither of County Pa's sons met his father's expectations. At last Carlton realized that it had never been Rudolph's fault.

County Pa had never set foot in a church. But when the boys were young, Laura had taken them regularly to Sunday school and church, taught them their catechism, and taught them to say their prayers. When Carlton was old enough to emulate his father, and independent enough to rebel, he had refused to go to church any longer, although Rudolph and his mother continued to attend regularly. Since then, Carlton had gone to church only when it suited his purpose, to see a girl, or to get out of the house when he was grounded.

When his head was throbbing after the accident, Carlton found himself praying for the first time in fifteen years. He prayed for the pain to stop, and promised God things in return that he would never be able to honor. Dr. Waldrop had explained that no pain killers could be prescribed, because they might mask other symptoms which could develop. So Carlton suffered through on his own. He determined that he would never forget the pain, or its cessation.

Carlton would never again be able to turn from the suffering of others the way he had before. When he was better, he thought back to the pain he had been in, and he felt pity for the person he had been, who had endured such suffering. He did not realize it then, but the quality of mercy had been born in him, not just for himself, but for others. It would change his life.

He had thought of Dixie Lee, too, during this time. He was in love with her, he knew that now, but it did not bring him the joy of the challenge, the determination of victory that it did before. Now it was a confusing state of affairs in the light of his new respect for Rudolph. He didn't feel the same about anything anymore, it seemed. His mind was strangely peaceful, devoid of bitterness, quiet. He wondered if he was out of his mind, for old habits and old attitudes clamored at times for attention from somewhere deep in his consciousness. He was convinced of his derangement when he realized that he had decided not to interfere in Rudolph's romance with Dixie Lee. He was in love for the first time in his life, and he wasn't going to do anything about it? He must be crazy.

When he saw Dixie Lee that night, his heart swelled so in his chest that he was sure it would burst. It had been a mistake to come, he thought, as he made his way to his table with Woody and Rudolph. He was not yet strong enough to endure *this* pain.

Woody stood talking with Rudolph, but Carlton comprehended nothing they said, so determined was he to avoid looking at Dixie Lee, and to hide the pain he felt. He found this behavior strange in himself, for being noble was Rudolph's forte, not his, and he sank deeper into a state of confusion and mixed emotions. The rest of the patrons had returned to their places at the bar or the tables, and when Rudolph walked out of the room with Woody, no one approached his table. Rudolph must have told them to let him rest, for under any other circumstance, his table would have been overrun with merrymakers.

He looked up and found Dixie Lee standing next to him. He did not expect this, and made a fumbling attempt to rise from his chair. She put a hand on his shoulder to stop him.

"Don't get up, silly," she said. "You shouldn't even be here, you know."

He gathered his wits to answer as she sat down, but when he looked in her eyes he could think of nothing to say.

"Do you mind if I sit down?" she asked.

"No," he said, his eyebrows knitting together for a second. "Of course I don't."

Dixie Lee had been worried about him. Too worried. She had wanted to visit him, but she hadn't gone. She didn't like the way she felt when she was around him. He always made her feel sort of uneasy, and her heart would begin to race, just as it was racing now. She was never in control around him; she felt vulnerable, as if he could hurt her. She avoided him; it was the only thing she could do. But when she had seen him tonight, she found herself walking to him. And she felt a warm feeling creep over her when he spoke to her.

"I'm sorry you were hurt," she said. "I was going to look in on you, but Dr. Waldrop was so strict—"

Carlton said, "I looked for you." His eyes were on the table.

Dixie Lee was taken aback. She opened her mouth to speak, but could say nothing in her confusion at the tenderness in his voice. He looked up and they stared into each other's eyes for a few seconds. It seemed an eternity. Dixie Lee's heart melted, and she looked away at last. She drew a quick, deep breath.

"I'm sorry," she said haltingly. "I would have come, of course, if I had known you wanted me to come. It's just that, well, I haven't really seen you since that day . . . I mean, I was . . . well, we haven't been on the best of terms, and I—"

"Dixie Lee," said Carlton softly, "I want to apologize for what happened in the barn. Can you forgive me? I promise I'll never treat you that way again."

He was different. He was actually apologizing to her. It was not at all what she expected, and he seemed so sincere. She found herself responding to him before she could think her way out of it. She could have handled the man she had thought he was, or at least, she thought she could. But now he was so open, so different. He felt something for her, something real; she could see it in his eyes.

"Carlton," she said slowly, "thank you for telling me this. I forgive you. I had hoped we could get back on good terms for Rudolph's sake." She looked up at him and said, "He really loves you, you know?" His eyes held hers again in a long embrace, and she felt her cheeks flush as she thought of Rudolph, but in moments she was lost in his eyes, and Rudolph was forgotten.

"I won't—" said Carlton, "I mean, I don't want to do anything to come between you and Rudolph." He tore his eyes from hers and sat back suddenly in the chair, looking everywhere and nowhere. He took a deep breath and learned back on the table, his hands clasped in front of him. He voice shook as he said, "God, at least I think I don't want to come between you. I don't know anything anymore. Maybe you better go back to your table, Dixie Lee. Maybe I shouldn't be around you for a while."

Dixie Lee knew. He was in love with her! He must be. Why did it make her so happy? She was in love with Rudolph, wasn't she? She could not help herself. She had to know. She moved without thinking into her proven cloak of manipulation.

"Do I have to go?" she asked. "I promise I won't bite you."

The sudden anger in his eyes turned her blood cold.

He grabbed her wrist and whispered, "This is no time for games, you little fool. That stuff might work on my brother, but not on me. If you want me to tell you I'm in love with you, I will, but don't try your tricks on me. We don't need tricks, you and I, because I know you, Dixie Lee. I know you better than Rudolph will ever know you. I love you for what you are, not for what you pretend to be. Save your pretending for Rudolph, do you understand me? If you love him, then marry him, but if you do, you stay the hell away from me."

Dixie Lee was in trouble. She knew it. She was dizzy with the heady feeling of surrender to the first man who had ever managed to dominate her. She wanted him. She wanted to feel his strong arms around her, wanted to belong to him. Her emotions were out of control, but her mind was not. She rose from the table quickly and headed for the ladies' room, catching herself midway to slow her steps, so not to draw attention to herself. She passed Woody Price at the entrance to the hall, and walked by without a word.

Woody had been watching them from the doorway. He had sent Rudolph on a fool's errand to give them some time together. He knew that neither would be able to resist the other for long. He smiled as Dixie Lee passed, but she did not notice. His plan had worked.

After she left, Carlton glanced self-consciously around the room, hoping no one had noticed his talk with Dixie Lee. He caught sight of Woody standing in the door, and he knew Woody must have seen them. Carlton waved him over. Damn it, he thought, as Woody approached the table and sat down. What power did she have over him? He had planned to stay out of it, and now he had blurted out his true feelings. For once in his life, he had wanted to do the right thing, and he had only made matters worse.

"You saw?" he asked Woody.

"I couldn't help it," replied Woody. "But put your mind at ease. No one else did. And I can keep a secret, believe me."

There was a strange smile on his face.

"Well, don't jump to any conclusions," said Carlton. "You didn't see what you thought you did."

"I saw nothing," replied Woody. "Nothing at all."

"You're right, whether you believe it or not."

"Of course I'm right," said Woody, "and the pretty child is gone now, so let's turn our attention to other matters."

17

Early on the morning of December twenty-seventh Will Fable gathered his belongings and left Hayley. He did not say goodbye to Tori, for his heart would have broken at the tears. He left a letter for her the night before.

Darkness had fallen when Tori returned from her visit with Wendy the previous day. She had not discovered Will's surprise. She would see it today.

Will had stayed up late with Mrs. Cooper the night before, long after Tori had gone to bed. They had talked for hours, about his life, his future, and about Hayley and the people there. Will wanted to know all about Elizabeth Cooper, it seemed, her life, her friends, her beliefs. With each passing hour, their friendship was more firmly sealed, more deeply and permanently cemented.

Mrs. Cooper suspected rightly that Will was gathering more information for his writing, so she talked at length about Hayley and its citizens, keeping her own history to a minimum. She told him briefly of her background, her family, the agonies the Depression had brought them, and her move to the South. Mostly, she talked about Hayley. Without knowing it, she told Will as much about herself as she did about her neighbors, for in the realistic, yet kind, portraits she drew of others she revealed a wisdom and contentment Will admired greatly.

She told him of the struggles of the poor farmers, like Jake Potter, the man Tori had proudly pointed out to Will in church, and who had made the beautiful manger scene. Will did not meet Jake, for the Potters had come in after Tori and Will were seated, and had left hurriedly following the service, with scarcely a word to anyone, much to Tori's disappointment.

Elizabeth told Will of the Townsends, of the legacy of the late

County Pa, and of the strife between the two brothers that was now visible to all. She told of their great wealth, of the elegant country club at Radium Springs, and of the forbidden game preserve and the legend of the ghost which now inhabited it. Will realized this was the place where he had spent the night less than a week ago, and he remembered vividly the eerie feeling of dread the woods had given him, as well as the haunting face in the portrait, the young County Pa.

By the time their long talk had ended, Will knew most of Hayley's people: stalwart Bubba James and his beautiful, headstrong daughter; the miserly, greedy Sam Gates and his questionable business dealings; even Mr. Buford was described with gentle amusement, for he so fit, in appearance and demeanor, his chosen profession.

Will learned, too, of Tori's friends. Jessie Potter, whose courage and innate sweetness withstood the assaults of prejudice and poverty. Little Boozie, who got her nickname from her fear of ghosts and boogey men. And Wendy, with her shy spirit and gaudy clothes, trying to survive in a world of grown-up tinsel and decadence. Long after he said good night, Will burned the lamp in the barn, writing down all he could remember of their conversation. Of all the people he had met vicariously through Mrs. Cooper, it was Jake Potter that interested him the most, for Will had seen a look of desperation in the man, a look with which he himself was well acquainted. It was Jake who did not fit the description Mrs. Cooper had given, who did not seem capable of creating such beautiful, sacred carvings, at least from the brief impression Will had gotten from him that night. Will saw only a tumultuous, twisting spirit, reflected through hollow eyes of rage and despair. Strangely, Mrs. Cooper did not seem to know the Jake Potter Will had seen. But Will knew him well— Will had once been a Jake Potter.

The sun had not yet risen as Will Fable walked into Hayley. Dressed again in the clothes of an aimless wanderer, Will was free for the moment to explore the little township. He could not afford to be seen, for the two-day stubble and tattered clothing would not be sufficient to disguise him. What a shock would await the people of Hayley if they learned that the well-to-do Mr. Fable from New York City was not really on his way to his winter home in Florida. Will chuckled at the thought.

Will drank the town in, creating a vivid picture in his memory to carry with him, as Hayley had become a place of great importance to him. When the sun threatened to slip above the horizon, painting the gray landscape again with colors, Will made his way to the railroad tracks, just below the depot. Here he would wait, hidden, for the train to arrive, so he could slip unnoticed aboard one of the boxcars. He had no idea when the train would arrive, so he settled himself among the weeds on the embankment and waited. He was warm, for he wore the long underwear and wool sweater of the late Mr. Cooper beneath his tattered jacket.

In ten minutes the sky had turned from purple to pink to blue. Above him, Will heard the sounds of the town awakening. An automobile pulled up to the depot, and he heard the sounds of someone walking up steps and opening a squeaky door. Bubba James was opening up the post office and jail. Soon there was activity in the warehouses, doors being thrown open, and cargo being rolled out to the landing on carts and lorries.

If he craned his neck a bit, Will could get a glimpse of the loading dock of the first warehouse. He looked up and saw four Negro workers straining to lift a dark-grained casket onto a lorry. They deposited the burden with great difficulty, as if the casket was filled with lead. A man approached them from the deserted landing shed, a man with a sour face and a long, pointed nose. Will recognized the dour mortician, Mr. Buford. The man began barking orders at the Negroes, and two of them turned and left. Buford returned to the shed, out of Will's view, but the demeanor of the two remaining Negroes told Will that Buford remained close by, watching the casket and the men.

Not many minutes later, Will heard the whistle of a train. He was pleased, for his wait had been short, and it was still early enough that he was assured of few onlookers to discover him. Soon the Katy Flyer rumbled in with a long string of freight cars and flat cars behind her. She chugged to a thunderous halt at the depot, her lonesome whistle nudging sleep from the town.

Will did not stir. He would wait and catch the hand bar of an empty boxcar far down the line when the train was pulling out. He had learned the hard way not to hitch on until the train reached a respectable speed of fifteen or twenty miles per hour, having been dragged off slower moving trains. He looked back to the warehouse and saw Buford directing the loading of the heavy casket, which the two Negroes pushed up the grade of the boarding slant. The two men must have had to struggle to get the casket off the lorry once inside the boxcar, because they did not emerge quickly.

Unknown to Will, another man climbed slowly into an empty boxcar near the end of the train. This man was familiar enough with schedule and security to know how far below the depot he could board an empty car with no danger of discovery. Will Fable, observing the loading of the casket, saw nothing of the man, and waited patiently for the train to pull out.

Bubba James, boots shining and buckle gleaming, strode the length of the depot while the train took on cargo and cars were unloaded. The morning was crisp and clear, and patchy sheets of frost covered the ground. Bubba took a deep breath and relaxed his body, ignoring the cold. As usual, he wore no jacket. His uniform was the same both summer and winter, although he allowed himself the luxury of long johns in weather such as this.

Bubba fought all aspects of weakness in himself. Cold was a challenge to him. He believed it was a state of mind, like pain, which could be ignored. His forty-fifth year saw no end to the demands he put on himself, as if someday he expected to be put in a desperate situation, where his survival would depend solely on tough mental discipline.

Bubba stood, ever observant, on the platform during the stopover. As the train pulled out, Bubba watched the cars go by one by one, checking for loose anchor lines or open doors on the cargo cars. All seemed secure. Bubba continued to watch until the open doors of the empty boxcars at the end of the train came into view.

He was turning to leave when he caught sight of a ragged hobo, struggling to pull a knapsack away from the open door of an empty car. The hobo looked up and saw he had been discovered. The train was passing swiftly, too late to halt. As if the hobo realized the chief's powerlessness to stop him, he stood up in full view, removed his hat, and bowed jauntily to Bubba as the train sped past.

Bubba frowned slightly, but the stranger's boldness amused him. He did not mind hobos really, the poor fools. When the hobo stood up straight again, a spark of recognition came into the chief's eyes. Bubba was famous for remembering faces and names. He had seen this man before. Damned if it didn't look like that rich visitor from New York—the one at the church. The train sped away. Bubba shook his head and turned to face the street. No, he thought, hell no. He removed his cap and ran his fingers through his thick blond hair, then replaced the cap. He must be seeing things. Rich Yankees don't turn into ragged hobos overnight. Elizabeth Cooper's friend was just what she had said he was, a friend. Nothing that woman did could possibly be questioned.

Bubba sighed. He reached into his breast pocket and retrieved the ever-present sunglasses. Maybe he was getting old. His mind was playing tricks on him. Somewhere deep within him, Bubba knew that something wasn't right. For the first time in his life, he suffered from insomnia. It would be many months before the chief would realize that his secret vendetta against Carlton Townsend was at the bottom of it. His dislike of Carlton violated the prime directive of his moral code, equal justice for all under the law. Putting his cold hands into his pockets, Bubba turned his face toward the sun and began his morning rounds.

18

Will Fable laughed softly as he retrieved his sack. He knew the chief did not recognize him. From the far end of the boxcar, a voice startled him.

"You're lucky, friend," said the voice.

Will turned in surprise. At the anterior end of the car he saw a thin form, reclining against the wall of the structure. The man made no threatening move. Will relaxed a bit from the natural defensive tension he felt. The unwelcome companion had called him friend.

"That lawman's not one t' play with," continued the man.

Will pulled the door of the boxcar partially closed against the cold.

"You know him?" asked Will casually. He was still cautious.

"Know *of* him," the man replied. "Know enough."

Will walked to the front end of the car and deposited his knapsack a few feet from the man. With a safe distance separating them, Will sank down and settled himself for the ride, out of the wind. Following the hobo code of anonymity, he did not look the man in the eye or intrude too closely upon his territory. Will stretched his muscled arms and yawned, watching the other out of the corner of his eye. After a time, he spoke.

"Where you headed, friend?" Will asked.

"Nowhere," replied the other sullenly.

Like Will, the man did not look at his companion. There was a gloom about him, an isolation and a sadness Will recognized at once. Will grinned knowingly at the man's answer.

"Nowhere, huh?" he repeated. "I've been there."

Will glanced over at his companion. With a start, he recognized the lonely face of Jake Potter. He turned away quickly, hoping Jake had not noticed the recognition in his eyes. Would Jake remember him from the church? He did not think so. He continued his lazy attempt at conversation.

"Yeah, I've been nowhere and I've been everywhere. One's much the same as the other." He looked at Jake. "What's your name, brother?"

"My name?" Jake paused. "I'm nobody," he mused, as if talking to himself. "Mr. Nobody. First name, No-count."

Will stretched his arms again and looked away, confident now of his own anonymity.

"That's quite a name," said Will. "I know what you mean. I've used that name myself, more times than I care to recall. But those days are behind me now. I've been through the dark valley and lived to tell about it. Will Fable's the name, friend, and I travel all over this great country by the rails."

Jake Potter was not impressed. He said nothing. His thoughts were his own, and he was deeply entrenched in them, like a man trapped long hours in a deep pit, too exhausted to try to escape.

So this was Jake Potter, the man who had put such love and care into a sacred sculpture, the man Elizabeth Cooper described as a man of integrity, with a clear head and high principles. A man who never accepted a handout, who worked hard and struggled to keep his own land, and his dignity. A man with a loving family, the father of Tori's best friend, Jessie. And yet, this was the same man whose eyes had been a mirror to Will, a mirror of Will's own misery. Mrs. Cooper cared about this man, and now Will did too. Something was wrong, very wrong.

"Where are you headed?" asked Will.

"Not far." Jake reached into his pocket and drew out a pocket knife and a wooden figure he was whittling.

"I figured as much," said Will. "I've been a bum too long not to know an innocent when I see one."

"What d'ya mean by that?" asked Jake.

"You know exactly what I mean," answered Will. "If you're a bum, I'm Franklin Roosevelt. You can't fool a veteran, friend. You don't belong here."

Jake opened the pocket knife and began to work on the little wooden figure. He never looked up.

"I don't care what you think," said Jake. "Who are you t' know anything about me. For all you know I could be a murderer, out t' kill you with this here knife."

Will smiled.

"That's some weapon."

"Look," said Jake with irritation, "I don't know you, mister, I don't care t' know you, and I didn't come here t' listen to a lot'a fool talk. Why don't you jus' sit there and mind your own business, and I'll mind mine."

Will looked at Jake. Jake felt the other man's eyes pierce him with a strange power. It was unnerving. Jake felt exposed but not threatened. The eyes of the hobo burned into him, but not with fire; they burned him with quietness, with peace, and most frighteningly, with wisdom. It was a strange feeling, and a stranger fate, to find such strength in the person of a hobo.

"You know, kid," said Will, "it's a real shame, but I'm afraid providence has seen fit to stick you with me for a while, and if ever there was a man full of fool talk, it's me. I'm sorry, but it looks like you'll just have to suffer, because you and me, we're going to have a little talk. I'm a fool that's just full of opinions and stories, and I like to talk. Besides, looks to me like you need a friend."

"I don't need no friends," said Jake. He shifted uneasily. "I don't need nuthin'."

"I'd say you're wrong about that," said Will. After a while he continued, "Tell you what, Mr. Nobody. How about if I tell you a story? Just to pass the time, you know."

Jake whittled and said nothing.

Will looked at the younger man's hands moving gracefully, skillfully, creating a thing of beauty from a piece of wood. It was the figure of an elephant, with wide ears thrown back, trunk raised. It was neatly finished and beautifully, delicately carved.

"Okay then," Will said, "if you have no objection. I'll tell you a story. It's a sad tale, too, about a man, a decent man." Will clasped his rough hands behind his head and leaned back. "He was what most people would consider poor in material things. He had to work hard to make it in this life. He had a good wife who loved him, and children who adored him. He had friends, too, friends who knew they could count on him when they needed help. He was never too busy to lend a hand.

"This man learned a hard lesson early in his life, that there were people who looked down on him and his family because of his poverty, people with small minds and dull senses, people who held themselves above him. But this man accepted things as they came. He knew who he was, he knew what was right and wrong, and he wasn't afraid of an honest day's work. He was proud and he knew what was important in life. He found life difficult, but he was not bitter.

"But then, one day, something happened. Something that made him resent his lot in life. He got angry. He began to question everything he had once believed. He thought himself a fool, and he decided things would be different. He didn't care what he had to do to make it so.

"All of a sudden, he found it easy to do things he never thought he was capable of doing. He started stealing. He started lying to his wife. He became a criminal.

"He had money then. It made things easier at first. He no longer worried about putting food on the table, or clothes on his back. But he couldn't escape from his conscience. He felt dead inside. He lost himself. He found he was holding those he cared about most away from him. He couldn't be the same to his family, because he wasn't the same to himself.

"He was in too deep, now, to go back, but he knew he couldn't go on. He thought he had known trouble and misery and want, but now he knew something worse. He knew guilt, and loneliness, and a pain in his spirit that made life not worth living."

Jake started to cry. Bitter tears stung his cold cheeks, and suddenly he threw the carving at the wall of the boxcar. He stood up angrily and faced the meddling stranger, pointing the knife at him, his face distorted with rage, his knuckles white upon the knife.

"Shut up!" he cried. "Just get away from me!"

Will Fable sat calmly. He made no move to protect himself from the man who stood over him with eyes red and blazing.

"Get out of here," said Jake. "Get out of here now, or I'll—"

"You'll what?" asked Will. "Kill me?" Will paused. "I don't think so. You're no murderer. I'm staying."

The two men stared at each other for a long moment. Again Jake felt those piercing eyes, reflecting only peace and kindness. At last Jake threw the knife on the floor and turned his back on Will Fable. His heart was pounding and a searing heat cut his brain in two. He grabbed his temples and pressed hard, as if trying to force out the throbbing pain.

"It's all right, son," said Will finally. "You didn't want to hurt me. You wanted to hurt yourself."

Jake sat down heavily. God in heaven, how did he get to this place? What was he doing here? Had he lost his mind? The tears came again, against his will.

"Who in God's name are you?" he asked.

"I'm you, kid," came the calm voice, "five years ago."

Jake looked up at the other man in surprise, and a chill ran down his spine. There was something unearthly and fearful about this strange man who seemed able to see into other men's souls, who seemed to know all things secret and profound.

"I don't know who you are," said Jake, "but you've told me things no man has a right t' know. I don't want t' hear any more." He hung his head wearily. "Just leave me alone."

"I can't do that," said Will. "You're at a crossroad, son. You've gotten yourself mixed up in something illegal, and you know you can't go on. Like I said before, you're an innocent. You don't belong here."

"I guess you're right," said Jake. He began to laugh slowly, a terrible deadly laugh, a laugh of desperation and confusion. "God help me," he said. "I don't know what t' do."

"Tell you what," said Will. "I'll give you a little advice. No charge. Whatever it is you're mixed up in, whatever you've been doing, stop it now. Go back home."

Jake hesitated. He suddenly realized that he had as much as admitted to a perfect stranger that he was a criminal. He turned cold eyes on the other man. Who was he? Jake wondered. He was no ordinary tramp.

Could he be a federal agent or a revenuer? Was he a policeman in disguise?

Will read Jake's mind easily.

"Relax," he said. "I'm not the law. I don't know what you're involved in, and I don't want to know."

Will stood up and walked to the other end of the boxcar. He bent over and picked up the carving Jake had thrown. Will inspected it carefully in the light of the slightly open door. He recognized the same style, the same skill he had so admired in the manger scene. Will walked back to his place and sat down. Jake watched him warily, but in his heart, he was drawn to Will Fable. His instincts told him that Will was a friend.

"You have a gift," said Will, holding up the carving.

Jake smiled sarcastically.

"What good is it?" he asked. "It don't keep my head above water."

"You sell these?"

"I sell them."

"Who buys them?"

"The travelers at the depot, mainly."

"What do you ask for them?"

"Fifty cents."

Will smiled. The man had no idea what a talent he possessed. Will had seen lesser works at novelty shops in the East sell for five dollars or more. And the art galleries often displayed larger works by less talented sculptors, asking hundreds of dollars for each piece.

"Let me guess," said Will. "You sell every piece you make, right?"

"Yeah."

"And if you raise the price, the buyers offer you less, right?"

"Right."

"What's the highest price you've asked for?"

"A dollar."

Will shook his head. In New York, even this small piece would sell for at least ten dollars.

"Tell you what," said Will, "next time ask for ten dollars and see what happens."

"You're crazy," Jake replied. "Nobody will give me that."

"Maybe not," said Will. "But that's what it's worth. If the wealthy people on the train have any sense, they'll offer you at least half that price, and know they got a bargain."

"If I could get five dollars apiece, I wouldn't need to ride boxcars," said Jake dejectedly.

By this time, Jake had forgotten his apprehension that his mysterious fellow traveler was a threat to him. He found himself strangely comforted by Will's presence. How could this man seem to know so much about him? Will had once been in Jake's shoes, he had said, at war with himself, full of the same pain. Could he really understand?

"What makes you think you know so much about me?" asked Jake. "What makes you think you can give me advice? You don't know me. You don't know nuthin' about me."

"I know you're troubled," answered Will. "I know you're hurting inside. And I know why."

Jake said nothing. He was amazed at Will's ability to read every thought, every feeling.

"You've forgotten something very important or you wouldn't be here," continued Will. "What other people think of you is not as important as what you think of yourself. You knew that once, but something made you forget it. What it was, I don't know. But I can imagine it came at a time when you were already at the breaking point."

Through Jake's mind passed the vision of Mabel, weak and feverish. The drought, the ruined crop, the empty cupboard, and the gnawing hunger. He saw the blank stares on the faces of the men sitting around the stove in the General Store, and the little boy in the depot. They're trash, his mother had said. Trash. Jake felt the tears forming and covered his face with his hands.

He saw other faces, all of them looking at him with vacant eyes, tolerant eyes, belittling eyes. But then, he saw the face of his wife, warm and trusting. He saw the happy face of Jessie, sitting on his lap and reading, and the kind smile of Elizabeth Cooper. He remembered those who had always treated him with respect, people like Bubba James and

Crawford Welch. He knew Will Fable was right.

As if he knew Jake had come to the point of accepting his words, Will spoke. "You've seen the dark valley now," he said, "and I think you've learned, like I have, that the dark valley isn't out in the world. It's inside each of us. There's not a man alive who's not capable of evil, who's not capable of stealing or cheating or lying. But there's a light inside each of us, too, a light that tells us right and wrong. You can try to hide from it, but it will eat you alive if you do. No matter what happens to you in this life, nothing is worth living with yourself in that dark pit.

"You're not the only one who has broken his back to earn a living, who has wanted to make life good for the people he loves. Half the world is in your shoes, boy. Shoot, more than half. Life is hard. Life's going to hand you one problem after another; that's just the way it is. When one problem is solved, another will take its place.

"You're a lot better off right now than you realize. I've seen people without a living soul to care about them, some of them crippled with age or infirm with disease. You've got a lot to be thankful for, even now. Just open your eyes. You're not blind, that's the first blessing you can count. Count the rest. If you still think you don't have much to be thankful for, then listen to me for a while. I'll tell you a hundred problems you don't have that you don't want."

The train let out a roaring whistle, signaling its approach to Albany. Jake reached over and picked up the knife he had dropped. He closed it and put it in his pocket.

"This your stop?" asked Will.

Jake nodded. Will took the little elephant from his lap and offered it back to Jake. Jake shook his head.

"Keep it," he said. "A gift."

Will smiled and nodded, setting the carving aside.

"Remember what I told you about the depot," said Will.

"I'll remember," said Jake. "This is Albany. I'll be getting off here. I don't know how you got here, but I'm glad I met up with you. Thanks for the advice." He extended his hand.

Will smiled and shook his hand.

"It's been a pleasure, Mr. Nobody," he said.

"My name's Jake. Jake Potter."

"Glad to know you, Jake," said Will. "One more thing before you go."

"What's that?"

"I never told you my story, son," said Will. "There wasn't enough time. Maybe it's enough for you to know it was much the same as yours. But I want to tell you that I learned something else in my journey. I learned that you and I are both in the hands of a higher power. Don't forget that, ever. It was no accident that we met here today. I'm sure of it."

Jake went to the door of the boxcar and pulled it back. He peered out, seeing the depot far in the distance.

"So long," he called to Will. "Friend."

"Good luck, Jake," replied Will.

Jake jumped from the slow-moving car and was gone.

Quickly, Will jumped to his feet, snatching up his belongings.

He hurried to the door of the car and looked back. Jake was there, climbing up the slope. When Jake disappeared over the ridge, Will took a deep breath and jumped. With a well-practiced roll, he landed safely in the brush. He retrieved his knapsack and stealthily climbed the slope. In the distance he saw Jake, walking by the road to the depot. Without a sound, and keeping well back, Will followed him.

19

Tori awoke still determined to find a way to convince Will Fable to stay. She did not know that he had been gone for hours or that he and Mrs. Cooper had stayed up late, talking, after she had gone to bed. Neither did she know of the gift Will had left for her, or the real reason her grandmother had robbed her of Will's company the day before, insisting that she spend the afternoon with Wendy Hamilton at Radium Springs.

It had been fun, but Tori would rather have stayed home to talk with Will, her new best friend. Mrs. Hamilton had seemed glad to see Tori, but promptly deposited the girls in the care of the kitchen Negroes. Wendy and Tori had gone exploring in the clubhouse, with Wendy as the guide, showing Tori all the rooms, the poolroom, the golfers' locker room, the snack bar, the dining rooms, the party rooms, and, of course, the grand ballroom, where they had watched the Labor Day dance. Tori shivered when she saw the portrait of County Pa staring down at her from the wall of the ballroom. She tried not to look at it, and examined instead the statues in the alcoves of the walls.

Most of the Christmas decorations were intact, although the maids were adapting them for the New Year's Eve ball. Tori was amazed at the size of the huge Christmas tree at the far end of the room, hung with shiny ornaments and candles. The maids began to take down the decorations from the tree, declining the girls' offer to help. The ornaments, it seemed, were fragile and valuable. For the New Year's Eve party, the ropes of greenery, hung in tiers along the walls, were to remain, and also the poinsettia plants. The red candles on each of the side tables, in their nests of holly, were to be replaced with white candles. The maids agreed to let the children take down the wreaths.

When the girls returned to the kitchen, Tori overheard one of the maids talking about Jack Hamilton, Wendy's father, but the words made no sense to her. A greater impression was made by the fact that the woman stopped speaking, in midsentence, when she saw the girls. Wendy's face had turned red, but she said nothing. More and more, Tori was becoming aware that something was wrong between Wendy's parents, and that Wendy was keeping it to herself.

But Wendy was not on Tori's mind when she got out of bed, Will Fable was. He just couldn't leave today. She had to think of something quick that would convince her grandmother. In four short days, Tori had come to love Will Fable. He was so kind and so much fun. He was full of surprises and stories, and he talked to her as a friend. What would make him stay? Talking didn't help, begging didn't work. She had begged to stay home the day before, but was whisked off to Wendy's anyway.

Tori heard her grandmother in the kitchen, humming as she prepared breakfast. Tori bathed and dressed quickly. As she put on her shoes, she thought of it—surely Will would stay if she was hurt! Tori took a marble from her marble pouch and put it in the heel of her right shoe. She put all her weight on it. It hurt a little. It was perfect. With great pain etched in her face, Tori limped to the door of the kitchen.

"Good morning, dear," called Mrs. Cooper. She turned to Tori with a smile.

"Meema," said in a small, hurt voice, "I think I hurt my leg."

"Why, honey," said Mrs. Cooper, "what did you do?" She dropped the toast and knife in midbutter. "Did you turn your ankle when you got out of bed? Let me see." The thought of polio came to her, but Mrs. Cooper pushed the thought from her mind. Be calm, she told herself; surely it's nothing serious.

Tori sat heavily on one of the kitchen chairs, and Mrs. Cooper bent to examine the imaginary injury. She pressed here and there along the ankle, hoping the problem was there, not in the muscles of the calf.

"Does that hurt?" she asked.

Tori winced, half from guilt at her deception.

"There's no swelling, honey, and I see no bruise."

Mrs. Cooper pressed the ankle again below the bone. Tori's lips formed a silent ouch as she drew away. Mrs. Cooper breathed a silent prayer of thanks. The child had turned her ankle, nothing more.

"My goodness, child," she said, shaking her head. "You can get yourself into more trouble than a brainless turkey gobbler." She rose and went to the cabinet for a basin.

Tori knew her tone well. Whenever Mrs. Cooper was afraid for her safety, whenever Tori fell or cut herself, Mrs. Cooper fussed at her for a minute or two. It never took long for good sense to take over, however, and for Mrs. Cooper to realize that a child will be a child, and suffer little hurts no matter how well taken care of they are. She was very liberal with Tori, letting her run free as much as possible, as a child should, making her own mistakes, learning by experience to be careful. But when something did happen, the natural protective instinct of a mother rose within her, and she scolded, more herself than Tori.

"You'll have to keep an ice pack on that ankle for a little while," said Mrs. Cooper, opening the icebox. She began to chip away at the big block of ice with an ice pick.

An ice pack. Tori had not bargained on that. She hated ice packs almost as much as castor oil.

"It's not that bad, Meema." she said. "It's not swollen up, you said so."

"Not yet, it isn't," replied her grandmother, "but it probably will be if we don't put ice on it immediately. Stop your protesting. You're going to have an ice pack and that's all there is to it, understand?"

"Yes, Meema." Tori pouted.

Mrs. Cooper prepared the ice pack with a dishcloth, tied it around the ankle, removed Tori's shoe and sock, and set her foot in the basin to catch the water as it melted. The marble rolled secretly to the toe of Tori's shoe, unnoticed.

"Know what would make me feel better?" Tori asked innocently.

"What, honey?"

"I know I'd feel a lot better if Will could come in and tell me a story. Can he, Meema, please?"

Mrs. Cooper was silent. She knew Tori would be crushed to learn that Will had gone. The child adored him. She, herself, had become very fond of him as well. She also hated to see him leave so soon, but what could she have done? It would have been improper to ask him to stay any longer. Besides, he had a new life to build for himself. She had bid him goodbye the night before, wished him well, and told him she would pray for him. Will had promised to keep in touch, and insisted that she keep him abreast of all the news of Hayley with regular letters. He had promised her the very first copy of his book, specially autographed. They would meet again, he had said, and that was a promise. She smiled fondly as she thought of him, sighed, and turned to Tori. She had to be told.

"Darling," she began, "Mr. Fable is gone. He told me last night he was going to leave early this morning, before sunrise. He gave me a letter to give to you."

Tori was out of her chair and opening the kitchen door before her grandmother could stop her.

"Wait a minute, young lady," said Mrs. Cooper. "Where do you think you are going?"

Tori raced out the door, down the steps and out into the yard, coatless, one foot bare, the ice pack bobbing around her ankle.

"Come back here this instant!" cried Mrs. Cooper.

She started out the door to catch Tori, watching her run across the large yard to the barn, the dishcloth falling from her bare foot midway. Suddenly, she realized the child wasn't limping, she was running full speed, strong and steady. Mrs. Cooper stopped at the screen door. She understood. The hurt ankle had been a ruse, a plan to make Tori's new friend too concerned to leave.

Mrs. Cooper was angry at Tori for deceiving her, and furious that she had run out into the cold, but her heart ached for the child. She listened to Tori calling Will's name desperately as she ran, and she knew the girl's heart was breaking. She had wanted Will to stay, and was willing to try anything to make it so. She watched as Tori disappeared into the barn, rushed out again, then ran around the side of the barn, searching for Will. She appeared from the opposite side of the barn, still calling him, sobbing. She ran slower now, her feet becoming leaden with disappointment and hurt.

Tori was crushed. He was gone, and he didn't even say goodbye. She looked up at the house and saw her grandmother watching her from the screen door. She knew! And she hadn't told her. Tori turned her back and sat down on the cold red earth in front of the barn. She started to cry. Bessie the cow lowed at her.

Mrs. Cooper went back to the kitchen and reached for her shawl. She walked out to Tori, her anger forgotten, feeling only sympathy for the child. As always, she could never stay angry at Tori for long. She placed the shawl around Tori's shoulders and knelt down beside her.

"I'm sorry, honey," she said gently. "Maybe he should have stayed to say goodbye to you after all."

Tori said nothing, her sobs coming softer, deeper, from the very pit of her stomach, her shoulders jerking with each.

"He knew you would be upset. He didn't want to see you cry, honey." Mrs. Cooper reached up and stroked Tori's hair softly. "Please don't cry. You know he couldn't stay. He's going home at last. After six years, he's finally ready to go home again. We couldn't keep him from that, could we?"

Tori looked up at Mrs. Cooper and said through her tears, "I didn't want him to stay forever. Just a few more days, that's all."

"But then, it would have been even harder to say goodbye, don't you see that?"

"No," Tori sobbed, "it would have been easier."

"Shhh," said Mrs. Cooper. "Please try to understand. Mr. Fable brought a lot of joy and excitement to our lives. He was like someone out of a fairy tale to you, with all his stories and his secrets. But he wasn't meant to stay with us."

Tori knew she was right. The realization that he was gone began to sink in. Slowly she became accustomed to it. She knew he would have to leave, she just didn't expect it so soon.

"He didn't tell me goodbye, Meema."

"Sweetheart, Mr. Fable had gotten very attached to you. It was just too hard for him, he told me so."

"What did he say?"

"He told me he would write to you, and that he would always wish you were his own little girl."

"He did?" asked Tori, sniffing, her tears drying.

"And he promised he would come back to see us one day."

"He did?" Her voice was lighter.

"He certainly did. Now, come on, let's go back to the house before we catch pneumonia. I'll bet breakfast is cold by now."

They rose and walked to the house. Mrs. Cooper picked up the dishrag on the way, saying nothing. Tori remembered her lie, and glanced up apprehensively at her grandmother. There were no scolding words. No mention of the fact that Tori no longer limped. Tori walked the rest of the way with her eyes glued to the ground, waiting.

When they came to the porch, Mrs. Cooper discarded the dishcloth on a chair, as if it were nothing of importance, just something she found lying in the yard. She knew, and Tori knew it.

But she did not mention it again. Her silence spoke more clearly to Tori than any words could have. Tori vowed never to deceive her grandmother again.

Conversation between them came slowly back to normal as they ate their breakfast of grits, toast, and peach preserves. They had both slept later than usual, and it was after nine o'clock when the breakfast dishes were washed and put away. Mrs. Cooper had not told Tori about Will's surprise. He had wanted her to find it for herself.

"Tori," said Mrs. Cooper casually, "run put on your coat and your mittens. I need you to go to the General Store and get some flour for me."

Tori smiled and nodded. She loved to go to the store for her grandmother. There was always an extra nickel for herself. Having donned her coat, Tori took the money from Mrs. Cooper and started off. The store was not far, within sight of the huge oak tree at the edge of their property.

This was the tree Tori had pointed out to Will, the tree she loved to climb in the warmer months. It afforded her a view of the town square, and of all the comings and goings of the good folks of Hayley. In the spring it would again burst forth with fresh green leaves, forming a happy green armor for her sanctuary, protecting her from discovery as she watched the little world of Hayley turn far below her lofty perch. It was her tree, hers alone, a special place. She could stay there for hours, pleasantly weaving tales and mysteries to fit the observations of the day.

She rounded the side of the house and the tall tree came into view, its formidable limbs reaching heavenward, bare and patient, waiting for the spring, its huge trunk solidly rooted, a strong, silent sentinel. Tori walked half the way across the yard, kicking stones, deep in her own thoughts, before she looked up in the direction of her summer retreat.

She stopped short suddenly, her mouth dropping open in amazement. There was a tree house! A homemade ladder, quite narrow, stood against the trunk, reaching to the level of the first great branching of the tree. Above it, a rope ascended ten feet higher to a wide wooden platform, with low walls at its edges. Tori was too excited to question how the wonderful structure came to be. She let out a joyful yelp and ran. She climbed the narrow ladder and grabbed the rope, easily navigating the thick, solid branching limbs until she reached the platform, eighteen feet above the ground.

It was at least five feet square, strongly braced, and sturdy enough for a dozen children. Built-in box-seating lined the edges of the platform on all sides, the backs of the seats being formed by the three-foot walls. She tried one of the box seats with joy as she looked out over the side walls toward the square. She jumped up and pulled in the rope, feeling for all the world like the captain of a great sailing vessel setting out to sea.

She twirled and laughed, realizing that by some miracle, this tree house belonged to her. Then she saw something tacked to a nearby limb. It was a white envelope. She reached up and grabbed it carefully, seeing her name written on it in a beautiful, round, slanting hand she recognized as belonging to Will Fable.

He did this for me, she thought, he did this yesterday while I was at Wendy's. She tore the envelope carefully, extracted the note, sat down on the seat, and opened it.

It read: "Dear Tori, I'm sorry I didn't stay to tell you goodbye. Will you forgive me? I hope you like your tree house. I wanted to do something just for you. It's a couple of days late, but Merry Christmas! I learned to do a lot of things in my travels, and nailing boards together is one of them. You have your grandmother to thank for the lumber. Yes, you'll find the planks gone from the barn. Be sure you do thank her, as she may have been saving the wood for another purpose. When I was your age, my father built a tree house for me, exactly the same as this one. I hope you enjoy yours as much as I did mine.

"I must be on my way, but I want you to know I will never forget you. I will write to you soon. One day you will see me coming down the path to your door again, I promise. Don't forget me, little one. Just look up at the stars any night and know that I am looking up and seeing them with you, wherever I am. And if I see Betelgeuse, I'll see you. I will always be your friend. Love, Will."

Tori felt warm tears stream down her cold cheeks as she read the letter over and over. Will was the best friend she had ever had, except for Jessie. And he promised to write, and even better, to come back again for a visit. He promised. She knew she would see him again some day.

At last she put the letter in her pocket and admired her new castle. She tried to imagine it in summer, shielded from all eyes in a cloak of green. She stayed for more than an hour, until she realized her grand-mother would be looking for her. Meema. Dear Meema. She had done this, too. Tori dropped the rope and descended the tree quickly, with well-practiced agility. Remembering her errand, she ran to the General Store and purchased the flour, not even pausing to get her usual treat. She raced home to thank her grandmother, who had known all along, who planned for her to find Will's wonderful present on her way. What fun she would have, what fun. There was not another child in the world happier than Tori Tanner that day.

20

Will Fable was a stranger in Albany. It was a little after ten in the morning when Sheriff Jock Morehouse approached him. He was sitting on the end of the wooden porch of Bailey's Feed and Seed, facing an alley, shielded from the view of the street by bales of hay. He was waiting for Jake Potter to emerge from the barber shop across the street.

Sheriff Morehouse doubted that this scruffy stranger had anything to do with the string of burglaries in Albany, but he would check him out, nonetheless. He was acting kind of suspicious, and loitering besides. People in town were nervous, skittish, wary now of strangers. The sheriff would be looked upon as lax in his duty if he did not check out any suspicious character, no matter how unlikely a suspect he was.

Will sat calmly as the sheriff approached him. He had seen him coming, and expected the questioning as a matter of course.

"Mornin', Sheriff," said Will.

The sheriff was blunt. "What's your business around here, mister?"

"No business, Sheriff," Will replied with a grin. "Just passin' through."

"You'll find no friends and no handouts in this town," said the sheriff. "I think it would be best if you just move along."

"I understand, Sheriff," said Will. "I'll be on my way directly, as soon as I rest my feet a bit and get myself a bite to eat."

"You have money to buy it with, I assume?"

"Yessir, I've got money."

"Where'd you get it, boy?"

Will was distracted momentarily as he saw Jake Potter emerge from the shop across the street. Jake was agitated. He seemed to scan the street, then he began to walk, with an attempt at casualness, toward the hotel at the end of the street.

Will could not waste time with the sheriff now. He would have to tell him more than he planned to if he was to keep an eye on Jake.

"I earned the money, Sheriff," Will said, "A kind lady in Hayley, down the road apiece, let me do some work for her. Elizabeth Cooper is her name. If you need to check up on me, call Chief James. He can get Mrs. Cooper to vouch for me."

Sheriff Morehouse was satisfied with this answer. It was obvious that the man must have spent some time in Hayley, to be familiar with Bubba's name. The sheriff had an instinct about men. He knew that this stranger was a harmless wanderer. There would be no need to check up on him.

"I'll do that," said Jock Morehouse. "When I come back this way, I want to find you gone. Understand?"

"Yes sir, thank you, sir," said Will, rising. He caught sight of Jake entering the hotel as he stood up. "I'll get something at the hotel restaurant down the street to carry with me on the way out of town. Thank you, Sheriff."

Sheriff Morehouse watched as Will Fable walked to the hotel and went up the steps. Will looked back and gave a wave of compliance to his observer as he entered the hotel lobby. Once inside, Will quickly scanned the room and spotted Jake standing at the far end of the lobby, using the telephone. Jake's back was to him. Will walked carefully in the direction of the restaurant, having to pass Jake on the way. Jake was speaking in a low voice, trying to appear inconspicuous to the people who milled about the lobby. Will passed by unobserved.

"There's nuthin' else we can do," Will overheard Jake say as he passed. "You'll have t' come up here tonight. Bring Mose and the wagon, too. I'll check into a room here and we can wait for it t' be over. Bring some money for the room."

Will walked into the restaurant and headed for the kitchen, knowing his unkempt appearance was unwelcome in the dining room. He ordered a lunch to go from the cook and waited as it was prepared, as he knew the sheriff would probably check up on him. He could no longer afford to play the hobo in this town if he was to remain to keep an eye on Jake. He took the sack from the cook, paid for it, and left by the kitchen door. He knew he had time because Jake was checking into the hotel. There had been some kind of trouble.

Will headed for a clump of woods behind the hotel and disappeared into them. In about thirty minutes, a well-dressed stranger emerged empty-handed from the woods. Will had transformed himself into the wealthy New Yorker who had visited Elizabeth Cooper on his way south. He had left his knapsack and backpack under a clump of brush, carrying nothing with him save his wallet and identification.

Not even Sheriff Morehouse, who had looked him in the eye an hour ago, would have known him now, hatless, clean-shaven, and displaying the genteel manner of the life to which he had been born. Indeed, not even Jake Potter would have known him. He entered the hotel and approached the desk.

"Morning, sir," said the desk clerk pleasantly. "What can I do for you?"

"I'd like a room for the night."

"Yes, sir," said the clerk, turning the register toward him and offering him a pen. "Just passing through, sir?"

"Quite," replied Will. "Although I'd like to be able to stay longer in your fair city. I've come halfway across the country on that blasted coach car and I just couldn't face another night of traveling. My business will wait long enough for me to spend one night in a real bed."

"Where you headed?"

"Miami."

"Ah, Miami," replied the short, bald-headed clerk. He traveled vicariously with the patrons of the hotel, having never left the state of Georgia. "I hear the weather is lovely down there this winter. You'll be leaving in the morning, then?"

"Probably," Will replied, "but let's keep that option open, shall we?"

Will signed the register with his real name, the name on his identification papers, a name he had not used for six years. The entry above his on the ledger was that of Jake Potter, Hayley.

The clerk rang the bell and a uniformed, tousled-haired bellboy sprang to attention.

"Take Mr. Neill's bags to three-sixteen, Jeremy," he said.

Will thought fast.

"There are no bags, my good man," He said with irritation in his voice. "The fool railroad sent them to California, from what I understand. That was another reason I decided to stop over here. I planned to replace the necessities this afternoon from some of your local storekeepers. I cannot stand this rumpled suit another minute."

Dollar signs filled the eyes of the clerk as he looked at Will's wrinkled suit. His brother-in-law owned a dry goods store on Court Street.

"What a shame," said the clerk sympathetically, "If I may, sir, I'd like to suggest to you Cunningham's on Court Street, just across the way. I'm sure you can find everything you need there. Jeremy can direct you there after lunch, if you would like."

"I appreciate that," Will replied. "I'll let you know."

The register listed Jake Potter in room two-twenty. Will made a mental note of the number and followed the bellboy. As they were going up the stairs, Jake Potter passed them on his way down, Will continued to the second floor landing before he turned to the bellboy.

"Son, I've changed my mind. I think I'll take a walk around town before lunch. Just give me the key to my room."

Will reached into his pocket for a nickel for the bellboy, and handed it to him as he took the key.

"Thankee, sir," said the boy, who sat down on the stair as Will descended to the lobby.

Will hurried out the door, unseen by the clerk, and saw Jake ahead of him, walking past the barber shop he had visited earlier. Will followed at a distance. Jake continued down the street, and turned when he reached the corner. When Will turned the corner, he saw a dozen cars at the far end of the block, clustered around a pretty little church of whitewashed stone.

Jake was walking toward the church, on the other side of the street. He slowed his pace as he neared the church, and milled around at the window of the hardware store opposite it, as if he was unsure of his next move. After a couple of minutes, Jake took a seat in one of the rocking chairs on the front porch of the hardware store. Will loitered in front of the shop windows across the street from Jake until he was sure it was the church that Jake was watching. It was clear that Jake had no intentions of entering the church, but the problem was there, Will was sure of it.

He decided on a bold move. Will headed for the church, in full view of Jake Potter. If he was lucky, Jake would not recognize him. How else could he learn what was going on? He had to take the chance.

21

From his seat across the street, Jake gave no thought to the well-dressed man who climbed the steps of the church and entered. Jake knew he would have to wait for the funeral to end and then follow the mourners to the cemetery somehow, out of sight, to see where they laid the coffin. He had to be careful that Sam Gates did not see him, for he had no business at the funeral of Viola's father. What a ridiculous situation it was. If it weren't so dangerous, Jake would have laughed.

Buford had been furious when he had told him, calling him a stupid fool. He wasn't going to blame it on Jake, no sir! It was his own fault and he should know it. He was the one who labeled the coffins. If they all got caught, Buford would have his own hide to blame.

Why did this have to happen now, just when he decided it would be his last run? If there was a God in heaven looking out for him as Will Fable had suggested, why did He let things go so wrong? Well, that didn't matter. What did matter was that he was going to get this mess straightened out and then he was calling it quits with Buford. What could he do to him after all, without exposing himself? Jake felt he was thinking clearly for the first time in weeks. He had thought he was in too deep to get out, but now he saw that it wasn't true. Buford couldn't touch him, for all his clever words and veiled threats.

When Buford had seen that Jake was having second thoughts about running the moonshine, he had used scare tactics on Jake, telling him that six Negroes in Clay County had died from drinking a bad batch. They were implicated in homicide now, he had told him, they could go to jail for life. Jake had spent many a sleepless night agonizing over his part in the deaths of these men, and had watched the newspapers for some mention of it. Wouldn't be in the papers, Buford had told him; they were only Negroes, after all. But the revenuers and Sheriff Morehouse were in hot pursuit of the moonshiners, he said. And if they were caught, they would be charged with murder, six counts.

As he sat there, Jake went over Buford's story in his mind. Ever since he jumped off the train that morning, he had felt different. He realized that he wasn't afraid of Buford anymore. The story about the deaths of the Negroes didn't make sense. Why wasn't there anything in the papers? Slowly, it became clear. Buford had invented the whole story just to keep him in line. How could he have been so stupid as to believe such a story? It was a blatant lie, a wretched, evil lie told by a wretched, evil man.

Jake hated Buford, hated him for the sleepless nights he had spent, for the torment he had endured. But these feelings were not uppermost in his mind. A new feeling of release, and hope, held him in its grasp, in spite of the mess in which he found himself.

Thanks to a strangely omniscient hobo, the way to heaven had opened a wee crack that morning, and Jake Potter had slipped in through the back door. Will Fable had helped him return to his senses, and he could see his way clearly again. He would get out of this mess, and nothing in heaven or earth could stop him.

As the funeral service continued across the street, Jake made his careful, determined plans. He would say nothing to Buford when he arrived that evening. They would do what had to be done and they would go home. After that, Jake would simply fail to show up, not even to pick up his last payment from the wretch. If Buford threatened him, he would pretend he didn't know what the devil the crazy fool was talking about. Jake would say the man was talking nonsense, that he was out of his head. Jake knew that if he did not admit his complicity, even to Buford himself, there was no way the mortician could take advantage of him. The surest way to hide a sin is to refuse to admit it to the only other person who knows it is true. Jake would deny it to the devil himself! The only one he would not deny it to was to God, but that was just between the two of them now.

Yes, the dirty little mortician was in for a surprise. For the first time, Jake realized he knew enough to put the man in prison if he wanted to. The court might even grant immunity in exchange for his testimony.

They didn't want the errand boys, they wanted the man behind it, and that man was Buford. Jake smiled. Buford just better watch his step from now on.

WILL FABLE sat silently in the back pew of the church. He had entered without anyone's notice, and saw that he had walked in on a funeral service. A closed coffin, draped with flowers, sat before the altar as the preacher extolled the virtues of the departed soul. Will knew immediately that this was the coffin he had seen loaded onto the baggage car in Hayley, for it was quite distinctive; jet black with silver mountings and handles. It had been unusually heavy.

There could be only one explanation for Jake Potter's behavior. He was to accompany some illegal cargo hidden in this coffin to Albany, and see it safely delivered to the barber shop. There must have been a mixup. Whatever was in the coffin was not, Will knew, the body of a man named Jacob Banner, whose life the pleasant-faced parson was detailing. Could it be stolen property? Could Jake be involved in fencing the booty from the cat burglar's raids? It was possible.

The wails of the dead man's daughter reached a new height, and the distraught woman, middle-aged and black-haired, rose from her seat and rushed to the coffin, clutching its side in desolation. With a start, Will recognized the woman. It was Viola Gates. Will had spoken with her for more minutes than he had cared to at the Christmas Eve service. She had been intrigued with him, and had only been snatched away from their conversation of New York stage productions by her impolite, bossy husband, Sam. Yes, there he was, sitting in the front row next to the seat Viola had vacated, his half-scowl visible even from the side.

Will realized he must leave before they recognized him. How could he explain his presence? He was to have been in his nonexistent Florida home by now. Will started to get up, but the church doors behind him opened. A latecomer, a portly gentleman with a broken arm, entered the church and hurried down the aisle. When the stricken Viola saw him, she ran up the aisle to meet him, crying, "Brother, brother! Our father is dead!" They embraced awkwardly at the center of the church, she wailing, he comforting.

"What has kept you?" she asked through her tears. "What has happened to your arm?"

At that moment, Viola looked past her brother and spotted, in the back pew, a surprising guest. Her face noted instant recognition of Will Fable, and she nodded to him graciously, with a look of both surprise and pleasure. Caught, Will nodded back. The bereaved pair made their way back to the altar, the brother explaining the reason for his delay, an accident on the way in his journey from Savannah.

Will had to think of something. Who did he know in Albany? He searched his mind for a name mentioned to him by Mrs. Cooper or Tori. He could only think of one. It would have to do.

When the service was over, the casket was removed by eight stout pallbearers to the hearse waiting in front of the church. The eight young men had a strange look on their faces, as if irritated that some of the others were not bearing their fair share of the burden. As the family filed past him, Viola nodded again to Will. When he joined the mourners on the steps of the church, she approached him immediately.

"How kind of you to come, Mr. Fable," Viola gushed. "How utterly, completely kind. You must ride with us in our car to the cemetery—or do you have your own car?"

"No, Ma'am, I don't," replied Will respectfully. "I shall be honored to accompany you."

They all got into a long, black Oldsmobile coupe, Sam Gates, Viola, the portly brother, and Will. The bereaved Viola seemed to lose much of her misery with the presence of such an unexpected guest, and she glowed as she introduced him to her brother, Butch Banner. She turned to Will and asked, with fluttering eyelashes, how he came to be in Albany.

Will seemed a bit embarrassed when he answered.

"Well, Mrs. Gates," he said, "I wouldn't want this to get around, but the truth is, I met a young lady while I was visiting Albany with my dear friend, Elizabeth Cooper, the day after Christmas. I delayed my trip to Florida for a few days, you see, to . . . to call on her."

Viola's eyes lit up at the prospect of learning this juicy bit of gossip so unexpectedly.

"Goodness me," she said. "Who is it? Do you mind my asking? I know many of the young ladies in Albany. Perhaps I know the dear girl."

Will looked out the window and spotted Jake Potter hurrying along the sidewalk as the car slowly followed the hearse.

"I don't suppose she would mind my telling you," replied Will. "I know you are not the sort of woman who would bandy idle gossip about. She's a lovely schoolteacher named Rebecca Rigsby."

A momentary frown formed a straight line between the eyebrows of Viola Gates. She was flabbergasted. Rebecca Rigsby, she thought. That plump partridge? Why, she's an old maid. How in the world did she charm this rich Yankee? Her face relaxed.

"Miss Rigsby?" she repeated. "Of course! How charming. Why, you'll never believe this coincidence, but my precious little Marvin is one of her pupils."

"Viola," came the stern voice of Sam Gates, "you forget yourself."

Viola looked at her husband in surprise, and, meeting his stony eyes, turned back around in the front seat. In a moment, she turned back to Will.

"Forgive me," she said. "I was so happy to see you. We must talk later, when it is more proper. At the reception, perhaps? Certainly you'll join us?"

"I'd be honored."

At the Eternal Rest Cemetery, a casket full of moonshine was respectfully laid to rest, while the body of the late Jacob Banner lay cold and silent in another casket in the back room of Billy Harper's barber shop on Front Street, two miles away. Jake Potter, having made the two-mile hike in record time, watched as the coffin was prayed over, caressed, and finally, with some difficulty, lowered to the bosom of mother earth. It was only because Will was looking for Jake that he spotted him, standing among the stand of pines that bordered the far edge of the cemetery. Will left with the others, confident he knew Jake's only possible course of action. It would be tonight. They would have to make the exchange. Then Will would learn what was in the coffin, and what Jake was involved in.

A welcome and petted member of the funeral party, Will moved unrecognized among the mourners at the reception. All afternoon, he played the part which had been forced upon him with the skill of an accomplished thespian, hoping against hope that the gossip that would inevitably result would be withheld as a courtesy from the ears of poor Miss Rigsby.

Viola Gates was in her element, introducing Will to all as her dear friend from New York City, only releasing her lock on his gentlemanly arm when absolutely necessary. As it turned out, he had to talk very little, as Viola did most of the talking for him. When, at last, he said his goodbyes, she stole away with him to the parlor door and demurely offered him her hand, which he kissed with the utmost sincerity as he took his leave.

At last, alone in his hotel room, he dashed off a note to Elizabeth Cooper, explaining that he had been caught out of his hobo garb by Viola, who was in town for her father's funeral, and that he had been forced to play along. Realizing that Viola would spread the gossip all over Hayley, Will also told Mrs. Cooper of his story of a romance with Miss Rigsby. She would probably get a kick out of it, he thought, and she would understand that there was nothing else he could have done. Tori would have to be let in on the secret as well, he told her. He knew that Tori would enjoy the continuation of the little deception they had perpetrated on the town. He just hoped, he wrote, that Miss Rigsby did not find out and start asking questions.

Will Fable posted the letter and returned to his room to wait. He would stake out the cemetery after dark.

22

Will Fable slept late the next morning. The transfer of the contents of the coffins had taken place, as he expected, the night before. Darkness had not hidden the identity of the tall, gaunt Hurd Buford, although he had not recognized Young Mose or the barber, Billy Harper. It was close to three in the morning when Will crept from gravestone to gravestone, close enough to hear the hushed conversation of the men as they dug up the new grave and switched the contents of the coffin, at last laying the late Jacob Banner to rest. They had come with a wagon of empty cartons, and beneath them, the body, covered with blankets.

When the deed was done, Jake had taken Buford aside for a private conference, leading him within ten feet of Will's hiding place. Will listened as Jake told Buford he was through. At last Will understood the extent of Jake's misery, as Buford threatened to expose him as a perpetrator in the deaths of the Negroes.

"There never was anyone dying, was there?" Jake had asked. "No, you're not going t' say nuthin', cause nuthin' never happened like that. Jake Potter's not as stupid as you think he is, not anymore. You're not going t' say nuthin', cause if you do, it's you that's going to jail, not me."

When he knew he was beaten, the moonshine-running mortician had laughed. "All right, Potter," he had said, "you'll be easy enough to replace. But it goes both ways. You keep your mouth shut or we'll both be behind bars."

The foursome left the cemetery on the wagon, and Will followed on foot as they turned off into a wooded area where Buford had parked the hearse. The boxes were loaded into the back of the hearse, and Jake and Young Mose parted company with the other two, to ride the mule-drawn wagon back to Hayley.

What happened to the booze, Will did not know, but as he walked the mile back to town, he was satisfied that Jake would be all right. He was not mixed up in the burglaries after all, and he was ending his short-lived life of crime. It was funny how things worked out, Will thought. It could not have been just chance that brought him together with Jake on that boxcar. They both walked under the same heaven, and heaven had seen fit to save them both.

SOMEWHERE BETWEEN the last days of that December of 1938 and the beginning of 1939, Will Fable was laid to rest as surely as was Jacob Banner. The man who wore the new suit of a man he never knew, a man long dead, was a new man, or rather, a man reborn. It was Forrest Neill, not Will Fable, who wore the late Mr. Cooper's suit as he rode first-class on the train to New York City.

Will Fable was at last relegated to the pages of a novel. He was just a character in the mind of Forrest Neill now, like a person he had met somewhere a long time ago. The fact that they had once been one and the same person didn't seem possible. Nor did it seem possible that in the space of two short weeks, the man who had been Will Fable had found the courage to return to his home, to his name, and to his new life.

It was a new year, and a new life for a formerly bitter, wandering outcast who had found himself in the home of a kindred soul, a woman who was a bit of an outcast herself, a New Yorker in Georgia. She had lost her money, her position, her mate, as he had, but it had not broken her spirit or her faith. He owed a lot to Elizabeth Cooper, and he would never let time or distance be a barrier to their friendship. Tori had become the child he had lost, and Jake Potter the semblance of Will Fable, the man he had been. These three lives would forever be a part of his, and they did not even know his name.

On the tenth of January, Forrest Neill walked into the plush Manhattan office of the publisher who had financed his travels for the past year. He was told by a bespectacled, businesslike secretary that Mr. Wesley G. Yesterhouse of Yesterhouse Publishing Company saw no one without an appointment, and that there were hundreds of would-be authors waiting ahead of him. Forrest handed the last few chapters of his book to the prim woman, and told her to tell the publisher that Will Fable wanted to see him.

The woman's cold stare melted away at the mention of the name of their most eagerly awaited new moneymaker, and she blushed and apologized profusely as she rose and welcomed him.

"Please," she said, glancing down at the name he had given, which she had written down thoughtlessly and automatically on her notepad, "Mr. Neill, take a seat. I'll tell Mr. Yesterhouse you are here. He will be delighted to meet you at last. Please sit down."

She took the envelope he offered and went to the door of her employer's office with practiced dignity, revealing her agitation only by a subconscious pat of her tightly pinned hair. She knocked and, after a pause, entered the office without waiting for an answer, closing the door behind her. Forrest acquainted himself with the office as he waited, inspecting the framed posters of Broadway plays and Hollywood movies which lined the walls of the sunny, twenty-third floor office. Forrest had not thought of the possibility that someone might want to make a movie or a play from his book; indeed, he was still wondering if the book itself would be a success.

Millie Rhodes, Mr. Yesterhouse's secretary, was a forty-year-old spinster who had devoted her life not to husband and children, but to books. The books published by the firm were her children, and she was an integral part of each, working, as she did, late into the night reading final drafts, and acting as liaison between author, editor, and publisher. In her sixteen years with Yesterhouse Publishing, she had never been as much in love with a work as she was with the ragged longhand pages of Will Fable which had arrived on a monthly basis for the past year. She had long looked forward to meeting this genius, this unfortunate who could write poetry for the masses with such subtlety and grace that the Bard himself would have been impressed with the turn of his phrases.

Whatever she expected when she met the man known only to the Yesterhouse firm as Will Fable, it was not the tall, handsome, well-dressed and well-spoken young man who had walked through the door that morning. Only her years of strict discipline in dealing with the public had saved her from making a complete fool of herself. She was in love with him already, it seemed, for she had fallen in love with first his thoughts, then his handwriting, and ultimately, with the mystery of his spirit. That he could be young and handsome too never entered her mind. It was almost too much to bear as she stood, breathless, on the other side of the door. She felt dizzy, unable to walk for a moment, to the man who sat behind the big oak desk and summoned her in with a wave of his hand as he continued his telephone conversation.

"I don't care what he told you," said Wes Yesterhouse into the phone, "the deal was for twenty percent. We agreed on that when you came to me, and I made no bones about the fact that it applied to all mediums of the work. If you will take a moment to check your contract, you'll find it spelled out in black and white. And another thing, are you forgetting the work Jean and Marty had to go through to get that mess of yours in shape to publish?"

Millie's heart was pounding as she walked to a chair beside the desk and sat down, the envelope on her lap, her eyes burning with excitement. Her mind raced. How could a man like this have written what he had written? Could he have been only an observer of the life he wrote about? Was that possible? He was more of a mystery now than ever, and twice as exciting.

"That's more like it," continued Yesterhouse. "I'm sorry it had to come to this. I must say I'm a little disappointed in you. If you want to survive in this business, you've got to be smart enough to separate the sheep from the wolves. You ought to know who your friends are at this late date. Tell you what. You call me when you make up your mind, okay?"

He hung up the phone and turned to Millie, rolling his eyes and sighing, "I told you that guy was an ungrateful wretch, Miss Rhodes. The next time we hear from him, his lawyer will do his talking for—Say! What's put a flower in your bonnet?" He finally noticed the soft sparkle in the eyes of his usually hard-boiled secretary.

"There's a man to see you," she began, in her best professional voice, "named Forrest Neill." She intended for her boss to suffer the same shock she had suffered, and maintained her deception with great difficulty. But her eyes gave her away. Wes Yesterhouse had known her too long to be fooled.

"Neill?" repeated Wes, playing along with the act. Somebody important was here, he was sure. Someone important enough to the firm to change this lioness to a kitten, and that took some doing. "I don't know any Neill. And you know I see no one without an appointment."

"Yes, I know," Millie continued. "He just walked in the door and handed this envelope to me. I told him we don't accept unsolicited manuscripts, sir. Should I tell him to leave?"

Wes took the envelope and opened it, pulling out the pages inside. "Look, Millie," he said, "what's the deal? I know you're up to something."

He recognized the handwriting of Will Fable immediately. On the top was a short note: "Mr. Yesterhouse: Enclosed are the last three chapters of the book. Thanks for your support. Will Fable."

"Is he here?" he asked quickly. "Is this Neill a delivery boy, or what?"

Millie laughed.

"We've been hoodwinked, sir," she said delightedly. "Apparently we've been doing business with a fictitious character. There is no Will Fable. The author's name is Forrest Neill, and he's outside waiting to meet you."

"You're kidding!" Wes said. "Listen Millie, you better be right about this or I'll have your hide."

"Wait till you meet him." she gushed. "You're in for a shock, I can tell you."

"My God!" the publisher replied. "He must be a terrible sight for you to get such a kick out of it. Forrest Neill? What kind of name is that for a drifter? Is that the high-class pen name he's dreamed up for himself?"

They both laughed, but for different reasons.

"Well?" said Wes, "what are you sitting there for? Bring the old codger in!"

Millie's lips were cemented together with glee as she rose and went to the door to admit the old beggar Wes expected.

"Mr. Neill," she called softly, "Mr. Yesterhouse will see you now."

Forrest walked into the office and strode to the desk of the publisher with the same dignity and sense of purpose which had betrayed him to Elizabeth Cooper. He extended a clean, work-toughened hand to the man who had become his friend through their correspondence, which Wes had mailed to post offices all over the country, always designated General Delivery.

"Will Fable, sir," he said in his hobo voice, "at yer service."

Wes took his hand and shook it heartily, his powers of observation at their sharpest, feeling in the warm grip of the calloused hand the friendship and honesty of the man he had known only on paper. Wes Yesterhouse was a better judge of people than his harried secretary, for he saw at once in this young man's eyes the hope and wisdom of a man who had lived with pain and endured hardship. He was doubly pleased to find a look of peace in those eyes, and to find that the public relations man he had planned on hiring to turn a ragged genius into a respectable author would not be necessary.

"Damn, boy!" he said. "It's great to meet you at last! Have a seat! Have a seat!"

Forrest and Millie sat down, and Wes picked up the papers before him. "This is the last of it, then?" he asked, smiling.

"Yes sir, that's it. What do you think? Will it sell?"

Wes and Millie looked at each other and smiled. In that instant they had communicated to each other unbelief at the man's ignorance of his own talent, and relief that he would, unlike most writers, be a joy to work with.

"Let me get something out of the way, first," Wes said. "Your name is Forrest Neill, not Will Fable, correct?

"Correct."

"Forrest Neill is your real name?"

"You think I should change it?"

"Hell, no!" Wes laughed. "It already sounds like you made it up to put on a book jacket! It's fine. Now, I don't want any more of this 'sir' business. We already know each other too well for that. You call me Wes, agreed? And this is Millie Rhodes, in case she forgot to introduce herself, of which I have no doubt. Call her Millie. I do, except when she's in the doghouse."

Forrest rose respectfully and shook Millie's hand.

"Nice to meet you, Millie."

Millie shook his hand and nodded, her heart fluttering. She looked at the floor or at Wes for the remainder of the interview, for she knew better than to look again into Forrest Neill's warm green eyes.

I appreciate your kindness, Wes," said Forrest as he took his seat again. "And I appreciate your confidence in me. I hope it will be rewarded."

"Son, I must admit, I wasn't exactly straight with you in my letters. It's hard for a man in my position to do business through the mail with a man I've never met, but let me put your mind at rest. I told you your work was promising, didn't I? Promising enough to warrant a cash advance. Well, that's sort of how we play the game here. We never tell a new writer he's God's gift to the world at first, even if he is."

"There are just too many that fold up on us and die in the trenches. I was guarded with you because you were sending in bits and pieces, a little at a time. I didn't know who you were, or if you would ever get it finished. But every chapter you sent convinced me more and more that you are the most talented new author to come our way in twenty years. Don't you worry about a thing, Will—uh, sorry, Forrest. You're going to make us both a great deal of money."

There was a little pause as Forrest tried to accept the truth of the publisher's words, tried to grasp that he would indeed begin life anew, without financial worries. "I had hoped it would turn out that way," he began, "but it's hard to be your own critic. It's a lot easier to believe your work is good when someone else tells you it is, especially someone like you."

Millie could remain silent no longer. "I can't wait to read the end," she said. "I must tell you, Mr. Neill, your book is brilliant, absolutely brilliant."

"Thank you, Ma'am," said Will, smiling at her.

"She should know, Forrest, my boy," added Wes. "Her instinct has been a mainstay of this company for sixteen years, and she's gotten sharper all the time. She told me after the third chapter came in that we had a best-seller on our hands if we could rope in the deal."

Forrest sat back in his chair and rubbed his chin thoughtfully. He nodded as he digested this statement, then shook his head and stared at the ceiling for a moment. "This is . . . " he stopped midsentence and tried to put his feelings into words. "This is wonderful. I don't know what to say."

"Better get used to it," said Wes with a smile. "You're going to have hard-boiled critics calling you a genius when we release this book, and lots of society dames at your door. Say, by the way, I still don't know much about you. Are you a married man? Do you have a family? Where are you from? Tell us about yourself."

"No," replied Forrest. "I'm a widower. My wife and son were . . . they died, let's see, five, no, six years ago."

Millie's heart went out to him, for the experience was still plainly a painful one. But she could not suppress some pleasure at the thought that he was single. She found this feeling shocking in herself, and took a deep breath and drew herself up sharply in her chair, determined that she would conduct herself in a businesslike fashion if it killed her.

"My home is Philadelphia," Forrest continued, "but I left there after my—well, to be honest, I saw my mother—I mean, I went back home again a few days ago for the first time in six years. You know me better than you think you do, you see. Will Fable isn't somebody I made up. He's me. I called myself Will Fable for six years, and the life you read about was my life. You know everything except the reasons why, and maybe the ending. You've got that on your desk, there."

Wes accepted this statement easily, having seen the truth in Forrest's eyes, but Millie was further devastated. The poor darling, she thought, how he must have suffered. Still, now it made more sense to her. But the effect he had on her was the same, if not more so, for she felt the long-suppressed instincts of a protective mother as well.

"If the book does well," Forrest continued, "like you say it will, there's another book inside me, and you've got the rights if you want them."

"Millie," said Wes, "go draw up a new contract. And call Miller. Get him up here with a draft for the amount we discussed for the completion of the first book."

"Right away, sir," said Millie, already halfway out the door.

Wes looked at Forrest and smiled. He stood up and extended his hand. "Deal?" he asked.

Forrest laughed as he shook the man's hand. "Deal," he said.

Behind the chair where Forrest sat was a vertical stand filled with large, stiff, cardboard frames that opened like the pages of a book. The frames, each more than a yard long and a yard wide, held more of the movie and play posters Forrest had seen lining the walls of the outer office. The stand was opened to a poster for a play called *The Lord of Rain*. The cold eyes of the star of the play, in full costume, stared at Forrest as if he recognized an evil enemy.

Forrest was too heady with pride and excitement to notice. But if he had seen those eyes, he would have recognized them. He would have seen the truth. And maybe a child he loved would have been spared a terrible ordeal she would remember the rest of her life.

23

A couple of weeks later a large package arrived at the post office in Hayley, addressed to Jake Potter, in care of General Delivery. Bubba James was busy that day, for there had been a disturbance at the Robinson place. Bubba didn't have time to ride out to Jake's place to tell him to pick up the package, so he stopped at the Cooper place and left the message with the widow Cooper.

Tori was sent to carry the message to Jake, and she had been given permission to stay and play with Jessie. Tori wondered what Jake had at the post office, as she skipped the distance to Jake's house. It was heavy, Bubba had said, and it came in on the train.

When Tori rounded the curve and the Potter place came into view, she ran the rest of the way. She saw Jessie and yelled, waving, as she neared the yard.

"Hey," said Jessie when Tori joined her on the steps. "Can you stay and play for a while?"

"Uh huh," Tori replied, "but is your daddy here? Meema sent me over with a message from Bubba."

Jessie frowned. "From Bubba? What is it?"

"It's something good, I think," said Tori. "There's a great big package at the post office for Jake. Do you know what it is? Did he order something from the catalog?"

"Gee, I don't know," said Jessie in amazement. "I don't think he did. I bet it's not for us. Pa never got a package in the mail as far back as I can remember."

"Bubba said it came in this morning on the train," Tori countered. "And you know good and well Bubba James doesn't make mistakes. It's heavy too, too heavy to carry. Jake will have to bring it home on the wagon, Bubba said."

195

"On the train? Jumpin' catfish, Tori Tanner! It can't be for us. Whose going to send us somethin' on the train? We don't know anybody farther than Albany."

"Well, maybe it's from somebody in Albany, goose," said Tori. "Where's Jake?"

"He's off somewhere," said Jessie. "Maybe Mama knows. Come on, let's tell her about the package."

They ran through the dog-run to the kitchen door. Mabel was as surprised as Jessie to hear the news, but sent them to get Jake, who was chopping wood in Cutter's field down the road, aptly named, for the timber was free for the cutting.

It was more than a mile to Cutter's field, but the girls had their excitement to speed them, and they reached the field in minutes. They spotted Jake's mule and wagon and ran to it, yelling Jake's name.

Jake was in the timbers when he heard them calling. He put down the ax and yelled, "Over here." The girls rushed up, both talking at once. He could make no sense of it.

"Hold on, now," he said. "What are you trying to tell me?"

"Let me tell," insisted Tori. "Bubba sent me."

"Bubba?" repeated Jake. "Sent you for what?"

"There's a big package for you at the post office," Tori continued. "A great big one. You'll have to use the wagon to carry it home, Bubba said so."

"I ain't expectin' no package," he said, half to himself. "It must be for somebody else. I got no package comin'."

"It's for you," Tori insisted. "Bubba came by the house special, just to send word to you to come get it. It has to be for you. It has to!"

"All right, all right," Jake said. "I guess we'd better go into town and check it out. Hop on the wagon, both of you. We can leave this wood till I get back."

The girls jumped with glee and ran to the wagon, jumping on. Jake put the ax in beside them and climbed up on the seat. They rode into Hayley as quickly as the mule would take them, and stopped at the little combination jail and post office next to the train station.

"You have a package for me?" Jake asked the postmistress, Cora Jane Oates.

"Yes, Jake," replied the widow Oates. "It's that big one there, in the corner. Came in on the train from New York City this mornin'. What is it?"

"New York?" asked Jake, walking to the box. "I don't even know anybody in New York."

He inspected the package and read his name on the label. "It's from somebody named Mr. Forrest Neill."

"I'll take it, Cora," he called, "but if it's some kinda mistake, I'll bring it back t' you. You'll have t' send it back."

"Sure thing."

Jake lifted the package, a wooden crate, with some difficulty, and carried it out to the wagon. The girls were ecstatic and carried on unmercifully until Jake told them to settle down.

They stopped at Tori's house instead of going back out to Jake's to open it, for Jake saw no reason to tote it all the way home if he was going to just bring it back to Cora after all. Tori ran in to get Mrs. Cooper for the unveiling, and Jake met her at the front steps to tell her he would need to borrow a crowbar from the barn. Elizabeth Cooper was as curious as the girls, and went out to the wagon with them to wait for Jake.

When the box was pried open, Jake found a letter addressed to him on top of packing straw, and managed to quiet the girls long enough to read it before they examined the contents. The letter was typewritten, and when Jake opened it, he found the envelope to contain not only a letter, but also five twenty-dollar bills. He was dumbfounded.

"Here, Miz Cooper," he said, handing her the letter, "you read it for me. I'm too jumpy t' read it."

Mrs. Cooper took the letter and read aloud:

"To Mr. Jake Potter, General Delivery, Hayley, Georgia. Mr. Potter, you may not remember me, but we have met briefly. I bought some carvings from you some time ago when my train paused in Hayley. I was very impressed with your work, and asked your name of a passerby. I would like to commission you to carve a larger elephant for me like the one I bought from you, from this block of rosewood which I have sent. I realize that you may not have worked on large pieces before, but I believe you have great talent, and can master the art with little difficulty. I am an art dealer in New York and I believe I will be able to sell the piece here for a great deal of money if I am correct in my estimation of your talent. I am also sending along the tools you will need, as an investment, along with a book by a wood sculptor who teaches art classes here.

"Take as much time as you need. I am paying you in advance. If it doesn't work out as I hope, the money will still be well spent, as I am willing to take a chance on developing talent. If I sell the finished piece at a profit, I will commission more works from you in the future.

"By the way, I took the liberty of also enclosing several smaller pieces of rosewood in the crate, for you to practice on. I hope you will make us both wealthier. Good day to you.

"Sincerely, Forrest Neill, P.O. Box 1187, Grand Central Station, New York, New York. P.S., Send the finished work to me COD at the address above."

"Lord in heaven," said Jake. "Do you suppose this is a joke?"

"Apparently not," said Mrs. Cooper. "Now, Jake don't get scared and doubt that you can do this. This man is obviously a professional, and he knows what he's doing. Why, he probably already sold your wood pieces for more than you could imagine."

"Please," Tori begged, "can't we look in the box now?"

"Pa, come on!" Jessie chimed in. "Please, let's see what's in the box."

Jake had completely forgotten even to check out the carton's contents, but having been reminded, his curiosity matched that of the children, and he jumped up on the back of the wagon. The three gathered around the crate as if it were the lost ark of the covenant.

"I'll do it," said Jake. "You girls just don't touch nuthin'."

Elizabeth Cooper picked up the envelope Jake had dropped on the ground when she read the letter aloud, and looked again at the return address. She said nothing, and put it on the back of the wagon. Bless him, she thought. She had guessed the truth.

Beneath the straw were indeed the tools, the book, and pieces of wood described in the letter. Jake lifted one of the smaller blocks out for the girls to see, and the feel of the smooth, cool wood in his hand was to him like holding an infant newborn. From that moment, Jake had no more doubts.

24

As in all small towns, news traveled fast in Hayley. There was not much that went on that could be kept secret for long, or so it seemed. The truth was that since the fall, secrets bloomed in Hayley like azaleas in the spring, but they were known only by one man.

A few days after the package arrived for Jake, Elizabeth Cooper wrote the following letter to Will Fable: "Dear Will, I hope all is going well for you in New York. Unless I miss my guess, I believe you will know to what I refer when I tell you that the package for Jake arrived safely. I had been worried about him this past month, he seemed so troubled and unhappy. But whatever was worrying him is over, now that he has been given the chance to develop his talents by a mysterious benefactor named Forrest Neill.

"Tori tells me that he has been diligently studying the books you sent, and spends most every morning working on the sculpture. Jake takes a commitment seriously, and he is committed to earning every penny you sent him. I think you will not be disappointed. Thank you for your generosity and kindness to him. The Lord will have a good steward for his wealth in you.

"I was pleased when I found from your last letter that you had returned to New York at last. I assume that you have finished your book and are in the midst of editing it and working with the publisher you mentioned. Godspeed to you. I know it will be a great success.

"I read Tori your letter about Viola Gates and Miss Rigsby, and she was tickled beyond words at the continuation of our little deception. She, of course, told no one. She tells me that the children at school have heard that Miss Rigsby now has several suitors, who, I'm sure, want to find out what charms allowed her to catch your eye. The gossip was all over town, of course, but I think the Southern tradition of discretion will keep it from Miss Rigsby.

"Tori misses you. She loves the tree house more than I can tell you, and now that the weather is getting milder, she spends all her free time there. I hope you will write her soon.

"I have learned more about the problems out at the Townsend plantation. If you remember, I told you the Townsend's barn burned down, and then Carlton, the younger brother, was hurt in a car crash. He had a severe concussion and some cuts and bruises, but he will be all right. He was pulled from the wreck by a man named Woody Price, who turns out to be a wealthy newcomer to Albany. All of the society belles have been chasing him with great enthusiasm, but so far, he remains unattached and something of a mystery. I understand he spends a good deal of time at Radium Springs (the Townsends have adopted him, so to speak). I have heard he is quite a gentleman, extremely polite and courteous. He will be a great success if he chooses to settle here.

"There seems to be something going on between our police chief and Carlton Townsend. Bubba had a man come down from Atlanta to investigate the burning of the barn. The investigator determined that either carelessness with cigarettes or arson was the cause.

"There has been some talk that Chief James believes Carlton is involved in the robberies which have been going on here, and also blames him for fire. This is strange, if it is true, since his daughter is engaged to Rudolph, the older brother.

"Such are the goings-on here, which you asked me to record for you. I hope we will hear from you soon, and see you sooner. By the way, shall I call you Will or Forrest now?"

VALENTINE'S DAY fell on a Saturday. Most of Tori's classmates were invited to a party that afternoon at the home of Marvin and Veda Gates. Everyone was invited, that is, except Tori and Jessie.

Wendy had told Tori about the party a week ago, and every day since, Tori had waited for either Marvin or little Veda to invite her. They didn't. When Friday came, Tori realized she and Jessie weren't going to be asked to come at all, and she ran home with tears in her eyes.

Mrs. Cooper was wise enough to realize Tori's hurt feelings could not be healed with words, but still, she tried, telling Tori they were still considered outsiders in Hayley, and that eventually it would change.

"I hate Marvin!" Tori sniffed, eyes red and lips pouting. "He's mean and ugly. All he ever does is pick on me and call me names."

"You don't hate anyone, young lady," said Mrs. Cooper, with more sternness than Tori was expecting.

"Why not?" Tori countered. "Why shouldn't I hate him?"

Mrs. Cooper was silent for a moment.

"Hate is something that will hurt *you*, honey, not Marvin. If you hate Marvin back, you're no better than he is."

"But, Meema—"

"I don't want you to hate anyone, because if you do, I won't have the same little girl I love anymore. I'll have a little Viola Gates!"

"Ugh!" said Tori, drying her tears.

"You are sunshine, and happiness, and warmth itself, and I don't want you to change. You will if you let yourself hate Marvin. Do you understand what I'm saying?"

"I guess so," said Tori. "I guess I don't really hate him. But I sure don't like him much."

Mrs. Cooper smiled. "You don't have to like him, dear, as long as you don't hate him."

With a child, this was all Mrs. Cooper could hope for. It was enough for now.

The next day, Mrs. Cooper surprised Tori with a cake. She had decorated it with colored icing of red, white, and blue. Letters of icing on the top read, "50% Rebel, 50% Yankee, 100% All American!"

It lifted Tori's spirits and she was herself again. She spent the afternoon in Will's tree house, watching the Saturday afternoon activity in Hayley. The train came and went on schedule. Ladies came to the beauty shop and the General Store, and old men sat in clusters around the square, whittling, smoking, swapping stories. Around three o'clock, children began arriving for the party, and Tori's heart winced. But she didn't let herself get unhappy, and she didn't hate Marvin like she thought she would.

When most of the children had arrived, she climbed down the ladder and walked slowly to the General Store. She sat down on the steps and watched Marvin's house. A few customers came and went as she sat there, and all who knew of the party felt sorry for her. Most of the mothers who saw her promised themselves that she would never be uninvited to their children's parties, and muttered to themselves against Viola Gates, who had scaled new heights of boorish behavior in this obvious slight.

After a while, Daniel J. Smith hobbled across the square to the General Store and nodded to Tori as he went in. When he emerged, he approached Tori and sat down in one of the rocking chairs opposite her on the porch.

"You be Victoria?" he asked casually, drawing a pouch from his jacket. Mr. Smith seemed to know all the goings-on of the community.

"Yes, sir," she answered, "but you can call me Tori if you want."

"Suits you better, Brown Eyes," replied Smith, as he began to roll a cigarette.

Tori jumped up at this and came to his side, remembering dimly that her grandfather had rolled his own cigarettes; it was a pleasant memory. She went to his chair and watched with great interest as he filled the paper and licked the sides, and then deftly rolled up the slim cylinder. She smiled as he lit the cigarette, and his eyes gleamed back at her. They were funny eyes in such an old face, full of spark and fire.

"You can call me Dan," he said.

Tori laughed.

"Meema would have a fit, Mr. Smith," she replied. "She says it's disrespectful to call a grown-up by his first name."

"You call the chief 'Bubba,' don't you?"

"Yes," said Tori. "How'd you know that?"

"Heard you."

"Oh. Well, I don't do it around Meema. I just do it to Bubba 'cause it makes him so mad. He always corrects me, but he never gets after me 'cause he likes me. None of the others dare to do it, but I do." She laughed again. "It's fun. But Meema would skin me if she heard me."

Well, then, you can call me Dan when she's not around, agreed?"

"It's a deal, Dan," Tori said.

"Why aren't you at the party, Brown Eyes?"

Tori's face fell. "I wasn't invited. Marvin and I don't get along too well, I guess."

"Shush!" scoffed Smith. "Marvin's a real cracker, just like his old man. Don't you upset yourself over him. You're too good to go to any party of his. He's not worth a dime, and that's the truth."

"Maybe so," said Tori, "but Meema said he doesn't know any better and—"

"And that mama of his," interrupted Smith. "A gossiping witch if ever there was one. Believe me, if you're the only kid in town not invited to that party, you're the only kid in town with any value."

"Well," said Tori, "I still wanted to go at first. Meema told me that—"

"And that father of his! What a crook. Why, he'd take milk from a baby. If I were you, I'd stay away from all of them."

Smith continued talking, but Tori's happy smile faded as she listened to his grumblings. She realized Dan was saying things her grandmother had told her not to. But he was nice, too, taking up for her about the party, and talking to her like a friend. She was confused by him, and for some reason, suddenly a little bit afraid. She decided she'd better go home.

"Dan?" she interrupted him.

"Yes?"

"Don't you like the people here?"

Smith realized he may have said too much.

"Sure I do, Tori," he replied. "I just don't like some of them. I like you, though."

"I like you too, Dan," said Tori, and she did, really. "I guess I'd better go. Meema doesn't know where I am."

"Okay, Brown Eyes. Maybe I'll see you again sometime. I live over on Hemon Road."

"I know," said Tori.

"Do you?" asked Smith. "Well, there's not much goes on around here everybody don't know. Right?"

"I guess so," Tori said. "Bye."

25

Shortly after Valentine's Day, word came that Amos Brown, Boozie's father, had escaped from the chain gang in Savannah. Chief James paid Ottis a call and told him they expected Amos to head for home. The best thing Ottis could do for his son-in-law would be to convince him to turn himself in, Bubba said.

The dogs had been set on Amos, but the Savannah prison-farm guards had come up empty. It was the first time a man had made it through the swamps in ten years. Amos seemed to vanish into thin air. The Georgia officials suspected that he had met his death in the swamp, but police officers in three states were on the lookout for him, nonetheless.

Ottis went into Hayley that Saturday for supplies, as he always did. He walked with his head held high, ignoring the stares and the whispers. No one spoke to him of Amos, and everyone nodded to him as he passed, just as usual. Ottis was hurt by his son-in-law's crimes, hurt that the boy had brought shame to the family and trouble to his house. The town was, for the most part, sympathetic. Ottis was respected as much as a black man could be in Georgia, and his own character was above reproach.

He walked into the General Store and stared at the goods on the shelves, his big hands deep in the pockets of his overalls, his mind preoccupied. After a while, Crawford Welch approached him.

"What'll it be, Ottis?" he said.

Ottis turned to him with pursed lips and furrowed brow.

"I done forgot, suh," said Ottis.

Welch was not to be done out of a sale. "How about if I just get your usual order together for you then, Ottis?"

"That be fine," Ottis replied.

Early the next morning, Ottis went fishing at Froggy Bottom Pond, next to the Townsend game preserve. He was after catfish, and set out a trot line in the darkness. He sat alone in the creaky community rowboat, in the middle of the pond, as the first purple and orange streaks of the approaching dawn stole across the horizon. Fishing was like a soothing balm to Ottis. He could pray here as in no other place. Dawn was the best time for praying, or twilight, when the cicadas sang.

The lonely sound of the whistle of the early train moaned in the distance, and joined the first twitters of the lake and forest birds. The train tracks skirted the far side of the pond, and the train lumbered past, with a trail of freight cars stretching out a quarter mile long.

Ottis watched as the caboose passed by and the train began to wind away. He saw a man jump from one of the trailing boxcars, tumbling like an acrobat as he hit the ground beside the tracks. Ottis, silent and hidden in the blackness of the pond, craned his neck to see as the man stood upright and moved stealthily toward the forbidden game preserve. The man was clad in black from head to toe, and Ottis could not tell if he was white or colored. A chill went over Ottis as he realized the man was about the same size as Amos. Could his fool son-in-law actually have been stupid enough to come back here? Did he think he could hide out in the preserve, where no Negro dared set foot?

Ottis said nothing as he watched the man reach the south side of the preserve and climb over the fence. Maybe it wasn't Amos after all. He remembered the bag Tori had tripped over, containing black clothes and tools. Ottis had assumed those clothes belonged to Carlton Townsend. And now here was a man dressed in black, acting mighty suspicious. What could Mistah Carlton be doing stealing onto his own property, jumping off trains in the dark? It didn't make sense. It couldn't be Carlton. Merciful heavens, maybe it was Amos.

Ottis rowed silently to the bank and jumped out of the rowboat. He followed the man's trail to the fence and, with a deep breath and a prayer, jumped over. He was on a trail he did not know existed, and he followed it slowly in the semidarkness of the dawn. The woods were deathly quiet, like Ottis remembered from the day he taunted Boozie. His bones went cold at the thought of her recent tales of the ghost who was bold enough to walk in daylight. He had to take the risk. If it was Amos he had seen, he had to catch him and send him away, or convince him to give himself up. He'd be killed if the law spotted him, and Mary Lee's heart would be broken. Ottis caught himself mumbling that Jesus had been right when he warned that this life would be full of trouble.

The trail led to a high ridge above a clearing. Below him, Ottis saw the dirt road and the ragged cabin that held County Pa's secrets. He had come to the same place that Tori and Jessie had hidden the summer before, and he crouched down as they had done, and waited. It was getting light quickly now, and in the light of day he would be able to see whether the man was black or white. Ottis did not have to wait long, for the man was obviously in a hurry to leave. He walked out of the door with a package under his arm and walked down the steps. With a fright Ottis recognized the face he saw.

"Almighty God!" he whispered. "Out o' the mouth of babes!"

Boozie had been right all along. She had not been seeing things. The man Ottis looked upon was not Amos. It was County Pa! Ottis was over a hundred feet away, but he recognized the face, the carriage, and the body of the man all thought dead.

That ain't no ghost, Ottis thought, that flesh an' blood, same as me. His barrel chest swelled against the pounding of his heart. He was scared. He had never seen a ghost, so he wasn't quite sure if they could look so human. But that was County Pa, and he looked as alive as he could be.

The man had changed his clothes. He sat down on the bottom step and opened the package under his arm. From the package he brought out a mirror and what would prove to be, in the next few minutes, a disguise. Quickly, the man was transformed.

Nobody goin' to believe this, thought Ottis. He bin livin' among us all the time. He ain't dead. He up to some craziness like he always was.

Ottis froze when he realized that, if County Pa left by the same trail by which he had come, he would stumble right on top of his perch. Quickly Ottis looked around for a way out, but he was trapped. He turned his anxious eyes back toward, not a ghost, but a lord of men, who shot intruders without a breath of hesitation.

The man went back into the cabin and Ottis jumped up, scurrying off the trail, into a clump of dead leaves. In a few moments the man emerged again and, sure enough, started for the trail. He climbed the ridge and headed toward the southern fence, as he had come. Ottis lay still as he passed, hardly daring to breathe.

Ottis listened and heard the sound of the man's footsteps fade away through the brush. He remained motionless for a long time after the strange silence of the forest returned. He wanted to get out of there, but he was afraid to move. What County Pa did was none of his business. If the man wanted to pretend to be dead, it had nothing to do with Ottis or his family. When Ottis got out of there, he would wash his hands of the matter. Who in blazes would believe him, anyway?

In about an hour Ottis left his hiding place and ran as fast as he could to the fence. He hopped over and headed for Hayley, leaving his trot lines and his catch. He headed over the fields and hit Southland Road midway between Jake Potter's house and the Cooper home. He heard someone call his name, and spotted Tori Tanner and Jessie Potter waving to him from the ditch on the other side of the road. The sight of the children was especially comforting to him in his present state of mind, and he walked over to them.

"What you babies doin' diggin' in de dirt?" he asked with a broad smile.

"Look," said Tori, pointing to a dead bird they had found. "We're going to bury it."

"Well now, ain't that nice," replied Ottis.

A soft rattle sounded at Tori's feet. Ottis looked down and saw what Tori did not see. In an instant, before the child could scream when she saw the rattlesnake poised not a yard from her, before she could draw its fangs with a sudden movement, Ottis lunged at Tori, knocking her clear. The snake struck him twice in the leg, and again in the hand, as he grabbed it and smashed its head beneath a rock. The girls screamed and ran to Ottis when the snake was dead, crying and terrified. Ottis shook Jessie's shoulders to bring her out of her terror.

"Run!" he yelled at her. "Git your Pa. Git a knife, do you hear me?"

He shook the sense back into her. "Run!"

Jessie ran for Jake, crying and screaming all the way. Tori pulled on Ottis's arm, pleading with him to get up.

"No, baby," he said. "I have to stay down. That poison be done gone all over my body if I stirs around. You jus' stay here with me until Jake come."

"Ottis!" Tori wailed. "Please don't die! You have to be all right, you have to!"

"Don' worry, chile," said Ottis, laying his head back on the red ground. "I ain't goin' no place unless the Lord be callin' me home."

"No!" cried Tori. "No!"

She glanced over at the dead snake and was filled with hatred for the creature. She jumped up and ran to it, picked up a rock and hit it over and over. When she returned to Ottis, he was moaning and covered with sweat.

In five minutes, Jake arrived with Jessie in tow. Immediately Jake cut away Ottis's pant leg, exposing the wounds. The girls watched in horror as he cut a gash above and below the bite marks and sucked out the blood. Jessie was now also afraid for her father, who was taking the venom into his mouth and spitting it away.

"His hand," said Tori.

Jake saw the marks on Ottis's hand and cut again. He had been bitten right on a large vein.

Tori looked up at the sound of hoofbeats and saw Mabel Potter, driving the mule wagon, pull up beside them on the road. Ottis was still conscious, and somehow Jake managed to get the huge man into the back of the wagon. The girls tumbled in after him. Jake jumped up to take the reins from Mabel and whipped the mule into his fastest gait. In two minutes they were beside the depot, and Jake slowed the wagon when he saw Chief James.

"It's Ottis," he yelled to Bubba. "Snake bit. Rattler. I'm taking him home. Get a doctor. Get somebody!"

Bubba ran to the wagon and looked at Ottis.

"Get him home," he said. "I'll be there directly."

Jake whipped the mule and headed out Hemon Road to the Washington place, past the little house of Daniel J. Smith.

There was nothing anyone could do. Within an hour Ottis was delirious. He kept talking about County Pa and the cabin. "He too close," he said. "Mistah Price, you stay 'way from my baby. Go back to the cabin, where you belongs. We don' want you round here." Nothing made sense to anyone, except to little Boozie. She knew. She too had seen the ghost who walked in daylight. He was there, and now Boozie knew where he lived—in a cabin she had never seen.

That night Ottis slipped into a coma. In the morning, the gentle giant was dead. He died as he had lived, loving and protecting a child. The Washingtons were doubly grieved that terrible February, for no word ever came of Mary Lee's husband, Amos. He was presumed dead, swallowed up by the swamp.

There had never been a man like Ottis Washington in Hayley, Georgia, and there had never been such a funeral at the Freedom Baptist Church. It was not the first time Tori had been to the church, for she and Boozie had played there when they had gone exploring the summer before.

There were people everywhere, it seemed, when Tori and Mrs. Cooper drove up to the little wooden country church far out on Hemon Road. Thirty or forty were standing around the grounds of the church, dressed in their Sunday best, speaking quietly among themselves, for the little church could hold no more. Mrs. Cooper had made the decision to break with tradition and attend the funeral, for Ottis had died saving her granddaughter's life.

She had told Tori that they would go, but how long they stayed would depend on the reception they were given, since it was possible they would be intruding on the grief of the family. Elizabeth Cooper was well thought of by the Negro community, and beloved by the Washingtons, but she was also aware that Tori might be blamed for the tragedy. It is always difficult to predict how grief will affect those it visits.

Tori was devastated by Ottis's death, and cried for hours. She knew that he had saved her life and she did not know how to deal with such a thing. She had wanted to come, and yet hated to go to the funeral. She stayed close to her grandmother as they walked to the door of the church. The crowd parted for them as they approached the door. Soft murmurings were hushed as they passed; the men tipped their hats and avoided their eyes. The crowd blocking the entrance made way for them as well, and no hint of offense was given by anyone.

Every seat was taken, and the aisles along the walls were filled with others standing. Tori had never seen so many Negroes together at one time, for they numbered in the hundreds. A line of people was moving slowly down the center aisle to view the open wooden casket, and to speak to Doreen, Mary Lee, and Boozie in the front pew. There was no music, but the choir, in long purple robes, stood behind the casket, singing "Swing Low, Sweet Chariot."

When Tori caught sight of the face in the casket, she froze and would go no farther. A loud cry came from the front row, as Doreen was greeted by a friend, and a chorus of wailing began. It was different from the two white funerals Tori had been to, her mother's and her grandfather's. It was emotional and loud, as grief was expressed openly. It was too much for her, and she began to cry.

"Go ahead, Ma'am," said a white-haired elderly woman in a flat black hat and veil, "I'll take de baby fo' you." She drew Tori into the aisle seat next to her when Mrs. Cooper nodded, and Mrs. Cooper joined the line moving slowly to the front.

As she advanced in the line, Mrs. Cooper was aware of the stares she was receiving from those she passed, and the whispers she engendered. She was glad she had come, for the mourners communicated to her only kindness and respect, as an honored guest.

Tori watched from her seat, her hand in that of the elderly woman, as her grandmother reached the front pew and hugged Doreen and Mary Lee. They spoke for several minutes and then Mrs. Cooper sat down between Mary Lee and Boozie. Boozie sat dry-eyed and straight, in the muslin dress Mrs. Cooper had made for her for Christmas, secure in the knowledge that her grandfather was home with Jesus. Mrs. Cooper took her hand, but Boozie looked straight ahead. She was a gifted child, intelligent and bold, and she had met her beloved grandfather's death with the control of a dowager who had seen it all. When Mrs. Cooper took her hand, the first tear she allowed herself welled up and fell down her cheek.

The choir ended their selection and began to hum. Boozie looked up at Mrs. Cooper and said quietly, "I'll be singin' Pap's song now." She rose from the seat and walked to the front of the choir. All eyes were on Boozie as she began to sing.

The church was filled with the strong clear voice of little Mary Bea Brown. Her voice was high and sweet, her pitch perfect, her timbre velvet. Those present must have heard her sing before, for none was surprised at the beauty of her voice. Tears flowed freely as she sang.

Mrs. Cooper was amazed by the child. She had long wished for a gifted student to teach, for her training was in voice as well as music. Boozie's voice would be operatic when she matured, of this Mrs. Cooper was sure. There was a way, then, to help this family. A way to thank them for her granddaughter's life. Mrs. Cooper had already decided. She would work with Boozie, giving her voice and music lessons. The child was gifted, and all she needed was love, training, and practice to lift her out of this life of poverty.

How strangely God works His will, Mrs. Cooper thought as she sat there, among friends.

26

It was a quiet spring. Tori was not herself for weeks after Ottis's death, and spent her time in Will's tree house, alone. She didn't invite her friends to join her, and got no joy from her old game of watching Hayley below her.

Nothing Mrs. Cooper could do or say seemed to cheer her up. It was something she had to endure alone, and, by the first blooms of the azaleas, she was again cheerful and playful. The turning point came with the arrival of a letter from Will Fable. Mrs. Cooper had written to him about the death of Ottis, and Tori's resulting depression. His letter arrived in the first days of March, when the air was fresh with spring.

Mrs. Cooper never knew what was in the letter, for Tori guarded it closely and would not let her read it. In Paul Tanner's absence, Tori turned more and more to Will as a father figure, and he did not disappoint her. She knew Will loved her, and she loved him more than she knew.

Her spirits changed overnight, it seemed. She was happy again, curious and daring, as always. Mrs. Cooper thanked the Lord for Will's friendship, and asked no questions.

Things quieted down in Albany, too. The robberies stopped. They had been regular, if erratic, since the October before, and since the middle of December, all was quiet. The cat burglar had gained a degree of notoriety in the area, for his daring exploits had baffled the police, and there were still no real clues.

People began to speculate about the fate of the thief. Some said he had moved on. Others said he had been hit by a train or died of the flu. No one entertained the possibility that he was still around, and that his actions had a purpose.

Bubba James continued to watch Carlton Townsend closely. He was surprised to find that, during the weeks since his accident, Carlton had broken with his old habits and his old cronies. He was no longer reported to be gambling heavily, and he abruptly ceased his legendary seductions. He still frequented the bar at Radium Springs, often in the company of the newcomer, Woody Price, but not one report of riotous behavior or drunkenness reached Bubba's ears.

It was difficult for Bubba to believe that the habits of a lifetime could change so quickly. Carlton was up to something, the chief thought. And it was strange that the change in his behavior was linked almost to the day the robberies had stopped. Bubba finally admitted to himself that he believed Carlton to be the cat burglar, and that he was doing everything in his power to prove it. He believed the boy was doing it for a lark, a prank to show that he could outwit the police. It was no secret that Carlton had little respect for the law, and no use for lawmen.

It was too soon for Bubba to wonder if maybe Woody Price was having a positive influence on Carlton. Bubba found it easier to believe that the two of them were involved in some kind of scheme which took all their time and energy. For this reason, Bubba began to keep tabs on Woody Price as well.

It was not as easy as it had been with Carlton, for Woody seemed to disappear for periods of time. No one he could enlist as an observer could account for the man's whereabouts from time to time. Woody became a familiar, if aloof, figure in Hayley, visiting his friend Carlton quite often.

Bubba was too entrenched in his suspicions to notice that his daughter had become very unhappy. Dixie Lee and Rudolph had not announced their engagement that spring, as planned. Rudolph was ready and willing, but Dixie Lee was not. She wanted to wait until June, she explained to him, when the brides section of the Albany paper was fringed with flowers. Rudolph thought it silly, but it was a fanciful, feminine suggestion, and it charmed him out of questioning her further.

Dixie Lee and Carlton saw each other often, as they moved in the same circles, but they never spoke to each other beyond the expected pleasantries. If they could graciously avoid each other, they did so, but with each casual meeting, the bond between them grew stronger.

Dixie Lee fought her feelings for him, but each day she found them harder to deny, and her feeling for the virtuous Rudolph growing dimmer. She wanted to *marry* Rudolph. It made sense. He would be a good husband, and she had thought she was in love with him. As the days passed, she realized she had never loved him at all. She had worshiped him, but never loved him.

The real reason she had delayed the announcement of her engagement was known only to herself and to Woody Price. Woody had seen the truth in silence. Dixie Lee was only now beginning to admit the truth to herself. The change in Carlton since the accident had only made matters worse for Dixie Lee, for she now saw good and admirable qualities in him she never knew existed.

Dixie Lee was probably the only person in the area who didn't like Woody Price. He was always a perfect gentleman to her, as he was to all the girls, but Dixie Lee sensed something underlying his gallant behavior. It was as if he was too kind, too polite, too good to be true. Dixie Lee found him false and shallow beneath his impeccable manners and expensive suits. It was a feeling, an instinct, more than anything else. She did not understand why, but she disliked him greatly.

AT THE end of March, a new book hit the bookstores around the country. It was called *Wandering Dreamer* and it was an instant success. The author, Forrest Neill, became an instant celebrity, if a reticent one. The *New York Times Book Review* heralded the work as the front runner for the Pulitzer prize, and reporters clamored for information about the new author. They met a dead end, for all press releases came only from the publisher, Wesley Yesterhouse. The usual picture of the author which graced the back cover of most book jackets was absent, and the news media speculated about the identity of the author.

Everyone in the publishing and entertainment industry of New York read the book and left request after request with Mr. Yesterhouse's secretary, Millie Rhodes, for a meeting with the author. At first Wes was not at all happy about Forrest's dislike of publicity, but after the mystery of the author's identity caused such a stir, he decided it was the best publicity stunt ever pulled. Millie dutifully delivered the messages to the reclusive author twice a week, but he never answered any of them.

Except one. A short telephone message came not for Forrest Neill, but for Will Fable, the name of the character in the book. A young lady had left her name, Camilla Goodson, and the message: "We met in Hayley at Christmas Eve, remember?" Millie was surprised when Forrest asked for the phone number she had left.

Camilla Goodson entered the Penthouse Restaurant at the top of Knox Towers. She was stunning in a kelly green linen suit and white silk blouse, with a matching green straw hat. Camilla turned heads everywhere she went, and the men in the restaurant envied the man to whose table she was led.

She extended a white-gloved hand to Forrest Neill, who had risen to greet her.

"So I was correct in my suspicions," she said to Forrest with an endearing smile.

"I'm afraid so," Forrest replied, taking her hand. "I was surprised you remembered me.

"Nonsense," said Camilla, taking the seat he offered her, "You're the talk of the town, and somewhat of a mystery man as well, I understand."

"No mystery," Forrest replied, "I just don't like publicity, I guess. I'm new to all this. I need some time to get used to it."

The waiter approached them with menus and took their order for wine. Forrest watched with detached admiration as Camilla removed her gloves and continued her conversation. She was one of the most beautiful women he had ever seen, with her long black hair, fragile features, and those wonderful, huge, gray-blue eyes. She was all things feminine, yet she was strong. In her eyes Forrest met a kindred spirit, a fellow traveler. She had known instinctively the gentle lessons of the heart that Forrest had understood only through suffering. He felt at home with her, as if he had known her as a little girl with long black braids, running through the fields of Hayley.

"I've read the book, of course," she was saying. "It's wonderful. I found myself reading parts of it over and over again. I was intrigued with the name of the character, since I had met a charming man with the same name back home on Christmas Eve. But to be honest, I thought it was just a coincidence. I never expected you to call. It was just a flight of fancy on my part to leave the message for you."

They both laughed.

"I'm so glad you did," he said. "For some reason, I feel like we are two conspirators, watching the rest of the world scurrying like mad to find a man who doesn't exist. Does that make any sense?"

"It's beginning to," she said. "I'll be happy to keep your secrets, dear Will." She shook her head and caught herself. "I'm sorry. I know your name is Forrest. But Will suits you better. Why were you using your character's name in Hayley? I've never figured that out."

"Please don't ask me to explain. I want to continue to be mysterious and charming to you, don't I? I'll even confuse you further by asking you to keep calling me Will. I'm more at home with that name than with my own. And I'm more at home with you than with anyone I've met since I came back to New York."

Camilla asked no more questions. She saw the truth suddenly.

As unbelievable as it seemed, she knew that she was talking to the character in the pages of the book. He had lived the life he wrote about, not just observed it. This was not Forrest Neill, famous new author. This was Will Fable, hobo, poet, wanderer.

"I think I understand you better than you may wish," she replied. "You are a remarkable person, Will Fable."

Forrest put out his hand, and Camilla reached across the table and took his hand in hers. They smiled and gazed into each other's eyes like a brother and sister reunited after a long separation.

"Are all the natives of Hayley, Georgia, unique?" he asked.

"Every one of us," said Camilla, smiling.

"So far, I would have to agree."

They ordered lunch and enjoyed the view as they ate, as, more and more, the conversation returned to Hayley. Forrest learned that Camilla was lonely in New York, and was tiring of her life there. She was thinking of returning to Georgia for good, to Atlanta or Albany. She did not say

Hayley, but he knew she wanted to go home.

She mentioned a man there she had once loved, who was now engaged to someone else. It was not hard for Forrest to understand that she was talking about Rudolph Townsend. Forrest thought she was still a little in love with him.

When they had finished eating, they stayed on, talking about Hayley. Forrest asked her about all those he had met, and she knew them all, except Tori and her grandmother. Camilla had left Hayley about the time the Coopers arrived, but she knew Paul Tanner well, and also Mary Catherine, Tori's mother.

She told him about the Townsends, but never admitted Rudolph had been her lover. Her tales of County Pa were the stuff of legends.

"How did he die?" Forrest asked at last.

"Plane crash," replied Camilla. "It was a big story down there, because a state senator also died in the crash. They were in a private plane that went down over the marshes. There was a big investigation after the crash, and allegations of missing funds from the state treasury. It was a mess. Nothing ever came of it though. County Pa was too powerful for anything to stick. Had too many friends. Everybody knew he was guilty, though. They were all guilty."

"This might sound like a stupid question," said Forrest, "but were they sure . . . . " He hesitated.

"Sure of what?"

"Sure he was killed."

"Why do you ask that?"

"You'll laugh," he said.

"No, tell me."

"Is there any possibility that he could still be alive?"

"Well, maybe, but not really. What do you know that I don't?"

"Nothing," said Forrest. "It's just that it seems like the man is still alive down there. They still do things as he wished them done. I could almost feel his presence once. I stayed in a cabin one night that I later learned was his private property on some forbidden wooded area."

"The Townsend game preserve?" asked Camilla in surprise. "Lord!

And you a stranger? You're lucky you didn't get shot."

"See what I mean?" Forrest said. "Even you seem to perpetuate the influence of the man."

"I wasn't referring to County Pa. Carlton would have shot you. He's just like his daddy."

"I felt something that night," Forrest continued. "It was cold and frightening. I felt like someone was watching me. And there have been reports of sightings."

"You mean the ghost," said Camilla. "Hayley loves ghosts and legends. The ghost of County Pa is alive and well, all right, if that's what you mean."

"No, someone has seen him."

"Who?"

"She's just a child, but she insists she has seen the ghost. I figure she has seen a man, not a ghost. Is it possible he's alive? Tell me about the crash."

"There were three bodies: the pilot, of course; the senator; and County Pa. They were burned, but not beyond recognition. The pilot and the senator were identified by dental records."

"And County Pa?"

"They knew he boarded the plane. He chartered it. It had to be him."

"So they never really identified the remains."

"There was something else."

"What?"

"The plane was off course. They were supposed to be flying to Miami. They went down near Savannah."

FORREST WALKED the short distance to Rogue's Gallery later that afternoon. He paused at the window and admired a two-foot-high wooden sculpture in the window. It was of a lion reclining. The proud head of the lion gazed out of the plate glass window, as if all New York were his domain. Forrest smiled. Rarely had he seen a sculpture which so captured an animal in a pose of casual rest. It seemed almost alive.

The proprietor of the gallery had seen him admiring the sculpture through the window, and rushed to meet him at the door.

"Ah, Mr. Neill," he gushed. "I was hoping you would stop by today. The lion has sold already. I have a check for you. Come in, come in."

"My protégé will be pleased," said Forrest.

"Sir, you must convince him to let me handle his work." the owner continued. "He will receive no better percentage in all of New York, I assure you."

"I think that can be arranged."

JAKE POTTER went to Albany on the Katie Flyer the first day of June. He opened a new account at the Farmer's National Bank with a deposit of five hundred dollars. The check had come three days before, and he had sat holding it with wonder for hours. Mr. Neill had written that the sculpture had sold for over a thousand dollars, and that more raw material would be arriving for him shortly.

Jake had bought a new suit for his trip to Albany, with the rest of the first hundred dollars. He looked like a new man when he walked into the bank. The bowed head was gone, the dirty hands clean. For the first time in his life, Jake Potter was free of worry.

He spoke very little as he opened his account. He was being treated with respect, as a person of worth, by the bank clerk, and he did not know how to respond. Yes sir, no sir, thank you sir, said the man. Jake nodded and left as quickly as he could.

He felt odd, uneasy. He did not deserve this good fortune. He had to escape from the clerk before the real truth about him was discovered. That he was an ignorant farmer, a poor man, a man the clerk would never consider addressing as "Sir." Jake didn't want him to know.

Elizabeth Cooper paid a call to the Potters the next day. She asked to see Jake alone, and the two walked out to the stand of bamboo that lined the stream behind the house. She carried a package under her arm, and handed it to Jake.

"What's this?" he asked. "You done enough for me, Miz Cooper. It'll be me doin' for you from now on."

"Take it," said Mrs. Cooper. "It's from Forrest Neill."

Jake looked at her in surprise.

"Yes," she continued, "I know him. And you do, too."

"How do you know him, Ma'am?" asked Jake. "I don't remember meeting him at the station, like he said in the letter. I wouldn't know him if he fell on me."

"You never met him at the station, Jake. He told you that to make his proposal seem logical."

Jake was puzzled. What was she talking about? If he wasn't a passing traveler who had seen his carvings, who was he?

"You talk like you do know him, Miz Cooper. How do you know about all this? And why do you say I know him too?"

"Let's sit down over there, Jake," she said, pointing to a couple of large tree stumps, "and I'll tell you."

They walked to the stumps and sat down, and Jake took the wrapping from the book Mrs. Cooper had given him. He saw the author's name.

"He writes books?" he asked. "I don't know this man, Miz Cooper."

"You do, Jake. Open the cover. He wrote something there for you."

Jake opened the cover and read these words: "To my friend Jake, from Will Fable."

Jake stared at the words. He never forgot the man he had met on the train that day. Will Fable had turned his life around, given him the strength to turn away from an evil path. Jake had wondered afterwards if he was sent from God, one of those angels the Book said people meet unawares.

Jake shook his head in confusion.

"I know this man," he said. "I met up with him on a boxcar once. "He's no rich writer of books. What does he have to do with Forrest Neill?"

"He *is* Forrest Neill, Jake," said Mrs. Cooper gently. "Let me explain."

27

It was Saturday morning. Tori propped her head on her hands and sighed as she looked over the edge of the tree house.

"There's Dixie Lee James," she said.

"Where?" said Jessie, jumping over to Tori's side of the tree house.

"You missed her," said Tori. "She went into the beauty parlor."

"She live in there," said Boozie, who was reclining on one of the benches Will had built along the walls. "She never gonna come out one day."

"Oh, hush up, Boozie," said Tori impatiently. "She'll be out by eleven. Then she'll go riding in the fields like she always does on Saturdays."

"She's so pretty," said Jessie dreamily, as she returned to her bench opposite Boozie. "I wonder if I'll be pretty when I grow up?"

"Pretty be as pretty do," said Boozie.

Jessie frowned.

"What does that mean?" she asked.

"Hush up, both of you," said Tori again.

"What's the matter with you?" asked Jessie.

"Look," said Tori. "He's watching her again."

"Who's watchin' who?" asked Jessie, springing back to the wall that faced Hayley's square.

"Carlton Townsend, that's who," said Tori. "I told you he's been following her around."

"Where?" asked Boozie, joining them at the wall.

"See?" said Tori, pointing to the group of men playing checkers on the green. "That's him with his back to us. He's watching the door of the beauty parlor, see?"

"That's him, all right," said Jessie. "But why's he watchin' Dixie Lee?"

"He's trying to take her away from Rudolph, that's why," said Tori. "That Carlton is always trying to mess things up for Rudolph. If I was Rudolph, I'd kick him right in the shin."

"I thought you didn't want Rudolph to marry Dixie Lee," said Jessie. "If Carlton steals her away, then he won't marry her. That would be good, wouldn't it?"

"No, goose," Tori replied. "How would you like it if somebody stole your boyfriend?"

"I got no boyfriend," said Jessie.

"I do," said Boozie.

Tori and Jessie stared at the younger girl. Her statement was dismissed quickly, as was most of Boozie's crazy talk.

"If you had one, silly," said Tori, turning back to Jessie, "and you were going to break up, you'd want to break up on your own, wouldn't you? Not because someone else made you do it."

"I guess so."

"If Rudolph is stuck on her, he's stuck on her," said Tori. "If she ends up with Carlton, he'll get a broken heart."

"Poor Rudolph." said Jessie.

"Don't say that!" said Tori. "Carlton will never win. Besides, he's acting mighty funny about the whole thing. He doesn't really act like he wants to win, like he used to. Well, look at him."

"What he gonna do now?" asked Boozie.

"See," said Tori, "that's the funny part. He never does anything. He just watches. Half the time she doesn't even see him. It's like he's a birdwatcher, looking at a new bird with his binoculars."

"Does she ever see him?" asked Jessie.

"Sometimes. She stares at him a minute, then goes the other way," said Tori.

"She know a rat when she see one," said Boozie.

"Look, he's leaving," said Jessie.

The girls watched as Carlton lazily walked from the green, and mounted the steps of the General Store. He sat down in one of the chairs on the porch and started up a conversation with Daniel J. Smith, who spent most Saturday afternoons sitting there.

"Maybe he figures she'll go next door to the General Store when she gets out of the beauty parlor," suggested Jessie.

Tori turned a superior eye to Jessie and said tolerantly, "You'll never be a detective, Jessie. That's not why he moved."

"And I reckon you think you know?" said Jessie.

"Yes, I do."

"Why?"

"Because of Bubba, of course."

Tori looked with satisfaction over to the depot. Boozie and Jessie followed her gaze and saw the chief leaning up against the wall of the post office.

"How long he been there?" asked Boozie.

"He came out of his office a couple of minutes before Carlton. He watches Carlton like Carlton watches Dixie Lee. Something's going on, I can tell."

"Well, Carlton better leave Dixie Lee alone, if he knows what's good for him," said Jessie. "Bubba will thrash the daylights out of him if he don't."

"Carlton ain't scared of him," said Boozie. "He ain't scared of nuthin'. He go out to the woods all the time, with his daddy's ghost walkin' round in the sunlight."

"Oh, Boozie," said Tori with exasperation, "are you ever going to stop talking about that ghost? Nobody believes you anyhow."

Boozie said nothing. One did, she thought silently. Pap done seen him, too. Boozie flopped back down on the bench and put her head to the wall.

"You hurt her feelings," said Jessie.

"I don't care," said Tori. "Somebody's got to tell her."

"You don't have to be mean," said Jessie.

"Okay," said Tori. "We're going to settle this once and for all. Let's go see the ghost. Let's all go out to the preserve after church tomorrow and see if we can find him."

"You talk foolish," said Boozie. "Your granny forbid you to go there."

"Who's going to tell her?"

"Just wait a minute," said Jessie. "I'm not going anywhere near that evil place, and you're not either."

"Oh, Jessie," Tori said, "you of all people should know better. Nothing happened to us before, did it?"

"Ha!" replied Jessie. "We almost got caught, and you say nothin' happened? You're crazy."

"Don't you want to know what's down there?" Tori asked.

"Where?"

"In the secret room."

"Tori," Jessie cried, "there is no secret room. You dreamed that, remember?"

"Then I'll go myself."

"Go ahead," said Jessie. "I don't care."

Boozie sat up. "Don't do it," she said. "Only human can walk those woods safe is the son of County Pa."

AS THE noon hour approached, Woody Price sat waiting a couple of miles from Hayley, concealed behind a thick clump of brush near Rainbow Ridge, a lovely hollow in the forest off Hemon Road. He was waiting for Dixie Lee. She was a creature of habit, it appeared, and for the past four Saturdays, Woody had followed her to this place around noontime. She had ridden Highpocket here faithfully every week, as if it were some kind of ritual.

Rainbow Ridge was a beautiful, peaceful retreat in the springtime, massed with blooming azaleas and wisteria. A huge fallen tree trunk arched over the field like a rainbow. Blown down by a tornado years before, the huge oak somehow managed to survive, and sent a new growth of green leaves heavenward from its grounded branches every year. The azaleas were gone now, but daffodils and blooming clover carpeted the ground beneath the trunk.

It did not take long for Woody to realize that this was Dixie Lee's dreaming place. She would climb the huge trunk and sit with her legs dangling, shaded by the tree's new branches. This was to be the last week Woody would follow her before making his move. If she came again today, he could count on her presence here next Saturday as well, and he could put his plan into action.

It would be a simple matter to maneuver his friend Carlton to the place. If the two were ever alone together, Woody knew, they would not be able to keep up their present masquerade. One chance meeting would be all they needed, and Woody planned to provide that chance meeting for both of them.

AT THREE o'clock the train from Albany pulled in. Tori and her friends were jolted out of their lazy afternoon high in the treetop by the surprise arrival of Camilla Goodson, who stepped off the train in a dazzling red dress. Camilla apparently had told no one of her visit, for nobody met her at the depot. The girls watched as Bubba James approached and offered to help her with her luggage.

"She brought enough suitcases to stay for a year," Tori commented, as Bubba loaded the bags into his patrol car for the short drive to Brother Goodson's house next to the church. "You suppose she's going to stay awhile this time?"

"No," answered Jessie. "She never stays long. Dixie Lee would die if she did."

In a strange, quiet voice, Boozie said, "There's powerful magic in dis here."

"What are you talking about now?" asked Tori, who had learned to recognize Boozie's fortune-telling tone.

"There's three of them," continued Boozie, as if she were talking to herself. "No, there's four. It change shape, three sides, four sides. Miss Camilla, she bring it with her."

"Bring what?" asked Jessie, eyes wide. She believed in Boozie's predictions. It was generally accepted that Boozie would be the natural replacement for her elderly Aunt Colley, the Delight Diviner.

"Yesterday," said Boozie. "She bring yesterday in her bags."

"Boozie!"

The girls heard a voice below them, looked down, and saw Mrs. Cooper coming toward them.

"Come on down, Boozie," she said. "It's time for your singing lesson."

"Meema," said Tori, "can't you wait five minutes? Boozie's right in the middle of a saying."

"Nonsense, " said Mrs. Cooper. "Come, Boozie, let's get started."

Boozie came out of her trance and returned to the present, dutifully climbing down for her lesson, which she loved dearly. Mrs. Cooper had never worked with such a talented child, and Boozie was progressing at remarkable speed for one so young.

"Well," said Jessie, as she and Tori returned to their post facing the square, "one thing's for sure."

"What?" asked Tori.

Jessie nodded in Camilla's direction.

"They'll be a big crowd for church come mornin'."

They both giggled.

28

Camilla Goodson relaxed in the late afternoon sun. It was Friday. She had been home nearly a week. She was alone, sitting in a wrought iron chair in her father's backyard, beneath the shade of a huge pecan tree. It was so good to be home, really home at last. For the first time in years, she let the warmth and comfort of Hayley reach out and reclaim her.

During her years in New York, Camilla had held herself aloof from all she loved in Hayley. It was easier that way: easier than to miss her parents and friends, easier than to be homesick, easier than to admit she was still in love with Rudolph. The excitement of her career and her friends in New York had made home seem dull, and she had fed upon the adventure of it. She had kept her visits short, and for good reason. Her heart ached for Rudolph, and for Hayley. But as time went by, coming home had become easier. Eventually her trips to Hayley were perfunctory; her mind and her emotions never really left New York.

Until she decided to end it, until she stepped off the train, Camilla had never realized the extent of the barriers she had placed between herself and her hometown. But now she knew how much she had missed Hayley and its people. And Hayley had missed Camilla. People gravitated to her, because she had the uncommon gift of making everyone feel they were her friend. She was warm and friendly, at ease with everyone she met. She was unhindered by her beauty, the same person in blue jeans that she was in satin.

Camilla felt the warm pull of the land she loved reaching out for her. She was a part of Hayley, as much a part of it as the red clay beneath her feet, or the towering pines.

Here she was complete, content, where all was familiar, all was comforting. She knew every meadow, every road, every stream. All she looked upon was full of meaning, full of memory. Here she learned to swim; here she romped with her beagles; here was the tree that was once her castle. She visited the graveyard where she had spent many hours speaking silently to her beloved grandmother. She walked wistfully through the bower where Rudolph had first kissed her.

She sighed as she lay in the shade. As much as she had tried to deny it, now she knew she was still in love with Rudolph. She smiled fondly as she remembered her new friend, Forrest Neill, back in New York. What lovely evenings they had spent together. He had taught her much about herself, and much about the friendship that can exist between a man and a woman. She had thought herself a little bit in love with him at first, and indeed, love him she did. He had shown her tenderly, wisely, the difference between friendship and love. Somehow, he had known the truth: she had always been in love with Rudolph. Forrest had convinced her to face her feelings, to confront them.

But now, what was she to do? Rudolph was engaged to Dixie Lee James, and, by all accounts, deeply in love with her. How could Camilla intrude upon his life at this point? She knew that she must accept the situation and erase him from her life forever. She had only herself to blame. It was she who had let her ambition come between them. She had broken his heart.

Now he was happy again, in love with someone else. He deserved to be happy, and she would not interfere. Forrest had told her that she would never be free of Rudolph unless she accepted the truth. Dear, dear Will, she thought. She had continued to call him by his character's name, as he had asked her to, but only when they were alone. Dear, wise, generous Will. If she ever got over Rudolph . . . .

Comforted by the warmth of the afternoon and the feel of Hayley grass beneath her bare feet, Camilla became drowsy. All thoughts left her, and she dozed peacefully. The back door of the Goodson home opened, and Moira Goodson nodded toward her daughter. Rudolph Townsend walked past Camilla's mother and into the yard. He smiled at Moira, who shut the screen door and discreetly returned to the den. Rudolph walked slowly toward Camilla. Seeing that she was asleep, he was relieved, for that gave him a little time to gauge his feelings, time he had not counted on. Silently, he took the seat opposite her and sat back to look at his former love. Her mother had confirmed the rumors he had heard, that Camilla would not be returning to New York. Whether she would settle here, or in Albany or Atlanta, was not decided, Moira had said. But she was definitely back in Georgia to stay.

Rudolph was an acute observer of the human heart, and he had seen a change in Dixie Lee in the last few months. The carefree, lively girl who had enchanted him now seemed troubled, leaden. He was beginning to have reservations about their marriage, for her moods troubled him. Perhaps Rudolph loved Dixie Lee because she was so like Camilla; not physically, for Camilla was tall and raven-haired, Dixie Lee petite and blue-eyed, with light brown hair. They were alike in temperament, though, both a far cry from the helpless, frilly, empty-headed belles of Albany. Dixie Lee was Rudolph's last hope of breaking free of the memory of Camilla, but lately, when he looked into his fiancée's eyes, he read kindness and caution, not love and commitment.

When he realized he was looking for the same things in Dixie Lee's eyes that he had found in those of Camilla long ago, Rudolph knew he had some hard thinking to do. He could not be unfair to Dixie Lee, and marry her, if he was still in love with Camilla.

Rudolph smiled as he looked at Camilla. She was barefoot, dressed in a flowered skirt and white sleeveless blouse. She sat back in the chair, her head resting against the back of it, her legs crossed at the knees, her hands in her lap, her eyes closed. She had not stirred with his arrival. This was his Camilla, he thought. She wore no makeup, her black hair pulled back with a white ribbon.

She was a natural beauty. When she wore elegant fashions, and her hair and makeup were done by New York professionals, she was transformed into a glamorous woman Rudolph almost failed to recognize. He was surprised at the way his heart wrenched to see her as he knew her best, natural, honest, accessible.

He had come to face her, to face himself. He had to learn the truth before he married Dixie Lee. If he was still in love with Camilla, he would know it. He had no idea how Camilla felt about him. If she wanted no part of him, which he suspected, yet he found he was still in love with her, he would still have to break off his engagement. He would rather break Dixie Lee's heart now than live a lie with her.

He sat watching Camilla, thinking, trying to understand his feelings, seeing so much of the past, living it over in his mind. His life with Dixie Lee faded into the background. He tried to pull his feelings for Dixie Lee to the forefront, but was met again and again with the pervasiveness that was Camilla.

So. It was true. He was still in love with her. Rudolph swallowed hard and felt a tightness in his chest that seemed to crush his heart. The truth brought him no pleasure, for he knew he would hurt Dixie Lee terribly, and, there seemed little hope that this worldly, headstrong creature who sat before him wanted him back.

Camilla opened her eyes. With a start she saw Rudolph sitting across the table from her, his eyes closed, his hands clasped, looking for all the world like he was praying. She didn't move or make a sound. Her heart began to beat wildly and she tried to collect herself. What was he doing here? How long had he sat there, watching her sleep?

She watched in wonder at the way he was clenching his hands together. He tightened his hands into a taut grip and then relaxed, over and over again, as if he were in some terrible struggle with himself. His eyes clenched together now and then, and the muscles in his jaw tightened. Something was wrong. Her eyes filled with concern for him and she fought back tears. She started to speak, but stopped. She needed time, a few moments to think. She retreated to her pose of slumber; wiping all expression from her face.

When Rudolph opened his eyes he saw she was still asleep. He had to know.

"Camilla," he said gently. "Wake up, honey."

She opened her eyes and smiled at him lazily, warmly, with no surprise in her expression.

"Hello, Rudolph," she said. "I've come home."

"I know," he said. "Your mother told me."

They looked deeply into each other's eyes for a long moment. Then Camilla reached out and took his hand.

"You never could keep secrets from me," she said. "What's the matter?"

He dropped his eyes and stared at the hand he held. He caressed her hand, rubbing his fingers over it gently, tenderly.

"I won't be getting married after all," he answered.

Her heart leaped at his answer, but she struggled to retain her poise.

"Why not?" she asked softly.

He raised his eyes to look at her. He did not try to disguise his feelings. It was all there for her to see: love, pain, longing, hopelessness. She felt her throat tighten.

"I should thank you for coming home," said Rudolph in a strange, sad voice. "You've kept me from making a terrible mistake." He paused and looked back at her hand. "I've always been able to tell you everything, haven't I?"

"You know you have," she answered. "You always will."

He smiled.

"I can't marry Dixie Lee because I'm still in love with you. I don't know how you feel about me now, after all this time, but it doesn't matter. I had to come today, to see you again. I know now that I only loved all the things about Dixie Lee that reminded me of you, Camilla. It's you I love, just as I always have. I love you beyond reason, beyond all else."

She began to cry. Rudolph misunderstood and went to her, kneeling at her feet.

"Please," he said, "don't cry. How I feel doesn't matter. I won't interfere with your life."

She looked at him with a strange incredulity.

"You big oaf," she said. "Why do you think I came back?"

Her eyes were red, but somehow, he saw the gladness and relief they held. A terrible weight fell from him as he found the love he remembered, shining back at him in those glorious, swollen, gray-blue eyes.

29

The last week of school was a strain on all. The children were too excited about summer vacation to keep their minds open or their mouths closed.

Teachers were trying their best to make it until the thirty-first without going crazy. Parents struggled to keep the children at their books until the last test was given, but it was an impossible job.

When the day finally arrived, Miss Rigsby surprised the class with the announcement that she would be getting married in June, to a widowed banker with seven children. The day was spent in celebration, and, for once, the children decided Miss Rigsby was a real person after all.

Tori had not seen much of Wendy that spring, other than in school. She had become sad and listless, and never had much to say, even to Tori. On the way home, the last day of the school year, Wendy told Tori her daddy was gone.

"JACK HAMILTON'S a damn fool," said Carlton as he took his regular seat in the bar at Radium Springs.

"Who is this that he's run off with?" asked Woody, taking the chair opposite Carlton.

"Some empty-headed hostess he met at his last tournament," Carlton replied. "I'd like to wring his neck if I could get a hold of him. He's left us in a hell of a mess here. Marie's too upset to come to work, and the members are all screaming about their golf lessons being paid up for the summer."

"I take it he will not be welcome here again?"

"He better not show his face, if he knows what's good for him. Marie told me tonight she'll be leaving, going back to Atlanta. The place is a madhouse. Mother's having to supervise the cooks, for God's sake."

"Is there anything I can do to help, old man?" asked Woody.

"What's your handicap?" asked Carlton, amused.

"Don't ask," laughed Woody. "I'm afraid you'll have to advertise for a new golf pro."

"And a club hostess as well," said Carlton, rubbing his forehead.

"Hey, don't go overboard with this thing," said Woody. "You'll be flooded with resumés in a week, I'll wager."

"Maybe," said Carlton. "I need help fast. This club can't run itself, and I sure don't want the job."

"Tell you what," said Woody. "Let's change the subject. Get your mind off things. I've been wanting to talk to you about something."

"What?"

"Rainbow Ridge," said Woody.

WHEN THE first day of June arrived, Tori was not as jubilant with her summer freedom as she had planned to be. She was upset. True to Wendy's prediction, she would be moving away, and soon. Tori knew a little about what happened, that Wendy's father had deserted Wendy and her mother, and broken their hearts. Tori was deeply torn by this turn of events. She felt sorry for Wendy, but also she wondered if this could happen to her as well. What if her own father decided he didn't want her anymore? His letters were few, and his visits fewer. Here it was, June, and she hadn't seen him since October.

It was almost noon, a beautiful warm day. Honeysuckle was heavy in the air as Tori walked slowly down Southland Road, kicking pebbles. She reached the gully where Ottis had saved her life, and stopped to stare at the place where he had fallen. It all came back in an instant, the shock, the guilt, the grief. Suddenly she started to run. She ran wildly down the road, tears streaming down her cheeks. Everything was wrong, it seemed, and she ran until she could run no more. She came to a stop in front of the forbidden game preserve, panting, but feeling better for her exertion.

When she got her breath back, she looked at the fence and the entrance to the preserve. Her mood was reckless and rebellious, and she needed something else to think about. What better diversion than a new adventure? The more dangerous, the better.

Today's the day, she thought matter-of-factly, and turned without hesitation onto the dirt road. She scurried under the fence and took off down the road to the cabin. The trees were thick with green, and the branches arching above her made the path to the cabin shadowy and ominous. Whereas the forest had been alive with the sounds of birds and small creatures before she came, they were silent now, and not a breath of wind stirred the smallest leaf. It was hot and still, and with each step the forest seemed to swallow Tori deeper into a fantasy land. The eeriness, the element of danger was exciting, and Tori's mind flew from one role to another. First she became a detective on the trail of a cat burglar, then a maiden lost in a magical kingdom, then a big game hunter stalking a lion.

When the cabin came into view, Tori realized for the first time that she was on forbidden ground. The voice of Boozie came back to her, with the tales of the ghost that walked in daylight like a man. She watched the cabin for a while. There was no sign of life. Carlton's car was not there. She looked down the road and listened for the roar of an engine. All was still. It was now or never.

From inside the cabin, a man watched Tori as she hesitated. He could not have planned it better. Behind him, in the back room, the rug had been pulled back and the door to the cellar stood open. In one corner of the cellar, the booty of the cat burglar was stacked neatly. The wealth of Albany now occupied the place where the stacks of County Pa's money had been. The money was in a sack at the man's feet. Over two hundred thousand dollars; he had counted it. Now if only the little girl would come in, he thought.

Tori started toward the cabin, and the man hastily placed the bag of money in one of the cardboard cartons along the wall. He went silently to the pantry, the same place Tori and Jessie had hidden themselves. He waited.

Tori mounted the steps to the cabin and crossed the porch to the door. Something was going to happen, she knew. This was no fantasy, this adventure was real. Instinctively she knew that she was about to discover a secret. Maybe the secret of the ghost of County Pa. She boldly pulled back the latch and opened the door. The room was dark and musty, just as she remembered it. Her heart began to beat wildly as she listened for any sign of life. She heard nothing. She stepped inside and waited for her eyes to become accustomed to the dim light.

It was the same. The cardboard cartons lined the wall. The faded portrait of County Pa stared down at her. She looked into the eyes of the man in the portrait, expecting him to come alive. To her surprise, the eyes looked dull, benign, even friendly. Suddenly she knew. There was no ghost. County Pa was just a man, and he was dead and buried. She would never be afraid of him again. Tori stared into the eyes of the man in the portrait and felt sorry for him.

Tori walked slowly to the entrance to the kitchen, creeping like a cat upwind of a hound, listening for any sign of life. She crossed the kitchen to the entrance of the small back room where Carlton had gone, and stopped in surprise when she saw the open hatch in the floor.

"Holy cow!" she said softly, as exhilaration flooded her. She had been right all along. It was there, just as she knew it would be: County Pa's secret. It was a cellar where no one would dream of building one. But this was no fruit cellar. It was a secret room, a room for hiding things, a room no one knew about except Carlton and County Pa.

She walked to the opening and looked in. There was a sturdy set of wooden stairs leading down. She got on her knees and looked down, but it was too dark to see anything. What if somebody or something was down there in the dark? But excitement and curiosity beckoned her, overpowering her fears. I'll never get this chance again, she thought. I'll never know the secret if I don't go now.

She inched her way down the steps, slowly, cautiously, as if she would meet a demon any second. Halfway down, something flimsy hit her in the face and she cringed, batting it away. It came back and she saw that it was a string hanging from the ceiling. She looked up and saw, in the dim light, that it was connected to a light bulb. She pulled the string and the cellar room was flooded with light. She blinked the brightness out of her eyes and saw at last, the secret. She gasped.

The room was large and looked like the study of a rich man. County Pa's sanctuary! The floor was covered with a thick brown carpet and the walls were lined with chestnut paneling. A huge rolltop desk spilled papers from each pigeonhole, and a leather desk chair was pushed slightly aside, as if County Pa had just risen from his place. An easy chair stood at the opposite end of the room, with a table and large lamp beside it. The wall behind the chair contained built-in bookcases above cabinets. Books and stacks of papers filled the shelves of the bookcases. A tall gun cabinet with a glass door stood empty opposite Tori, and beside it, what looked like a liquor cabinet.

Tori descended the rest of the steps and immediately spied a neat pile of boxes. She walked to the boxes and opened one. She jumped back when she saw what looked like a dead animal in the box. She gathered her courage and looked again. It was fur, all right. She reached in and pulled out a soft mink stole.

"Jiminy," she said, as she saw that the box was filled with fur pieces, jackets, coats, and stoles. She replaced the stole and opened another box. In it she saw small velvet-covered boxes. She drew one out and opened it, finding a beautiful diamond necklace. She dropped the box to the floor as realization flooded her. This was the hiding place of the cat burglar! This was his booty. And she had discovered it. It was Carlton. He was the thief, and if he caught her—

The door above her slammed shut and the light went out. Tori screamed and crouched down, covering her head with her hands, as if to ward off some imaginary blow. At first she panicked and stumbled toward the staircase, screaming to be let out, but she realized she might be in even more danger if he did let her out. Above her she heard footsteps. He was whistling a tune, the same naughty tune she had heard him sing here long ago. Then there was the sound of hammering, and she heard him drag the rug across the floor.

He was covering up the hatch. She was trapped! She climbed the steps slowly, silently. She couldn't believe Carlton would leave her here. Maybe she could reason with him. Maybe if she promised she would never tell, he would let her go. Maybe if she pretended she didn't know it was Carlton. Something told her to remain silent. Then she heard a sound which chilled her to the bone. He was laughing, and his laughter faded away with his footsteps. She was his prisoner and nobody in the world knew where she was.

30

Carlton was late. He cantered his gray mare down Hemon Road towards Rainbow Ridge. It was just past twelve, and Woody had said eleven thirty. Why Woody wanted to buy this piece of land from him, Carlton had no idea, but he was willing to listen. Land was something the Townsends held sacred. They owned thousands of acres in and around Albany. The Townsends rarely sold their holdings; usually they acquired more. If Woody Price succeeded in buying Rainbow Ridge, it would be the first sale of land by the Townsends in twenty years.

Carlton need not have hurried. Woody Price was not there. He never had any intention of buying Rainbow Ridge or of meeting Carlton there. He wanted Carlton to meet the chief's daughter, his brother's fiancée, instead. She was there, doing her Saturday dreaming, just as usual. Woody planned to give fate a little push.

Woody had timed it perfectly. Dixie Lee's defenses against Carlton had been breaking down over the past months. She had been thrown together with him more times than she had bargained for, at Radium Springs functions, at lunches and suppers at the plantation, at trail rides and picnics. Always they had been civil to one another, but always taking seats as far away from each other as politely possible.

It was not working. As the days wore on, Dixie Lee found herself watching him secretly. Whenever he was around, she felt a strange excitement, a feeling of exhilaration. The Townsend family functions were becoming a chore. She found herself dreading them.

She had witnessed a rare occurrence of nature in the past months, a blossoming of personality in a hard shell of a man. The Carlton she thought she knew would have been easy for Dixie Lee to handle. He was cold, selfish, totally self-centered, and incapable of loving anyone but himself. The old Carlton would have tried to take her away from

240

Rudolph for the fun of it, just for spite. For this, Dixie Lee would have been ready.

But now, every time he was stiffly polite to her, every time he determinedly sacrificed his own feelings for the sake of his brother, Dixie Lee's confusion grew. Everything she believed to be true of him came into question. She had hardly thought him capable of love, much less nobility.

To make things worse, Carlton was still all the things she originally found exciting: ruggedly handsome, dominant, witty, reckless, and charming. To these masculine traits now seemed added the fatal blow to Dixie Lee's defenses: honor. It was what she had found so attractive in Rudolph. Slowly, inevitably, like a fallen leaf carried downstream by a gentle current, the desires of Dixie Lee's heart had changed.

The control of her emotions was slipping away, carrying her further and further from Rudolph, ever closer to the irresistible challenge that was Carlton. Her feelings for Rudolph had distilled into the sweet wine of their true nature: friendship, protection, fantasy, and loyalty. But not love. In spite of herself, in spite of her plans, in spite of her every desperate attempt to change it, Dixie Lee knew she had fallen in love with Carlton. And God help them both, he was in love with her. The strain was becoming unbearable.

Rainbow Ridge was surrounded on all four sides by a thick stand of shortleaf pine, poplar, sweetgum, and white oak. There was a trail through the north stand, which led to Hemon Road. The meadow was not visible from the road, and its isolation was its principal attraction to Dixie Lee. Now, it seemed Rainbow Ridge was the only place she could be herself. Here she had no one to impress, no feelings to guard against, no dreams to suppress. It was always a happy place for her to be. But today not even her dreaming place could lift her spirits. She sat on the old downed tree trunk, dangling her legs and watching Highpocket graze. Her life was a mess. She was engaged to a wonderful man, and in love with his brother.

Carlton was more a threat to her than ever. Even though she loved him, he was a scary proposition. She could not be totally sure he wanted her, for he had avoided her at every opportunity. But he had said he was in love with her. She could never manipulate him, she knew that. Why did she love him so? Why couldn't she be in love with Rudolph? She started to cry. She began to hit the tree trunk gently over and over in frustration. She was not use to losing control of herself, even in this place of safe seclusion.

From the trail, she heard the sounds of a horse and rider approaching. She looked up and caught her breath as she saw Carlton riding in on his mare. Her hands went immediately to her face and she tried to wipe away her tears. She felt her face flush, which just make matters worse. Carlton pulled up the mare in surprise at seeing Dixie Lee. Woody was nowhere in sight. He hesitated, but then walked the horse out to her.

So it finally happened. Dixie Lee had wondered what she would do if she ever ran into him alone. She had even subconsciously set herself up for such a meeting, going where she knew he might be, pretending to herself she had reasons to be there. She never dreamed she would be given such an isolated place as this. And more, she wasn't ready.

"Hello," he said, as he drew up to the fallen trunk.

"Hello, Carlton."

Dixie Lee held her head high, knowing he was staring at her tear-stained, red face.

"What's the matter?" he asked gently.

Her heart was pounding. She could not trust herself to answer. She stared at him with eyes of fear and longing. She shook her head no, and fought desperately to keep back the flood of tears that seemed to well from every part of her being.

As if he knew she needed some refuge for a moment, Carlton turned sideways in his saddle and looked away from her.

"It's a beautiful day," he said. He took a long breath and let it out slowly. "Much too pretty a day for tears." He paused. "Is there anything I can do to help?"

His back to her, he waited for an answer. The mare put down her head to graze, and he let loose the reins. Dixie Lee said nothing. He heard her sniff once, twice. His heart was aching. He clenched his teeth and then caught himself, consciously relaxing his body. He made a decision. They could not go on this way. She could not marry his brother, she did not love him. Rudolph would be the loser either way. None of them could go back now.

He reached behind him and held out his hand to her. Take it, he cried silently to her, as he kept his eyes on the meadow.

Dixie Lee stared at his outstretched hand. Her breath came in short gasps. She felt herself surrendering. She could not fight him anymore. She touched his hand and the tears came. His hand closed around hers, and he turned at the sound of her sobs. His eyes were soft, knowing, accepting. He released her hand and jumped from the mare. He lifted his arms to her from the ground below.

"Jump," he said.

Dixie Lee jumped down to him, and was caught in his strong arms. She sobbed fitfully into his chest as he embraced her tenderly. Her hair smelled of flowers and lemon. He closed his eyes tightly and held her until she was quiet. Her taut body relaxed against him. For the first time in his life, Carlton felt complete. It seemed as if they were one. He knew he would never love another. He stroked her hair and murmured her name softly. She held him tighter.

"It's a dangerous game we've been playing, my darling," he said at last. "I just can't do it anymore." He lifted her chin and raised her face to his. "I love you too much." He bent to her and their lips met. He kissed her softly, deeply, completely.

He pulled her down with him to the soft ground. Dixie Lee was defenseless. She could not think. All she could do was feel. She had never known such ecstasy. Her soul was poured out to him. Her blood was hot wine, her bones limp. Whatever he wanted of her at that moment, he could have. She lay in his arms forever, it seemed, and he made no move to take her further. At last she tilted her head back and closed her eyes, heaving a deep sigh. She opened her eyes and, by degrees, brought her glance to his. It was almost painful for her to look into his eyes, for she knew he could see into her soul. This she had never given to anyone.

He looked into her eyes and said, "You're so beautiful."

She raised her lips to his, but he caught her gently by the chin and she looked at him questioningly.

"Tell me you love me," he said.

"I love you."

"Tell me that you'll marry me."

She could hardly breathe. What was left of her reason rejoiced. Her eyes flooded again with tears.

"Tell me." he demanded.

"Yes," she sighed. "Yes, yes."

He kissed her again and again. For how long she didn't know. She only knew she loved him and he loved her. She had forgotten Rudolph, forgotten herself, forgotten everything except the man who held her. Desire for him swept through her as his kisses grew more passionate. She turned her head from his kisses and gasped for breath. He looked at her, knowing that she was willing, that he could take her if he wished.

He drew back and sat up, and she looked at him in surprise. Suddenly she regained her senses and looked around the meadow as if someone could see them. The tender moment was gone, but in its place was a full, warm feeling that filled every part of her being. She dropped her eyes and wondered at herself.

He laughed softly.

"Don't worry," he said. "We're alone." He pulled her to him. "You're going to be wonderful, but now is not the time or the place. You deserve better."

She could not help it. She started to giggle. The months of frustration were over. She felt a release, a relief that was dizzying.

"What must you think of me?" she asked.

He smiled. It was a smile full of tomorrows. Her question needed no answer.

"It's hot," he said, "and we need to talk. I know a little spot beside Caloosa Creek. We can be there in five minutes. Come on."

He stood up and offered her his hand. She rose to her feet and brushed the grass from her clothes. The world seemed somehow a different place.

"I'll get the horses," he said. "Get your bag and we'll go."

"No bag," she said absently, as she marveled at her feelings.

Carlton paused, and Dixie Lee followed his gaze to the ground beneath the downed tree trunk. He was looking at a black bag with a shoulder strap, a knapsack of some kind.

"What's that?" she asked.

"I don't know," answered Carlton. "I thought it was yours."

"No," said Dixie Lee, "I've never seen it before. I didn't know it was there. Who could it belong to?"

Carlton picked up the bag and heard a soft clink of metal on metal.

"It's heavy," he said, setting it on one of the low branches.

Carlton opened the bag and pulled out a pair of black pants and a black pullover in a strange material. Black gloves and a black knit cap followed, as well as a number of hand tools, a rope, flashlight, wire, and a lock-picking kit.

"What is all this?" asked Dixie Lee.

"Oh, I'd say it was everything your friendly cat burglar needed for an evening's work," said Carlton with an amused grin.

"The cat burglar?" said Dixie Lee, eyes wide with excitement. "Let me see."

Carlton showed her the various items, and she fingered them with a strange fascination. Dixie Lee was among those who had a grudging admiration for the daring exploits of the mysterious thief.

"But he hasn't done anything in months." she said in wonder. "People say he moved on or died of the flu."

"Maybe he did, but he left this behind. Your daddy will be mighty interested in this."

Bubba James. The mere mention of Dixie Lee's father was enough to bring a feeling of uneasiness to them. He would never approve of their relationship. Carlton was more aware of Bubba's recent surveillance of him than was Dixie Lee.

"We have to keep this bag in a safe place and try to catch this phantom ourselves," said Carlton.

"Catch him? What do you mean?"

"If I hand this over to Bubba now, he'll try to pin this thing on me. He's been watching me for months. He thinks I'm the cat burglar."

"But that's silly!" Dixie Lee protested. "Why would he think such a thing?"

Carlton grinned.

"Let's face the facts, honey. I've been a real cutter in my day. I've grown up a little, but your daddy doesn't know that. To be honest, I guess I really don't blame him. If I was him, I'd keep a close eye on Carlton Townsend myself."

"How can you joke about something like this?"

Carlton smiled and took her hand. "How can we not joke about it?"

"This is serious," she said. "There's no way Daddy can blame this on you. I was here with you when you found the bag. We found it together."

"No," said Carlton, "the best thing would be to expose this guy and present him to your father all tied up with ribbons."

"How?"

"Let's hope he plans to come back for the bag. I'll put Kirkland on it."

"Who's that?"

"You've seen him. He's that Atlanta security guard Rudolph hired to watch the house for Mother. I'll stake him out here and he can lie in wait for this fellow."

"Oh, Carlton, do you think it will work?"

"It's worth a try."

A FEW miles away, in the cellar of the cabin, Tori sat alone in the dark. She had remained motionless at the top of the stairs for a long time after her captor left. She fought her feelings of terror, but she could not stop shaking.

At last she summoned the courage to try to open the hatch. She reached up and pushed as hard as she could. The hatch did not move. She pushed again and again until she was exhausted. She finally gave up and made her way down the steps in the dark. The string hit her face again, and she yanked on it. It came loose. She felt her way to the table beside the big chair in the corner. She felt for the switch on the lamp and pulled the chain. Light flooded the room, and Tori breathed a sigh of relief.

She needed an ax. A knife. Something to chop her way out. Feverishly she began searching the cabinets, the desk, the booty. There was nothing to help her get out. She did discover food. The cabinet contained all kinds of canned goods and jerky, even some bottles of wine. It was a small comfort, although at the moment, food was the last thing on her mind. She had to have a plan. He would be coming back sometime, maybe today, maybe tomorrow. She had to decide what she would do when he did. For the next few hours, Tori tried to think of a plan. Maybe she could hide herself somehow, so he would think she got away. Maybe someone would find her before he came back. But what if no one found her? What if Carlton never came back? Exhausted, Tori lay down on the thick carpet and drifted off to a fitful sleep.

IT WAS nearly five o'clock when Carlton returned to the Townsend plantation. He and Dixie Lee had taken the horses to a lovely shady spot beside Caloosa Creek and talked for hours. They talked of many things, of their future, of Rudolph, and more about catching the thief. Their fates were sealed in one afternoon, and neither could have imagined the heartache which lay ahead for both of them.

Carlton cantered the mare to the battered structure that served as shelter for the horses while the new barn was under construction. He carried the black bag securely on his saddle horn. He brushed down the horse and fed and watered her in the late afternoon light, then took the bag and hid it at the back of the lower shelf of a rough workbench in the shed. He placed an old paint can and several sacks of nails in front of it. No one had seen him. Carlton walked to the house and found his mother in the kitchen, cooking eggs.

"Mother, what in the world are you doing?"

His mother looked up and gave him a welcoming smile.

"Why, making dinner, of course."

"Where is Daisy?"

"I had to send Sally and Daisy over to the club. Juanita didn't show up again, son."

"Damn!" said Carlton. He looked a bit apologetic for his outburst, and said, "Excuse me mother, but this is getting out of hand. I'll not have you reduced to a scullery maid for that club. We can't do without Daisy here. If you can, I can't. Where in God's name is Rudolph, anyway?"

"Now calm down, dear," replied Laura. "It's not his fault. He went to Atlanta this morning to see about . . . something."

Carlton caught her tone. It was something she did not want to tell him.

"Well," he said with narrowed eyes that could not hide their amusement, "what's all the mystery?"

He grabbed an apple from the fruit bowl and sat down on a stool beside the stove.

"Oh dear, I wasn't supposed to tell you," said Laura.

"Oh? My, this gets better all the time. Come on now, dear heart, you know you could never keep a secret from me. I won't let on that you told me. What's he up to?"

"All right, but it's to be our secret. Do you promise?"

Laura, like Dixie Lee, could not resist his charm. Over the years, they had plotted to bring Price Townsend around to Carlton's way of thinking. And she had always been the buffer between the brothers. Laura was the foundation stone of the family, gently constructing a home in the midst of clashing temperaments.

Rudolph had always been a joy to her, but for a long time Carlton's wild nature had been something she had struggled to understand, and his actions something she overlooked. Still, she loved both her sons equally. Since his accident, however, Laura believed that Carlton was coming into his own at last. The barriers were falling away from the kind and generous heart that she alone could see.

"Rudolph went to see Thomas Moore about breaking your father's will."

"What? Breaking it how?"

"He wants to divide the property equally among the three of us. He thinks it should have been done that way all along."

"You're not serious?"

"Yes, I am."

"Well, I'll be damned."

"Your brother has come to have a lot of faith in you, darling. He wants you to have your fair share, and so do I. I think your father had what he thought were everyone's best interests at heart, but I always thought he went about it the wrong way."

Carlton's heart ached for Rudolph, who would surely be devastated by the loss of Dixie Lee. He loved his brother more at that moment than he had ever loved him, and wanted to prevent him from being hurt almost as much as he loved Dixie Lee.

"Mother," he said softly, "can you forgive me for the way I acted after Father died? I was bitter and hurt, and I know I brought great pain to you and Rudolph. I feel like I was another person then. I don't know how I could have been so selfish and cruel. I'm so sorry."

"Darling, I know. I know you were hurt. Your father was . . . well, he was like a hero to you. I don't believe he meant to hurt you the way he did. I understand, really I do."

"I love you, Mother."

"I know you do, darling. I love you, too."

They gave each other a peck on the cheek and a brief hug.

"Now run along, dear," said Laura, making an attempt to erase the emotion of the moment, "I'll be fine. Someone has to keep an eye on the club until we can hire a replacement for Jack. I'm sure Rudolph will be home shortly. He's overdue now."

"Yes, Ma'am," said Carlton. He bowed gallantly. "I'll go check out Daisy's cooking for you."

Carlton preferred to supervise things from a stool at the bar. He entered the softly lit lounge and smiled, seeing his friend Woody Price there. Carlton walked to the bar and sat down next to Woody.

"What happened to you today?" asked Carlton.

"I was at the appointed place at the appointed time and you were not," replied Woody. "What happened to you?"

"You were there? I wasn't that late, I must have gotten out there about twelve-thirty."

"We must have just missed each other. I'm afraid it's a habit of mine to arrive fifteen minutes early for an appointment. I waited thirty or forty minutes, then I left. I thought you had been detained."

"No, I was there. I was just delayed a bit. Did, um, you see anyone there today?"

"Should I have?"

"Well, I guess not. It's just kind of strange that you didn't see . . . oh, nothing. Forget it."

"Well," said Woody, "we can always do it another time."

"Maybe not," said Carlton. "Maybe it's for the best. I realized while I was out there today that I've grown attached to that place. I don't think I'll be wanting to let it go."

Woody sighed.

"C'est la vie," he said. "I don't blame you in the least. It's a lovely little spot."

"Yes," said Carlton with a faraway look, "it's lovely."

Woody smiled knowingly. It was as if he could read Carlton's mind. His plan had worked.

WHEN TORI had not returned for supper at five o'clock, Mrs. Cooper had begun to worry. At six o'clock, she got in her car and drove to Jake's house, thinking that Tori may have lost track of the time. The Potters had not seen her all day.

"Did you look in the tree house?" asked Jessie.

"She could be asleep up there, Miz Cooper," added Jake.

"No," replied Tori's grandmother. "That's the first place I looked. She's not there."

"Well, maybe she went to Boozie's house," Jessie offered, "or fishin' at Froggy Bottom."

"Jessie," said Jake, "go on with Miz Cooper. Y'all two can find her sure if you go together."

"There's still an hour of light left," said Mabel confidently. "You can cover all of Hayley in that time. I'm sure nothin' is wrong. She's just not used to summer light yet."

Elizabeth Cooper and Jessie drove back into Hayley, asking those they met if they had seen Tori. No one had. Jessie led the way to the old railroad tracks, Blackberry Glen, Froggy Bottom Pond, and back past her house to Cutter's Field. They went out Hemon Road to the Washington place, but Tori was not there either. Boozie was gone for the weekend, staying with her Aunt Colley, the Delight Diviner, in the backwaters, so she was of no help in the search.

"Maybe she went to see Wendy," said Jessie.

"No, honey," said Mrs. Cooper. "She can't be all the way to Radium Springs. It's too far to walk."

"She was upset about Wendy's daddy leavin', though," said Jessie. "I bet she did walk out there. I bet that's where she is."

Five miles? Mrs. Cooper thought to herself. It was possible. But this was not like Tori. She had never stayed out alone this late. It was getting dark. Still, she had been upset about Jack Hamilton.

"Maybe she met Rudolph on the way, and he gave her a ride over on his horse," Jessie suggested.

"You may be right, dear," said Mrs. Cooper. "Let's give it a try before the light fades."

At the clubhouse they talked to Wendy and Marie Hamilton, but neither had seen Tori. Another dead end.

On the way back they stopped at the Townsend plantation. Rudolph and Carlton were not there, but Laura Townsend promised to ask them about Tori as soon as they returned home.

"Don't worry," Laura had said. "I'm sure she'll turn up."

But Elizabeth Cooper was beginning to get a sinking feeling in the pit of her stomach. Tori was in trouble, she could feel it. She went to the chief's house at seven-thirty, just as darkness settled over Hayley. It was to be a dark night with no moon. Clouds rolled in from the south, cutting even the starlight from view.

Bubba James listened patiently to Mrs. Cooper's story as they sat in

Hedda James's immaculate front room. Dixie Lee and her mother listened silently from behind the kitchen door. Bubba never allowed them to be present if ever business should, of necessity, cross the threshold of their home.

They overheard Mrs. Cooper telling Bubba that she and Jessie had covered all the places Tori could have gone. Mrs. Cooper spoke calmly, as if she did not fear the worst.

"Did she say anything this morning that seemed unusual to you?" Bubba asked Mrs. Cooper.

"Not really," replied Mrs. Cooper. "But she was a little upset about Jack Hamilton deserting his family. Wendy Hamilton is a friend of hers."

"But you've been to Radium Springs already?"

"Yes. She hasn't been there."

"She has never done this before?"

"No, Chief."

"Has she been unhappy lately?"

"Why, no," replied Mrs. Cooper. "You know Tori, Chief James. She's a happy, well-adjusted child."

"Yes, I agree," said Bubba, "but I have to ask you these questions. There is no possibility in your mind that she could have run away?"

"None."

"Not even to her father?"

Paul. Mrs Cooper had not thought of him. Surely, he would not have come for her without any word. No, it was impossible.

"No, Chief. Tori would not have tried to go to him. And Paul would never have picked her up without letting me know. It's inconceivable. But if you like, I'll put in a call to him."

"I'm afraid you'll have to. We must exhaust all the possibilities, no matter how far-fetched. I doubt he had anything to do with it, but he'll have to be told sooner or later anyway. It can't hurt to check it out. You go on home now. I'll take it from here. Try not to worry."

"Thank you, Chief."

Mrs. Cooper and Jessie got up to leave. Jessie had been silent and shy, saying nothing unless she was asked to a question. She lingered for a moment after Mrs. Cooper had gone out the front door.

"Chief James?" she asked weakly.

"Yes?"

"The snakes are high this time of year, aren't they?"

Bubba hesitated.

"No," he lied. "Don't be thinking like that. Tori will be okay. I'll find her, and she'll be fine. Go on home now."

Mrs. Cooper went to the depot to put in a call to Paul Tanner. He had not seen Tori, or been out of town for weeks. He wanted to come down immediately, but Mrs. Cooper told him to wait at least until morning. Maybe she would turn up before then.

Mrs. Cooper stopped at her house, and she and Jessie checked every room, the barn, the yard, and the tree house. Tori was not there. Mrs. Cooper resigned herself to a long night, and carried Jessie home. But Mabel, Jake, and Jessie insisted on riding back to her house to wait with her, and Jake was sure he could be of some help in the search.

Bubba went from house to house, questioning everyone. No one had seen Tori all day. The chief enlisted the help of several of the men to help him in the search, should it become necessary.

As soon as Rudolph returned from Atlanta, Laura told him of Tori's disappearance. He told her to send word to Carlton at the club, and rode immediately to the Cooper home to offer his help. Bubba arrived shortly thereafter to check with Mrs. Cooper about Paul Tanner, and to make sure the child had not turned up in the interim.

It was nine o'clock. As the hours had passed, everyone concerned became silently convinced that something must have happened to Tori. If she could have made it home on her own, she would have by now. Bubba, Rudolph, and Jake were discussing their next course of action when Carlton arrived with Woody Price. They offered their concern and encouragement to Elizabeth Cooper, then joined the others on the front porch.

Bubba was speaking in low tones. He was as wary of Carlton as ever, but in the present crisis, he found it easy to suppress his feelings. He accepted Carlton and the mysterious Mr. Price simply as two more bodies to aid in the search.

"There's not much doubt that the child is lying hurt somewhere," Bubba said to the two newcomers. "We've got to find her as quickly as possible."

"We've decided to go for Jock Morehouse," said Rudolph. "His bloodhounds are the best in the state."

"We'll be back in an hour," Bubba continued. "One of you go get Reese Jones and Crawford Welch, and we'll meet you back here shortly."

"We'll need lanterns or torches," said Woody.

"You three take care of that while we're gone," said Rudolph. "Crawford can probably help you there."

A few minutes after ten, the men were ready. Mrs. Cooper remained calm when Sheriff Morehouse asked her for an article of Tori's clothing for the dogs. A pair of shoes and unwashed socks were produced and given to the dogs. Mrs. Cooper, Mabel, and Jessie watched from the front porch as the dogs took the scent. All four dogs began to bellow at once, and dragged their handlers out the front gate, straight down Southland Road.

The leashed animals quickly led the men past the Potter place without stopping. It was about a mile farther to the entrance of the Townsend game preserve, and the dogs pressed on without faltering. They turned off the road at the entrance to the preserve, but were barred from entry by the gate.

All the men were surprised by this turn of events. What could the child be doing here? Carlton opened the gate and the dogs howled louder, straining against their leashes as they entered the woods, leading the men up the narrow dirt road. The forest was dark and still. It was hot. Beads of perspiration broke out on Carlton' forehead as the dogs continued up the road. They were headed straight for the cabin. Carlton felt uneasy. He wanted to find the girl, but for now, the cellar must be his secret.

They would not find it. Rudolph had been there many times and never suspected a thing. Carlton had not told Rudolph about the secret room, and now he regretted that he had not. He had not decided what to do with the money. He felt now that he should have moved it to a safer place, a bank vault or safety deposit box. Before the events of this unusual Saturday, the money had given him a feeling of power and independence, as had the knowledge of his father's secret business deals and political ties. The evidence of his father's misdeeds was known only to Carlton, he believed, and he wanted to keep it that way. His mother and his brother knew a man named Price Townsend. Carlton knew County Pa.

Ever since he had come to see the error of his ways, Carlton had no longer wanted to use his father's secrets to his own advantage; but he had not been willing to let go of the money. Until he learned of Rudolph's generosity toward him earlier that day, he had seen the money as his inheritance, a bitter birthright that he alone was strong enough to claim, with the full knowledge and acceptance of its source. He must never let them know. His mother and his brother must be protected from the harsh light of reality. It was all up to Carlton. His family's honor was in his hands. His heart beat faster as the cabin came into view. The dogs led the men to the steps and onto the porch, howling louder than ever, knowing that their reward of fried chicken livers was at hand.

The sound of the dogs woke Tori from her restless sleep in the cellar, and she stumbled to the bottom of the stairs and listened. She heard only the dogs howling, and she slumped on the step, disappointed. It was just a pack of dogs.

"All right," said Rudolph, "Bubba and I will go inside. The rest of you wait out here. Jake, give me your lantern."

Sheriff Morehouse held two of the dogs and started down the steps with them. He turned to Woody Price, who held the other two, and yelled, "Price, get those dogs off the porch."

Jock's order to Woody startled Rudolph. He stared at the dogs for an instant, then at Woody Price. He had heard those words so many times when he was growing up. His mother scolding his father about the dogs in the house. The memory of his father suddenly swept through Rudolph like a chilling wind. Price Townsend's spirit was present in this place, strong and haunting. This had been his hunting lodge, his private domain. When they were young, his sons had been considered trespassers here, just like anyone else. Even now, it was no different.

Bubba looked questioningly at Rudolph, who was staring blankly at Woody Price. He cleared his throat purposefully. Still Rudolph stared.

"Shall we go in now?" Bubba asked pointedly.

Rudolph recovered himself. "Let's go," he said, and opened the door. He held the lantern before him and entered the dark cabin, with Bubba following.

From her prison below, Tori heard the creak of rotting floorboards and sprang to her feet. Carlton could be coming back! She had not decided what she would do. She ran behind the bar and crouched down, listening.

"Tori!" called Rudolph. "Tori Tanner! It's me, Rudolph, and Chief James. Are you in here? Tori!"

It was Rudolph! Her rescuer of old! Tori's fears melted away and every taut muscle relaxed. She ran up to the top of the steps and began pounding on the hatch.

"Rudolph!" she cried. "Here I am! Down here! Rudolph, let me out!"

Rudolph and Bubba heard soft pounding and Tori's muffled cries.

"Come on," said Rudolph, as he headed toward the kitchen.

"She's here!" called Bubba to the others as he followed.

A cheer went up from the men outside. Jock Morehouse proudly patted the dogs and pulled out their reward, causing a new round of yelping. Carlton remained in the yard with Woody and Jock, hoping that his secret would remain undisturbed. Jake followed the others into the cabin.

Rudolph and Bubba walked toward the sounds of Tori's pounding, through the kitchen and into the small back room. It was empty, except for a rug and a small pile of assorted rusty tools in one corner.

Tori pounded again and called to Rudolph. The two men looked at each other in surprise. The pounding was beneath their feet.

"Tori, are you all right?" asked Rudolph.

"Rudolph, I'm okay. Get me out of here."

"Where are you, girl?" called Bubba. "Under the house?"

"Pull the rug back," called Tori. "There's a secret room down here. You're standing on the door."

"What in God's name?" said Rudolph in astonishment as they stepped off the rug and pulled it aside, revealing the hatch.

"Don't worry, Tori," said Rudolph, "we'll have you out of there in a minute."

"Look, it's been nailed shut," said Bubba, fingering a nailhead nearly flush with the floor. "Somebody put her down there and apparently didn't want her to get out."

Jake picked up a hammer from the corner and offered it to Rudolph.

"Here, use this," he said.

Rudolph pried the nail free.

"Who on earth would do such a thing?" he asked as he opened the hatch. To the surprise of the men, light from the room below flooded the room.

Tori flew out and jumped into Rudolph's arms.

"Rudolph," she cried, "you found me! I was so scared. Please take me home."

"How did you get here?" asked Bubba.

"What happened?" said Jake.

"Please don't be mad at me," said Tori, fighting back tears. "I was trespassing. I came to find the secret room and I found it. Look, see?" She pointed to the room below.

"Who locked you in like that?" asked Rudolph.

Bubba continued to stare down the stairs at the lighted room. This was beginning to smell of Carlton Townsend.

Tori did not answer Rudolph's question. Bubba repeated it. "Who locked you in, Tori?"

"I think it was the cat burglar," said Tori frowning. She didn't want to tell Rudolph that Carlton did it.

"What?" asked Rudolph. "What in the world are you talking about?"

"Go and look," said Tori. "All his stuff is down there. The things that he stole. I read about it in the paper, and I found his hideout. He caught me and locked me in."

"Come here, Tori," said Jake.

Tori ran to Jake and hugged him. Bubba and Rudolph went down the stairs.

"Come on," said Jake. "Let's go outside and tell the others you're okay. We've all been worried about you."

They walked to the front door. Tori was met by a round of relieved applause. She looked in the yard and saw that the bloodhounds were being held by Woody Price and Carlton. Jake was relating the discovery of the secret room to the men on the porch. They did not notice that Tori's eyes widened and her body stiffened at the sight of Carlton.

Carlton was also staring at her. He was hearing what he had hoped against, that they had found the secret room. His heart sank. If those papers were made public, it would break his mother's heart. And the money. They had found it by now. His hopes of sparing his family were in ashes. There was nothing he could do about it now. And maybe if he played innocent, he would not be dragged into his father's mess. He could stand it no longer. He had to know what was going on. But the girl—why was she staring at him like that?

"Here," he said to Woody, "tie up these beasts or something. I'm going in there."

He handed the leashes to Woody and started for the stairs. Tori ducked behind Jake and let him pass. The rest of the men followed Carlton inside. Jake pulled Tori along by the hand.

When they climbed down the steps into the secret room, Rudolph and Bubba knew immediately that they had stepped into the secret sanctuary of County Pa.

"Would you look at this place," said Rudolph in disbelief. "I always wondered what happened to that trophy."

"Never mind that," said Bubba tersely. "Look at this."

He had found the stack of stolen goods immediately. He drew out a fur stole and several jewel boxes.

"I know this brooch," he said to Rudolph. "It belongs to the rich widow. Morehouse has a picture of her wearing it in his files."

Bubba went to the stairs and called, "Jock! Come down here!"

Jock and Carlton came down the stairs.

"Got a little surprise for you, Jock," said Bubba, motioning him over to the boxes. "Recognize this stuff?"

Carlton was staring at the boxes. The money was gone. Someone had stolen it, and stashed this booty in its place.

"What the hell?" said Carlton in surprise.

Bubba turned and faced him.

"I don't suppose you know anything about this, do you, Carlton?" Bubba asked. His eyes were deadly, but his tone was casual.

Carlton brushed past him, ignoring his question.

"Rudolph, what the hell is going on here?" he demanded.

"I would think that was obvious," replied Rudolph. "Father must have built this place years ago. Someone discovered it and has been using it as a hideout. The infamous cat burglar of Albany, I'm afraid. He must have found Tori here and locked her in to keep it a secret."

Carlton was visibly agitated. Bubba was observing his every move, as he stood with Sheriff Morehouse over the stolen loot. Carlton walked to the rolltop desk and eyed the papers nervously. He had none of Rudolph's amazement at the existence of the place. He seemed uneasy. Too uneasy.

Bubba walked over to one of the chairs and sat down. "I need a drink," he said nonchalantly. "Anything to drink down here, Carlton?"

"Why do you ask me that?" Carlton asked with some measure of control. "I've never seen this place before in my life. How would I know what's down here?"

It was the wrong answer. If Bubba had asked Rudolph the same question, Rudolph would have laughed and said he needed one, too, let's look around for something. Carlton had known. Strike one.

In one corner of the room was a coat rack. Hanging there, in plain sight, was one of Carlton's hunting jackets. There was no doubt. It was Carlton's, and he had worn it last winter, long after Price Townsend's death.

My god, thought Rudolph, if he had anything to do with this . . . .

It could be possible. A hundred images tumbled through Rudolph's mind as he struggled against believing that his brother was capable of burglary and kidnaping. Carlton laughing at Chief James, taunting him. Carlton spending money far beyond his means. Carlton swaying on drunken feet, hissing threats. Rudolph saw again the look of triumph in Carlton's eyes when he held Dixie Lee in the stable, and his grin when he lay beaten at Rudolph's feet. Bubba's words came back to Rudolph: it was either deliberately set, or carelessness with cigarettes. He saw again the image of the burning car, and Carlton lying day after day on his bed, unable to bear even the slightest sound. And, from the day of the accident, there had been no more burglaries.

If he had committed the burglaries, why did he stop after the accident? There could be only one reason. The change of heart in his brother was so obvious, the difference so radical, he must have come to his senses. Carlton was not the same person he had been. But if he had changed, how could he have locked up a child and left her to die to hide his crimes? It did not make sense. Rudolph refused to believe it. He looked again at the jacket. What Carlton's part in all this was, he did not know, but he would find out.

Carlton saw Rudolph glance at the jacket, and he knew his brother had not been fooled by his lie. Rudolph turned and looked at Carlton. His eyes were questioning. Carlton returned his gaze squarely, and briefly shook his head no. Rudolph nodded and looked away.

Bubba started up the stairs. He turned and said, "We'll have to cordon off the area. Looks like we've got a long night ahead of us. All this will have to be impounded and tagged as evidence. Rudolph, can I count on your help?"

"Of course," said Rudolph. "Anything I can do."

Bubba looked at his brother. "Carlton?"

Carlton nodded.

Bubba continued up the stairs and asked Tori to go outside with him. They went out and sat down on the steps. They were alone, for the rest of the men had gone inside to inspect the loot.

"Do you feel like answering some questions for me?" he asked gently.

"I guess so," said Tori, "but I really need to go home. Meema will be so worried about me."

Bubba called to Reese Jones, and Reese appeared in the doorway.

"Reese, I need to talk to the girl for a few minutes. Would you go back to town and tell Mrs. Cooper she's all right? You can ride back here with her in her car."

"Sure thing," said Reese. He grabbed a lantern and started up the dirt road.

"Reese has gone to get your grandmother," he said. "She'll be here for you soon, okay?"

"Okay," said Tori.

"Now," he said, "I want you to tell me exactly what happened, from the beginning. Everything you can remember."

"I came in from Southland Road."

"What time was that?"

"Just after lunch. About one o'clock, I guess."

"Good. Go on."

"I got to the cabin and I didn't see anybody, so I went in."

"You've been here before, then?"

"Yes, last summer. Jessie and me, we followed Carlton one day and found the cabin. We waited for him to leave, then we went in."

"Did you find the secret room last summer?"

"No, Chief," said Tori. "We were in the cabin and we heard Carlton coming back, so we hid in the pantry. He came in and we heard him go down to the room. We just wanted to get away. When he left we ran all the way to Jessie's house."

The chief made a mental note. The Potter girl could corroborate the fact that Carlton knew about the secret room. Bubba would have Jock Morehouse and a stenographer present when he questioned her.

"So you went into the cabin shortly after one this afternoon," said Bubba. "Then what happened?"

"I just walked into the back room and I saw the hatch standing open," said Tori. "I knew it would be there and it was. I listened for a few minutes and I didn't hear anybody, so I went down the stairs. There was a light on the stairs, so I put it on."

"Then what?"

"Well, I just saw the room and I went down to look. I hadn't been there five minutes when I heard the door slam shut and the light went out."

"You never saw him?"

"No, sir."

"Then what?"

"I heard him whistling a tune, and then he started laughing."

"Do you remember the tune?"

"Yes."

"What was it?"

Tori hummed it for him.

Strike two. Carlton's theme song.

"Tori," he asked slowly, "did Carlton lock you up in there?"

Tori's eyes widened.

"You can tell me, Tori," said Bubba. "Don't be afraid."

"But Bubba," said Tori in confusion, forgetting her manners, "I can't tell you. I didn't see him, really I didn't."

"But you thought it was Carlton, didn't you?"

"Yes," said Tori. "I thought it was."

31

Jock Morehouse left the cellar in response to Bubba's call. Bubba nodded toward the door, indicating that he wanted to speak to Jock alone. The two lawmen walked through the cabin and down the steps, past Jake Potter, who was sitting hand in hand with Tori, and past Woody Price, who leaned against the rail. They walked into the yard where they could not be overheard.

"What have you got?" asked Jock in a low voice.

"Enough for a search warrant of the Townsend place," answered Bubba. "The girl said that she and Jake Potter's daughter followed Carlton out here last summer. They can testify that he's been using the cellar all along."

"The testimony of two children isn't going to convict him."

"I know. It's all circumstantial now. If we don't turn up some hard evidence, he'll never even go to trial. We'll have to move fast. The girl is scared to death of him, but she won't say she saw him do it. Scoundrel or not, he's still Rudolph's brother to her."

"What difference does that make?"

"Ah, she's a funny kid. She's got more guts than boys twice her age. Now that she's safe, I have a feeling she won't want to do anything that will hurt Rudolph. He's been kind to her. You know how he is with kids. He's like some kind of hero to her. She'll talk herself out of believing Carlton did it, for his sake."

"She thinks he did it?"

"She heard him whistling. But I had to drag it out of her."

Jock sighed.

"Bubba, we ain't got nothing," he said. "In the first place, we'll have to do some mighty fancy talking to get Judge Allen to issue anything against the Townsends. He was in deep with County Pa, and he's mighty fond of Carlton."

"I wasn't thinking of going through Allen," said Bubba. "He's a lost cause. He's gotten Carlton out of more scrapes that I can count."

"Who else is there?" asked Jock. "Judge Allen is the District Judge. We'd have to go through him."

"For the burglaries, yes," replied Bubba, "but not for the kidnaping. That's a federal rap, and all the evidence indicates that the burglaries and the kidnaping were committed by the same man. We can go to the federal judge on kidnaping charges."

"Cunningham? We've got no pull with him. It'll take a couple of days to go through him. Carlton won't be stupid enough to leave evidence around for us to find. We can't lock him up while we sit on our tails in Albany waiting."

"We won't have to," said Bubba with a smile. "I know a way we can get those warrants tonight. Who do you know that is Cunningham's protégé?"

"You mean Baxter Brooks?"

"And who's sick of seeing Carlton Townsend get off with a slap on the wrist from Judge Allen? And who's running for governor next year?"

"Bringing a Townsend to justice would cinch the election for him, wouldn't it?" mused Jock. "I believe you're right. With Brooks on our side, we could pull it off."

Bubba started to smile.

"What is it?" asked Jock.

"Maybe we can save ourselves a lot of trouble. Maybe we don't need Brooks or Cunningham. You said Carlton won't be stupid enough to leave evidence around for us to find. You're right. If he's got anything incriminating, he'll get rid of it before morning. All we've got to do is catch him with it."

"Shadow him tonight? What if it doesn't work?"

"Then we'll go to Cunningham."

"All right, Bubba," Jock agreed, "it's worth a try."

Bubba and Jock descended the stairs to the secret room. Rudolph was standing at the bookcase with a book in his hands. Carlton sat in the desk chair, looking through the contents of the desk drawers.

"Mrs. Cooper is on her way," Bubba said to Rudolph. "Jock and I will have to go to Albany to get the necessary papers to impound the evidence."

Carlton turned in his chair and listened to Bubba's conversation.

"It will take about an hour to get a couple of Jock's deputies down from Albany. He can call them from my house. Would you and Carlton mind staying here until they arrive?"

"Of course not, Bubba," said Rudolph. "Is there anything else we can do?"

"When the men get here, they'll have to cordon off the area for a while. Do I have your permission?"

It was not necessary for the chief to ask permission to do his job, but he had asked the question out of respect for Rudolph.

"Certainly," said Rudolph.

The sound of an engine rumbled in the distance.

"That'll be Elizabeth Cooper and Reese," said Bubba.

Bubba climbed up the stairs, with Rudolph and Jock following him. Carlton remained behind. When the others were gone, he began rifling through the contents of the desk in desperation.

His casual examination of the desk in the presence of witnesses had failed to turn up County Pa's ledger. The book was a private record of illegal payoffs, kickbacks, bribes, stock swindles, and illegal deals. If County Pa ever fell, he planned to take everyone else with him. There were names, dates, account numbers: all County Pa's secrets in black and white. And it was gone.

Whoever planted the loot and stole the money also stole the ledger. Carlton was relieved in one sense, for the ledger had not fallen into the hands of Chief James. But he worried that now he would have to deal with a blackmailer.

As soon as she heard the car approaching, Tori jumped up and ran to meet her grandmother. Reese had explained the situation as well as he could on the way. Mrs. Cooper was shaken by the story, but managed to keep her composure as she greeted Tori. Chief James and the other men came out to the car, and Mrs. Cooper listened quietly as Bubba related what he knew. She appeared calm, but the hand which held Tori's shoulder trembled.

It was decided that Jock and Bubba would ride back to Hayley with Mrs. Cooper and Tori. Reese, Crawford, and Woody would walk back with the dogs. Rudolph and Carlton would stay with the stolen goods, as agreed, until the deputies arrived.

When the others had left, Rudolph returned to Carlton in the cellar. It was cool there, and sleep was the last thing on their minds.

Rudolph watched as Carlton walked to the liquor cabinet and reached for a bottle of sour mash with a practiced hand.

"You've known about this place all along."

"Yep."

Carlton pulled two glasses from the cabinet and poured a shot for both of them. "Have a belt, brother," he said. "You look like you really need it."

"I want the truth," said Rudolph, taking the glass. "I want an explanation, and I want a damn good one."

"I know how it looks," said Carlton. "Somebody has gone to a lot of trouble to make it look that way. I'd like to know what the hell is going on here myself."

He pulled out a Lucky Strike cigarette and lit it.

"All I can do is tell you everything I know," Carlton continued, "and that's going to be hard enough for you to believe."

"What are you talking about?"

"County Pa and this room, mostly."

"Father?" said Rudolph. "What in God's name does he have to do with a child being locked up here and left to die?"

"All right, damn it!" said Carlton. "Let's get one thing straight. I knew about this place. I've spent a lot of time here. But I never locked up that girl and I never stole anything in my life. I don't know who did this, or how he found this place. He must have followed me here. So why did he put all this stuff down here? Why didn't he just sell it? He must have known I would find it, don't you see that? He must have wanted Bubba to find it down here before I did. It doesn't make any sense unless he wants to pin it on me."

The two brothers stared at each other.

"Nobody's accusing you of anything," said Rudolph quietly. "And nobody but me knows that you knew about this place. They can't pin something on you without any evidence. Just tell me what you know. Everything, from the beginning."

"I don't know anything about these crimes," said Carlton. "All I know is what our father did in this room. And now, someone else knows, too."

You're talking in riddles again."

"Papa was a crook, Rudolph."

"What are you saying?"

"I'm saying that every penny we have was gotten illegally, through some scheme or other. Wake up, Rudolph. Look at this place! This was his lair, his secret sanctuary. He conducted all his secret business here, kept all his records here. He put out that story that he would kill any trespassers to *protect* this place. Hell, he didn't even have to lock it up. He scared everybody away."

"How do you know this?" asked Rudolph.

"There was a ledger," Carlton answered, stubbing out his cigarette. "It was full of names, men you know. There are a lot of crooked men in politics, you know that. So did papa. He knew every crooked politician in this state."

"This is nothing new," said Rudolph. His tone was cautious. "I've heard the rumors about him. Politics is fraught with bad apples. You have to deal with some of them. That doesn't make you one of them."

"I'm not talking about small change," said Carlton.

"What *do* you mean, then?" asked Rudolph impatiently. "If you have something to tell me, then do it."

"All right," said Carlton. He walked to the bar and poured himself another shot. "Remember the Farmers Land Bank? How it went under?" His tone was deadly serious. "It went broke because Papa and a couple of others stole most of the money."

Rudolph's head began to throb and his stomach wrenched. He knew that if Carlton spoke the truth, Price Townsend was a criminal who had brought ruin to a great many people.

"You have proof of this?" he asked.

"Yes."

"My God," said Rudolph. He got up and walked to the bookcase. "What else?"

"He got whoever he wanted elected, then got most of the bids for land development and contracting at ungodly high rates. Minus the kickbacks to the man in office, of course." Carlton paused and lit another cigarette.

Rudolph felt his muscles tighten. He stood stiff and straight, looking at the titles of the books in the bookcase.

"Is there more?" he asked.

"It was all there in the ledger. Bribes, kickbacks, payoffs, even a couple of bond swindles and a bunch of illegal loans. There were bank accounts all over. Serial numbers and deposits were in the ledger, but the bank names and locations were in code."

Rudolph realized that his brother was speaking in the past tense. The knot in his stomach tightened.

"May I see this ledger?"

"It's gone. I've looked everywhere. Whoever put that stuff down here and locked up that child took the ledger too. I imagine he thinks we'll pay a lot of money to get it back, more than he stole from us already."

"Stole?" echoed Rudolph. "What do you mean?"

Carlton laughed bitterly.

"The last time I was here there was a suitcase full of County Pa's money. Over two hundred thousand dollars. He must have died before he could do whatever it was he did with his cash. That's gone, too."

"Ah," said Rudolph. He rubbed his forehead and winced. "Your gambling money, I presume?"

"Yep," Carlton admitted. "You knew about that?"

"Oh, yes," said Rudolph absently. "You were discreet enough, but there's not much that didn't get back to me one way or another."

"You never wondered where I got the money?"

"I assumed you were lucky and won now and then. I also know that you stopped gambling months ago. You've stopped a lot of the things that I'm sure you'll agree were nothing but self-destructive. That's why I couldn't believe that you were mixed up in this mess here tonight."

"Thank God you believe me. I don't really care if anyone else does."

"You'd better care," Rudolph snapped. The strain was beginning to tell. "I told you before that if anyone finds out you knew about this place, there will be the devil to pay."

"Damn it, I know that," Carlton answered. "But no one does know. No one except the man who did this."

"Why?" mused Rudolph. "Why would he do this? Who is he and what does he want from us?"

Carlton shook his head. "I don't know. Maybe he just wants someone else to take the blame for him."

"No," said Rudolph. "The man was free and clear. There were no clues. He could have fenced this stuff, just as you said. But he didn't. He set you up, and he must have a reason."

"Why did he stop the burglaries, then? I figured he had moved on months ago, but he didn't. He's been hanging around here, waiting."

My God," Rudolph said. "It's beginning to make sense."

"What is?"

"Think about it," said Rudolph. "The burglaries stopped the Saturday you smashed up your car."

"So what?"

Rudolph shook his head in wonder.

"Don't you see? After the accident you stopped doing a lot of things. This man has tied the end of the burglaries to you, as if you had a change of heart or a change of plans. A smart lawyer could make a case that you had some reason to stop stealing, just like you stopped gambling."

"No," said Carlton, unable to see the sense of it. "When he stopped the burglaries has nothing to do with my accident."

"It does if you were guilty of them," said Rudolph. "Look at it this way. You were stealing from the rich for a lark. You were smart enough to outwit all the lawmen in the state. But then you got hurt and what? Let's say you saw the error of your ways."

"Wait a minute," Carlton interrupted.

"No, it makes sense. Look at it like a lawyer would. You turned over a new leaf, or it just wasn't fun anymore, so you stopped. You didn't just stop the burglaries, you stopped gambling and carousing, too. Maybe you wised up and knew the authorities were hot on your trail, so you decided to quit for a while. You didn't need money, you were a rich Townsend. You just did it all for a lark, to see if you could get away with it. So you stashed all the stuff you stole down here. In a secret room on your property that nobody knew about."

Carlton was silent. It did make sense.

"Good Lord," he said. He picked up the narrative where Rudolph left off. "So when the child discovered my hiding place, I locked her in, to keep her quiet, right?"

The brothers looked at each other with a terrible understanding.

"We have to be very careful," Rudolph began, but when Carlton looked at him suddenly, as if he just remembered something, Rudolph asked, "What is it?"

"The bag," said Carlton. "It's there, at the old barn. If anybody finds that, I'm sunk."

"What are you talking about?" asked Rudolph.

Carlton stood up and put his hands in his pockets. He began to chuckle.

"If I ever find out who did this to me," he laughed in frustration, "I'll . . . ," his voice became serious, "I'll kill him with my bare hands."

"What else is there, for God's sake?" asked Rudolph.

"I found a bag today, a black knapsack. It's his gear. Lock-picking tools, black clothes, flashlight, rope," he remembered his words to Dixie Lee, "everything your friendly cat burglar needs."

A flicker of doubt crossed Rudolph's mind. A shadowy figure loomed before him, turned, and laughed at him with Carlton's face.

Carlton was suddenly aware of Rudolph's silence, and somehow he saw himself through Rudolph's eyes. The realization of how guilty he must look hit him like a hammer. He knew the strength of his unknown enemy for the first time, and he was full of hate and fear. Until that moment, his mind had not admitted the possibility that he could be made to suffer for a crime he did not commit. Now he knew the full extent of his vulnerability.

But Rudolph saw everything in his brother's eyes: the sudden shock, the realization of his vulnerability, the uncertainty of his future. Rudolph settled once and for all in his own mind that Carlton was innocent.

"Carlton," he said quietly, "pour me another shot of this poison."

Carlton took the glass and went to the bar. His voice was shaky as he asked, "Do you still believe me?"

Rudolph answered, "Yes."

Carlton's shoulders relaxed, and he poured the whiskey.

"But I'll be honest with you, boy," said Rudolph slowly. "A minute ago, I wasn't so sure."

Carlton turned and met his gaze. "But now you are?"

"Yes," answered Rudolph, "but that's not the point. If you have trouble convincing your own brother, what will others think?"

"What are we going to do?" asked Carlton.

"Get a grip on yourself," said Rudolph matter-of-factly. "The dogs aren't on your trail yet. The first thing to do is to get rid of that bag, tonight. Take it back wherever you found it, and be sure you wipe all your fingerprints off anything you touched."

"Right," agreed Carlton. "I found it under the old tree at Rainbow Ridge. Wait a minute, wait a minute," said Carlton, his eyes lighting up suddenly.

"What?" asked Rudolph.

Carlton had forgotten Dixie Lee. His heart began to pound. He did not dare tell Rudolph about their love. Rudolph was his only ally. What if the loss of his fiancée turned Rudolph against him? Maybe he would not need her to vouch for his whereabouts that day. He would say nothing for now.

"When did the girl get snatched?" he asked.

"She came up missing after lunch." said Rudolph. "Why?"

"I have an alibi, then. I was with someone. A woman."

"Can you trust her?"

"Of course."

Rudolph studied his face. Was there a hint of gallantry there? Or was it a guilty conscience?

"Don't tell me," said Rudolph. "You'd rather not drag her name through the mud?"

"Not unless I have to."

Rudolph threw up his hands. "I give up," he said.

The sound of a car approaching the cabin broke the stillness of the night.

"That will be the deputies," said Rudolph.

32

Bubba James and Jock Morehouse stood in the shadows of a stand of pecan trees at the edge of the Townsend plantation, their horses waiting behind them. It was after two o'clock in the morning when Reese Jones dropped the Townsend brothers off at the front door. The lawmen watched as Reese drove off and the two men entered the mansion. Lights were turned out on the first floor. Lamps were switched on in two of the upstairs bedrooms.

"Do you know his room?" asked Jock quietly.

"No," replied Bubba, "but someone is still downstairs."

Shortly after the bedroom lamps were turned off, a light at the back of the house came on, and a figure emerged.

"There he is," whispered Bubba. "Let's go."

Carlton walked swiftly to the old barn, opened the door, and was greeted by gently whinnies and snorts from the horses, who recognized the scent of their master. Carlton lit a lantern by the door, bathing the barn in a dim light. He quieted the animals and retrieved the knapsack from its hiding place. He led his mare from her stall, saddled her, and tied the bag to the saddlehorn. The mare nuzzled him affectionately as he led her out of the barn.

Bubba and Jock had seen him saddling the mare in the dim light of the open door, and raced to their own mounts. When Carlton mounted and headed the horse for Hayley, across the open fields, they were ready for him, and followed from a safe distance. The clouds that had hampered the search for Tori earlier had lifted, and the light of the moon now enabled the lawmen to follow from well back. The horses were held at a slow canter, and their hooves made soft gentle thuds on the soft, moist clay as Jock and Bubba followed Carlton.

Carlton crossed Albany Road and kept going. He came to Rainbow

Ridge and broke into the meadow. The men who followed him paused behind the thick stand of trees which bordered the meadow, and watched as Carlton dismounted at the fallen trunk. They saw him take something from his saddle and place it under the arch of the trunk. As he mounted again, he looked around as if he were fearful of discovery. He turned the mare and headed out of the meadow.

The lawmen had left a wide berth for his return, should he take the same way back, and waited as Carlton passed. When they were alone, they walked the horses to the trunk in the meadow, and Bubba dismounted and retrieved the knapsack. If it had been another man, the lawmen would have confronted him openly. But Carlton was a Townsend. Jock and Bubba were risking their careers if they were wrong, and maybe even if they were right.

Bubba gave a low whistle and swung the bag up to Jock. The sheriff examined the contents of the bag.

"We've got him," said Jock.

Strike three, thought Bubba.

BY MONDAY morning the news was all over Hayley. Carlton Townsend had been arrested and charged with the kidnaping and the burglaries. The story was told and retold, and elaborated upon to the point that one could no longer separate fact from fantasy. The story broke big in the Albany papers that morning. Scores of Carlton's former girlfriends were thrilled at the possibility that their Carlton was the daring cat burglar. Locals made jokes about it. Politicians found themselves strangely threatened, and scurried to learn the whole story. It was the biggest bombshell to hit south Georgia since the death of County Pa.

Dixie Lee was shocked. She knew Carlton's plan to catch the thief had backfired. Her father had not been home since she learned of the arrest. She had to see Bubba, to tell him he was wrong. She had been with Carlton that day; he could not have kidnapped the child. They were fools, her father the chief among them. She would not let this happen. She must tell them about finding the bag. She took the first train to Albany.

Rudolph convinced his mother that it was all a mistake, and that it would soon be straightened out. She had been shattered by the arrest Sunday afternoon. Chief James and Sheriff Morehouse had explained the facts to her briefly, as they held her in high regard, although they were not legally obliged to say anything.

Carlton had gone with them calmly, and did not seem surprised that they had come for him, although he remained silent. The lawmen were wary of him, for he seemed like a caged animal, waiting calmly to escape and tear them limb from limb.

Rudolph's behavior also puzzled Bubba and Jock. He had made no protest to the arrest. He accepted what was said without interruption, as if he expected it. His manner was calm and cold, with the same leashed outrage they sensed in his brother. Bubba found himself affected by this, as his respect for Rudolph was total. There was more to this than he knew. Something was going on between the brothers that had a direct bearing on the case, and he was determined to find out what it was.

Rudolph told his mother everything he knew. She had to be told about County Pa, because Rudolph fully expected a blackmail attempt by the man who was behind the framing of his brother. There was a possibililty that the man intended to let the ledger fall into the hands of the authorities, if his motive was to ruin the Townsend family. So he told his mother the truth. The color had drained from her face as she listened, saying nothing. The seriousness of Carlton's situation became clear to her, and seemed to remain foremost in her thoughts, even as the truth about her husband was revealed. She asked Rudolph to get her a cup of tea, but he poured her a brandy instead, and she accepted it.

She would speak only about Carlton, and refused to discuss Price Townsend with Rudolph. Rudolph could not tell how much his mother already knew about the extent of her late husband's crimes, and he had no wish to know. He chose to interpret Laura's reaction his own way, that her silence about County Pa was a type of shock. It was too much to face all at once, and she chose to concentrate only on her son's release. She insisted that Rudolph immediately contact their lawyer, Thomas Moore in Atlanta, which he did.

AT EIGHT-THIRTY Monday morning Rudolph was on his way to meet Moore in Albany when he stopped off at the home of Elizabeth Cooper. He wanted to explain to Mrs. Cooper that Carlton was innocent, and to talk to Tori. Rudolph sat with Mrs. Cooper in the living room. She listened to him intently, carefully, as he told her as much of the story as he felt he could. She was still shaken by the kidnaping, and fiercely protective of her granddaughter, but she was open to Rudolph, and did not seem to have condemned Carlton as many had done.

"I'm very worried about her," Mrs. Cooper replied as Rudolph asked about Tori. "She won't tell me much about it. She keeps insisting that she is all right, and that she doesn't know who did it. She's insisting too much. She's holding back something, and it worries me terribly. She should not carrry such a burden."

"May I talk to her?" asked Rudolph.

"Paul is coming. He's on his way now. I hoped that when he got here, she would—"

She did not finish her sentence as she stared thoughtfully into the face of Rudolph. He was a good man, a kind man, and he had been like a big brother to Tori. A flash of insight told her the truth. Tori was trying to protect Rudolph. If that were true, then she must believe, like Chief James, that Carlton was guilty.

Elizabeth knew Carlton. He was wild and irreverent, but he was not capable of this horror. She had always been able to see people as they truly were, beneath the surface cruelty or false pride. She had always thought of Carlton as an unhappy, bitter young man, but not without principles, not without loyalty or honor. Carlton himself would have scoffed at her assessment of his character only a year before, but it would have been accurate then, as it was now.

"Rudolph," she said carefully, "I think Tori may be trying to protect you. She must think Carlton is guilty. It would explain her behavior."

"Mrs. Cooper, the whole world seems to think he is guilty. I cannot blame her. I don't want her to protect me. She must tell the truth. I have to make her understand that. And you as well."

Mrs. Cooper agreed with him. If Carlton was innocent, he must not be convicted. If he was guilty, the facts would condemn him. In either case, the truth must be told with nothing withheld.

"You may speak to her," she said, rising.

She went to Tori's room and came back with her. Tori came slowly to Rudolph and hugged him. Her brown eyes were troubled and cautious.

"Sit down, honey," said Rudolph. "I want to talk to you. Your grandmother tells me you are frightened, that you are not telling her everything. Is that true?"

"I don't know," she replied. Her voice trembled.

"That won't do, Tori," he continued gently. "I'm going to ask you a question now, and I want you to tell me the truth. You must tell the truth, because if you don't, you will be lying to me, and to your grandmother, and to God. You must not lie to me, Tori. Now tell me, do you think that Carlton locked you in the cellar?"

Tori's eyes filled with tears. She wanted to run out of the room. She could not deny it, not now, not after Rudolph had summoned God Himself as a witness. She did not answer.

"Answer him, child," said Mrs. Cooper.

Tori didn't understand why they wanted her to admit this. She looked at Rudolph, with a shadow of her old defiance in her eyes.

"Yes," she admitted, finally. "It was Carlton."

Rudolph said, "Good. Now that's over with, and I can ask you the things I really want to know."

Tori was puzzled. "But Rudolph, don't you care that Carlton . . . ." Her voice trailed off, her question half-posed.

Rudolph looked at her intently. "Of course I care. I want to see the man who did this to you punished. If my brother did it, he will be punished. But if he didn't, we have to find out who did. I don't blame you for thinking it was Carlton. A lot of evidence points to him. The only thing in his favor is that you didn't actually see him do it."

"I know," Tori interrupted. "I didn't see him, so nobody can make me say he did it. I wasn't going to say that he—"

"Stop it," said Rudolph, "and listen to me. You will not help me or

my brother if you are not absolutely truthful and honest about everything that happened. Not just to me, to everyone, do you understand?
This is not a game, Tori. You must do as I say."

"Okay," said Tori quietly, her eyes wide.

"Why do you think Carlton locked you in?"

"It was his secret room," she said. "No one but him goes there."

"You went, didn't you?"

"Yes."

"Then someone else may have too, right?"

"Do you think so?" she asked.

"What I think isn't important," answered Rudolph. "What else
made you think it was Carlton?"

"I guess the song he was whistling."

"What song?"

Tori couldn't whistle, so she hummed it for him.

"He always sings that song," said Tori. "It has naughty words, too."

She was right, of course. Rudolph looked at her thoughtfully.

"Have you ever heard Carlton whistle it before? Not sing it or hum
it, whistle it."

Tori's forehead wrinkled. She had not thought about it. She thought
of him always humming the song.

"I don't think I have. Is it important?"

Rudolph glanced at Mrs. Cooper. She nodded.

"Tori, if he sang it you would have recognized his voice for sure. But
anybody can whistle a tune." He paused for a moment. "Except you, or
Carlton. He never could learn to whistle either, Tori."

Tori was stunned by the truth of it. Could she have been wrong? It
was the tune that had convinced her. But she remembered that the man's
laugh had been so deep and strange. It didn't sound like Carlton at all.

"Rudolph," she said slowly, "maybe it really wasn't Carlton."

"Why, honey?"

"Because he laughed, and it was a laugh I never heard before. It was
deep and scary. Carlton's got a high, funny, laugh. You know how
Carlton laughs. He makes everybody else laugh, too."

Rudolph looked at Tori and waited. She had to realize it herself.

Tori's mind raced, coming back to the same facts again and again. She really didn't know who it was, she really didn't! It was even beginning to make more sense that it was not Carlton. The evil laugh. It was deep, sinister, it chilled her to the bone. It was like the laugh of a demon, like the laugh of the ghost of County Pa! A look of shock came over her face.

"What is it?" asked Rudolph.

Tori wanted to ask him, but she didn't want to sound foolish. Could it have been the ghost of County Pa? No, ghosts aren't real. Ghosts can't slam doors and hammer nails and make the sound of footsteps when they walk. But Boozie had said the ghost of County Pa walks like a man in the daylight. Boozie claimed to have seen him many times, spoken to him even.

Suddenly the truth hit Tori like lightning. It wasn't a ghost Boozie saw. It was a real, live man. A man who trespassed on County Pa's land. A man who needed a hiding place, where no one else would dare to set foot.

"Boozie!" Tori exclaimed. "Boozie has seen him, the man who walks on the preserve. She claims he's the ghost of County Pa come back to life, but he looks like a human being during the day when she sees him! She's not seeing things, like we thought. She's seen the man who locked me in there. She's seen the real cat burglar!"

33

When Dixie Lee James stepped off the train in Albany, it was just past ten in the morning, but the heat was already stifling. The heavy humidity wilted the stiffest collars, and weighted the city down to a slow stroll. Dixie Lee's light brown hair, streaked with gold from the sun, was damp against the back of her neck as she walked to the center of town. More than once she turned the head of an appreciative male, for she wore a fetching sundress which left her shoulders bare.

She paid no notice to anyone, and her steps were quick and sure. There was a strange mixture of fear and determination in her blue eyes. Well acquainted with the town, she soon found her way to the Albany police headquarters. She paused at the door, composing herself, and then walked in.

"Good morning, sir," she said to the uniformed man behind the desk, flashing her prettiest smile.

The man got to his feet politely, smiling at the lovely young visitor.

"Mornin', Miss. What can I do for you?"

"I'm Dixie Lee James. I'm looking for my father, Chief James from Hayley. Can you tell me where I might find him?"

"I haven't seen him this mornin', Miss James," replied the man, "but it's most likely he's over to Sheriff Morehouse's office in the courthouse basement, across the way yonder."

"Oh," said Dixie Lee with a pretty pout, "I see." She looked around the room for a moment, then returned to the man. "Are you in charge here, sir?" She batted her eyes at him innocently.

"Yes, Miss," the man smiled. "Sergeant Larry Hardy, at your service."

"Well, Sergeant," she said, "it's so nice to meet you. I wonder if you might do me a small favor?"

"Anything, Miss James, if I'm able."

"You have Carlton Townsend here in one of your cells, do you not?"

"Yes, I do," the man beamed proudly. "Locked up good and tight, he is."

"You know Rudolph Townsend, his brother?"

"Oh, yes, everybody knows Mr. Rudolph."

"Sergeant," said Dixie Lee in a low voice, as if she were granting a confidence, "I don't have to tell you how distressing this whole matter has been to Mr. Rudolph. It's all a terrible mistake, of course. Why, just this morning, Judge Allen was fit to be tied over the whole thing."

The man saw the drift of her meaning, and changed his attitude appropriately.

"Yes, Miss James," he answered conspiratorially, "it was a whale of a shock to all of us, them bringin' Mr. Carlton in under a federal warrant and all. The whole town's buzzin' with it."

Dixie Lee turned eyes full of childlike confusion to Sergeant Hardy.

"I don't know what to do, Sergeant," she said helplessly. "I have a message for Carlton from Rudolph. Mr. Rudolph is my fiancé, you know. I hoped to find my father here, so he could arrange for me to see Carlton for a moment, but—"

The man came from behind the desk instantly.

"Don't think another thing about it, Miss James," he beamed. "I'll be glad to let you see the boy. He ain't goin' nowhere."

"Why, Sergeant," Dixie Lee smiled, "how kind of you. You will save me oodles of time."

"No problem at all, Miss. You just set yourself down for a minute and I'll take care of everything."

"Thank you, Sergeant. I'll be sure and mention your kindness to my father."

The man hurried out, to take the prisoner to the small conference room. No daughter of Bubba James was going to trek past the drunks to Carlton's cell if he had any say in the matter. Besides, what could be the harm? He'd just keep the cuffs on Carlton and stand outside the door. It wasn't policy, but nothing would happen, he'd make sure of that.

He led Dixie Lee to the conference room usually reserved for interrogations and lawyers.

"Now, I'll be right outside the door here, Miss James," he said. "Take all the time you need."

"You're a darling, Sergeant Hardy," replied Dixie Lee. She had not dared to look at Carlton, who sat waiting, his cuffed hands resting on a table. Dixie Lee kept the false smile on her face until the sergeant closed the door.

She turned to Carlton, her face flooded with concern. He looked at her with quiet awareness and calm restraint. His caution was an unspoken signal to her, and she walked to him casually, aware that the sergeant would be glancing through the window now and again. She sat opposite him.

"Darling," she whispered, but he cut her off.

"I don't want you here," he said quietly. "It's no place for a lady."

"I had to see you," she whispered. "I can't believe this is happening. It's a mistake—a horrible, ghastly mistake." Her voice choked. "I don't understand what's happening."

"There's no time," he said quickly. "I know you don't understand, but I do. I don't have time to explain it now. Go to Rudolph. He can explain everything. I'm here because someone has set me up as the cat burglar. Set me up carefully and patiently. Rudolph can fill you in later, but now I want to tell you something."

She fought back tears and looked at him expectantly.

"Listen to me very carefully," he continued. "You must not go to your father; not yet."

"But why?" she gasped. "You were with me when the child disappeared. I'm your alibi. I must tell them."

"In good time," he replied.

Dixie Lee saw the finality in his eyes. She nodded, waiting for him to tell her more.

"We're in a touchy situation, you and I. Rudolph is my staunch defender at this point, and I don't want to drive a wedge between us by telling him about you if I can help it. Not yet.

"Your father already has it in for me," he continued, with a mocking smile, "no doubt because I had the poor taste to kiss his daughter in a barn once. If he finds out I've managed to steal you away from Rudolph on top of everything else, he'll want to hang me himself."

"You're wrong," she pleaded. "I can make him understand. I know I can."

"You may have to, before this is over," Carlton said. "Listen to me. I don't know what evidence they have against me. Hell, I haven't even talked to my lawyer. He's on his way from Atlanta now. Let's don't show the prosecution all our cards. If we have to, we'll play the hand out, when the time is right."

"But—"

"No arguments, Dixie Lee. I will not have you dragged into this unless I must. You have to trust me. I'm not telling you to lie, just to keep silent for a time. Do you understand me?"

"Yes, Carlton, I understand. But I don't agree with you. If they knew you had an alibi, none of this would be necessary."

"Are you so sure they would believe you?"

"Why, of course they would. Why wouldn't they?"

"You're a woman in love," he said. "Maybe you'd say anything to save the man you love. Women have perjured themselves before."

"You can't be serious," she said, with hurt and incredulity in her voice. "I would never—"

"I know you wouldn't," Carlton interrupted. Their time was short. "I wouldn't break in houses or terrorize children either, but look where I am."

Tears filled Dixie Lee's blue eyes. She reached across the table to touch his hand. Her eyes dropped and she caught the beginning of a sob in her throat.

"Carlton, I love you so much."

He waited for her to raise her eyes to his. He held her eyes with a long, possessive gaze that seared her soul. She was filled with him, and her heart beat wildly.

He spoke the words, unnecessarily, "I love you, too. And I'll never let you go. Never."

He pulled his hand away and sat back in the chair. He could not bear this exquisite torture, for he longed to hold her. He contemplated her with sudden amusement.

"Maybe I would have made a hell of a cat burglar," he said, letting his eyes roam over her appreciatively.

Dixie Lee, conscious of the sergeant outside, gathered her wits and replied with a weak, knowing voice, "To what are you referring, sir?"

They both knew the answer. He smiled that old, irreverent Carlton smile, and his eyes twinkled. Dixie Lee could not help herself. She was bewitched, and she found herself smiling too. She was amazed by his undaunted confidence. In this desperate situation, he was making jokes.

There were voices outside the door. Carlton recognized the voice of his brother with a sinking heart. So did Dixie Lee, and she looked at Carlton, her eyes filled with confusion.

"It's too late," he muttered. "Let me do all the talking. Just play it by ear."

The door opened and Rudolph strode in, curiosity and caution etched in his face, having been told by Sergeant Hardy that his fiancée was delivering his nonexistent message to the prisoner. He was followed by a tall man in a dark gray business suit.

"Thank you, Sergeant," said Rudolph. "We would appreciate a little privacy for a few minutes, while my brother confers with his lawyer."

Sergeant Hardy nodded and closed the door. He looked back at Rudolph through the glass, nodded again, and padded back to his chair at the front desk.

Rudolph took in the scene at a glance. There was an undeniable tension in the air, a strange sense of conflict. He knew Carlton too well, and had known Dixie Lee too dearly not to understand what was going on. Unbelievable as it seemed, they had fallen in love with each other. He could see that they were afraid for him to know. His emotions were too complex to explore at the moment, for gaining his brother's release was foremost in his mind, but in the depths of his consciousness he felt a sense of relief.

"I'm glad you're here, Dixie Lee," he said calmly. "You may be able to help."

Dixie Lee was surprised at his greeting, for he asked no questions and demanded no explanations. She stole a look at Carlton, who avoided her glance. Carlton's face was carefully blank. Dixie Lee called upon the actress in herself, and looked back at Rudolph with strained innocence.

But her initial reaction was observed by Thomas Moore. He read both guilt and confusion in her eyes, and guilt was his business. He realized he was watching a drama between these three people unfold before him. His success as a criminal defense lawyer depended on his ability to understand the complexity of human nature and human relationships. His instincts told him that his clients were engaged in role-playing, and his instincts were never wrong.

"Tom, you know Carlton," Rudolph said, and Carlton nodded to the lawyer as Rudolph added, "and this is my fiancée, Dixie Lee James. You've met her father, I believe, Hayley's chief of police."

"A pleasure, my dear," said Thomas.

As he and the lawyer sat down at the table, Rudolph said, "I'm afraid I was a little late meeting Tom this morning, and I haven't gone over many of the facts with him. Carlton, just start at the beginning and tell him what you know."

Carlton began to relate his side of the story. It was a whitewashed version, for he said nothing of the ledger or of his liaison with Dixie Lee. Dixie Lee could not help observing Thomas Moore with curiosity. She knew who he was, of course. He was the only lawyer in the state of Georgia whose name was a household word. He was not what she expected, for he seemed neither imposing nor impressive. He was tall and slender, and had the look of academia about him. She could easily picture him in a library, surrounded by stacks and stacks of musty old books. He was not a young man, but his smooth, unlined, boyish face belied his age.

His face was pale and his hands were smooth and white, as if he never saw the sun. Dark-haired and clean-shaven, his features were so regular they bordered on the nondescript, the type of face that is hard to remember. His eyes were his one compelling feature, large brown eyes that were at once sharp and kind. He was almost apologetic in his manner, and his bearing was humble. As the lawyer listened patiently to Carlton, Dixie Lee was flooded with hope and calm feelings. There was something about Thomas Moore that seemed to flow to those around him: confidence.

As Carlton told his story, Rudolph found himself putting pieces of his own puzzle together. Dixie Lee's strange moodiness. Her hesitance to announce their wedding date. It all fit. He remembered the way Carlton and Dixie Lee avoided each other at parties and dinners, their strained politeness. He had mistaken it for dislike. In truth, they had been fighting their feeling for each other.

Rudolph was amazed at the depth of change this implied in his brother. He had never known Carlton to sacrifice his feelings before. In all those moments, he knew that Carlton had made no move toward Dixie Lee. How they finally came to be together, he did not know, but if they could have prevented it for his sake, Rudolph knew they would have done so. So Dixie Lee was the mystery woman Carlton was reluctant to reveal as his alibi.

If they only knew, he thought, that I am just as guilty. He had not told Dixie Lee that their romance was over. He had not told her he was in love with Camilla. There had not been time.

The calm intelligent mind of Thomas Moore took in every nuance of Carlton's whitewashed tale. When Carlton finished, he said, "I would like to speak to each of you alone. I will take Carlton first. Rudolph, please take Dixie Lee into the lobby. I will call you back in a few minutes."

When they had gone, Thomas turned to Carlton.

"Son," he said pointedly, "I will ask you once. Are you guilty or innocent of these crimes?"

"Innocent," Carlton replied.

The two men measured each other for a moment. Thomas seemed satisfied with Carlton's plea.

"Yes," he said, "I believe you are innocent. I will take your case, but I will tell you now what I tell all my clients. If you are guilty, I will find you out. If you have lied to me about your innocence, I will not defend you. I am free to chose whom I defend. I have never chosen to use my skills to help a guilty man go free.

"And now, if I am to defend you successfully, there must be no secrets between us. You are withholding information that is vital to this case. You cannot hope to protect others and come out of this unscathed. If you cannot be truthful with me, I cannot help you." He met Carlton's gaze squarely. "Trust me, son. Let's have it, warts and all."

Carlton hesitated. He was searching the lawyer's eyes, looking for any sign of duplicity. He found none. An unspoken agreement passed between them. Carlton would trust him with the truth.

He told the lawyer of County Pa's crimes, and the theft of the damning ledger and the money. He told of his scandalous lifestyle after the death of his father, of his accident, and of his change of heart. He told of his former bitter rivalry with Rudolph, which had lately undergone such a radical change. And he told the truth about Dixie Lee, and that he had been with her when the child was kidnapped.

Thomas listened dispassionately. The relationships became clear. The shadowy figure of the real culprit began to take shape. The Townsend brothers were perhaps too close to the situation to see their enemy clearly, but the lawyer was not. Their enemy was close to them, and diabolically clever. He was close enough to know their habits, their feelings, even their secrets. He had instigated the robberies for the sole purpose of setting up Carlton as a thief. For some unknown reason, this mysterious man hated them, and now he seemed to hold all the cards. County Pa had made many enemies, but this enemy seemed to go beyond the norm. Why did he hate the sons of County Pa? Thomas had some deep digging to do. He nodded silently, stood up, and extended his hand to Carlton.

"Thank you for your confidence," he said. "I have a good many people to talk to before I can tell you how we are to proceed. Be patient and try not to worry."

Carlton shook his hand as best he could in view of the handcuffs, and got to his feet.

"You believe me, don't you." It was statement of fact, not a question.

"Yes," Thomas replied. "I certainly do. Now go back to your cell and speak to no one about the case, with one exception."

Carlton stiffened as he felt the lawyer's penetrating stare. He knew already what he would ask him to do.

"You want me to tell Rudolph about Dixie Lee."

"You must," Thomas replied. "She's your alibi. You've held it back only for his sake. Get it out in the open, now. You can't throw barriers in your own path." He paused and looked at the floor. Putting his hands in his pockets, he continued, "Besides, he knows already."

Carlton was taken aback by this statement, and waited cautiously for the lawyer to look up. "How could he?"

"How could he not?" Thomas smiled sympathetically. "It was written all over you both when we walked in. Even I guessed."

Carlton sighed. "God," he muttered. "He didn't say a thing."

"Talk to him. I'll get back to you tomorrow."

Thomas went to the door and called for Sergeant Hardy. Carlton was taken to his cell and Dixie Lee was brought in. The lawyer told her that Carlton had told him of their relationship. Thomas confirmed with Dixie Lee that she had been with him on the day in question, from about half past noon until around four-thirty. She also confirmed that she had been with him when he found the black bag, and that Carlton had planned to try to catch the thief himself, using the bag as bait.

Thomas dismissed Dixie Lee, and Rudolph came to the conference room.

"He told you the rest of it?" asked Rudolph as he seated himself opposite Thomas.

"He did."

There was a strained silence for a moment, then Rudolph continued,

"I haven't had a chance to tell you, but something new turned up this morning. It may be important."

"Yes?"

"Tori Tanner. She seems to think that a friend of hers has seen the real thief."

34

After lunch, Rudolph and Thomas Moore rode to Hayley to talk to Boozie.

"She should be home by now," said Rudolph as he turned the car onto Hemon Road. "I stopped by this morning. That's why I was late meeting you. Boozie's grandmother said they expected her around noon today."

"How old is the child?" asked Thomas.

"Eight, nine. Something around there."

"You know her well?"

Rudolph smiled apologetically and glanced at Thomas.

"They're country people, good people. I know her mother well, Mary Lee. She's been a maid at the club for years. She used to bring Boozie along with her sometimes. The child's grandfather was a sort of hero around these parts, to the children anyway. Ottis was his name. He died a few months ago of snakebite. Saved Tori and Jessie Potter from a rattlesnake."

Thomas caught something behind Rudolph's tone.

"What is it about Boozie that you want to tell me?"

Rudolph laughed at his perceptiveness.

"She's the county's next Delight Diviner."

"Say again?" asked Thomas.

"Delight Diviner," said Rudolph. "The local fortune teller and prophet of sorts. Supposed to see the future and grant wishes. There's supposed to be some secret potion handed down that makes wives irresistible to their husbands, and so forth. Big stuff to the local Negroes."

"I see," said Thomas. "And Boozie is the chosen successor?"

"To her old Aunt Colley. Lives up in the backwaters somewhere. Boozie is blessed by the spirits, they say. This area is fraught with legends.

I guess it was natural for the ghost of County Pa to spring up."

"Many legends have their basis in fact, my friend," said Thomas wryly. "We shall see."

They reached the Washington place and turned into the front yard. Doreen watched from her chair on the wide wooden porch as the car came to a stop. Mary Lee appeared at the front door, which was standing open, with a bowl in her hands. Rudolph and Thomas walked up to the porch.

"Afternoon, Doreen, Mary Lee," said Rudolph. He spoke to them with respect, as he always did.

Doreen nodded, her hawk's eyes fixed on them with curiosity.

"Afternoon, Mr. Rudolph," said Mary Lee warmly. "What brings you here?"

"I'd like to speak to Boozie, Mary Lee, if you don't mind. It will only take a few minutes."

Mary Lee leaned her head to one side and considered them.

"To my baby?" she asked. "What about, suh?"

Thomas Moore answered for him. "About the ghost of County Pa."

"Lawd have mercy!" muttered Doreen, who shook her head and returned to shelling peas.

Mary Lee was surprised as well, but was glad to oblige Rudolph, who had always been kind to her.

"She be inside, Mr. Rudolph. I'll get her."

Mary Lee disappeared into the weather-beaten house. Rudolph exchanged glances with Thomas.

"Let me handle it," said Thomas in a low voice.

Rudolph nodded.

Mary Lee returned with Boozie, and shooed her down the steps. Thomas smiled as he saw the prissy child descend the wooden stoop. She sat down on the middle step.

"Hello, Boozie," said Rudolph. "This is Tom. He wants to ask you some questions."

Thomas sat down on the bottom step and Rudolph followed suit. They were just about eye level with the child.

"Boozie," Thomas began, "Mr. Rudolph tells me that you have seen the ghost of County Pa. Is that true?"

Boozie looked pleased, and answered, "Yes, suh."

"You saw him in the Townsend game preserve?"

Boozie nodded and threw Doreen a superior glance.

"What did he look like?"

"He look like his picture," she whispered conspiratorially, her eyes narrowing with confident knowledge.

"What picture?" asked Thomas, glancing at Rudolph.

"The big one in the hall," Boozie said. "The one with the dogs."

"You mean the portrait in the ballroom at Radium Springs, Boozie?" asked Rudolph.

Boozie nodded.

Rudolph glanced quizzically at Thomas. Surely the girl couldn't mean the man really looked like his father.

"You saw him clearly? How close was he to you?" Thomas asked.

"Close as to the door," said Boozie, looking behind her to the front door, ten or twelve feet behind them. "He close enough to get me if he want."

"And he looked just like the man in the picture?"

"It the ghost of County Pa, all right. Just like the picture."

"Boozie," said Thomas carefully, "did he look like a ghost or like a man?" He stressed the last word.

"He look like a man in the daytime. Ghost at nighttime."

"Did he speak to you?" asked Thomas.

"He tell me who he be."

"Tell us what he said."

"He say, 'Boozie'," she scowled and shook her finger menacingly, "'you keep yo kin off my land. You keep everybody off my land'."

"How did he know your name?" asked Thomas.

"He know everybody's name." answered Boozie simply, as if Thomas should have known this. "Ghosts know things, know all things."

Rudolph and Thomas exchanged glances.

"What else did he say?"

"He say nobody but me can see him in daytime, but he wrong."

"Someone else saw him?"

"Pap."

Thomas looked questioningly at Mary Lee, who answered, "Her grampa, Ottis."

"Ottis saw the ghost, Boozie?" continued Thomas.

"He saw him the day he . . . went home to Jesus."

"All right, Boozie," said Thomas. "One last question. Are you sure he looked exactly like the man in the picture?"

Boozie nodded. "He the same. But he come back strong and fit again, like all ghosts do."

"What do you mean?"

"He came back in years, he leave his age behind."

"He was young again?"

"Yes, suh. Like Mr. Rudolph."

A chill swept over Rudolph.

"True," a chilly voice seemed to whisper to him, "it's all true."

It was like a warning, a supernatural omen. His eyes widened and he felt a strange force surrounding him. He questioned his sanity. Boozie was staring at him. Her gaze held him transfixed and for a split second he sensed magic in the child. Then it was gone.

Thomas questioned Doreen and Mary Lee and found that Ottis had spoken of seeing the ghost when he was delirious. They had given it no thought, the women said. He had been out of his head. They could not remember much of what he had said, only that County Pa was too near to Ottis's family. Ottis had wanted him to "go back to the cabin" where he belonged.

RUDOLPH STARED at the road ahead as he drove back to Albany. Thomas was speaking, but Rudolph wasn't listening. Something, a feeling, a gnawing answer, struggled for recognition at the back of his mind. He could not throw off the feelings he experienced at the Washington house.

"He's young," Thomas was saying, "we know that much. He's agile and strong. I went over the evidence with Sheriff Morehouse this morning. They didn't call him a cat for nothing. He scaled walls up to three stories. And he's an expert with locks."

Rudolph was not listening. He had a sickening feeling in the pit of his stomach. The answer. It was there, somewhere in his mind, and he was afraid to let it surface.

"We cannot discount what the child said about his appearance," Thomas went on. "Her grandfather apparently recognized him, too."

Rudolph forced himself to listen, and he said, "Ottis was a religious man, Tom. He was never known to tell a lie. If he said he saw my father, he did. He wouldn't be capable of lying, even in madness."

"Then there are two possibilities," mused the lawyer. "Either the man has gone to great pains to disguise himself to look just like your late father, to perpetuate the legend of the ghost; or he *does* look just like your father."

Rudolph sensed it again, the dangerous truth, the terrible answer. It was deep and strong within him. It was just out of reach.

Thomas contemplated his silent companion.

"Rudolph," he said, "you look like *you've* just seen a ghost."

"Maybe I have," he said. "I have the strangest feeling about this. I can't explain it."

Thomas nodded and looked to the road. His mind was like a machine, sorting facts and cataloging data at a dizzying speed. If the most logical explanation was the correct one, it would break many hearts. He knew he would concentrate first on finding this vision of a dead man.

35

That evening Thomas Moore hurried to keep an appointment with County Pa's friend and associate, Judge Jacob G. Allen. The judge's estate was called Springvilla. It was about ten miles north of Albany, not far from the rented home of Woody Price. Judge Allen's house sat high on a hill whose slopes were covered with huge, hundred-year-old oak trees placed as though they were meant to frame the mansion like a necklace of emeralds. The slope led to a large pond, large enough to contain, in its center, an island, also covered with huge trees. Bathed in moonlight, it was an arresting sight to Thomas as he turned into the entrance and drove around the pond to the house.

Judge Allen and Thomas were old sparring partners, friendly enemies in the strange rivalry that lawyers have with judges or police officials who contend with them from opposite sides of a courtroom. One could not be in Thomas's position in the state and not be aware of the powers that be. For the past twenty-five years, the power was County Pa in south Georgia. Neither Rudolph nor Carlton could have known that Thomas Moore was aware of the corruption of their father's power. He was also aware of County Pa's relationship with Judge Allen.

They were the untouchables, Judge Allen and County Pa, and hundreds like them in every state. They were political brokers, buying and selling the law, always for a profit, always behind closed doors. It was a closed society, and Thomas moved within its confines only by virtue of his nonacknowledgment of its existence.

He needed Judge Allen's help. Revenge was the powerful motive of the real cat burglar, revenge against Carlton or revenge against County Pa. Thomas's instincts told him to look first for an enemy of the father, and for that, there was no better place to start than Judge Allen. The enemies of County Pa and the enemies of Judge Allen would be the same.

Thomas's knock at the front door was answered by a pretty teenage girl.

"You'd be Mr. Moore," she said in a soft Southern drawl. She leaned against the door jamb. "I'm Audrey," she said. "Daddy's expecting you, I believe."

"It's an honor to meet you Miss Audrey," he said. "You are a rare and beautiful flower, and indeed most charming." He kissed her hand.

Audrey's eyes widened at this unexpected attention. She was usually ignored by the grown-ups she knew, especially the serious, harried associates of her father who called from time to time.

Thomas smiled tolerantly and entered the hall. A gruff voice bellowed from nearby.

"Audrey Jane! Shut the damn door!"

The girl closed the door meekly, embarrassed to be treated as a child in front of Thomas.

"Come on down here, Tom," the voice bellowed. "I haven't got all night."

Thomas nodded to Audrey, giving her his full attention.

"Thank you, Miss Audrey. I can find my own way."

He turned and headed in the direction of the judge's voice, finding the study easily.

Judge Allen looked up at the familiar figure hesitating in the doorway. Thomas Moore never failed to irritate the judge with his unpretentious manner. He scowled. The lawyer was a crafty genius, a bedeviling pest, but the judge was crafty himself, and was used to burying witch hunters. But you never knew where you stood with this one. He never overplayed his hand. For that, Thomas had earned the judge's grudging respect.

Thomas walked to the big walnut desk and extended his hand to the stocky, balding man. Judge Allen was fiftyish, with horn-rimmed glasses and a short bristly beard. His manner was brusque, irritable, and authoritative. He was sharp and impatient, a formidable, no-nonsense opponent.

"Thank you for seeing me on such short notice, sir," said Thomas.

He smiled apologetically and sat down opposite the judge in a large leather wingback chair.

Judge Allen was never sure if Thomas's manner was simple condescension or actual humility. It always caught him off guard, and usually amused him, as it did now. He fixed his hawklike stare on the lawyer and nodded appreciatively. The faintest shadow of a smile twisted the corner of his mouth.

"You're defending Price Townsend's boy," he said, leaning forward and clasping his big hands together, resting them on the desk in front of him. "What do you want from me?"

"I will not waste your time asking for your help," Thomas answered. "I know I have that, as you are fond of young Carlton. I also know that there is not much which goes on in this district of which you are unaware, so I assume you are familiar with the major facts of the case."

Judge Allen raised one eyebrow in acquiescence, and waited silently for the lawyer to continue.

"I intend to try to set the date for a bond hearing before Judge Cunningham tomorrow morning," Thomas went on. "I would like to get the boy out of jail as soon as possible, of course, but you and I both know that the judicial process is fraught with delays."

The Judge sat back in his chair, impatient now for the man to finish, as he understood his meaning.

"With your considerable influence, sir, you could be of great help to us in getting the case on the docket within the next few days. I realize that—"

Judge Allen interrupted him.

"I'll see what I can do," he said impatiently. "That's small potatoes, Tom. What do you really want?"

There was a brief silence as the two men contemplated each other.

"Information," Thomas answered carefully. "Perhaps information that only you can give me."

A hint of amusement flickered in the older man's eyes. This was what he was waiting for—the beginning of the game. Now we will see, he thought, how well the mouse can bargain with the cat.

"My appraisal of the case thus far," said Thomas, "is that the Townsend boy has been set up by a man bent on revenge, a man willing to risk his own life to bring ruin to this boy or to this family. I suspect that it is the Townsend family name that this unknown man is out to destroy. I suspect that the motive of revenge was engendered by some argument with the late Price Townsend, rather than with either of his sons."

Judge Allen smiled slightly. He knew what the lawyer would ask. He knew also how difficult it would be for him to answer Tom's question. To name the enemies of County Pa would be to list the dead man's offenses, many of which were joint ventures with the judge himself. He felt almost a twinge of sympathy for the lawyer. The mouse was cornered. There was no way Tom could ask, and no way he could be answered.

Thomas paused expectantly in his statement, knowing the judge was clever enough to perceive the dilemma. A look of complete understanding passed between them; the facts were accepted, the problem evident, the question unspoken. If there was any knowledge which could be helpful to the case, Thomas knew, it could be passed to him indirectly, anonymously, by a third party. There were many ways to do it without involving the judge directly. It was only left to the lawyer to make this option clear to the judge.

"Sir," said Thomas, "I have given this matter a great deal of thought. The motive of revenge usually stems from one or two things; love or money. The scope of this unknown man's vindictiveness leads me to believe that money is not the issue here." He paused. "I believe, sir, that we are dealing with betrayal, and betrayal on the very deepest level of human experience."

Judge Allen frowned, his interest rekindled. He realized there was great perception in this train of thought.

"If your friendship with Price Townsend was such that he was able to confide in you, sir," Thomas continued cautiously, "perhaps you may be aware of some information that could help me. Of course, money is also a powerful motive, and I may be wrong."

Thomas stood up to leave.

"You are a powerful man in these parts," he said. "Perhaps a word in the right ear is all the help I will need. In any case, I shall not bother you again, sir. If you think of anything, please let me know. I know you are a busy man. You may get word to me in whatever way is most convenient for you." He extended his hand. "Thank you for your time."

"I'll do what I can, Tom," he said. He rose from his chair. "I'll walk you out."

"Thank you, Judge," Thomas replied, "but I can find my own way."

Thomas turned to leave, and walked from the room. The judge watched him disappear through the door, resumed his seat, lit a cigar, and puffed it pensively. He had not even considered that Carlton's enemy could have a motive involving something deeper than financial ruin. It was an interesting thought. Betrayal. Thwarted love and revenge. That meant a woman was involved. Perhaps there was one wild possibility. But that was thirty years ago. He interrupted his musings with a gruff snort when he realized he had been bested once again by the quiet, bookish lawyer. Moore was going to get the information he wanted after all.

"Check," he muttered with an amused nod, "but not mate."

36

The next day, Tuesday morning at nine o'clock, Rudolph met Carlton in the conference room of the Albany jail. Carlton had asked him to come.

Carlton entered the room, escorted by Sheriff Morehouse, who saw no need for keeping him handcuffed. He looked a little tired, as if he had not slept well. Rudolph smiled at him and thanked Jock. Carlton sat down at the table. For the first time since his arrest, Rudolph detected a slight break in his brother's confidence.

"Rudolph," Carlton began, "I need to talk to you about something."

"Can it wait?" asked Rudolph. "I have to get something off my chest."

Carlton looked at him with a frown, and shrugged.

"All right," he said, rubbing his temples as if the interruption of his own confession had given him a sudden headache. "What is it?"

"I need your advice," said Rudolph casually. "You're a man of the world. You know how to handle women. I've gotten myself into a bit of a mess this time. Maybe you can help me get out of it."

Carlton's hands froze at his temples, and he stared at his brother suspiciously.

Rudolph continued, "Did you know that Camilla Goodson came back to town last week?"

Carlton nodded cautiously, still trying to figure out what Rudolph was up to. Thomas Moore had told him that Rudolph had guessed the truth about his relationship with Dixie Lee.

"I went to see her a few days ago," Rudolph continued. "And I learned something about myself that I truly didn't . . . . ”

He paused and smiled wryly at his brother. "Let me start again," he said. "You see, for the past few months, I've noticed a change in Dixie

Lee. She seemed moody, preoccupied, not herself."

He glanced at Carlton to see his reaction. His brother was staring at him. He sat motionless. There was a hint of alarm in his eyes.

"I began to wonder if Dixie Lee was happy with me," he continued, his face turned in profile to his brother. "I began to wonder if I was happy with her. Something was wrong, but I just couldn't put my finger on it."

He turned and met Carlton's questioning eyes. In that moment, Carlton read his brother's meaning perfectly. Thomas Moore had been right. Rudolph knew that Dixie Lee was lost to him. But there was no reproach in his eyes. No anger.

"Rudolph," Carlton began, wanting to explain, but he was met with a hand held up in interruption.

"No," said Rudolph, with a strange lightness, "let me finish. As I said, my relationship with Dixie Lee has troubled me for some time. When Camilla came back, I found myself thinking about her more and more. I realized that all the things I loved about Dixie Lee were the things I had always loved in Camilla."

Carlton listened expectantly.

"To make a long story short," Rudolph continued, "Camilla and I are back together. We're getting married."

"Are you serious?" Carlton asked.

Rudolph ignored his question. "So, that leaves me with quite a problem," he said. "I'm engaged to marry two women." He looked at Carlton. "This is where you come in. Tell me, how can I break the news to Dixie Lee? She'll be heartbroken."

The irony in Rudolph's tone was unmistakable.

"My God," said Carlton. "You're serious."

"As a judge," answered Rudolph, his light tone fading.

"You're not just doing this just to let me off the hook?" Carlton asked.

"You're the one," said Rudolph, "who has let me off the hook."

"I'll be damned," said Carlton.

DIXIE LEE was ushered down the corridor to the conference room by

Sheriff Morehouse. Again she had been lucky enough to avoid meeting her father, and again had managed to come up with a plausible excuse for seeing Carlton. She approached the room with caution, for she had learned that Rudolph was there. Her mind raced, but she could think of nothing which would explain her presence to Rudolph. Play it by ear, Carlton had told her yesterday.

The door opened and she walked in. The two brothers, sitting at the table, looked up in surprise at her arrival. She took a deep breath and swept forward, meeting them both with a carefully relaxed smile. The brothers rose to their feet.

"Rudolph," she said, as she rose on tiptoe to place a kiss on his cheek. She looked at Carlton and extended her right hand to him across the table, as she held Rudolph's hand with her left. Her eyes were for Carlton as he took her hand and she asked, "Is there any news?"

The two men looked at each other and said nothing. Dixie Lee saw that something had passed between them.

Rudolph released her hand and said, "Sit down, Dixie Lee." His voice was gentle, knowing, protective.

"What is it?" she asked, her voice almost a whisper. "What has happened?"

Again the two men spoke to each other with their eyes. Carlton nodded to his brother. Dixie Lee looked from one to the other, becoming more confused.

Rudolph spoke.

"Don't worry, honey," he said in his deep confident voice. "Nothing bad has happened."

Something warned her that he knew. She looked to Carlton for some sign.

Carlton nodded, the love in his eyes no longer concealed from his brother. He reached for her hand.

"There's no need to pretend any longer," he said calmly. "He knows everything."

She dared not look at Rudolph. She felt lightheaded. A piercing pain shot through her temples and her throat tightened. Until that moment, she did not realize how deeply devoted she was to Rudolph. She wrenched her hand from Carlton and covered her face. Her perfect control deserted her as her eyes filled with tears. She was not prepared for this.

Carlton half rose from his chair, but Rudolph put out a hand to stop him. It was Rudolph who rose and went to her, pulling her to her feet and wrapping her in his arms. She held onto him, sobbing softly into his chest.

Rudolph was deeply moved by her response. He had loved her more than he knew. He stroked her hair gently.

"It's all right, honey," he whispered. "Everything will be all right, I promise you."

She became quiet in his arms. When she raised her tearstained face to his, she met eyes filled with kindness.

"I'm sorry," she whispered.

"I know."

"I'll always love you a little," she said. She was trembling.

Rudolph smiled at her.

"I know, honey." He bent and kissed her lightly, and for the last time. He was kissing her goodbye.

Carlton sat silently, watching them as though through a glass. He was an observer, for the moment, and an outsider. It was their time together, and he had no wish to interfere.

He understood so much now. Rudolph had tried to spare him by telling him first about Camilla. And now, he spared Dixie Lee by saying nothing of Camilla. Carlton stood up when Dixie Lee turned to him, and she stepped into the protective circle of his arms.

"Enough of this sentimentality," Rudolph said. "Let's all sit down and find out where we are in this thing."

Dixie Lee smiled at Carlton as he patted her shoulder and pulled out the chair for her.

"Tom thinks that he can get me out on bail since I have an alibi," said Carlton, resuming his seat. "You'll have to go to the hearing, Dixie Lee."

"I'll have to tell Daddy," she said. "As soon as possible."

37

Thomas Moore was on his way to the Albany courthouse when a teenage boy called to him. The youngster was hurrying down the street after him, waving a white envelope.

Thomas paused and waited for the boy to catch up.

"I have a message for you, sir," the boy gasped, out of breath in the noonday heat. He handed the envelope to Thomas.

"Who is it from?" asked Thomas.

"Don't know, sir," answered the boy. "I'm just a messenger." He nodded and walked off.

Thomas opened the envelope and pulled out a scrap of paper. On the paper were words scrawled in pencil: Rosellen Daniel, 1908. Thomas folded the paper and put it back into the envelope. He smiled. The date was just about right. He put the envelope in his breast pocket and patted it. Judge Allen had come through.

"The game," he quoted his favorite mystery writer aloud, "is afoot."

ACROSS THE square, in the basement office of the Sheriff, Bubba James drummed his fingers on the arm of the chair. He did not like waiting. Across from him, Jock Morehouse seemed busy enough, shuffling through a mountain of papers on his desk. They were waiting for a call from the FBI in Washington, D.C. Carlton's black knapsack had been shipped to them Sunday night for fingerprint analysis and forensic examination. They had been promised the results by this morning, and Bubba was tired of waiting. He had wanted the bag and the results back yesterday. Red tape, he thought. Damn red tape will be the end of us all. He jumped as the shrill bell of the telephone rang. Jock picked up the receiver.

"Dougherty County Sheriff's office, Sheriff Morehouse speaking."

Bubba leaned forward in his chair. In a moment Jock nodded to him, indicating that it was indeed the call they had been waiting for. Bubba could hardly restrain himself from questioning Jock before he hung up.

Jock listened, then grabbed a pad and a pencil as he said, "You're sure? Yes, I've got it."

Bubba walked over, stood behind Jock's desk, and leaned over his shoulder. On the pad he read: Fingerprints match. As he watched, Jock wrote: Hair sample.

"You'll send it back today, then?" Jock asked.

There was a pause, then Jock thanked the man and hung up. He turned to Bubba with a smug smile twisting down one corner of his mouth.

"The boy's fingerprints were found on one of the tools," he said. "They also turned up a blond hair sample. They need us to send them a sample of his hair immediately. They also found flakes of tobacco at the bottom of the bag. Lucky Strike."

Bubba nodded. A flicker of relief showed in his eyes. Now they had concrete evidence linking Carlton to the bag. Before, it had been assumptions and circumstantial evidence—their word against his. Now they had proof. The Townsend family was powerful, and Bubba and Jock had their necks on the chopping block if anything went wrong.

The evidence ran through Bubba's mind. Carlton had denied knowledge of the secret room, and the girls could testify they saw him there the summer before. The loot from the robberies was stashed in the secret room. The fact that nothing had been fenced had been one of the reasons there had been no leads in the case. They could place him with the black bag, and now had proof that it belonged to him. The child had heard him whistle a tune Carlton was especially fond of. Then there was the cessation of the robberies when Carlton realized he was the object of police observation. The case was airtight. Bubba smiled at Jock.

"Want to make a small wager that the hair sample will match?"

"Hell, no," said Jock. "I don't bet against a sure thing."

There was a knock on the door.

"Come on in," said Jock.

Rudolph Townsend entered the room. The circumstances apparently had failed to affect him, for he strode into the office as naturally as he would have if he had come to make a donation to the Sheriff's Orphans' Fund. His manner was the same as always, calm, confident, and friendly.

Bubba was wary of him. Rudolph was suppressing the feelings of silent outrage Bubba had sensed the day they took Carlton to jail. It was a difficult situation, for Bubba respected Rudolph and valued his friendship. There was also the realization that an unnatural bitterness against Carlton had led Bubba to pursue him. He was not willing to admit that his feelings had influenced the outcome, but he could not deny their existence. It was a weakness he found bothersome in himself.

In the end, it was his duty which mattered. He was just doing his duty. He gave Rudolph enough credit to understand that, but the uneasiness still ate at him. So did Rudolph's manner. The coldness was gone, and he didn't seem bothered by the fact that he was addressing the men who had apprehended and charged the younger son of County Pa with kidnaping and burglary. In his own way, Bubba decided, Rudolph was as much of a threat as Carlton.

"Good morning, gentlemen," said Rudolph.

He was facing them for the first time since they had come to the house for Carlton. He extended his hand to Bubba, who shook it somewhat nervously, and then to Jock, whose response was more serious and professional, unhindered as he was by any personal involvement with the case. Rudolph pulled up a straight-backed wooden chair close to Jock's desk and sat down.

"Since you are both here, let me say something that needs to be said." Rudolph looked squarely at Bubba, then Jock. "I have counted you both as friends, and I have never had reason to doubt your abilities or your devotion to your duty of upholding the law."

He paused as Bubba's glance flickered to Jock, who was listening intently to Rudolph and did not return Bubba's glance.

"I want you both to know," Rudolph continued, "that I understand why you had to arrest my brother. Under the circumstances, there was nothing else you could do. If I had been in your place, I would have done the same thing."

Jock's eyebrows arched slightly at this statement. The older Townsend brother was running true to form, a reasonable and honorable man in any circumstance.

Bubba made no reaction. Unlike Jock, he was defensive, and waited for the ax to fall.

"You have evidence which appears to incriminate Carlton and you have acted accordingly. You have done your duty, and now we all find ourselves in an unpleasant and uncomfortable situation. I bear you no animosity, but understand this: it is essential that we remain open and cooperative with each other," he looked pointedly at Bubba, "if justice is to be served, which I know is your aim."

"I appreciate your candor, Rudolph," said Jock, "and I assure you that finding out the truth is our goal as well as yours. I expect you think your brother is innocent, and that's perfectly understandable—"

"No sir!" interrupted Rudolph, his balled fist crashing down on the desk. "It most certainly is not understandable. If my brother is guilty, I'll help you convict him myself. The fact that he is my brother has nothing to do with it."

Rudolph's eyes blazed, daring them to doubt him.

Jock was taken aback by Rudolph's outburst, and realized that he had misjudged him by inferring that he would be unable to accept criminality in his brother. Bubba said nothing.

Rudolph recovered his attitude of calmness and confidence. After a brief silence, he spoke again.

"I'm afraid we misunderstand each other. When I said I wanted justice to be served, I meant just that: justice. If my brother is guilty, he'll take his punishment. But if he is innocent," he stared coldly at Jock, "I expect you both to do your damned best to find the guilty party."

Rudolph's righteous anger had found its mark, and Jock found himself wondering for the first time if it were possible that Carlton could have been set up.

Rudolph rose and extended his hand to Jock, with a pleasant smile on his face.

"If you will excuse me now, I have some things to do."

Jock shook his hand and said, "Of course. Rudolph. I appreciate you stopping by."

THAT AFTERNOON, Dixie Lee caught up with her father at Sheriff Morehouse's office. They needed a private place to talk, she said. Bubba led the way to the back room, which was a kitchen of sorts. He indicated a chair at the dining table to Dixie Lee, and sat down in the opposite chair, facing her. Her attitude was cold and distant, and he wondered what she was up to.

There was a feeling of tension between them, it was undeniable. Dixie Lee knew that Bubba was the real fish they needed to hook. What she was about to tell him wouldn't make matters any easier. Still, Bubba was a man of principle. Dixie Lee counted on that.

"I have to speak to you about Carlton, Daddy," she began. "You see, I am involved in this case."

Bubba frowned and his eyes narrowed cautiously at the mention of Carlton. "Involved? What do you mean?"

"I was with Carlton all afternoon the day the child disappeared. I can give him a solid alibi, and I'm ready to testify to his whereabouts in court."

Bubba glowered at Dixie Lee. What had Rudolph talked her into?

"We asked Carlton where he was that day," he said through gritted teeth. "He said he was out riding all afternoon. Alone. He has no alibi."

Dixie Lee paused before answering.

"I know he told you that," she said. "He was lying."

"And now he's telling the truth?" asked Bubba sarcastically.

"Now we are both telling the truth, Daddy," Dixie Lee said. "Both of us have something to confess. Carlton's half-truths and lies are the reason he's in jail. He lied only because he didn't want you to know he was with me."

Bubba considered Dixie Lee. She was deadly serious and what she said made some sense. Carlton would have good reason not to want to involve the daughter of his primary accuser. But why were they together all afternoon? What were they doing together? A pulse began to throb in Bubba's temple. A possibility began to form which he dared not consider.

"If you were together," he said cautiously, "and I'm not sure I believe you were at this point, why was he afraid to tell me he was with you?"

"He didn't want you to know why he was with me."

"And why was he?"

She took a deep breath and blurted it out.

"Carlton and I are in love with each other, Daddy."

A bead of perspiration formed on Bubba's brow. His eyes filled with rage, but he moved not a muscle. After a stony silence, he asked, "And how long has this been going on?"

"I'm not sure," answered Dixie Lee, her voice rising defensively. "I don't know when it started. Months ago, weeks ago, I don't know. But that day we realized we were in love and wanted to be together."

There was another silence.

"You certainly are cool about this," said Bubba finally. "The last time I looked it was Rudolph you were in love with."

Dixie Lee looked thoughtful, as if she was measuring her words.

"I was mistaken," she said, looking at Bubba. "I can't marry Rudolph. I'm in love with Carlton."

Silence. Then Bubba said, "How convenient."

"Daddy," Dixie Lee began, "I know your opinion of Carlton. He's been wild and irreverent. He's been a drunk, a rascal, and a ladies' man. Believe me, in those days, I would never have looked at him twice."

Bubba was struggling to control his rage. His eyes bored into her, but he was looking beyond her, seeing someone else, directing his rage at someone else. Dixie Lee's heart sank. She had to make him understand.

"Carlton is not the same person he was. He's changed."

"Oh," said Bubba, "he's a regular saint now, is he?"

Dixie Lee's patience was beginning to wear thin.

"Look, Daddy," she said, a hard edge creeping into her voice, "the deeper we get into this awful thing, the worse it gets. What it comes down to is that Carlton has an alibi: me. I was there, I was with him. He could not have kidnaped the girl, don't you understand? How you feel or how I feel doesn't matter anymore. What matters is that you are sworn to uphold the law. You've never let personal feelings interfere with your job, and I'm not going to let you start now."

"Don't tell me what I am or am not going to do," thundered Bubba, rising from his chair, his restraint gone. "And don't tell me how to do my job."

He walked out of the room, slamming the door behind him. Jock looked up in surprise as Bubba stomped past him, through the office and out the door.

Dixie Lee emerged from the back room and shot an urgent look at Jock.

"Go after him," said Dixie Lee. "There's no telling what he might do."

"GIVE ME the cell keys," hissed Bubba to a startled Sergeant Hardy.

"They're on the nail yonder, Chief James," said Hardy, pointing. "If you need the conference room I can—"

Bubba grabbed the keys and was out of the room before the sergeant could finish his sentence. He covered the distance to Carlton's cell in moments, and paused to look through the bars at him before he fumbled with the lock.

Carlton sat on his cot with his back against the wall, waiting. He watched as Bubba opened the door and stared at him. Bubba unbuckled his gun belt and threw it down the passage. His gold badge followed. Bubba was a full four inches taller and forty pounds heavier than Carlton. Carlton knew he was going to get the beating of his life.

Bubba lunged into the cell and dragged Carlton up by the collar. Carlton allowed himself to be hauled close to the chief's face, but offered firm and measured resistance. Bubba was surprised by the strength of the younger man, for he had rarely met a man he could not best. They glared at each other eye to eye.

"Stay away from my daughter," hissed Bubba. "Stay away or I'll kill you."

His threat was answered by a deadly calm voice.

"Then kill me now, Chief. Having her is more than worth whatever you can do to me."

Bubba raised his fist and slammed it into Carlton's face, sending him sprawling across the floor of the cell. Jock Morehouse flew through the cell door and grabbed Bubba before he could do any more damage. Sergeant Hardy looked at the prisoner in dismay as Dixie Lee rushed past them and bent over Carlton.

"Have you gone crazy?" Jock was saying.

"Get out of here," screamed Dixie Lee. "Leave him alone!"

Sergeant Hardy was enlisted to help pull the raging Bubba from the cell. Some semblance of sanity returned to the usually nonviolent Chief James and he shook off Jock and Hardy and walked out to the office.

38

Thirty miles away, Sam, Rudolph Townsend's Negro butler, and sometime chauffeur, carefully guided the yellow and black Packard over the rough patches and gulleys of the trail leading to the backwater cabin of Colley Washington, the Delight Diviner. Thomas Moore had borrowed both the car and Sam for the afternoon, telling no one of his destination. Sam's eyes had widened in curiosity when Thomas had told him where he wanted to go.

"We almost there now, Mr. Thomas," said Sam over his shoulder. "The house be down at the water's edge, yonder, past them trees."

"That's fine, Sam," said Thomas. "Just get me as close as you can without tearing up Mr. Rudolph's fine car."

Sam grinned. "Yes, suh."

The car lurched slowly around the bend, and a weather-beaten cabin came into view. It was small and devoid of color, blending in with the grayish brown of the forest. On the neat porch were six lovely blooming geraniums. The car rumbled to a halt.

"I won't be long," Thomas said to Sam.

Sam looked nervously at the cabin.

"I be right here, Mr. Thomas. I wait right here for you."

Thomas turned and walked toward the cabin. His approach had been hardly silent, so Boozie's aunt was surely aware of his presence by now, if she was home. He walked slowly, noting the abundance of animals which seemed to inhabit the place. Birds of every description roosted in the branches of the trees, but only the softest twitters were heard. Grazing nearby was a large doe, with her fawn at her side. The deer raised its head at his approach, then returned to her grazing, as if used to the sight and smell of man. Squirrels and rabbits watched him pass, and, everywhere, wildflowers bloomed. He paused at the top of the steps and knocked loudly on one of the porch rails.

"Aunt Colley," he called. "I've come with Sam, from Mr. Rudolph's house. I need your help."

He waited. From his wallet, he retrieved the scrap of paper that had been given him anonymously, bearing the words Rosellen Daniel, 1908.

The door creaked open. Aunt Colley, short of five feet tall by several inches, stood in the doorway.

"Come in, Mr. Thomas," she said. "I been expectin' you."

Thomas smiled. He was not disappointed. She had already learned his name, and of his visit to Boozie. If anyone knew who Rosellen Daniel was, it would be this powerful slip of a woman.

JUDGE JACOB G. Allen was a good man to have in one's corner. He managed to get Carlton's hearing set for Wednesday afternoon at two o'clock. This rankled the federal prosecutor, Baxter Brooks, to no end. He had barely had time to get the evidence against Carlton organized.

Thomas Moore knew Judge Allen could outmaneuver Brooks and get the case presented to the federal grand jury currently in session. Carlton was bound over for trial, but in view of Dixie Lee's testimony and Rudolph's influence, Carlton was released on a ten thousand dollar bond. This was an excessive amount for that area of the country, but Judge Cunningham felt it was warranted, considering the charges.

The date for Carlton's trial was set for a month and a day hence. This unusually speedy trial date was due to the eloquence of the determined Mr. Brooks, who wanted this trophy on his wall well before the November election, if not in time for the primaries.

Baxter Brooks was in his third successful year as south Georgia's federal prosecutor. He was forty-one, dogmatic, distinguished, ambitious. His style was flashy, his mind cunning, his voice deep and mesmerizing. He looked forward to the legal joust with his eccentric peer, the eminent Mr. Moore. Brooks considered himself a worthy opponent to the pedantic genius, and this case had all the earmarks of fame for the winning lawyer. If he had to pull every last marker that anyone owed him, and call in every political favor, Judge Allen's influence would not hinder him further in this case. This Baxter Brooks vowed silently as he watched Carlton Townsend go free.

There was little fanfare as Carlton, dark glasses covering his swollen left eye, descended the steps of the courthouse with Rudolph, Thomas, and Dixie Lee. They were unaware of the many eyes which followed them as they drove away. The shops and offices lining the street were filled, however, with onlookers, many of them starstruck young girls, who were convinced they were watching the release of the cat burglar.

One of the onlookers leaned against the wall of Billy Harper's barber shop, shaded from the sun by the red and white striped awning. Chief Bubba James watched the departure from behind spotless sunglasses, slowly chewing his gum. He had elected to skip the hearing. Jock Morehouse was fully capable of presenting the facts. Bitter and disillusioned, Bubba knew he needed to separate himself from the case.

The depth of his emotional estrangement from his daughter had taken him by surprise. Because he loved Dixie Lee so deeply, he found the estrangement intolerable. It was forcing him to examine his own position, to face the vindictive feelings he held against Carlton. Also intolerable was the lapse of his ability to separate his emotions from his job. Bubba fought against any sign of weakness in himself, challenging and overcoming physical infirmity or emotional fear. He was also able to accept his limitations. He was human, he was not perfect, he made mistakes. Bubba demanded more of himself than he ever demanded of others. When he found himself in the wrong, he accepted it without resentment or self-incrimination. He acknowledged his error and resolved to learn from his mistake.

This time it was no different. He had allowed personal feelings to interfere with his job. He had some explaining to do to the only judge that mattered, himself. Still, as he watched the car disappear, he felt a twinge of regret, knowing that he would shortly have to cancel this vendetta, and release this rage. He knew he would do what was right, what was just. He always did. His hatred of Carlton was wrong, and it would have to be dealt with if Bubba wanted to live with himself.

But for these few minutes, Bubba clung to his bittersweet hatred, as the inevitable waves of justice swept closer and closer, to drown him again in his damn lofty principles, his damn unforgiving duty.

"WELCOME HOME, darling," said Laura Townsend as Carlton came through the front door, followed by Rudolph, Dixie Lee, and Thomas Moore.

"Mother." Carlton gathered her to him, giving her a firm hug. "God! It's good to be home."

Laura released him and turned to Thomas.

"We have you to thank for this," she said, her eyes misting.

"Don't worry, please," said Thomas, taking her hand. "We have a lot of work ahead of us, but your son will not be taken from you again. I am sure of it."

Laura nodded, blinking back the tears. Holding her head high, she smiled at them all and said, "Sam has set up one of his famous teas in the dining room. Come, I feel like celebrating."

They followed Laura into the dining room, their talk frivolous, their gaiety forced. Thomas smiled and said little as tea was spiked with sour mash, and finger sandwiches and small cakes consumed. It was a time of escape. They talked of horses, crops, rain, anything and everything except the one thing that was foremost in their minds, the trial. Ever the observer, Thomas saw the look of concern cross Laura's face as she watched her younger son look into the loving eyes of Dixie Lee. At last Carlton rose and excused himself, saying that he could wait no longer for a hot bath.

Taking Rudolph aside, Thomas said, "Your mother wonders what is going on between your fiancée and your brother."

"Lord," said Rudolph. "She doesn't know. I'd forgotten." He laughed in frustration. "So much has happened. I'll tell her. Take Dixie Lee out to the garden or something, will you, Tom?"

39

It was after seven when Dixie Lee arrived home. She was relieved that her father was still out. She was furious with him, and she was in no mood to play games.

She had come home in tears the night before and told her mother everything. Hedda, unaware of Bubba's intense dislike of Carlton, had been incredulous, but as she cared only for her daughter's happiness, she had not questioned Dixie Lee's sudden change of affections. She was concerned only that the man her child loved was in such dreadful trouble.

When she heard of Bubba's attack on Carlton, she had difficulty believing her husband was capable of such a thing, in spite of his affection for his daughter. It was totally out of character for the cool, levelheaded, fair-minded Bubba James.

He had come in and found them talking, seen Dixie Lee's tearstained face, and stared at her with the eyes of a stranger. Hedda knew then that everything her daughter had said was true. Bubba had sat down in his easy chair, with his back to them, and read the paper without a word. Dixie Lee had burst into tears, ran to her room, and slammed the door.

Hedda had known better than to approach him. She had retired to the kitchen and occupied herself with dinner preparations while she tried to sort out her feelings.

Bubba had not moved from his place, nor turned a page of the paper, when Hedda had put up her sewing and retired. She loved Bubba James, and she was a good wife to him. She knew when she could approach him and when she could not. They rarely argued, because she knew there was no point. One did not argue with Bubba James. The man was of such a temperament, and possessed such a sense of right and wrong, that he needed no wifely prodding to sort out his problems.

In many respects Bubba was a loner, an unreachable entity. Hedda had always respected this invisible barrier between them, not daring to trespass further, knowing that he gave as much of himself to her as he was able to do. Because she loved him, it was always enough.

WHEN DIXIE Lee came home that night, Hedda sensed trouble. "You're so late, honey," she said, following her daughter to her room. "Is everything all right? Did they release him?"

"Yes, Mama," replied Dixie Lee, as she reached in her closet for a small suitcase. "He got out around noon. I've been over at the house all afternoon. I'm sorry. I should have let you know." She went to the dresser and began pulling clothes from the drawers.

"What are you doing?" asked Hedda in a small voice. She did not want to hear the answer.

"Packing. I've got to get out of this house, Mama. I'm going to stay with Janie in Albany for a while."

"Darling, you can't leave, not now," Hedda pleaded. "You must stay and try to work this out with your father. I've never seen him so broken up about anything. If you leave, you'll break his heart."

"He has no heart!" snapped Dixie Lee, going to the closet. "If he had one, he would never have done what he did. He might have killed Carlton if they hadn't dragged him away. He doesn't care about me. He doesn't care that I love Carlton. All he cares about is that badge of his." She threw a dress at the bag on the bed.

Hedda shook her head, hurt that her daughter could speak so. "How can you say that?" she asked. "How dare you say that about your father? Sweet Jesus, child! Your father thinks the sun rises and sets on you."

"Maybe he did once," Dixie Lee said stiffly, "but not anymore." Her throat tightened and she felt on the verge of tears. No, she vowed silently, I will not cry. He will not make me cry again. Ever. She turned from her mother and took another dress from the closet.

Neither of them heard the front door open. Bubba walked into the house and heard their raised voices. He took off his hat and unbuckled his gun, listening.

"I'm sorry, Mama," Dixie Lee was saying, "but I just can't stay here right now. I'm so upset I just can't. I never thought I'd feel this way about my own father, but right now I don't know if I'll ever be able to forgive him."

"Forgive him for what?" Hedda asked. "For trying to protect you? For wanting what's best for you?"

"He has no conception of what's best for me," replied Dixie Lee, her voice rising. "None of you do! Why don't you just leave me alone? I have my own life. I'm a grown woman, for God's sake. I'm not a child anymore. Can't you understand that?"

"It's not always that easy," came a deep voice behind them.

Dixie Lee looked up and saw her father standing in the doorway. He put a gentle hand on Hedda's shoulder, a silent signal to leave him alone with Dixie Lee. Hedda left without a word or a backward glance.

How typical, Dixie Lee thought, how absolutely typical! He waves his wand and mother disappears. She gritted her teeth and looked back to her suitcase, her anger rising as she folded the clothes and packed them neatly.

Bubba stood there, watching. He felt the anger churning again, deep in the pit of his stomach, but his chest was burning. No one, not even Hedda, owned as much of his heart as Dixie Lee. He took a deep breath, and automatically tried to put the pain out of his mind. But this was not a crushed hand or a sore back he was trying to ignore; this was despair, desperate sorrow, separation. It took all his strength not to let it rip him apart.

"Where are you going," he asked, "now that you're so all-fired grown up?"

Dixie Lee stopped her packing and glared at him with eyes of smoldering fire. He returned her gaze evenly.

"To Janie's house," she answered with quiet determination.

"I wish you wouldn't," he said.

It was the same voice he used to keep drunks in line. It meant, "No you won't," and Dixie Lee knew it.

"Ohhhh!" she raged, slamming down the lid of the suitcase. She marched over to him, her eyes spurting fire. "And I wish," she hissed, "that my own father didn't call me a liar!"

"You watch your mouth, young lady!" he retorted. "I never called you any such thing. I don't know what the hell you're talking about!"

"Oh?" said Dixie Lee, turning her back to him and walking to the bed. "Just what would you call it? I told you I was with Carlton all afternoon! I told you he couldn't have kidnaped the child!" She began throwing clothing into the suitcase, her eyes wild.

"All I knew was that he had got his hooks into you somehow."

She continued as if she did not hear him. "But did you believe me?" She arched her brows in an exaggerated fashion before answering her own question. "No," she said, mocking, "you didn't believe me. I'd say that's the same as calling me a liar, wouldn't you? You didn't believe me then, and you don't believe me now. You think I made the whole thing up."

Suddenly she stopped her violent packing. She stood looking at her suitcase, shaking her head as if she knew a sickening truth.

"What's the point of this," she asked. "Just tell me this, Daddy. Do you still think he's guilty? If you do, then you are most certainly calling me a liar."

Her barb hit home. She was right, and inside, Bubba squirmed. His frustration only heightened his anger.

"I don't want you involved with him!" he thundered.

"I knew it!" cried Dixie Lee, triumphantly. "You still think he's guilty."

"He's guilty of something, all right! How much, I don't know, but I'm sure as hell going to find out!"

Dixie Lee snapped the lid of the suitcase shut.

"You just do that!" she hissed, grabbing the heavy bag as if it were a feather. She tried to brush past him, but he caught her. His other arm barred her way.

Dixie Lee felt angry tears spring into her eyes. She was weak from the violence of the argument, and she had spoken as much from disappointment in her father as from anger. She hated herself for her tears, for the unwelcome urge she felt to throw her arms around him as she did as a child. It was too late for Daddy to make everything better.

"Daddy," she said softly, her voice calm again, "let me go."

He hesitated, then dropped his arm and stepped back from the doorway. Dixie Lee walked out of the room and down the hall. She paused at the end of the hall, and looked back at her father.

"You know the worst part?" she asked, her voice trembling. "I told Carlton he was wrong about you." Her voice broke as she continued, "Wasn't I a fool?"

She ran from the house, lugging the heavy case. Now it seemed to weigh a ton, and she struggled against it as if she were dragging a ball and chain. She headed for the General Store, where she knew she could flag Janie down on her way to pick her up.

Bubba stood in the doorway of Dixie Lee's room, leaning heavily against the doorjamb. He was exhausted, but his mind was clear. He wasn't thinking about Dixie Lee, he was thinking about Carlton. Dixie Lee had managed to do what Bubba had fought against, convince him that Carlton's alibi was solid. Disgusted, he wondered how long he had known the truth, and how long he had buried it. He would call Dixie Lee tomorrow. Then he would get to work, and find out the truth.

40

The day after Carlton's release, Thomas Moore began his slow, painstaking investigation. He was on the trail of the ghost of County Pa. If he had not been a lawyer, like his father, Thomas would have been a good detective. He was a consummate researcher. He did not know everything; the secret was knowing where to go to find out what he needed to know.

Boozie's Aunt Colley, as he suspected, knew the history of Hayley and its people as well as anyone in the county. She confirmed that County Pa did, indeed, have an illegitimate son, born to one Rosellen Daniel in 1908. This was Boozie's ghost, a man now age thirty, a man who so closely resembled his late father that, from a distance, Ottis Washington had mistaken him for County Pa himself.

Thomas knew the face he was looking for. He could not be sure of the height or the weight, but it was not unreasonable to assume that the dimensions were close to those of the father. He knew the man was nearby, perhaps in hiding, perhaps in disguise.

Perhaps he would be caught, perhaps he would not. Catching him was not Thomas's aim; establishing that he existed, and that he had committed the crimes out of revenge, was. If he was to prove Carlton innocent, he would have to learn everything he could about this man. It would have to be enough to convince a jury that the mountain of circumstantial evidence against Carlton was just that: circumstantial. Thomas knew that when Dixie Lee's relationship with Carlton was established, her testimony would be questioned by the prosecution. The case did not rest on whether the jury believed Carlton's alibi, it rested on exposing a shadowy figure.

Colley had told Thomas who the Daniel girl was, but did not know what had happened to her or to the child. Rosellen Daniel was the only child of the Reverend Darenger Daniel, who served as pastor of the Good Shepherd Baptist Church from 1901 until his death in 1913. He was a widower and a strict disciplinarian. The girl was remembered as being uncommonly pretty, with a natural seductive quality which was, to her father, a curse of the devil. She was just seventeen when she left town, never to return. Colley was one of the few who knew the girl had been disowned by her father when he learned she was pregnant. Her father died of a heart attack five years later—shortly after, Colley believed, he learned of his daughter's death.

Most of Colley's information had come from a cousin, Derry Franklin, who had worked as a maid for the preacher. Derry was still alive, living in Tifton. Colley had given Thomas a note to give to Derry, and as he drove to see the elderly woman, Thomas prayed she could remember what happened to the child she had told Colley about so long ago.

The house was in the country, a tired gray structure like hundreds of others in the rural South, but devoid of that which seemed to give the others life—children. Derry lived alone, as did her cousin Colley. How she sustained herself was a mystery to Thomas. He knocked at the door but there was no answer. Talk loud, Colley had said, she's deaf as wood. He knocked again, loudly.

A surprisingly clear, melodious voice answered, "Come in, child, I'm here."

Thomas opened the door and entered hesitantly, not wanting to alarm the old lady. He was surprised to find the room alive with warm colors and light. The long windows bathed the bright-yellow room with sun. The wooden floor was painted cherry red and bordered with stenciled flowers.

She sat in a bright red rocking chair, small and fragile, her white hair a cloud around her unwrinkled face. Beneath her long cotton skirt, her tiny brown feet were bare, and did not touch the cherry floor.

"Aunt Derry?" Thomas asked.

"Yes, child," she answered in the same musical voice, "come closer."

Thomas walked up to her and smiled. She was lovely. Her face lit up as she smiled back at him with perfect white teeth, and eyes deep and kind. She looked much younger than her seventy-five years.

"Who are you, child?"

"My name is Thomas," he answered, keeping his voice clear and distinct. He did not raise his voice, for he had come to understand in his dealings with the elderly that clarity, not loudness, was the problem. "Aunt Colley sent me to see you. I have a note for you." He fumbled in his pocket and handed it to her.

She took the note and read it, reaching for no spectacles.

She looked at him again and said, "Pull up that chair and sit with me a spell."

Thomas drew a ladder-back chair with a cane seat from against the wall and placed it next to hers. Like everything else in the house, it was painted brightly, this one yellow, like the walls.

"What you need to know?"

"Everything you can remember about Rosellen Daniel," Thomas replied, "and the child she had thirty years ago. I'm trying to find the child."

"Lord, he be a man now," said Derry, arching her brows in remembrance. "It all a long time ago." She shook her head thoughtfully.

"You worked for Rosellen's father?"

"Yes, Lord. He was all hellfire and brimstone. Didn't any more know the love of Jesus than that chair you sit in. He turn her out."

"Aunt Colley said you knew of her baby?"

"She had no place to go. I half raise that poor girl. She come to me. I knew a place, a woman who would take her in. Sent her there, to Macon, to Miz Walcott's house. Miz Walcott in heaven now. I won't say the same for the Reverend."

"She had a son?"

"A lovely child he was, too. Miz Walcott sent me word he born in the new hospital, only the fifth baby born in that shiny new place."

"Do you remember the name of the hospital?"

She smiled regretfully.

"No. She never name it for me, that I recollect. But it was new back then. You jus' find the one they open then."

Thomas nodded appreciatively. Apparently the years had not dulled the woman's memory or her mind.

"Can you tell me anything more?"

"Some," replied the tiny woman. "Rosellen was pretty. She say to me, I'm going to be on the stage, Derry. I'm going to run away and go to New York one day. She full of dreams. She be run off by her father and run off by her man. She didn't want that baby. Miz Walcott send word Rosellen left the baby behind and run off to the stage like she always say she gonna do. They put the poor little baby in the orphan home."

"In Macon?"

"Maybe. I never knew any more."

"You said she was run off by her man. Who was he?"

Derry looked at Thomas suspiciously. She blinked and considered her answer, wondering why he asked if he already knew the answer.

"You know it. Why you say for me to tell it?"

"He's dead now, isn't he?" asked Thomas patiently. "You can speak of him now, can't you?"

"He was an evil man," she said. "We knew him. He fool a lot of people, but we knew."

"Will you tell me his name?"

"Did Colley tell you?"

"Yes."

"Then you know."

Thomas paused. He did not understand the woman's reticence. Surely she did not believe in the ghost.

"Aunt Derry," he said at last, "do you know what happened to Rosellen?"

"She died." The old woman looked away and balled her hands as she realizing something. "Wait. I do know more. Miz Walcott told of money that came into Rosellen's hand. She use it to fly away."

"I see," said Thomas. "And you know of Rosellen's death?"

"I see the telegram the Reverend got the week before he die. Ottis, Colley and me, we all can read. It say she gave his name as kin before she die of pneumonia in the charity hospital. It say she dead and did he want her body. He throw it away. He sit there for a week. I found him dead in his chair. He killed that girl. He knew it, too."

"And the child?"

"Know nothing of her baby. Never heard nothing."

41

Woody Price walked into the wide entrance hall of the Radium Springs Country Club and saw the Townsend brothers at the entrance to the bar. Crossing the Alabama marble floor, he waved and called to them. The brothers grinned and welcomed him with hardy handshakes.

"Damn good to see you," said Woody to Carlton.

"Damn right," replied Carlton. "Come on, join us for a drink. We were just about to go in."

Woody followed them into the softly lit bar. Brothers. He envied them. They were there for each other in this crisis, in spite of all the bickering, the competition, the arguments and clashes of the past. Nothing could break the bond of blood.

"Not much of a crowd tonight," remarked Rudolph wryly as they sat down at a table. Except for the bartender, they were alone in the room. Woody looked at Rudolph, puzzled by his tone.

"What?" asked Carlton sarcastically. "No welcome home party? No band?"

"Apparently not," said Rudolph. He looked at Woody. "Some fairweather friends, huh?"

"You're not serious, surely?" Woody asked in disbelief. "I can't believe your friends would believe these lies."

"You don't live here," said Carlton with a knowing grin. He winked at Rudolph. "I can see it all now," he continued, "outraged mothers locking their tearful daughters in their bedrooms. Snobby fathers strongly suggesting that junior join him and mother for dinner tonight."

"Yes," agreed Rudolph solemnly, "it's done with such subtlety, you see. No one mentions it in polite company. The shame, you know. They just suddenly find there are so many things to do."

"Why go to the club for dinner again, Mildred?" asked Carlton in a mock voice, "Let's try that new restaurant over on Fox Street."

Woody laughed at the two of them.

"Come now," he said with amusement, "you exaggerate. It's Wednesday night. There's never a crowd here on Wednesday night. And it's still early besides. I'll be most disappointed if what you say is true."

"Oh, it's all true," said Carlton, eyes narrowed. "Not a soul will show. As a matter of fact, you wouldn't be here either if you had a shred of decency."

At this, Woody roared. Carlton laughed too, and his infectious cackle sent both his companions into gales of laughter. Finally, their laughter quieted and they turned strangely sober, for they had good reason to wonder if their mocking was actually close to truth. The silence was heavy, uncomfortable, seconds dragging and hanging dead in the air.

"Let's drink to your release," said Woody, to break the silence.

"Hell," said Carlton quickly, glad the uncomfortable moment was ended, "I'll drink to kudzu, if you say so, boy!"

"Tony!" Rudolph called to the bartender. "Bring these men a drink!"

From the door of the bar came a jovial voice.

"Sounds like the best idea I've heard all day."

They turned and saw Alan Dunlap enter the room with a pretty redhead. Alan smiled his lopsided grin and shook hands with everyone. His date, Maryjean Penney, smiled shyly and stared at Carlton.

They were the first of many. By eight o'clock the bar was filled with the usual Saturday night crowd, celebrating as if it were New Year's Eve. Woody observed Carlton and Rudolph surrounded by their friends, exchanging jokes, offering their support, and toasting anything that came to mind.

Woody was as jovial as the rest, but inside, he held himself apart. He was not part of this community of familiar friends. His heart held none of the merriment of the others as he flirted skillfully with the girls and traded quips with the men. As always, he was a watcher, an outsider.

Woody slipped unnoticed from the crowded room and walked down the wide hall to the front porch of the clubhouse. He drew a cigarette from his coat pocket and lit it. The night air was surprisingly cool, and a light wind blew through the trees. Woody walked down the steps and out into the parking lot. He would not be missed.

CAMILLA GOODSON walked into the General Store looking fresh and cool despite the ninety-degree noonday heat. She smiled her brilliant smile when she caught the eye of Crawford Welch, who beamed at her in return.

"It's only me," she called to him affectionately. "Don't know if I came to look or to buy." She walked to the counter. "May end up just pestering you for a while."

"Anytime, darlin'," said Crawford.

"How about me?" came a smooth, deep voice from behind Camilla. "I wouldn't mind a little pestering myself."

Paul Tanner was at the other end of the store, pulling a Coke from the drink box. Camilla knew the lazy voice immediately. She turned and saw Paul striding toward her, with his broad shoulders and rugged features. Still the athlete, still her childhood friend.

"Paul!" she cried. "How wonderful to see you."

Impulsively, she hugged him.

"How long have you been back, princess?" he asked.

"Not long," she replied with a smile. "Only a week or two."

"Two whole weeks?" he asked. "My, my. You haven't stayed two weeks in this town for seven years or so, my dear young lady. What can it mean?"

"Get me one of those and I'll tell you." She nodded toward the soft drink in his hand. "Let's sit out on the porch for a while. It's been ages since we've talked."

Paul got her a drink and joined her on the porch of the store. They sat at the far end of the porch, as far away as possible from a grumpy-faced, hunched-over man with a white beard who sat at the other end.

"Who's that old fellow?" she asked as Paul sat down beside her.

Paul looked at Daniel J. Smith. "I have no idea," he answered with a shrug. "So, what's the big story? How did you escape from New York?"

"Never mind about me," she said. "Tell me about you first. I know why you're home. How is your little girl? Rudolph told me she seemed fine on the surface, but—"

"She's taking it better than I expected," said Paul. "Elizabeth is worried about her, though. Thinks she needs to express her emotions. She's tight as a drum. Won't give in to the fear she went through. It will hit her someday; when, I don't know."

Daniel J. Smith cocked his head toward the newcomers and listened. He knew who the woman was. She was the preacher's daughter, the pretty one from New York, the one so good for church attendance in town. The man, he realized, was the father of Tori Tanner.

Poor little Brown Eyes, he thought. In the wrong place at the wrong time.

Camilla and Paul continued to talk about Tori and about the case. Camilla saw Paul stiffen at the mention of Carlton's name.

"Listen, Paul," said Camilla earnestly, her eyes locking with his, "Carlton did not do this. He is not capable of it."

Paul frowned and shook his head.

"I thought I knew him, Camilla," he said. "He used to tag along after me and Rudolph all through grade school, you know that. But I've been away for two years. I've heard things. He's got a bad reputation in the county, in the whole damn state." He rubbed his forehead. "It wasn't hard to check on, believe me. Every place I've been, people have been telling me about him, more than I wanted to know. At this stage, I have no idea what Carlton Townsend is or is not capable of doing."

"What did Rudolph say?"

"I haven't seen him."

"Have you tried?"

"No."

"Oh, Paul," she said, understanding. "You must see him. He knows Carlton didn't do it." She lowered her voice. "He couldn't have. He was with Dixie Lee James all that afternoon. It's a mistake. He shouldn't even have been arrested."

Paul studied her carefully. He wanted to keep an open mind, but found it difficult. Camilla seemed convinced of Carlton's innocence. His friend Rudolph was nobody's fool, but if there was any possibility that Carlton had done this thing to his daughter . . . . He gritted his teeth subconsciously. He had been avoiding all contact with the Townsend family, trying to sort things out in his own mind. Now he knew he had judged Carlton prematurely. He would talk to Rudolph.

Daniel J. Smith could still hear every word of the conversation. He leaned his head back in the rocking chair and closed his eyes. Within minutes, a soft snore could be heard.

Camilla knew what Paul was feeling. Her eyes misted as she reached for Paul's hand.

"This is my fault," Paul said pensively. "I wasn't here when she needed me."

"Darling Paul," she said. "You must not blame yourself."

"When I left here and went out on the road, it was like tearing my heart out," he said. "But when Mary Catherine died, something died inside me, too. It was hard for me to go away, but I had no choice. Once I put this town behind me, Lord help me, I knew it was the best thing I could have done. It was so painful to be with Tori and Elizabeth then. I was so full of grief and bitterness. The traveling was a way to start over, a way to forget. It took a couple of years, but the pain finally went away.

"I have a new life now, in Alabama. I married again, and we just had a baby girl. I haven't even told Tori or Elizabeth about the baby yet. It's hard to explain, but I needed all this time to get my life back together. And just when I'm ready for my old life and my new life to come together, for Tori to come and live with me again, *this* happens. What kind of a father am I? I've been terribly selfish. All this has really brought it home to me.

"When I left, I asked Rudolph to look out for Tori. He's done that. Tori adores him. I owe Rudolph a lot for that. If you say he knows for a fact that Carlton is innocent, then Carlton must be innocent. I guess I've judged the boy without thinking, without trying to find the truth."

"Consider him innocent until proven guilty," said Camilla. "I think that is all Rudolph or Carlton could ask of you."

Paul smiled slightly.

"God, I feel better already," he said. "It's a hell of a strain being someone's judge and jury. Or your own, for that matter." He turned to her. "As always, running into you brings me luck, princess. I wasn't thinking clearly about any of this." He smiled and winked at her. "If I wasn't married already, I'd likely try to sweep you off your feet."

"If I wasn't engaged," she said, "I'd likely be swept away."

Paul's eyes widened.

"Ah," he drawled. "The old boy hit a home run at last, huh?"

Camilla smiled and her cheeks flushed.

"It's about time you and Rudolph tied the knot," said Paul.

Daniel J. Smith smiled and snored again.

THE MACON hospital which opened its doors in 1908 was called Johnson General Hospital. Thomas handed the subpoena to the hospital administrator, Dr. Glenn Webster.

"This gives me the right to examine your files, sir," said Thomas to the portly man behind the desk. "I will be out of your hair as quickly as I can, I assure you." He looked apologetic.

The doctor looked quickly at the papers and put them down on the desk.

"You may have some difficulty plowing through that mess, Mr. Moore," he said with a briskness that befit his profession. "The early years were a little unorganized." He stood up and put his spectacles inyo the pocket of his white lab coat. "They're in the basement. Come with me. I'll take you down."

Eight hours later, Thomas found what he was looking for. Admission record of Rosellen Daniel, it read, July 4, 1908. The word "charity" was struck through with a pencil at the bottom of the page. Her home was listed as the residence of Mrs. Via Walcott, Macon, Georgia. Age eighteen. Attending doctor, Frank W. Moss, M.D.

There was a birth certificate stamped "Copy," with no official seal affixed. Date of birth, July 5, 1908. Time, 8:20 a.m. Sex, male. Weight, 6 lbs., 6 oz. Color eyes, hazel. Color hair, blond. Race, white. Name of mother, Rosellen Daniel. Name of father, unknown. Name of child, John Price Daniel. Religion, Baptist.

The next paper of importance was the release signed by Rosellen Daniel, allowing the child to be placed in an orphanage. Thomas studied the signature of the young would-be actress. It was large and bold, with loops and flourishes. The ink was fading on the yellowed paper. Attached was a release allowing the orphanage to acquire custody of the child. The paper was signed by Mary Grey, RN, Yves Homes, Savannah, Georgia.

Thomas was taken aback by the name of the orphanage. It was a private institution, not a charity or church-funded orphanage as he expected. It was an expensive parking place for orphans of wealthy backgrounds, whose estates could pay the tuition. Strange that this unwanted, destitute child would be placed in a high-priced bed of convenience for the illegitimate offspring of the upper class.

He looked back to the admission record, seeing again the pencil mark through the word "Charity." Thomas was surprised by this, for he had assumed that Price Townsend would have nothing to do with the child or the mother, wanting no link to them. He took out his notepad and began making notes.

Thomas left the records with the clerk in the medical records department. Dr. Webster had agreed to place them in the safe the next morning, to avoid confusion when the subpoena for them arrived. Thomas dashed off a short note of thanks to Dr. Webster, handed it to the clerk, and left the hospital. It was nearly midnight.

His mind forgot his emotional reaction, and the researcher in him took over, compiling facts, recording data. He made no assumptions or conclusions. Once the facts were assembled, he assimilated them as a whole, dispassionately. Then he slept. When he woke, the conclusions were instinctive, and he went with them. This method rarely failed him.

42

Dear Will,

Tori is the same. Paul is still here, and has been a wonderful blessing to Tori through this ordeal. We have had several long talks, and have agreed that his absence from Tori's life will shortly be ended. He is a good man. I know you will understand why he took the path he did following my daughter's death.

He is at last coming into his own again, and has built a new life for himself in Alabama. Tori has a new little sister, one month old. Paul wants to take Tori back with him, but strangely enough, Tori has begged to be allowed to spend the rest of the summer with me. She has wanted nothing, for the last year, more than to be with her father again, but now that he has come for her, she turns away from him. I am very worried about her.

I don't believe it has anything to do with the new stepmother and sister or with her father. It is the experience of the kidnaping, I think. Outwardly, Tori seems much the same, but I have seen the subtle changes in her behavior. She rarely ventures beyond the tree house. She never asks "why" questions anymore, and, I suspect, she no longer plays detective or any other pretend adventure games. It seems that the side of Tori's nature which imagines, dreams, and dares is now dormant.

She has no conception, of course, of the real danger she was in or of the true evil involved. She is innocent, still, and unaware of the extent of man's capacity for sin. She has been loved and protected all her life; such children react differently when they are exposed to danger. They are incapable of true terror, because they are unaware of evil.

Still, the experience has changed Tori. She has not expressed the fear she must have felt. She is guarded, cautious. And now, she does not want to go back with her father. Perhaps she just needs time. Her spirit has been shaken.

As you know, Carlton Townsend has been accused of the burglaries and the kidnaping. I am quite sure he is as much a victim as is Tori. He is out of jail now and will be put on trial shortly. Tori will not be involved in the courtroom proceedings, but she must give a deposition to the judge in quarters. I dread even this for her.

I have decided to let Tori enter the talent contest at the end of August sponsored by the DAR in Albany. I'm hoping that planning her number will be a diversion. I miss my brave, inquisitive, enthusiastic Tori.

God bless you. I hope to hear from you soon.

Sincerely, your friend, Elizabeth Cooper.

P.S. Jake is building a new house on his land.

"WHAT'S IN these crates you send off to New York, Jake?" asked Cora Jane Oates, the postmistress, as she watched Jake Potter deposit a heavy wooden box on the lorry in the corner of the post office. "It's getting to be a habit, and a costly one at that."

"Nuthin' much," replied Jake, wiping his brow. "I'm just doin' some work for this New York fella, Mr. Neill. He sends me stuff, I fix it, I send it back to him."

"Well, it'll cost you another five dollars for freight," said Cora, "unless you want to send it COD."

"No," said Jake, "I'll pay for it."

Jake handed Cora the money. He was still not used to the feel of cash money in his pocket, money that he could spend on simple luxuries. He was strangely ill at ease with his good fortune.

Jake walked out of the post office into the bright summer sun. In the pocket of his new blue jeans he carried his bankbook, which recorded the sum of his account at the Farmers' National Bank of Albany as $737.68. Jake Potter now had more money than anyone in Hayley, except of course the Townsends, and maybe Sam Gates.

He walked across the square to the General Store. He had already spent so much, it seemed, paying off his debts, and buying lumber and other building materials for the new house. And still he had what seemed a fortune. The news of Jake Potter's sudden good fortune was all over town, and the curious were eager for any new bit of information. Where was the money coming from, they asked each other. It had something to do with the mysterious crates from New York, they were sure. Rumors abounded, but in the end, only getting some of "Mr. Potter's" business was uppermost in their minds. Jake's good fortune was beginning to engender as much tale-spinning and notoriety as the upcoming trial of Carlton Townsend. It was a glorious summer in Hayley.

Every sculpture Jake completed brought him another three hundred dollars, an unbelievable sum, and they sold as quickly as he could ship them off. There seemed no end to the demand. The first had been an elephant; the next three had been the same, a lion declining. The last one was something new, a doe at rest with a fawn at her side. Each work took about a month to finish, but it was time he spent happily, creating a thing of beauty. His overworked fields had lain fallow over the spring for the first time in a hundred years.

Jake began to have new dreams for his farm. He dreamed of a stable filled with brood mazes, a stallion or two, and quarter horses. If he loved anything more than sculpting, it was horses.

He needed tenpenny nails. Jake walked into the General Store, the tinkle of bells sounding above his head as he opened the door. It looked the same. The shelves stocked with items of every description, the men clustered around the old stove which lay dormant beneath the revolving ceiling fan, Crawford Welch behind the counter as usual, bargaining with a customer. It looked the same, but it was different. The shelves did not seem so high, the men did not seem so important, Mr. Welch did not seem so all-powerful.

Jake walked silently to the back of the store and gathered up the nails he needed into a small paper bag. He browsed around for a few minutes, looking at the tools and hardware, before he made his way over to the counter, past the men sitting around the stove.

"Afternoon, Jake," called a friendly voice as he passed the men.

Jake turned to see the curious eyes of Irwin Black, the owner of the warehouses at the depot, fixed on him. The other men seated with him also turned and looked at Jake with greedy smiles. It was so casual, as if they had always spoken to him thus, as if he were one of them, as if their past treatment of him was forgotten forever.

Jake frowned slightly in surprise at their greeting, and nodded. He kept walking. He did not want to talk with them, to sit down with them, to drink coffee with them. He did not want to pretend he did not remember how they used to treat him. He was not bitter, but he did not want to be bothered, either. Somehow, he knew he would never sit with those men around the stove, as he had once wished to do.

He had always thought those men were better than he was, that they were above him, maybe because he was conditioned to think it. They had treated him as something lower than dirt, and he had no reason to question them. They had everything, he had nothing.

Now that he had something they wanted, they treated him differently. He was suddenly on a first-name basis with men who had considered him dirt. A bittersweet truth had been dawning on Jake over the past couple of months, as those around him began responding to his sudden wealth. The truth was that these men were the ones who were nobodies.

Thank God there were enough Elizabeth Coopers and Bubba Jameses in the world to make life worth living. It was no accident, Will Fable had told him, that the two of them had met in the boxcar. Will was right; it was nothing short of a miracle.

"Hello, Potter," said Crawford Welch.

Good old Crawford. He would never call Jake by his first name. He would be the no-nonsense businessman in good times and bad. He would ask no questions as long as the bills were paid.

"Mr. Welch," Jake greeted him with an appreciative nod. "I'll take these nails."

"Put it on your account?" asked Crawford.

Jake had the money in his pocket. He smiled at the man who had always been fair to him.

"Yessir," he said. "Just put it on my account."

Irwin Black watched as Jake walked out of the store without a backward glance. Turning to his companions, he said, "What's the latest on that ignorant cracker, anyway?"

"If it was up to me," said old Doc Houston, "Bubba James would be impounding one of those crates of Potter's, instead of asking a bunch of fool questions about nonexistent strangers."

"Potter's up to no good, that's for sure," said Sam Gates. "That boy has spent a year's wages in the last three months. Now where do you think he got that kind of money? If Bubba James is so sure Carlton Townsend was set up, maybe he better start looking for the real thief in his own backyard instead of chasin' all over creation."

"Bubba James is soft in the head when it comes to the Townsends," said Irwin Black in disgust. "Carlton is guilty as sin. We all know it. No, Jake Potter has his fingers in another dirty pie altogether, you mark my words."

AS CORA Jane Oates was not exactly the soul of discretion, the name of Jake's mysterious contact in New York City, Mr. Forrest Neill, was no secret around Hayley. Especially to Viola Gates, who thrived on gossip, and who happened to entertain the widow Oates in her home every Thursday, along with the other members of her church circle.

This Saturday, Viola was in Albany doing her shopping, and was soon browsing among the bookshelves of the Golden Leaves Bookstore on Walnut Street. She finally settled on a classic, and made her way to the cash register at the front of the store. The bespectacled clerk greeted her cheerfully.

"Hello, again," said the woman. "What's it to be today?"

"Just this one, I guess," answered Viola with a sigh. "I haven't got time to really browse today."

"Ah," said the clerk, "one of my favorites. Dickens never disappoints, you know. Have you never read this one?"

"Yes," answered Viola, looking at the display behind the girl's head of the latest best sellers, "a long time ago. I hardly remember it now. It will be like reading a new one, I'm sure."

"Forget Pip?" said the clerk. "Or Miss Haversham? The wedding cake full of cobwebs? Come, now, no one could ever forget them!"

"Well, don't remind me of the whole story," snapped Viola. "I may as well not bother to read it again."

She barely noticed the new display as she stared at the featured volumes of the Civil War romance behind the clerk. "When are you going to change your display books?" she asked with some irritation. "I'm sick to death of looking at that foolish pulp novel." She waved a plump finger at the display.

"When it stops outselling everything else in the store, I guess," answered the clerk. "You've read it, haven't you? Didn't you love it?"

"Heavens, no," answered Viola primly. "It's obscene and vulgar." Her face reddened. "It paints a sorry picture of the South, I'll tell you that."

"You think so?" asked the girl in surprise. "Why, I don't agree at all. I think it is brilliant, just brilliant. They're making a movie of it, you know. I can't wait to see it."

Viola tapped her foot impatiently and directed her attention to the new book displayed beside the other novel.

"Well, what's this one then?" she said to change the subject. "Something new?"

"Oh, yes!" replied the girl delightedly. "That's *Wandering Dreamer*. It's selling like mad right now. We can't keep it in stock. Just got a new shipment in yesterday."

Viola's eyes widened as she caught the name of the author of the new book.

"Forrest Neill?" she asked in amazement. "Is that the author's name, Forrest Neill?"

"Of course," replied the clerk, handing Viola one of the volumes.

Hurriedly, Viola searched the flyleaf and the first and last few pages of the book, looking for the usual information about the author. She was disappointed. There was none. Not one word. No picture, no biography, no dedication, no credits, nothing.

"I did that, too." smiled the clerk, adjusting her horn-rimmed glasses. "There isn't a scrap of information on him. The newspapers in New York have made quite a thing of it, I'm told. The man gives no interviews, makes no appearances, wants no publicity, apparently."

"How odd," mused Viola, her interest piqued.

She thumbed through a few pages until her eyes rested in shock on the name of the main character, Will Fable.

She shut the book and said as calmly as possible, "I think I'll take this one, too, my dear. How much do I owe you?"

As soon as she was out of sight of the bookstore, Viola grabbed the book out of her shopping bag. She stared at the name of the author, Forrest Neill, as pedestrians passed her on the busy sidewalk. She realized she was standing in the middle of the walkway, and looked quickly around for some place where she could examine the book more closely.

She spotted a coffee shop nearby and walked to it, taking a corner booth with her back to the other customers. She ordered coffee from the waitress and settled in to try to figure out the mystery.

Gulping her sugary coffee, she opened the book to the first page. There it was, that name again. My name is Will Fable, she read, and I travel all over this great country by the rails. Will Fable. The handsome stranger she met on Christmas Eve, the guest of Elizabeth Cooper. An old friend, Mrs. Cooper had said, from New York. Just passing through on his way to his summer home in Florida. The man who strangely turned up at her father's funeral in Albany three days later. Dating Miss Rolypoly Rigsby, indeed!

She smiled smugly and closed the book again. Forrest Neill, she read again on the cover. The mysterious Mr. Neill who sends suspicious crates to that white-trash farmer, Jake Potter. And suddenly, Potter is spending money like there was no tomorrow.

She was on to something, she knew it. If the man she met was Forrest Neill, why did he call himself by the name of a fictitious character in a book he was writing? What was the need? What was he up to, something illegal?

And the widow Cooper, lying about the man's identity to everyone; what was her part in this scheme? She and that Jake Potter were in it together, that was for sure. Viola sniffed haughtily, thinking of the woman's gall, letting her grandchild—Paul Tanner's daughter, mind you—play openly with that ignorant Potter child. And the widow Cooper herself, letting that Jake Potter traipse all over her property like he was family. She shivered.

A cruel smile twisted down the corner of Viola's mouth. A hoax had been perpetrated on them, and she had stumbled on it. could it possibly have anything to do with the cat burglar mess? Bubba James was asking a lot of questions about strangers in town. A wild thought hit Viola. Could the kidnaping also have been a hoax?

She had to get home. Sam would know what to do. If Bubba James wanted a stranger, she sure as fire had one for him. Viola gathered up her possessions and raced home, as fast as her plump legs could carry her.

43

Time was ticking away.

It took time to get the court orders, the subpoenas, time to follow the thirty-year-old trail of paper. The trial was now only three weeks away, and Thomas was no closer to the real cat burglar than knowing his name. It was John Price Daniel.

Mary Grey, RN, had been a young woman of twenty-two when she first saw John Price Daniel in 1908, at the Johnson General Hospital. She had been little more than an assistant then. But now, after thirty years of dedication and hard work, she had risen to the position of Director of the Yves Home in Savannah.

It was the first bit of luck Thomas had, for the woman remembered John Price Daniel. It was not surprising that she did, for the boy had stayed with the home for eight years, longer by many years than any other child in the home's history. Most children stayed several months to a year before other arrangements were made for them. Mary Grey practically raised John Price Daniel.

"What's it all about?" she asked Thomas, holding the subpoena for access to the home's records. "Why do you need to find Johnny?"

"I wish I could be more forthcoming, my dear Miss Grey," said Thomas earnestly. "You've been extremely cooperative and of great help to me in what you've been able to remember about the boy. Unfortunately, I am not at liberty to discuss the case."

"Oh, I understand that," she said with a sigh. "I just hope the poor darling has not fallen in with the wrong crowd. I never heard from him again after he left the military school in Virginia."

"If you like," said Thomas, "I will get in touch with you when I can legally do so, and let you know what I can."

The matronly woman smiled at him.

"That's very kind of you, Mr. Moore," she said. "I would like that very much."

On his notepad Thomas had written down the name of the military school the boy had attended until he was fourteen, Hastings Institute in Richmond, Virginia. The trail was getting longer and longer. Unless he got a big break soon, he had no hope of tracing the boy in time for the trial to begin. He would have to ask for a postponement. If he couldn't get one, he was licked.

Miss Grey rose from her seat behind the desk.

"Let's just look at those records now, shall we?"

"Thank you," said Thomas, rising.

He followed her down a long hall with a shiny linoleum floor to a locked door marked Record Room. Miss Grey took a key from the pocket of her white uniform and opened the door. It was little more than a large walk-in closet, lined from floor to ceiling with shelves.

Neat file folders and labeled cardboard boxes filled the shelves to capacity. Thomas breathed a sigh of relief. At least Yves was more organized than Johnson General had been. But then, they could afford to be.

"Here we are," said Miss Grey, pulling a brown folder from the "D" shelf. "John Price Daniel." She handed the folder to Thomas. It was the largest file in the record room.

"Follow me," she said, "and I'll get you settled in a nice quiet room in a comfortable chair. It will take you hours to go through that file. Then we'll get started with the financial records."

Thomas held little hope that the benefactor of little Johnny Daniel would have revealed anything of his identity in the financial records. There were too many ways to conceal what was to be kept secret, too many legal labyrinths in which to hide. If there was to be a break, it would be somewhere in this file.

As he opened the heavy folder in the quiet library room, Thomas felt a tingle of anticipation. It was here, he could feel it, he could smell it. A small black and white photograph fell from the folder. Thomas bent down and retrieved it, bringing it to the lamp.

A shiver went down his spine as he looked into the fourteen-year-old face of John Price Daniel. He could have been looking at a photo of Price Townsend as a youth and never questioned it. He turned the photograph over and read the words written in pencil: "Miss Mary, thanks for the birthday card. Love, Johnny."

After an hour of reading progress reports, diet sheets, medical records, and academic programs, Thomas found the break he needed. At the age of seven, Johnny had a tonsillectomy. Attached to a copy of a report from a Savannah hospital was an authorization for surgery, signed by next of kin or legal guardian. He stared at the initials on the form in disbelief. "JJM," it read, in a bold dark pen, followed by the note, Permit #GEO-33579. JJM, in a loopy, exaggerated, blessedly familiar scrawl he knew as well as his own name.

"I don't believe it," he said aloud. "I don't believe it!"

He laughed and quickly gathered the contents of the folder together. He did not need them now. With a little luck, he may have stumbled onto everything. He opened the door of the study and walked back to Miss Grey's office. She was out to lunch, so he handed the file to the secretary and, as was his custom, scratched out a hurried note of thanks on his business card.

"Tell Miss Grey I'll be in touch," he said to the secretary, unable to suppress the excitement in his eyes.

JJM. John Jefferson Moore. It had never occurred to Thomas that his own father could have been the guardian appointed as benefactor of little Johnny Daniel. All his late father's files were intact. All the information he had so painstakingly unearthed had been right under his nose.

THE FIRM of Lincoln & Moore was his father's firm, brought to prominence by his own brilliant legal career. Randall Lincoln, his father's partner, still puttered around the office, retired from practice but not from the love of the law. He advised Thomas wisely from time to time, and kept the staff on their toes.

Thomas entered the front door of the Atlanta office and waved to

Jeannie, the redheaded receptionist, without waiting to hear her pleas to answer his messages. He rushed into his office and threw his briefcase on the desk, opened the drawer, and pulled out a chain of rusted keys. In minutes he was in the attic room, running his finger along the alphabetic index cards identifying the contents of the string of file cabinets which contained his late father's case files.

He found the drawer marked CO-DI, and continued his search for the drawer marked TA-TY. Unlocking the cabinet, he pulled the file on Price Townsend, and, seeing one in front of it on Laura Townsend, he pulled hers as well. He returned with some trepidation to the first drawer, and, with a sigh of relief, saw the file on John Price Daniel.

As he reached for the file, Thomas paused instinctively. The name on the file was clearly visible, the folder raised a bit above the others, as if it had been pulled and hastily returned to its place. This was such a small detail. Why did his mind tell him it was important? Thomas had learned years ago never to doubt his instincts, and he automatically, methodically, impressed the picture of the folder, slightly raised above its fellows in the drawer, into his photographic memory.

Thomas pulled the file and laid it on top of the other two. Carefully, as if he cradled a newborn baby, he carried the files downstairs to his office. Shutting the door behind him, he went to his desk and sat down, laying the file folders before him on the cluttered surface. He picked up the telephone and told Jeannie to hold his calls. He switched on the reading lamp on the desk and took off his jacket, throwing it on the chair to his left. With a sigh of anticipation, he opened the file on John Price Daniel.

It was all there. Trust account, established 1908. Name of benefactor: P. L. Townsend. Benefactor shall remain anonymous. Trust shall be administered by trustee, J. J. Moore. Principal to be withdrawn and transferred to the subject on completion of his college degree. All that Thomas had discovered in his investigation was documented, and more. There for him to examine were the hospital bills, the records of the Yves Home, the Hastings Military Institute, and beyond, to financial and academic records of the boy's enrollment in the School of Engineering at

Boston College. He scanned the file hurriedly, trying to determine the most recent mention of the boy. He was disappointed, for the records led him only to the boy's graduation from college and the final endowment, a generous nest egg for the young man, a head start as he began life in the business world.

That was eight years ago. Eight years! Thomas put the file down and wiped his face with his handkerchief. It was a blow to his hopes. His search would not be over so easily. He had to learn what happened to the boy up to the point that he became entangled with the lives of the Townsends. The picture of the file, raised above the others in the file drawer, flashed through his mind.

He picked up the file on Price Townsend and began to skim through it, looking for any mention of his association with John Price Daniel. There was nothing, not a misplaced memo, not a pencil scratch. He looked at Laura's file. She was apparently an independently wealthy woman, with many of her own holdings, but he learned nothing which could link Paulette Laura Townsend to—

Thomas froze. He got a lump in his throat as a wild possibility hit him. His heart pounding, he laid Laura's folder aside and looked at Price Townsend's file. Quickly he searched paper after paper for the man's full name. The benefactor was P. L. Townsend. A myriad of questions and answers deluged the agile mind of the lawyer. He was right, he knew he was right. And if he was, it explained everything. Feverishly, he examined every paper for the middle initial of the dead man. Again and again the same signature, Price Townsend, Price Townsend, the same typed name, Price Townsend. Then he saw it, typewritten at the top of a contract: Price (NMI) Townsend.

"My God," Thomas said aloud.

He sat back in his chair, his hands folded in his lap. NMI was the shorthand way of designating on a legal paper that a person had no middle initial, and that the full legal name was being used. Price Townsend had no middle name.

John Price Daniel's benefactor had never been his true father, as the boy surely must have assumed. It was a kind woman who no doubt signed a paper thirty years ago, and gratefully trusted the dispensation of her generosity to others. A woman whose loyalty to her husband defied understanding. A woman who could forgive almost anything. A wife who could let no part of the man she loved suffer. P. L. Townsend, the silent benefactor of John Price Daniel, was Paulette Laura Townsend.

Thomas removed from his briefcase the notebook in which he had recorded the facts of the case. With the detachment of a mortician, he began writing, listing every new piece of information he had learned. An hour later he was finished.

Thomas took a deep breath and brought all his forces of concentration to bear on the pages of the notebook before him. He scanned each page, committing it to memory. Then he closed the notebook and pushed back the comfortable padded chair. Putting his feet up on the desk, he leaned back and closed his eyes. In a moment he was asleep.

He was dreaming. He saw a man, his face in shadow, pacing back and forth in the lobby of a hotel. The man looked at his watch for the hundredth time. He cursed and left the lobby of the Savannah Savoy Hotel. Images flew, switching from one place to another, one time to another. "But why?" a young boy with blond hair asked tearfully, as he ran to the waiting arms of Mary Grey, RN The scene switched again, the images tumbling one into the next, almost too fast to comprehend. "Savannah?" Rudolph Townsend was saying. "That's impossible. He was going to Miami." The light faded. In a dark room, a hand reached into a pocket and drew out a slender pick. The man raised the pick to the lock of the file cabinet and opened the lock easily. He drew out the file. P. L. Townsend, he read, Townsend Plantation, Hayley, Georgia.

Thomas frowned in his sleep and shifted in the chair. He saw more in his dream. A sandy-haired man setting his briefcase on a desk. The young man turned to Thomas's father and said, "I'm looking forward to working with you, sir." The scene was swallowed up in darkness, and then the sleeping Thomas was moving along a sidewalk in his mind's eye. He was close to the ground, running swiftly, black paws carrying him gracefully to the light. He came upon two men, talking in hushed tones.

One was Senator George Richmond, the other, County Pa. "The resemblance is uncanny," the senator said to Price Townsend. "I've never seen anything like it in my life." The two men suddenly turned and looked at Thomas. County Pa pointed his finger and started toward their unwelcome observer. "Never," he said heatedly, his face suddenly beginning to decay. "You'll never get a cent!" He came closer to the cat that was Thomas, his clothes falling to dust, his body crumbling. He was menacing, horrible.

Thomas awoke with a start. He was perspiring and breathing heavily. His head ached, the familiar pounding thudding through his brain. He reached for a pen and jotted down the following: George Richmond's files, John Margolin. He relaxed against the chair and returned to his sleep, hoping the migraine would be gone when he awoke. It wouldn't be.

GEORGE RICHMOND'S widow lived in Albany. Thomas guided his car steadily toward the Avenue of the Azaleas, Mrs. Richmond's address. State Senator Richmond was killed in the same plane crash which took the life of his friend and associate, Price Townsend. If Thomas Moore's deductions were correct, Richmond, a practicing lawyer, was the man who was handling the case of the unwelcome and unexpected appearance of the illegitimate son of County Pa for his friend Price Townsend.

The boy had been clever. The puzzle pieces were fitting together. Thomas now knew that John Price Daniel had set himself up as a recent law school graduate two years ago, and managed to get himself hired into the firm of Lincoln, Moore, under the name John Margolin. He had stayed just long enough to learn the name of his secret benefactor, and then vanished. When Thomas had subsequently investigated the young man, he had learned that all his papers were forgeries.

Randall Lincoln had hired John Margolin, and neither he nor Thomas had ever figured out the young man's purpose. Nothing had been stolen. Thomas had deduced that he was a plant, sent to discover some confidential information, probably financial in nature. Thomas had filed the experience in his memory, knowing that he probably would discover the truth eventually. Thomas had not thought of the clever imposter in years, before he surfaced in the dream.

Thomas remembered the young man. John Margolin was tall and blond, but the features which would have revealed him as Price Townsend's son were obscured by thick glasses, a full, closely cropped beard, and what must have been a false nose. From this, Thomas knew that John Price Daniel was something of a master of disguise.

The six years between his college graduation and his appearance as John Margolin at the law firm were still a mystery, as was the contact that must have ensued between the boy and County Pa. Thomas hoped the late senator Richmond's files would provide the answers he needed. Thomas had learned much, but there was still nothing to link the young man directly with Price Townsend.

Thomas found the Richmond place easily. It was an old mansion with white columns, the type one often saw in the South. It had once been the main house of a plantation, surrounded by acres of farm land. The acreage had been sold off little by little after the war, so that now the large home was only one of a row of elegant smaller homes on a suburban city street.

Pamela Richmond was expecting him. She opened the door and smiled as she welcomed her visitor.

"Come in, sir." The title was more a habitual form of address than a sign of respect, for Mrs. Richmond addressed all men in this fashion. "You are prompt. My late husband placed great emphasis on punctuality."

"You were so kind to see me, Mrs. Richmond," said Thomas, removing his hat as he entered the entrance hall. "I knew your late husband. He was a fine lawyer. Please accept my sympathies for your loss."

As were most people, Pamela was a bit surprised at Thomas's appearance. She had met many men in the legal profession over the years, and most of them had one thing in common: a competitive drive, a brash aggressiveness, albeit within the customary boundaries of a polite Southern gentleman. Pamela sensed none of this in Thomas. Yet his reputation was legendary. The soft-spoken, scholarly man before her scarcely fit the bill.

"Thank you, sir," she replied. "Shall we go into the library?" Her eyes reflected no hint of her surprise that Thomas was not what she expected.

He followed her to the library, whose walls were lined with hundreds of books on built-in shelves. The brown paneled room was dominated by a massive desk, and furnished comfortably with couches and upholstered chairs. Pamela sat on a light blue couch before the fireplace, and waved Thomas to a matching chair on her right.

"Now," said Pamela, "what can I do for you?"

"I would like to ask you a great favor."

"Indeed?"

"Yes. I mean no imposition, but I am currently involved in a case which I believe also involves your late husband."

"The Townsend trial?" she asked quizzically. "What could George have had to do with that?"

Thomas leaned forward in his chair.

"Mrs. Richmond, I believe your husband was working on a case for Price Townsend when they were killed, a case which has a direct bearing on this trial."

"You intrigue me, sir," said Pamela carefully. "But surely you are not suggesting that George could have been involved in any wrongdoing."

"No, no," said Thomas, "of course not. There is no possibility of that whatsoever. It is only that he may have had contact with a man I am seeking. In fact, I believe that he and Mr. Townsend were on their way to meet this man when they died."

"I see," said Pamela. "And how may I be of assistance to you? I have been quite distressed over Carlton's trial. His mother is a friend of mine, and I would like to be able to do something to help her."

"Your husband's records, papers," said Thomas. "If I might look at them."

44

After two weeks at Janie's house in Albany, Dixie Lee was still not willing to move back home. It was not that she was still at odds with her father, she was not. It was just that being away from home for the first time was fun, and getting out of Hayley was exciting. She had seen her father several times and they had worked out their differences. Bubba was not happy that Carlton, rather than Rudolph, was to be his son-in-law. He determined to find the truth concerning the case of the cat burglar, however, without prejudice and without malice.

He had begun his own investigation, having learned that all the evidence against Carlton could be explained to his satisfaction. The returning of the black bag to the meadow in the middle of the night, Carlton's denial of his knowledge of the secret room, the lie about his whereabouts that Saturday, it all made sense when Bubba put himself in Carlton's shoes. The truth was that Bubba's new openness with Carlton was not because he believed Carlton was innocent, it was because he believed his daughter was telling the truth.

Neither Bubba nor his wife had asked Dixie Lee to come home. Bubba was too proud and Hedda too wise. She would come home when she was ready, but she would come home. This, all three of the Jameses knew.

Dixie Lee and Janie Parrish chatted happily as Dixie Lee looked through Janie's immense closet for something stunning to wear to dinner with the Townsend brothers and Camilla that evening. The two girls wore the same size clothes, and had traded dresses all through school. Dixie Lee had brought nothing appropriate with her in her hasty departure from home. It had to be something special tonight; Camilla would be there with Rudolph.

In her bedroom, surrounded by hundreds of ribbons and trophies she had won at horse shows over the years, Janie lounged lazily on her bed watching Dixie Lee try on dress after dress. She was amused by her friend's obvious sense of competition with Camilla Goodson.

"Poor Rudolph," Janie said with a sigh as she stared at the ceiling. "Going back to Camilla on the rebound." She tried not to smile.

"Well," said Dixie Lee, "it's only natural, I guess, since she's back in town for a while." She admired herself in Janie's full-length mirror. I want him to go out, you know," she continued, fussing with the lace collar of the dress. "He can't just pine away after me for the rest of his life."

Janie sat up. "I heard that she's not just visiting," she said. "I heard she's come back for good."

"Maybe she has," replied Dixie Lee. "I hope you're right." She went to the closet again, looking for another dress to try on. "Rudolph loved Camilla once. Maybe they can love each other again."

"You and Camilla, sisters-in-law," mused Janie. "Hmmm . . . . "

Dixie Lee's eyes widened at the prospect, but she replied calmly, "And why not?"

Janie laughed.

"You'd probably kill each other."

"What in the world are you talking about, you ninny?" asked Dixie Lee, turning to her friend with an irritated frown. "I have nothing against Camilla Goodson. She's a very nice person," she paused, "in spite of the fact that she's—uh, rather attractive."

"Oh, of course she is. I know that. I was only kidding. You know what they say about two women getting along in the same house and all."

Dixie Lee's eyes narrowed and she turned away from Janie to hide her irritation. The thought of Camilla with Rudolph was almost unbearable to her. She had to find a way to deal with these unwelcome feelings. Why should she be jealous of Camilla? She wanted Rudolph to be happy, didn't she? Besides, she was going to marry Carlton once he got out of this mess. She was marrying the man she loved. Why should Rudolph's life concern her now? She turned to replace a dress in the closet and bumped her wrist bone on the doorjamb.

"Darn it!" she cried.

Janie looked at Dixie Lee in surprise.

"What is it?"

"Oh, nothing. I hit my arm on the door."

Janie arched a knowing brow.

"Calm down," she said coolly. "It's not the end of the world, you know."

ONLY CARLTON and Laura Townsend knew the truth about Rudolph and Camilla, that they had rediscovered their love prior to Dixie Lee's confession. Both Carlton and Laura agreed to go along with Rudolph about his beginning to "date" Camilla again after losing Dixie Lee. There was no need for Rudolph and Camilla to rush announcing their engagement, with the specter of Carlton's trial so near. In a court of law, the withholding of truth is considered the same as a lie; in everyday life, the same may be considered a kindness.

That evening the Townsend brothers and their future brides were seated at the best table at the New Albany Hotel Restaurant. Dixie Lee looked stunning in a blue silk sheath dress, and Camilla was elegant in white linen. The patrons of the restaurant politely ignored their entrance, but their presence engendered conversation.

Dixie Lee's apprehension about seeing Rudolph with Camilla was made bearable in the face of Camilla's warm interest. On the surface, at least, they were at ease with each other almost at once. Again the actress, Dixie Lee's talents did not fail her, but underneath, she could not reconcile her feelings of conflict. Carlton's presence made it easier. There was no doubt which of the brothers had captured her heart.

Rudolph smiled as he listened to their cheerful small talk. It was right, finally, he thought. Happy with Camilla, Rudolph could not help but notice the change in his former fiancée, and in his brother as well. Carlton seemed more settled, more satisfied, even content, as he carried on as usual for his audience, cracking jokes and inciting them all to join in his infectious laughter.

Dixie Lee was different, too. Amazingly so. Ever insistent, ever in soft control, she seemed to melt under the spell of Carlton's charm.

Rudolph was jolted out of his private thoughts when the conversation turned to the trial. Carlton turned to him and asked if he had heard from Thomas.

"Not for about a week, I guess."

"Well, what's he doing, for God's sake?" said Carlton in a low growl. "Do you realize that he hasn't told us anything about my defense?"

"He's working on it night and day," said Rudolph. "I know that for a fact. You know he's trying to find the scoundrel who's behind this.'"

Carlton sighed. "I know, I know. But has he had any leads? I just wish he would keep us better informed, that's all. I've tried to call him, left messages. Hell, he's never there."

"He's not there because he's out beating the bushes, looking for your friend the cat," replied Rudolph calmly. "When he has something to tell us, he'll call."

"Don't worry, Carlton," said Dixie Lee. "If anybody can straighten out this mess, Thomas Moore can. He's the best there is, I really believe that."

Carlton nodded and drew a deep breath. "Y'all just look over me," he said. "I must be getting nervous."

"You have nothing to be nervous about," Rudolph replied confidently. "You've been reading too many newspapers."

"And now Daddy's on your side, too," added Dixie Lee softly, "don't forget that. He's checking up on all kinds of people, newcomers, drifters, strangers. He and Sheriff Morehouse are both working on it."

"This guy's no drifter," said Carlton. "He's got something against me, and he wants to see me nailed to a tree." He shook his head thoughtfully. "I can't figure it out. I never hurt anybody, not intentionally. I never punched anybody out or stole anybody's wife."

Rudolph arched a skeptical brow at this, and rubbed his jaw in remembrance. Carlton caught his meaning and smiled.

"Hell," he continued, his tone lighter now, "I'm the one who took everybody to lunch and bought everybody a beer. What is it? What could I have done to this guy?"

"Perhaps Tom can tell us that in time," Rudolph replied with a shrug. "I suggest we forget about it for a while, and enjoy the company of these two lovely ladies. The trial will be upon us soon enough."

"You're right," said Carlton with a decisive nod. "Let's drink to it."

"He reached for the carafe of wine beside him, cooling in a silver ice bucket, and poured out a fresh libation for each of them.

"A toast!" he said, raising his glass.

The others raised their glasses in anticipation, as Carlton's eyes suddenly looked beyond them, to the lobby of the hotel.

"What shall we drink to?" asked Rudolph, waiting.

Carlton put down his glass and rose hurriedly from the table. "I'll be right back," he said quickly, and he walked briskly through the restaurant, out into the lobby.

"What's going on?" asked Dixie Lee, lowering her glass as she watched him disappear through the doorway.

Rudolph looked at her and smiled wickedly.

"Old girlfriend, probably. He's got thousands of them."

Dixie Lee's mouth dropped open and her eyes widened. Then she snapped her pink lips tightly together and threw Rudolph a menacing look as he chuckled. She fought a smile as she slapped him playfully on the shoulder in protest.

"You beast," she said.

Camilla smiled at their antics. It would be a good relationship, she hoped. Rudolph and Dixie Lee would be friends. Camilla was not as sure about her own relationship with her future sister-in-law. Her instincts told her that there was more to Dixie Lee James than the Townsend brothers realized.

Carlton reached the bottom of the circular staircase at the far end of the lobby in plenty of time. The man who had caused his hasty departure was just ahead of him on the stairs, carrying a small suitcase up to his newly rented room. His strong shoulders seemed to sag wearily, and his gait was slow.

"Hold it right there, Mister!" Carlton growled. "I have business with you."

Jack Hamilton froze, recognizing the voice of the younger Townsend.

"I vowed I'd knock your block off if I ever got my hands on you," Carlton continued.

Jack, the philandering golf pro, turned on the stairs to face him.

"As I recall," Carlton went on, "wringing your neck was also a definite possibility."

Jack sighed.

"Tell you what," he said, "I've got some lovely Irish whiskey in this bag. Join me for one last belt before you do me in. Deal?"

Carlton glared at him, hands clenched into tight fists, irritated by Jack's nonchalance. He pounded the handrail sharply in frustration.

"Damn it, man! Don't you know what a mess you left us in?"

Jack glanced around the lobby. Carlton's voice was rising. They were attracting attention.

"Come on, sport," he said tolerantly. "Upstairs. You can have your choice of weapons."

He turned and left his former employer on the stairs. Carlton was furious.

In room 211, Jack Hamilton set his bag on the bed and unzipped the top. He glanced back at Carlton, who was standing stiffly just inside the open door.

"Shut the door, Junior," he said, pulling the bottle from the bag, "and sit down, dammit."

Carlton took no offense at this form of address. Carlton was just fourteen years old the first time Jack Hamilton called him Junior. Always irreverent, Jack told Carlton he was likely to grow up to be "Junior Pa" if he didn't change his ways.

Jack was the only man Carlton knew who called his father County Pa to his face. Carlton never understood the relationship between the two men, for although they cursed each other unmercifully, they always seemed to remain friends. When Carlton asked Jack about it once, Jack just laughed and said, "Hell, Junior, that's just business. Got nothing to do with being friends after business hours."

Jack was kinder in his address to Rudolph, dubbing him Rudy, a nickname Rudolph hated and tolerated from no one else but Jack. Only

Laura escaped Jack's wit, for he never called her anything but Mrs. Townsend.

When he walked out at the beginning of the summer, he left not only his wife and daughter, he left the employ of a family who depended on him, and boys who grew up with him. He was a handsome smoothie with a head for business, the perfect party mixer, the ultimate club promoter. Jack kept everybody happy and the dollars rolling in. He and Marie ran the country club with what seemed little effort. They made it look easy.

Something had happened between Jack and Marie when County Pa died. They began to have violent arguments, often terrifying Wendy. Jack started drinking heavily, and it was rumored that he was finally, after ten years of fidelity to Marie, accepting the inevitable propositions of the bored society matrons whom he coached in their backswing.

At the time, Carlton could not be bothered, embroiled as he was with his resentment of Rudolph and his rebellion against his father's will. Laura was, as always, protected from unpleasant staff problems, so it fell to Rudolph to call Jack to task. He never did.

Carlton knew none of this. He knew only that a man he considered family, a man he depended on, a man with a wife and child, had disappeared one day without a backward glance. Carlton stared at Jack Hamilton as he opened the bottle and poured himself a drink.

Jack looked up.

"Make up your mind, boy. Are you in or out? If you're in, shut the damn door and sit down!"

Carlton kicked the door shut with his foot.

"You've got a lot of nerve showing your sorry face around here again," he said.

Jack scowled.

"Have I, now?" he asked.

He offered the glass to Carlton, who made no move to accept it, and no move to sit down.

"Take it," Jack said wearily. "The last wish of a condemned man?" His tone was mocking. He had not been afraid of the father; he was certainly not afraid of the son.

Carlton was frustrated by his affection for the man. His anger left him, dissipating into the air. He grabbed the glass and sat down on the bed.

"Crap," he said.

Jack smiled sadly.

"I couldn't have put it better myself," he said.

"You look awful, Jack."

"Thanks." He sat down on the other bed, facing Carlton. "Got a cigarette?"

"Yeah." Carlton threw him the package. "What happened to the hostess?"

"She's back on the circuit, I guess, spilling her coffee on some other jerk." He lit a cigarette. "She served her purpose. Poor darlin' only knew how to do one thing, but she did it well, that I can tell you."

Carlton didn't smile.

"I hope it was worth it," he said. "Marie will never forgive you."

"You don't know that, Junior. I think she will."

"But why, Jack? Why did you do it? I thought you—"

"Loved her?" Jack shrugged. "Yeah, I love her. I wouldn't have come back if I didn't."

"You still haven't told me why," said Carlton.

"And I won't," replied Jack. "Some things are nobody's business, Junior." He took a swig from the bottle. "Let's just say I made a mistake, okay? Now I'm back to try to make it right. I'm forty-six years old. When your father died I came face-to-face with something I have avoided thinking about all my life. My own mortality. I think I went a little crazy."

Carlton sighed. "You're not the only one," he said.

The two men sat in silence, each considering his own folly. Carlton was at odds with himself about his father. He knew the man's corruption, his deceit, his selfish pride, his cruelty. Yet, he was a man who had sustained the love and loyalty of an extraordinary woman, a man who was capable of generosity and charity, a man who had collected scores of true friends, like Jack Hamilton. And in spite of all his faults, Carlton had loved him. So, apparently, had Jack.

Jack looked at Carlton.

"So," he stated flatly, "I'm back, now. I'd like my job back if it's still open—if you'll have me back." He put down the bottle. "I'll straighten out. Just give me another chance. How about it?"

Carlton paused before answering.

"Job's still open. Job's still yours. You forgot to resign when you left."

Jack smiled. "I guess I did. Thanks, Junior." He went to the window and looked out into the dark street. "You know, I missed this place. Anything interesting happen while I was gone?"

"Nah," grinned Carlton. "Same old stuff."

45

It was a cloudy night. Flashes of bright lightning lit up the eastern sky, but there was no thunder. The sun was gone, but the clouds seemed to hold a strange luminescence all their own between the unending, silent sheets of white lightning. It was tornado weather, a night for fear.

Elizabeth Cooper was finishing up the supper dishes when she heard a knock at the front door.

Tori put down her dish towel.

"I'll get it, Meema," she said.

"No, dear," answered Mrs. Cooper, "finish your drying. I'll go."

She wiped her hands on her apron and left the kitchen.

"Who is it, please?" asked Mrs. Cooper through the door.

"Chief James, Ma'am," came the reply.

She opened the door and admitted Bubba James. He towered over her in the narrow hallway.

"Sorry to bother you so late, Mrs. Cooper," said Bubba in his official voice, "but I have some questions for you. May I come in for a few minutes?"

"Certainly, Chief James," replied Mrs. Cooper. "Please, come in and sit down. May I get you some coffee? A cup of tea?"

She led the way to the front room as she spoke. Bubba followed.

"No thank you, Ma'am," he said, sitting down in the rocker opposite the couch. "This won't take long."

Mrs. Cooper watched as Bubba shifted nervously in his seat. He drew out a small notebook from his breast pocket.

"Mrs. Cooper, there's been some talk. A certain party came to me and made some, uh, disturbing suggestions."

Elizabeth Cooper looked at the man across from her with perceptive eyes. He was strangely stiff and formal.

"You mean accusations, don't you?" said Mrs. Cooper. "What kind of accusations?"

Bubba coughed and opened the notebook. He kept his eyes on the little book.

"Are you acquainted with a man named Forrest Neill, Ma'am?"

"Why, yes," she answered.

"Is this Forrest Neill the same man who visited you last Christmas under the name of Will Fable?"

Mrs. Cooper looked at him with a discerning frown.

"Yes, Chief," she said, a slight smile on her face as the unbelievable point of his question dawned on her.

He looked up, hearing the hint of amusement in her voice.

"Would you mind explaining to me what is going on here, and what his connection is to Jake Potter? Just for the record, Ma'am. Believe me, I wouldn't be here if I had a choice in the matter."

She looked at him sympathetically.

"Chief, I would be more than happy to. It's a bit complicated, but it's a wonderful story. But first, I will ask a favor of you."

"If it is in my power, Ma'am," smiled the chief.

"I am wary of your need to know about my friends. You said a certain party has made unkind suggestions. I do not wish to hear them, or the name of the person. I will tell you what you need to know, and I will ask you to make sure this goes no further."

Bubba James said that had been his aim all along.

"Now then, Chief," Mrs. Cooper continued, "the best way to learn about my friend Will Fable is to read the book he wrote, the book that has obviously made its way to some citizen here. I met him for the first time just before Christmas. He was dressed as a hobo, and he called himself Will Fable. I offered him shelter in the barn and he did some chores for me in return."

Bubba James listened intently as Mrs. Cooper related the tale of Will Fable. When she had finished, Bubba stood up and reached for his cap. He put the notebook in his pocket.

"Thank you, Ma'am," he said. The admiration in his eyes was clear, but unspoken, as he was there in an official capacity. "I'll take care of this little matter; don't you worry about a thing."

Elizabeth Cooper smiled at him in appreciation. She had always liked Bubba James. She walked him to the door and bid him good night, as the eerie weather rolled on above in silence. When he had gone, she walked down the hall to Tori's room, and saw her sitting on her bed in her gown. Mrs. Cooper smiled, walked over, and sat down on the bed.

"Why were you telling him about Will?" Tori asked.

"He has Will's book, honey," she answered. "He was curious, that's all."

A FEW miles away, John Price Daniel sat in the swing on the front porch of his rented home. He watched the strange silent lightning flashing across the dark sky. The wind blew through the trees, and there was a hint of respite from the heat of the day. It was so stinking hot down here. He had forgotten the humid, heavy, sticky heat of a Georgia summer.

He liked the isolation of the house. Quiet and peaceful, the old house was on a country road, hidden from view by a stand of scrub oaks and bushes. Even so, he dared not venture outside the house without his makeup. He was so close to his goal now. He could not afford to take any chances.

As the heavens danced above him, he opened the brown leather ledger on his lap and began to read. The book fascinated him. It was written in his father's hand, the father that rejected him, the father whose visage was his own. He had read the ledger many times in the secret cellar when he was shadowing his half brother, Carlton. It was as if by reading it, he could heal the past. But it only confirmed what he already knew about his father.

John understood him, even admired him. His father was like himself, superior to other men. In all his life, John had never met a man he could not outsmart; he wondered if Price Townsend could have been that man. If only he had not been born the spitting image of his father, John could have made it a real game, a true challenge. Matching wits with County Pa. If only there had been time.

He regretted revealing his identity to his father in that first letter. He should have done as he was doing now: living with them, eating with them, laughing with them.

Of course his father would reject him again, he had known that. What he had not anticipated was the violence and power of his father's rejection. John had thought himself above emotions. He had thought himself oblivious to rejection, to pain, to need, to love. But County Pa's final rejection had hurt him, and badly. Again.

All those years, his father had supported him, sent him to the best schools. John must have written him hundreds of letters. Did his father never read even one? Did his father never check on his progress? Even that would have been no surprise.

But when that lawyer, George Richmond, had met with John in Savannah, he brought a surprising response from County Pa. Price Townsend had denied knowing of him, denied knowing his mother, and denied ever giving him one cent.

No words could deny that he was Price Townsend's son. John had sent the lawyer back with a note threatening to show up in Hayley and let everyone see him. It was enough. A cash settlement was worked out. John was to receive cash, plus a share of the estate as his rightful inheritance upon County Pa's death, but only under the condition that John stay out of Georgia, and out of Price Townsend's life, permanently.

John accepted the offer, but only on the condition that Price Townsend hand him the papers personally. County Pa refused. That was what hurt. He didn't even want to see for himself. And John hated him for it.

From that point on, John's life was changed. He was eaten up with hatred. The more he thought about the wealthy half brothers he had never seen, about the pampered woman who should have been his mother, and most of all, about the vile man who was his father, the more tortured he became. County Pa became an obsession with him. He was bent on revenge, and on getting his rightful inheritance. He would take out his hatred on the Townsends and on the family name, which he had been denied.

There had been moments during the last few months when the game he was playing had actually been fun. It had been so easy once he discovered the secret room in the cabin. His plan had been perfect, even down to the notoriety of the cat burglar among the locals.

He had even been reckless and left clues for the fools. It had made the game more risky, more exciting. He had hardly disguised his name, for God's sake. He even showed himself to the little colored girl in broad daylight. It was different now, of course. The brothers knew they had an enemy, that he was out there somewhere.

John closed the ledger and sighed. It wasn't fun anymore. Ever since he locked up the girl in the cellar, he had felt a twinge of guilt. He didn't plan that, it just happened. He knew they would find her within twenty-four hours. There would be no harm done. But he kept hearing a soft cry in his memory. It was his own voice, a child's voice, crying for Miss Mary. The other children had locked him in a closet and left him there in the dark. He was six years old, but he never forgot his terror. For months afterwards he had nightmares, for years he was afraid of closets.

He hadn't thought about that experience in years. Now it haunted him. He regretted imprisoning the girl, Tori, and his feelings threatened him. He tried not to think about it, because such feelings were dangerously close to breaking through the hard callus he had placed over his heart long ago.

All of this he knew, but could not admit. He knew only that the joy of the kill had gone out of him. But he was determined to finish what he had started. Carlton would not be convicted, he was sure, but he would know how it felt to be trapped. John still had the ledger and the money. Rudolph would have to part with a large part of his fortune to get the ledger back and save his father's name. And what about Laura Townsend? What was his quarrel with her? She had been his father's wife; that was enough. Let her suffer for condoning his actions all these years.

John Price Daniel sat alone on his rented porch in the dark. He was thirty years old today. It was his birthday, and he was lonely. Not even his hatred comforted him anymore.

At the far end of the porch, a cardboard box contained his only companion, a large yellow puppy. Around its neck was a red ribbon. The pup had been sleeping, but now woke and sat up. Struggling to see over the wall of cardboard, it spotted John and immediately began yapping a squeaky, high, puppy bark.

THE NEXT morning, Tori awoke early. It was unusual for her to rise before her grandmother. She yawned and climbed out of bed, headed for the bathroom. When she reached the door, she heard again the lonely sound which had wakened her. She stopped and listened. Then she heard it again. It was a soft yapping.

Tori ran to the kitchen and opened the back door. On the porch was a cardboard box, and in the box was a big yellow puppy with a red ribbon around its neck.

In all her life, there was only one thing she had ever wanted desperately, that her grandmother would not allow, and that one thing was staring at her now.

She rushed to the puppy and brought it, soft and squirmy, to her chest. She sank down on the porch and squeezed the animal tightly. She sat holding the dog, rocking it, petting it. She did not realize that her grandmother had risen and had seen her on the porch with her wonderful companion.

It was the first time since the kidnaping that Mrs. Cooper had seen Tori smile. Without a word, Mrs. Cooper returned to the kitchen to make breakfast. The puppy would stay.

THOMAS WAS stalled. After days of sifting through a lifetime of paperwork in Mrs. Richmond's attic, he had found nothing. Without physical proof that John Price Daniel had contacted County Pa, Thomas had no case. He had the truth, but no case. And out in the late George Richmond's backyard was a garage full of paper yet to be examined. Thomas knew the file was there, if only he could find it in time. The trial was set for Wednesday, July thirteenth, one week away. He had to have some help.

He usually did his investigating alone, trusting no one to be as thorough as he knew himself to be, but this time he would make an exception and call on his staff. At eight-thirty on Wednesday morning, Mrs. Richmond found her garage filled with six fresh-faced young men. They were searching blind for three names: John Price Daniel, Price Townsend, Rosellen Daniel. Thomas had not disclosed his purpose or his theory to his staff, because until he had the proof in his hands, all he had was a theory.

At three o'clock that afternoon, theory became reality. Thomas scanned the discovered file, and then he dismissed the staff. The six of them piled into a borrowed car for the drive back to Atlanta, grinning, for Thomas had given them all the next day off in appreciation of a job well done.

Thomas got more than he bargained for. Not only did the file contain the letters to County Pa from his illegitimate son, and copies of a proposed financial settlement, there was also a lengthy report on John Price Daniel, compiled by a private investigator named Walter Montgomery.

Thomas knew the name. Montgomery was based in Washington, D.C., a former colleague of Elliot Ness. He had left the FBI after years of service, having no stomach for J. Edgar Hoover's tactics. In the legal community, Montgomery was considered a first class researcher— tough, thorough, shrewd, low-key, and very expensive.

Montgomery's report on John Price Daniel was worth the price. It was everything Thomas needed. Montgomery had traced John back to his college days. The report read like a fictional adventure story. After graduating with honors, the boy had come into a sum of money whose source was, in Montgomery's words, questionable. He did not immediately seek a job as an engineer, but instead had joined a traveling circus. A natural athlete, he had mastered the high wire and the trapeze with little difficulty, but his real love was makeup.

He became an expert with greasepaint, and created a hundred new faces for the clowns. Later he branched out to making up the faces of the female performers. After a year, he left the circus troupe and headed for Broadway. For the next four years, John had worked as a makeup artist for the stars by day, attending acting classes by night. He had the reputation of a near-genius with makeup; he could transform men into monsters, young into old.

At the beginning of 1935, John had become a Broadway actor, performing first in minor roles. He quickly rose to star in a play called *The Lord of Rain*. After a successful run of eleven months, the play closed.

And John Price Daniel disappeared.

46

Except for Sam and Daisy, Laura Townsend was alone in the big house when Thomas Moore called. A meeting had been set for two o'clock between Thomas, Laura, and her sons. Thomas called to ask if he could come an hour early to speak with her alone. Somehow she knew that Thomas would bring bad news to her that July day. It would be so like him to want to prepare her privately for a shock. All her life, men had tried to protect Laura from evil, from trouble, and from unhappiness. She must have appeared to them very fragile. The truth was that Laura was a rock, a well of strength. What she had endured over the years, she had endured because of her unshakable faith, faith in her husband, in her wayward son, and faith in God. She was a survivor.

She led Thomas to the brick patio at the side of the house. The sun was high and hot, the sky deep blue and filled with powder puff clouds of white. The heat of the day gave Laura strength. She bade him sit down at one of the wrought iron tables. Sam followed with iced tea and cake. She smiled at Thomas. She had known him slightly for more than twenty years.

"So," she said without joy. "You have found him."

"Yes, Ma'am," Thomas replied. His eyes were soft and sorrowful, but his voice was encouraging, even peaceful.

"And you believe the identity of this man will bring me pain?"

Thomas nodded.

"But it is not my son," she stated, waiting for his confirmation.

Thomas shook his head. Without a word, he withdrew a photograph from his briefcase. He handed it to Laura, the back side up. On the back were the words: Miss Mary, thank you for the birthday card. Love, Johnny. And below, in a different hand: John Price Daniel, age fourteen, 1922.

Laura took the photograph. Thomas saw only a flicker of surprise in her eyes as she read the words. She did not look at Thomas, but, after hesitating, she turned the photograph over. She said nothing as she looked into the youthful face of her husband's son, a face nearly identical to his own. She sat erect and silent, willing her heart not to beat faster as she realized who he was, and tried to understand the implications of his actions.

Thomas waited. He observed her closely, for her reactions would confirm or deny his interpretation of the facts. When her eyes filled with tears which fell unhindered down her cheeks, Thomas averted his eyes. He had seen enough. He looked at the red brick beneath his feet. It was as he suspected. She had provided for the boy, but had left him totally in the care of others. She had never seen him, never asked about him. Perhaps she had tried to forget he existed.

"You know of my sponsorship of this child?" she said at last.

"Yes."

"And you are saying this child has grown up to hate this family? And to perpetrate this terrible crime? But why?"

For the next few minutes, Thomas tried to explain. He showed her the documents he possessed, and wove them together in theory. She listened without question, without interruption, without denial. The truth was heartbreaking; the possibility that it would become public knowledge during the trial was shattering.

"Was I wrong to want to help him?" she asked finally.

"You should not have had to make such a choice," Thomas replied. "No one could say that you were in any way at fault." He paused and looked into her eyes. Somehow he knew she was strong enough to bear this, she was strong enough to bear almost anything.

"You are not responsible for the path this boy has chosen. You tried only to help him. You are a wise woman, Mrs. Townsend. You know this is true. You have lived with your own pain, the depth of which I do not begin to know, but you have transcended it. You have raised two strong sons who adore you. You are surrounded by friends who love you, and live in a town with people who respect you. You are not alone. Do not question now what lies before you. Nothing happens without a reason. I believe that something good can come of this, if we do not despair."

Laura reached out and took his hand across the table. She smiled, and in her eyes was fond affection and a bond of kinship, for she understood that the two of them were much alike in their beliefs.

"The boys will be here soon," she said softly. "I will be up in my room if you don't mind. I need to be alone for a while."

"Of course."

"I want you to tell them everything, just as you told me," she said.

"Are you all right?" asked Thomas, who stood up respectfully as Laura rose to leave.

"Yes, Tom," she said, "I believe I am, thanks to you. The things you have said to me have given me strength. I am very grateful, and I thank God you are here.

"My dear Thomas," she added sadly, "perhaps I am not wise, as you said. Perhaps I have always been foolish. Perhaps I have loved foolishly and forgiven unwisely. Perhaps I have clung to foolish hopes and closed my eyes to reality. You see, I always believed in my husband."

Tears filled her eyes.

"I felt I knew him differently than others did," she continued. She looked at Thomas again, her eyes beseeching him to understand. "He was a good man inside. He didn't want to be as he was. Things happened to him, changed him, but inside he—" She stopped abruptly and looked away.

Thomas placed his hands gently on her shoulders.

"Who is to say, Mrs. Townsend, that inside the hardest heart is not a soul which suffers? Perhaps yours is truly the path of wisdom after all. Maybe you did not close your eyes to reality, maybe you looked beyond it. And perhaps you alone were given the ability to see the truth."

She sighed, and when she raised her eyes again to him, he saw the flash of hope his words had rekindled there.

"Your husband was killed on his way to Savannah. Who is to say that he did not have a change of heart about this young man?" Laura's eyes widened as Thomas continued, "Listen to your own heart, my dear. In spite of everything, County Pa was loved by a great lady. And now, perhaps only she will understand his motives that last day."

RUDOLPH SAT in the desk chair in his father's library. He looked at Carlton when Thomas had finished his story, his eyes filled with regret. Carlton stared at the letter and the photograph before him on the coffee table. Their half brother's desperate search for County Pa's love and acceptance was too close to their own experience. Neither of them saw John Price Daniel as an enemy any longer. He was a brother, a brother of both flesh and spirit. All of their lives had in one way or another been shaped by the kind of man their father was.

"You don't know where he is, or who he is pretending to be?" Rudolph asked Thomas.

"Unfortunately, no." Thomas replied. "But I suspect he will not be far away during the trial, maybe in the courtroom itself. He is apparently, as I said, a supreme egotist. He will not believe he can be caught."

"Is there any way," said Carlton, "that you can get me off without bringing all this out?"

"I am a firm believer in telling the whole truth," said Thomas, "but exceptions can be made if the same result can be achieved with less than the whole. Let me think about it. In any case, you must trust me to do what must be done."

Rudolph stared at the photograph of the young John Price Daniel he held in his hands.

"I know this is crazy," he said, "but I wish I could find him, and pin him down, and make him listen to me."

"And what would you say?" asked Thomas sympathetically.

"That all this is wrong," Rudolph replied, "that it's not necessary. That he's still my brother, no matter what my father told him."

"None of that matters now," replied Thomas. "It will not undo the crimes, or get Carlton out of this mess. It is too late for reconciliation, it's life and death now."

"He's right," said Carlton with resignation. "We can't go back. We can't change what's happened. It's out of our hands, and if he's caught, we can't save him."

It was true and they all knew it.

47

Thomas Moore sat in the oak-paneled waiting room of Albany's district attorney, which had been borrowed for the Townsend case by the federal prosecutor, Baxter Brooks. His appointment was for one o'clock. Thomas looked at his watch. It was one-thirty. He looked up knowingly at the matronly secretary, who did her best to ignore him. After a few minutes, Thomas heard jovial voices and deep laughter in the hall. There was no mistaking that voice. Baxter Brooks was finally finished with his lunch. Thomas waited expectantly, his face calm and unruffled.

The door was thrown open and Baxter walked into the room, larger than life, filling every inch of the comfortable room with his mesmerizing presence. He walked over to his secretary and asked for his messages. The woman handed him a stack of small yellow notes, then discreetly mentioned that Mr. Moore was waiting. Baxter turned and searched the room for his visitor, as if he were unaware of his presence. A broad, practiced smile crossed his face when he spotted Thomas. He walked over to him and extended a great hand in greeting.

"Tom!" he said. "I didn't expect you until two."

Thomas stood up and grasped his hand.

"Hello, Baxter," he said. "I'm a little early."

The brown eyes which met Baxter's were calm and patient, and the smile on Thomas's face was tolerant. Baxter cringed inwardly at the other man, who had so neatly turned the situation to his own advantage. The federal prosecutor's eyes never wavered.

"Please," continued Thomas. "By all means take care of your messages. As I said, I'm a little early."

"I won't hear of it, Tom," replied Baxter. "I'll be right with you."

He called the name of his assistant and walked to the door of his office, throwing open the door as if Eden lay on the other side. The young man followed and closed the door. Soon, the assistant emerged, carrying the yellow notes.

When Baxter buzzed the secretary to admit Thomas, he picked up his briefcase and walked to the office door, opened it, and went inside. Baxter was sitting behind a massive desk whose surface was shiny and devoid of paperwork.

"Come in, Tom," said Baxter through his dazzling white teeth. "Have a seat."

Thomas settled himself on the edge of a stiff, uncomfortable monstrosity, with a hard wooden seat and a back which tilted too far back to offer any support.

"Now, Tom," said Baxter with deceptive warmth, "what can I do for you today?"

"I hope I have not gotten my dates mixed up again," Thomas replied with ease. "Was this not the date set by Judge Cunningham for the Articles of Disclosure?"

Baxter laughed. Thomas was beginning to make him nervous.

"Of course," he said. "The Articles of Disclosure. It must have slipped my mind." He opened a drawer and rummaged through it, closed it, and opened another. "It's here somewhere," he said. "I have so many cases, Tom. You know how it is. I rely on Mrs. Worsham out there to keep me straight, bless her heart." He continued searching, finally settling on a binder from the bottom drawer.

"Ah, here we are," he said. "Townsend, Carlton. Articles of Disclosure."

He handed the binder to Thomas. Despite himself, Baxter handed over the document with a measure of regret. He was required by law to reveal the evidence against the accused to the defendant's lawyer prior to the trial. He was showing his hand, but he was not incapable of keeping an ace up his sleeve. Baxter's every word, every smile, every action to his opponent that day had been planned, carefully designed to play down the eagerness with which Baxter approached the Townsend trial. He was used to controlling the world around him.

Thomas Moore was, in Baxter's opinion, highly overrated, having gained his formidable reputation by chance and by repeated good fortune. He had been in the right place at the right time, nothing more. His record was amazing to Baxter, in view of the man himself. Why, he had no personality, no charisma, no fire. He seemed so quiet as to border on the meek.

He would be so easy to take advantage of, or so Baxter thought. But surprisingly, Thomas Moore had not reacted once that day as Baxter had expected he would. Baxter was beginning to get the unwelcome idea that Thomas knew exactly what he was doing, and why he was doing it. It made Baxter uncomfortable.

"This is complete and up-to-date, of course," said Thomas as he took the binder.

"Of course."

Baxter watched as Thomas examined the binder. He glanced briefly at each page. Baxter shifted in his chair and pursed his lips impatiently as Thomas went through the file. He saw no need for the man to look at each page. The copies were typed for his use, he was free to take them. Baxter sighed and glared at the bookish lawyer. He had such meticulous, irritating habits. Baxter would have to put up with this all through the trial, no doubt.

At last Thomas finished his perusal of the documents. He looked up at Baxter Brooks and smiled. "You've done a lot of research," he said appreciatively. "My client was quite a rascal in those days, wasn't he?"

Baxter frowned momentarily. Thomas seemed unruffled by the mass of evidence against his client. He'll feel differently, Baxter thought, when he reads the reports more carefully. He smiled.

"Anything else I can help you with, Tom?" he asked.

Thomas replaced the documents in the binder and handed it back to Baxter. He stood up.

"No," he said. His eyes were soft, sympathetic. "I appreciate your help."

Baxter took the binder in some confusion.

"You are welcome to take the documents, Tom," he said. "It's standard procedure."

"That won't be necessary," Thomas replied in his confident, quiet voice. He extended his hand. "See you in court."

Baxter laid the binder aside and shook Thomas's hand. He watched as the lawyer turned and walked from the office, softly closing the door behind him. Baxter stared after him. Shaking his head, he scowled.

"The man's a maniac," he said aloud. "A maniac."

Thomas nodded to Mrs. Worsham and left the office, the Articles of Disclosure firmly imprinted on his photographic memory. Brooks had nothing Thomas had not expected, nothing he was unprepared for. Of course, there could be a surprise or two yet. Stepping out into the street, Thomas sighed as he thought briefly of the magnetic Mr. Brooks. Another raging Goliath to contend with. Giant egos—they always hit the ground hardest when they fell.

48

The courtroom was packed to capacity. Even the ancient balcony of the large city hall auditorium was full, as the trial of Carlton Townsend promised to be the best entertainment of the summer. Some of the onlookers had come to see the cat burglar himself. Some were there to enjoy the legal battle between Thomas Moore and the ambitious federal prosecutor, Baxter Brooks. A good number of young women were there, too, all former girlfriends of the accused, all convinced Carlton couldn't have done it, all thrilling to the possibility that he could have. If Carlton was lucky, Dixie Lee would not think to count them.

Dixie Lee James was there, sitting with Laura, Camilla, and Rudolph in the second row behind the defense table. Members of the gallery who knew Elizabeth Cooper could not miss the significance of Mrs. Cooper's chosen seat. In a show of support for Carlton, Elizabeth had walked in alone and headed directly for the Townsend party. She was sitting next to Laura.

Behind them, a few rows back, sat Jake and Mabel Potter, indistinguishable now, in their fashionable clothes, from the merchants and bankers seated around them. Jake received an envious and suspicious glance now and then from Viola Gates, who was sitting between her husband and Cora Jane Oates. Billy Harper, the barber, didn't seem to notice the faint odor of formaldehyde clinging to the black suit of the mortician, Hurd Buford. They sat together at the back of the room, speaking in low tones, as ladies nearby pressed white lace hankies to their noses.

Baxter Brooks made his entrance early, slapping his heavy briefcase down hard on the prosecution's table, followed by his stream of intense, clean-cut assistants. He filled the room with his presence as usual, and spent a few moments speaking with influential voters. No one in the room had reason to doubt that he would succeed in convicting Carlton.

Most of the spectators were still watching Baxter Brooks when Thomas Moore arrived. He was alone, and carried no briefcase, only a writing tablet. At the entrance of the auditorium, a moon-faced child, Horace Buford, offered Thomas a paper paddle-fan. A great box of the fans, all emblazoned with the name of Buford's Funeral Home, lay at the boy's feet. Thomas took the fan and thanked the boy politely with a gentle smile.

Jock Morehouse and Bubba James greeted Thomas solemnly at the door, and he spoke to them a few minutes in confident reassuring tones, for both the sheriff and the chief had come to respect him, and knew enough about the case to have given Carlton Townsend the benefit of the doubt.

Thomas paused as he entered the hot, crowded room. Then he walked down the center aisle and seated himself at the defense table with none of the fanfare of his counterpart. He nodded to Elizabeth and the Townsend party as he passed, but did not stop to speak to them. He was largely ignored by the townspeople who did not recognize him. The twelve jury members seated to Thomas's right nudged each other and exchanged knowing glances upon his arrival, and their interest began to alert the members of the gallery to his presence. Jury selection had taken four days. Mr. Brooks had found nearly all the jury candidates suitable, but Thomas Moore had sent many packing for what seemed the strangest reasons.

A plump matronly woman, wearing a broad-brimmed hat with a little papier-mâché bird on the side, fanned herself impatiently as she watched Thomas take his seat at the defense table. She leaned over to her companion and whispered, "Is that him?"

"No, of course not," replied the elderly woman beside her. "Mr. Moore is very handsome and distinguished. He wears hundred-dollar suits."

"Ooh, that's right," said the lady with the large hat. "I remember. He carries a cane and wears a red carnation in his lapel."

"The cane is hollow," replied the older woman. "He fills it with the finest Scotch whiskey."

"Really?" asked the other woman. "I wonder when he will arrive?"

The two women were no doubt disappointed to discover a few moments later that Thomas Moore was actually the bland man in front of them. All doubt to his identity was banished when Baxter Brooks approached the table and towered over Thomas.

"Hello, Tom," he said. His low voice was confident. "What's this? Forget your briefcase today?"

"Baxter." Thomas greeted him and rose to his feet. They shook hands briefly. Thomas was slightly taller than his opponent, but many of the suddenly silent gallery didn't notice. "I doubt I'll get more than a word or two in today, from the looks of your table."

Baxter glanced back at his table and the three assistants who were shuffling several tall stacks of paper.

"You may be right," he replied. He glanced at the gallery. "Quite a turnout for your boy, wouldn't you say?"

"Quite," replied Thomas. He arched a dark brow. "And every one legally registered to vote, too."

Baxter looked at him sharply. He was irritated by his opponent's confidence. It was time to put him in his place.

"Careful, Tom," he said coldly. "You don't want to lose the favor of the next governor of this state."

"Meaning you?" asked Thomas.

Baxter smiled. "Who else?" he answered. Then he lowered his voice and said, "I'm going to win this case. It's the last trophy I need for my collection. But don't worry. Losing this one will be no disgrace. The man's guilty, the case is airtight. Abraham Lincoln himself couldn't get this boy off."

Thomas seated himself again.

"I don't agree at all, Baxter," he stated. "Carlton is not guilty. Even the man who actually perpetrated these crimes is a victim here. The real villain in this case is dead and buried."

Baxter shook his head at Thomas. The man was talking in riddles.

"Well then, counselor," said Baxter, "if he's dead, how are you going to bring him to justice?"

Thomas smiled. He looked up at the federal prosecutor.

"Do you believe in ghosts?" he asked.

Baxter turned on his heel and returned to his table. Now he knew for sure. Thomas Moore was crazy.

The murmuring of the crowd was suddenly hushed as the door to the room was allowed to close with a loud thump. Judge Jacob G. Allen entered the room and walked solidly up the center aisle, nodding to acquaintances if someone happened to catch his eye, but otherwise rolling up the aisle like a freight train behind schedule.

Baxter raised an eyebrow and acknowledged the judge silently, as Judge Allen paused to shake hands with Thomas. The judge turned, met the eyes of his antagonist, Baxter Brooks, and offered a cold hand to the federal prosecutor.

"A little out of your territory, aren't you, Judge?" asked Baxter.

"Skip the politics, boy," replied the judge in a low voice, bringing his eyes dead level with the prosecutors. "You're fixing to be made a fool of by that little schoolteacher over there. If I were you, I'd keep my head out of the governor's mansion for the next few days and concentrate on saving your reputation."

Baxter's expression never wavered, but he paled at this appalling prophesy. Judge Allen smiled as if he had just wished Baxter luck, then turned and made his way to the seat next to Rudolph Townsend.

Something akin to a squashed wail of female voices accompanied the entrance of the defendant, Carlton Townsend, who entered the room at three minutes to nine from a door to the left of the defense table. Carlton tried not to show his amusement at the way the women greeted his entrance, because Thomas had instructed him in courtroom behavior. He was to be sober and confident, look all witnesses in the eye, make no outbursts or frantic movements. If in doubt, Thomas had said, just act like me.

Carlton had laughed at that suggestion, but now he found it helpful. He nodded to his family and his fiancée as he was led to his seat, then scanned the back rows of the auditorium. He spotted the private investigator, Walter Montgomery, almost immediately. Thomas had suggested that the former FBI man be hired to discover the disguise being worn by Carlton's half brother, John Price Daniel. Thomas was sure the real cat burglar would not be able to resist the courtroom battle. If he were not actually in the courtroom itself, he would surely be nearby, perhaps masquerading as a janitor or even a police officer. Bubba James had been working to discover the man's identity, but was close to exhausting all his leads.

At exactly nine o'clock, the court clerk rose and said in a loud voice, "Hear ye, hear ye. All rise."

Two hundred fifty spectators shuffled noisily to their feet as Judge Cunningham entered the room and took his seat behind the bench. Cunningham was respected in the district, in spite of the fact that he was a Yankee and had never managed to lose his Northern accent. It had always made him an outsider in the community. Nevertheless, he was accepted because he was tough and fair, and had more political enemies than political bedfellows.

As the clerk opened the session and called the case, Judge Cunningham scanned the major players in the drama, and sighed. It would be a loud, long trial from the looks of Baxter's table. He rapped the gavel and called for opening arguments.

Baxter rose and approached the jury box.

"Gentlemen," he said respectfully, "I have a little story to tell you. It's about power and recklessness and greed."

Dixie Lee felt a shiver of apprehension as she listened to the deep, resonant voice of the prosecutor.

"It's about a young man from a prominent family. A young man who thought he was above the law. A young man who lived fast and wild and used his family's influence to keep him out of trouble again and again."

Baxter leaned against the rail of the jury box and turned to join the jurors in their view of the defense table. All saw Thomas Moore sitting calmly, looking directly at the prosecutor. Carlton was doing the same, as Thomas had instructed.

"His name is Townsend," continued Baxter, "and in this little corner of the world, that was all this boy needed to get away with breaking the law. He was the son of County Pa! The son of the richest, most powerful man in Georgia. Like his father, this boy made his own rules. And like his father, he answered to no one. Many here in this courtroom today will be shocked as the state shows the evil and corruption of this boy's life." He turned again to face the all-male jury. "Yes, even your own wives and daughters will be shocked, if you allow them to remain."

Judge Cunningham raised an eyebrow at this statement and looked at Thomas Moore.

Thomas kept his eyes on Baxter, and Judge Cunningham thought he saw a slight smile on Thomas's face.

"It's quite a story," continued Baxter, "a story of gambling and drinking and womanizing. A story that leads to a terrible end, to corruption and blasphemy . . . "

Again the judge looked at Thomas.

" . . . to forbidden license, and finally to crime!"

Baxter was rolling now. He turned and pointed his finger at Carlton. "Gentlemen of the jury," he said, "the name of Townsend cannot protect this young man now. The prosecution will show that Carlton Townsend perpetrated a ghastly hoax on the members of this community for no other reason than a selfish thrill. He burglarized the homes of Albany twenty-three times, and stole priceless family heirlooms from widows and children."

Carlton frowned and looked at Thomas. Judge Cunningham smiled momentarily. Judge Allen coughed loudly.

"And when his secret hideout was discovered by an innocent child," Baxter continued, "he imprisoned her there and left her to die rather than risk discovery. Carlton Townsend is accused of burglary and kidnaping, members of the jury. But in my opinion, he should be tried for attempted murder!"

There was a loud murmuring in the courtroom, and Judge Cunningham pounded the gavel several times to restore order. Dixie Lee burst into tears.

Thomas spoke softly to Carlton, calming his client as Carlton's eyes blazed in anger. Judge Cunningham looked at Thomas, who nodded, indicating that he objected to the last statement.

"I won't wait to hear your objection, counselor," said the judge. "I object to that last statement myself. Jury is instructed to disregard the prosecutor's last statement. Counsel will approach the bench."

Baxter smiled smugly as he joined his colleague in front of the judge. Again the crowd whispered among themselves.

The judge looked at Baxter and said, "Mr. Brooks, the charges in this case are set and well-known to you. Do you intend to try this case or not?"

"I am sorry, Your Honor," replied Baxter. "You are right, of course, but my personal opinion is that the charges are incorrect."

"This court is not interested in your opinions, sir," said the judge. "Stick to the rules or face the consequences."

"Yes, Your Honor," said Baxter. He looked at Thomas, who was looking patiently at the judge with his hands in his pockets. He looked so benign, so untroubled. There was something familiar about his attitude. It was the same attitude Baxter himself had only yesterday, when he watched his stubborn young son make the same mistake over and over. Suddenly Baxter felt the chilling certainty of the man who stood silently beside him. My gosh, Baxter thought, he really does have something.

As if Thomas could read his opponent's mind, he turned and looked at Baxter.

"If we can return to the business of the court, I'll tell you exactly what you want to know," he said.

Their eyes met. Baxter was never at his best when he met with an unexpected difficulty. His mind began to fly in all directions. Could he have missed some piece of evidence after all? Could Moore have found a loophole, some way to get his client off?

"May we get on with it, gentlemen?" asked Judge Cunningham.

Thomas went back to the defense table and reclaimed his seat next to Carlton. Baxter walked back to the jury and began to speak.

"Gentlemen," he said, "the prosecution will show that the defendant, Carlton Townsend, had the means, the motive, and the opportunity to commit the crimes of which he is accused. The prosecution will show that he lied to the authorities, both about his whereabouts on the day of the kidnaping, and about his knowledge of the case. The prosecution will show that he had in his possession, at the time of the kidnaping, the tools used to commit the burglaries."

He paused and looked directly at Richard Webster, the head juror. In those few short minutes, Baxter Brooks had already learned much from Thomas Moore. He saw the value of restraint, of certainty. He would fight Thomas with his own weapons.

"The defense will tell you that much of our evidence is circumstantial, that we have no eyewitness who can testify that Carlton Townsend is guilty of these crimes. Circumstantial evidence simply means that a number of facts taken together lead to the logical conclusion of guilt when there is no eyewitness to the crime.

"It's true that we did not catch the defendant red-handed. But we believe the evidence will show that Carlton Townsend, and only Carlton Townsend, could have committed these crimes. There is a point at which circumstantial evidence does more than suggest a conclusion. There is a point where it demands a conclusion, and only one possible conclusion. The evidence in this case will lead you, gentlemen, to the undeniable conclusion that Carlton Townsend is guilty, and guilty beyond a reasonable doubt."

Baxter looked each man in the eye as he spoke. He restrained himself from smiling in satisfaction as he turned and walked back to his seat.

Thomas rose and faced the jury.

"Gentlemen of the jury," he said, "I come to you representing a man you all know, a man who has grown up in this community. The crimes of which Carlton Townsend is accused are serious crimes. This is something of a sensational case for this part of the country. It is inevitable, in a case like this, that rumors and gossip only add to the sensationalism. But this is a court of law. When you walk into this courtroom and take your place on this jury, you are expected to leave any knowledge of the defendant, or of the gossip, behind you.

"The opening remarks of the prosecutor were nothing short of sensational themselves. He has a story to tell you, he said, a story based entirely on circumstantial evidence. He was kind enough to define the term for you as well."

Thomas put his hands in his pockets and walked over to the jury.

"Stories have no place in a court of law," he said. "Here, we deal not with rumors, or gossip, or fairy tales. Here, we deal with facts. I have no stories to tell you. All I have are facts.

"Fact one: the crimes in this case have been committed by a man whom I will do my best to bring to justice. Fact two: the defendant, Carlton Townsend, is not this man. Fact three: each of these crimes was committed with the sole purpose of bringing blame upon an innocent man.

"In a court of law, the defendant is innocent until proven guilty. The evidence must show that the defendant is guilty, and guilty beyond a reasonable doubt. Gentlemen of the jury, Carlton Townsend is not guilty of the charges against him. The facts in this case will show that a wealth of contrived and circumstantial evidence has brought the wrong man to answer for these crimes."

As the quiet lawyer resumed his seat, a soothing calm settled over the courtroom. The raging ocean of Baxter Brooks's magnetic personality was quieted by the soft, warm soul of a man as quiet and eternal as the moon. Already, the tide had turned.

49

"Mr. Neill!" gushed Millie Rhodes. "I didn't know you were coming in this morning."

Forrest Neill smiled as he approached the spinster's desk in the plush reception area of Yesterhouse Publishing Company. Quite a change had come over the staid and stern Miss Rhodes in the past few months. Gone were the severe coiffure and the tailored suit. Forrest's gentle compliments and respectful treatment had buoyed the woman's confidence to the point that her natural femininity had found its way again to the surface.

"My, you look lovely this morning, Millie," said Forrest as he took her hand and placed a brotherly peck on her cheek. He noted with satisfaction the touch of makeup, the soft new coiffure, and the ruffled white blouse and light blue skirt. His gaze wandered to the low table beside her desk, which usually held a vase of fresh flowers.

"What's this?" he asked. "Something new?"

"Yes," Millie replied, "isn't it beautiful?"

They stepped closer to the wooden sculpture on the table, a delicate doe reclining with her newborn fawn at her side. Forrest already knew that Wes Yesterhouse had bought Jake's doe for Millie; he had taken the publisher to the gallery himself a few days ago.

"It's exquisite," said Forrest. "Has Wesley taken a sudden interest in art?"

Millie blushed. "Not really," she said. "He bought it for me, for my birthday. I decided I would like to keep it here where I can enjoy it all day."

Millie's infatuation with Forrest Neill had matured into a protective friendship. Her real love had always been her job, and she loved her job because she was devoted to her boss. It did not take long for Forrest to see that Wes and Millie were acting like an old married couple, laughing, squabbling, thinking each other's thoughts. As Forrest was all for love, he played cupid again. Maybe one day he would find the woman who could make his own heart sing once more.

"I don't blame you," said Forrest. "Just looking at it makes me feel peaceful. You could *use* some peace and tranquility around this place."

"Oh, no," said Millie, gazing contentedly at the sculpture. "I love the excitement. It's such a challenge, so fulfilling, and besides, I'd do anything for—"

"Mr. Yesterhouse?"

"Yes."

The door to the publisher's office opened, and Wes stepped one foot into the room. "What's going on out here?" he said. "I thought I heard your voice, Forrest, my boy. Come on in here. I have something to show you."

Forrest winked at Millie. He followed Wes into the office and took a seat opposite him.

"Before you get started," said Forrest, "let me tell you why I'm here. I wanted to let you know that I'll be out of town for a while."

"Where are you going?" asked Wes.

"To Georgia. Back to the town I'm writing about now."

"Something wrong?"

Forrest nodded. "Yes," he said. A tender look came into his eyes as he thought of Tori.

Wes saw that it was a private matter. He would not press him further. "When will you be back?"

"A week, maybe. I'm not sure. It depends."

"All right," said Wes, "we'll just put everything on hold until you get back. Don't worry about a thing. You just take all the time you need."

"Thanks, Wes," said Forrest. "Now, did you have something to show me?"

"Sure did!" replied Wes with a broad smile. "The Hollywood boys finally came up with an offer. Didn't figure they could hold out much longer. Look at this." He handed the paper to Forrest.

Forrest read the paper quickly. "They want to make it into a movie?"

"Great news, huh?" The publisher was beaming.

"I don't know," said Forrest, shaking his head.

Wes couldn't believe it. "This is great news," he said. "What's not to like?"

"No," said Forrest. "I'll have to think about this."

"You'll be turning down a fortune!" said Wes.

Forrest threw the publisher a sharp warning glance. "We'll talk about it when I get back," he said, handing the paper back to him.

"Okay, Forrest," replied Wes with resignation. "But at least tell me your objections before you go. Maybe I can be working some of them out."

"My objection should be obvious," said Forrest. "Most of the story takes place inside Will Fable's head, in his heart, in his soul. How can you put that on the screen?"

Wes stood up and walked to the bookcase. "Shakespeare had no problem with that, my boy," he said.

"I thought he was dead," said Forrest.

"He is," replied Wes with a grin, "but Joe Shores isn't."

"Who's Joe Shores?"

"Only the most brilliant screenwriter and playwright since the Bard himself," replied Wes. "And he wants *Wandering Dreamer*. Just look," he said, pointing to the floor file of movie and stage posters beside him, "Shores is the man who brought *Cloudy Way* to the screen, and a more touching film has never been made. He even made the author cry."

He turned a few of the big leaves. "You say it's all inside Will Fable's head. Well, what about the character of Robert Lord? Who else could have made *The Lord of Rain* such a knockout play?" He slapped the poster in satisfaction. "Believe me, boy, Shores will not disappoint you. Let me work on it while you're—"

Wes forgot what he was saying, and his voice trailed off, as he stared at the stunned face of his client. Forrest was staring at the poster in astonishment.

"What's the matter, Forrest?" Wes asked. There was concern in his voice, for the color had drained from his client's face.

Forrest was standing now, walking slowly toward the poster as if he were a blind man suddenly able to see for the first time.

"What is it?" asked the publisher in confusion.

"It's so simple," said Forrest to himself. "I can't believe the answer is so simple."

"What answer?"

Forrest did not hear the question. He was back in Hayley, back in the rundown cabin. He saw the face of the young Price Townsend looking down at him from the faded portrait on the wall, the same face that stared back at him from the poster. Quickly his mind moved to Christmas Eve, to the church. That's Daniel J. Smith, Tori had said of the little bent-over man. Nobody knows much about him. He's a stranger.

The poster for *The Lord of Rain* pictured the main character, Robert Lord, in full costume. He was a shriveled up, bent-over, bearded man. In the corner of the poster was a smaller inset photo of the young actor who portrayed Robert Lord. A young, handsome, blond actor named John Price Daniel.

Without a word, Forrest removed the poster from its sheath and folded it to a manageable size.

"What are you doing?" asked Wes.

"I must borrow this," he said quickly. "I can't explain, I haven't gone crazy.

He grabbed his jacket and headed for the door.

"I don't get it," said Wes, following him. "What the hell's going on?"

"I found him," yelled Forrest over his shoulder as he walked past Millie.

"Who?" called Wes in frustration.

"The ghost of County Pa." He slammed the outer office door behind him and was gone.

Millie looked at her boss questioningly. He was frowning after his client.

"What the hell is the ghost of County Pa?" he muttered.

Millie raised her eyebrows. A familiar bell tinkled somewhere in her golden instinct. She walked to Wes and stood beside him until he turned his attention to her.

"The ghost of County Pa?" she echoed. "Sounds like the name of his next bestseller to me."

Wes's eyes lighted up.

"Millie," he said appreciatively, "I'm gonna take you out to lunch."

50

At five minutes past one o'clock on the second day of the trial, Forrest Neill mounted the crowded steps of the Albany City Hall, carrying a brown envelope under his arm. Such a handsome and prosperous-looking stranger was a rare sight in Albany, and people stared at Forrest as he passed. Forrest saw no familiar faces until he edged his way into the great entrance hall. At the other end of the hall, Bubba James was standing beside the entrance to the auditorium, with another uniformed official. Quickly, Forrest walked to the two men.

"Chief James," he said. "Excuse me, sir, but may I have a word with you?"

Bubba and Jock Morehouse turned and gave Forrest the once-over. Bubba knew he had seen this man before, but he could not place him.

"It is very important that I speak with Carlton Townsend's lawyer, Chief James," continued Forrest. "Could you arrange it?"

Bubba's interest was piqued. This man was a stranger in town, and a Yankee by the sound of him. What possible business could he have with Thomas Moore?

"I'm afraid he's busy right now, mister," said Bubba. "He's right in the middle of Carlton's trial. You'll have to wait for recess, and that won't be for hours. They just now got started again after the lunch break."

"What I have to say concerns the trial, Chief," said Forrest. He indicated the envelope he held. "I have evidence here."

"Just who are you, friend?" asked Jock. He looked at the well-dressed stranger suspiciously.

Elizabeth Cooper had written to Forrest and told him about Bubba's visit to her home, inquiring about Will Fable. Forrest knew the chief would recognize his name. Before he could answer, Bubba's powers of observation unraveled the puzzle, and he realized who Forrest was.

"Wait a minute," said Bubba. "I know who he is. He's that New York fella."

"Yes, Chief," said Forrest. "Forrest Neill, from New York. I was here last Christmas."

"And using a false name, as I recall," said Bubba. "Are you mixed up in this mess after all, son?"

"What's going on here?" asked Jock.

"It's all right, Jock," said Bubba. "Let the man say his piece."

Forrest took a deep breath. He had not anticipated having to explain himself. Time was wasting.

"I have nothing to do with the case," he said. "But I have discovered some important evidence, quite by accident, which may bring this trial to an end. I must talk to Carlton's lawyer right away. Please. It is very important. If it were not, I would not ask you to interrupt the trial."

Bubba looked hard at Forrest. There was something very odd about this Yankee, he decided. Never in his life had Bubba James seen such eyes in a man as young as Forrest Neill. They were at once soft and strong, and filled with the wisdom of age. There was something else about him, too, a calmness, a sense of peace. In his own way, he reminded Bubba of another man who had gained Bubba's respect, Thomas Moore. Bubba remembered the story Mrs. Cooper had told him of Will Fable. This man fit the bill.

"I know about you," he said. "The widow Cooper told me. Your word is good enough for me. Wait right here."

Bubba pushed open the door to the auditorium and was gone.

Sheriff Morehouse looked at Forrest. "Will someone tell me what the hell is going on here?" he asked.

Bubba walked swiftly down the center aisle of the packed auditorium. He caught the eye of Baxter Brooks, who was questioning Dr. Waldrop on the stand. The doctor was one of Baxter's last witnesses. Himself a victim of the cat burglar, the doctor could tie the brand of tobacco found in the black bag, Carlton's brand, to the burglaries. The attention of the crowd was drawn away from the witness as Bubba walked over to Thomas Moore. The chief leaned over and whispered something to him. Thomas stood up and interrupted the doctor's testimony.

"Your Honor," he said. "The defense requests a five-minute recess. Some important new evidence has just been brought to my attention."

The crowd began to murmur. Judge Cunningham rapped his gavel several times.

"Order!" he commanded. When the gallery was quiet again, he spoke. "Go ahead, counselor. The court will take a five-minute recess. Doctor, you are excused."

The judge rose and disappeared out the side door for a cigar. The crowd began to buzz with excitement. Carlton glanced back at Rudolph. Rudolph shrugged slightly, indicating his ignorance of the reason for the interruption. Carlton turned questioning eyes to Thomas.

"I'll be right back," said Thomas. "Don't worry."

Thomas got up and followed Bubba down the aisle. Bubba led Thomas out the door and into the hall. Nodding to Jock Morehouse and Forrest, he kept walking toward a small office. "Come on," he said.

Thomas noticed the tall stranger's kind, anxious eyes and knew immediately that he was a friend. When they reached the office, Bubba ushered them in and then closed the door.

"What is it, Chief James?" asked the lawyer quietly.

"This man has asked for a private word with you," replied Bubba. "He said it couldn't wait. I can vouch for him. His name is Forrest Neill."

"Thank you, Chief," said Thomas. "I will speak to him."

Bubba nodded to Jock and the two officials left the room, closing the door behind them. Thomas turned to the stranger. Like Bubba James, Thomas was also struck by the man's wise, green eyes.

"My name is Thomas Moore," he said. "I am Carlton Townsend's attorney. Do you have something to tell me?"

"Yes, sir," said Forrest. "I am a friend of Elizabeth Cooper and little Tori. I know all about the trial, and I believe that Carlton was framed."

"As do I," said Thomas.

"I have something here I want to show you," said Forrest. He removed the folded poster from the envelope. "I believe it is the answer you are looking for. It is a long story, sir."

Thomas took the folded paper. "Very long," he responded. He did not look at the paper in his hands. "Thirty years to be exact."

Forrest studied the face of the lawyer, who was regarding him with a steady gaze. Somehow he knew that Thomas would understand the significance of the poster with no explanations. "Does the name John Price Daniel mean anything to you?" asked Forrest.

"Indeed it does," replied Thomas. He smiled gratefully at the tall stranger. He unfolded the poster and studied it silently. "Ah," he said. "The ghost of County Pa."

Forrest sighed with relief. "Yes," he said. "Little Boozie's ghost, in the flesh."

"And this character in the play," Thomas said, pointing to the bearded face of Robert Lord on the poster, "it is a face you know?"

"Yes," answered Forrest. "He lives in Hayley, down the road from Boozie. Tori pointed him out to me last Christmas. He calls himself Daniel J. Smith. Apparently he turned up out of nowhere and settled here about a year ago."

"'Daniel'?" repeated Thomas thoughtfully. "I should have known he would throw clues at us so blatantly. And living on Hemon Road. No wonder Ottis was afraid for his family."

Forrest looked at him questioningly, and Thomas could see that he was unfamiliar with the details of the case.

"Never mind," he said. "None of that matters now." He folded the poster. Forrest handed him the brown envelope and Thomas replaced the poster safely inside it. "If luck is with us," said Thomas, "and our clever adversary is running true to form, he is seated in the courtroom today." He offered his hand to Forrest. "Thank you," he said. "I knew everything about him except for the false identity he had assumed. I don't know who you are, sir, or what connection you have to this community, but you have done a great service to all of us."

Forrest shook the hand of the lawyer and smiled.

Thomas turned and walked to the door of the office. He opened the door and called to Bubba and Jock. The two officials entered the room and Thomas closed the door again.

"Chief James," said Thomas, "are you acquainted with an elderly man named Daniel J. Smith?"

"Sure," Bubba replied. "The old geezer lives in Hayley. Rents the old Bibb place on Hemon Road. Why?"

"Is he by any chance present in the courtroom today?"

"I think he is," said Bubba. "I saw him come in this morning. Why do you ask?"

Thomas glanced at Forrest and smiled.

"I must ask that you and Sheriff Morehouse trust me now," said Thomas. "This man must not leave the courtroom. I have learned for certain that Daniel J. Smith is the man we have been searching for."

"Old man Smith?" asked Bubba, incredulous.

"He is not an old man, Chief," said Thomas. "He is a young man wearing a very clever disguise. He must not leave the premises."

"Well, I'll be damned," said Jock. "You're sure?"

"Yes, Sheriff."

Bubba nodded. "Just leave it to us. He won't get away. Jock and I will see to that."

Jock turned to Bubba. "Get Buck Taylor in here," he said, "and anyone else on duty you can find."

51

At two-thirty the prosecution rested its case. The defense took over, and Thomas began with a radical and unexpected move. He called Carlton to the stand. Thomas had not planned to do this, because he feared that Baxter Brooks would reduce the volatile Carlton to a raging demon with his sarcastic accusations. There had not been time to explain. Thomas told Carlton only that he must trust him, and warned him to remain calm on the stand, no matter what the prosecutor said. Thomas would do Carlton's fighting for him with the flashy Mr. Brooks. That was his job, not Carlton's.

Carlton took the stand and was very convincing under Thomas's questioning. He told his story of the day of the kidnaping, naming Dixie Lee as his alibi. He told of finding the damning black bag in the field while he was with her, and explained why he did not turn it over the authorities. Carlton admitted he had known about the secret room in the cabin, but as Thomas instructed, he said nothing about the ledger or the theft of County Pa's money. He admitted he lied to the authorities about the cabin, explaining that he did not want to become involved with a kidnaping. He also said that he secretly returned the black bag to the place he had found it, for the same reason he lied about the cabin.

It was an almost unbelievable story, filled with the admission of lies and acts of poor judgment. Every statement was torn apart by Baxter Brooks during cross-examination. The evidence was indeed circumstantial, but there was a mountain of it. A man with a spotless record and a good lawyer may have been able to convince the jury that there was at least a reasonable doubt of his guilt. But this was Carlton Townsend, and his exploits were public record. Baxter's background witnesses were enough to convince the jury that they could not take the word of the younger son of County Pa.

If Thomas had not discovered the real culprit in time, he would never have put Carlton on the stand, in view of the prosecutor's skill. Carlton managed to keep his temper, but nevertheless, Baxter Brooks succeeded in making him look as guilty as Cain.

Thomas called Dixie Lee James as the next witness for the defense. She confirmed that she was indeed with Carlton that day, and that she had been with him when he found the black bag. Dixie Lee was easy prey for the district attorney, and he established her true relationship with the defendant immediately. Both her testimony and her honor were destroyed in minutes, as Baxter pointed out that she had taken up with Carlton while still engaged to the most respected man in the county, Rudolph Townsend.

Dixie Lee left the stand in tears. Carlton struggled to maintain the brave front of calm Thomas had demanded, but inside he was beginning to question his lawyer's handling of the case. How could Thomas possibly undo the damage that had been done? Still, something about Thomas's manner affected Carlton as he sat there next to him. The peace, the quiet certainty of the man, was like a calming voice that soothed Carlton's fears. Carlton sat still and said nothing. With great effort, he pushed aside the questions that ate at him.

Once the true whereabouts of his client had been established for the jury, Thomas began his attack. As his third witness, he called to the stand Walter Montgomery, the private detective. Baxter Brooks frowned as Montgomery took the stand, wondering what Thomas Moore was up to. The witness was sworn and seated, and Thomas approached him.

"You are Walter Montgomery?" asked Thomas.

"I am," replied the witness.

"And what is your profession, sir?"

"I am a private detective based in Washington, D.C."

"You have heard the testimony of the defendant concerning the existence of a secret room in a cabin on the Townsend game preserve, constructed by the defendant's late father, Price Townsend?"

"I have."

"Are you familiar with the name of Price Townsend?"

"Yes."

"Please tell the court of your relationship with Price Townsend."

"Objection," said Baxter, standing. "The defendant's father is not on trial here, Your Honor."

The judge looked at Thomas.

"I beg the court's indulgence," said Thomas. "It is true that Price Townsend is not on trial here, but perhaps he should be. The relevance of Mr. Montgomery's testimony will become clear in a moment. I propose to show that the late Price Townsend is a central figure in this case."

"Overruled," said Judge Cunningham. "We will expect such relevancy to be shown quickly, counselor."

"Thank you, Your Honor," said Thomas. Turning back to the witness, he said, "What was your relationship with Price Townsend?"

"I only met him once," said Montgomery, "to report the results of an investigation. In June of 1937, a man named George Richmond contacted me. He was Mr. Townsend's lawyer, and he arranged for me to investigate someone for Mr. Townsend."

"What sort of investigation?"

"To check up on someone, find out who he was, his background."

"What was the name of this man?"

"John Price Daniel."

"For what purpose did Price Townsend want this man investigated?"

"This Daniel had contacted Mr. Townsend with the claim that he was his illegitimate son."

The room was filled suddenly with excited murmurings. Rudolph took his mother's hand. Laura looked straight ahead, showing no sign of strain. Baxter Brooks stared at the witness, unprepared for this sudden turn of events.

"Order!" demanded the judge. The gavel pounded. When the crowd quieted again, every eye was on Walter Montgomery.

"Mr. Montgomery," Thomas continued, "can you tell the court what you discovered about John Price Daniel for Mr. Townsend?"

"Objection!" said Baxter. "This testimony is irrelevant, Your Honor. What has this to do with the case against Carlton Townsend?"

Judge Cunningham looked at Thomas.

"Counselor?"

"Your Honor," said Thomas, "if Carlton Townsend is innocent of these crimes, then someone else is guilty. If the court will permit me to proceed, I believe I will establish the identity of that person."

"Overruled," said the judge. "The witness will answer the question."

"I tracked the man down," said Montgomery. "He was quite a colorful character, actually. I found that he had been raised in some fancy orphanage. His college education was financed by some mysterious benefactor. He got a degree in engineering from Boston College, but he never put it to use. Whoever was financing him apparently left him pretty well fixed. He set himself up in a fancy apartment in New York City after he graduated, but he was never there. For some reason, adventure I guess, he joined up with a circus. After he left the circus, he began a career as a makeup man on the New York stage. Eventually he became an actor himself. He was in several plays, and starred in the last one. It was called *The Lord of Rain*."

"You say the last one," said Thomas. "What happened to him?"

"Nobody knew. He just dropped out of sight. Left a very promising career on the stage, too, I understand. According to Mr. Richmond, Daniel contacted Mr. Townsend shortly after the close of the play two years ago,"

"Mr. Montgomery," said Thomas, "were you able to prove that John Price Daniel was an imposter? That he was not in any way related to Price Townsend?"

"No, sir," replied Montgomery, "I was not. The records of his birth were not available to me. I tried to get them, but the orphanage's records on such matters are sealed by law. I had no real proof, but he was the son of Price Townsend, all right."

"If you had no proof, sir," said Thomas, "how could you be sure of this?"

Montgomery smiled slightly. "I got hold of a picture of him," he said. "I brought it with me when I gave my report to Mr. Townsend. The minute I met Price Townsend, I knew Daniel's claim was true."

"How?" asked Thomas.

"Daniel was the spitting image of his father. They could have been twins."

Again the crowd was stunned to excited whisperings. Again the judge was forced to call the gallery to order. "If this behavior continues," he said, "I will order the room cleared. The court will tolerate no further outbursts."

John Price Daniel, disguised as Daniel J. Smith, shifted in his seat. Casually, he looked behind him to the side entrance on the other side of the room. Standing there solidly was Sheriff Morehouse, looking back at him. John looked back at the main entrance. Bubba James was there, guarding the door, and also looking back at him. When he returned his gaze to the front of the room, he noticed that the Albany police chief, Buck Taylor, had entered the room by the door the judge had used, and was standing in front of it, his gun on his hip.

John raised his eyebrows in appreciation. He had underestimated the famous lawyer. The presence of the lawmen could mean only one thing, that Thomas Moore had learned not only his true identity, but his false identity as well. No doubt John would be unmasked shortly, before all of Albany. This put a new kink in the game. It did not matter. The end would be the same. It might even be fun. John settled himself in his seat, which was directly behind Rudolph Townsend, to watch the show.

"Can you tell us anything further?" asked Thomas of the witness.

"Well, as I said," answered Montgomery, "my association with the late Mr. Townsend ended when I gave him my report. I just know that he wanted to get rid of Daniel in some way, pay him off or something."

Thomas turned to the judge. "I have no more questions, Your Honor."

"Cross-examine?" the judge asked Baxter.

"No questions," muttered Baxter Brooks.

"The witness is excused," said Judge Cunningham. "Call your next witness, counselor."

"The defense calls Mrs. George Richmond."

Pamela Richmond took the stand and was sworn in. She turned to face Thomas Moore with perfect poise.

"You are Pamela Richmond," said Thomas, "the widow of the late state senator, George Richmond?"

"I am, sir. "

"And you have heard Mr. Montgomery's testimony that your late husband was acting as Price Townsend's lawyer in the matter of John Price Daniel?"

"Yes."

"You are a widow, Mrs. Richmond. How did your husband die?"

"He was killed in a plane crash two years ago," replied Pamela, "near Savannah, Georgia."

"Was anyone else involved in that crash?"

"Yes. Two others died with him. The pilot and Price Townsend."

"The father of the defendant?"

"Yes."

Thomas walked over to the defense table and picked up a small bundle. He unwrapped the papers and handed them to the witness.

"Do you recognize these documents, Mrs. Richmond?"

Pamela took the papers and scanned them briefly.

"Yes," she answered. "These are the papers you removed from my husband's files."

"Will you tell the court the contents of these documents?"

"Yes." She offered the first paper back to Thomas. "This is a letter to Price Townsend from John Price Daniel. In it he claims that Price Townsend is his father, and that his mother's name was Rosellen Daniel." She handed him the second paper. "This is a contract, detailing my late husband's agreement to act as Price Townsend's attorney in the matter of John Price Daniel." She handed him the third paper. "And this is apparently a rough draft of a financial agreement between Price Townsend and John Price Daniel."

Thomas took the last paper and held it up for the witness. "I have marked a paragraph here," he said. "Will you read it, please?"

"It says that a meeting will take place on July fifteenth, 1937, at the Savannah Savoy hotel."

"And that date has significance to you, Mrs. Richmond?"

"It was the day my husband was killed."

"Thank you, Mrs. Richmond," said Thomas. "I hope this has not been too difficult for you." He turned to the judge. "I have no more questions of this witness, Your Honor."

"Mr. Prosecutor?" asked Judge Cunningham.

"No questions," said Baxter.

Thomas approached the bench as Pamela Richmond left the stand. "I offer these documents as exhibits for the defense, Your Honor."

Judge Cunningham took the papers and looked over them. He handed them to the bailiff at his right.

"The bailiff will mark these as exhibits C, D, and E for the defense," he said. "Does the prosecution wish these documents to be read into the record?"

"That won't be necessary, Your Honor," said Baxter.

"Call your next witness, Mr. Moore."

Thomas stood behind the defense table. He paused before answering, and put his hands in the pockets of his trousers. Every eye was on him as he stood there silently. Baxter Brooks looked up at the delay and stared at Thomas like the rest. It was such a simple thing, the pause, yet it held everyone spellbound. Baxter smiled knowingly at the humble lawyer. Against his will, the prosecutor's regard of Thomas Moore had turned from disdain to respect. As if he knew his opponent's thoughts, Thomas glanced at Baxter. His eyes were apologetic. Baxter nodded to him slightly and raised an eyebrow. The gesture was a sign of appreciation.

Thomas looked at the judge. "I call Daniel J. Smith to the stand."

Carlton looked at Thomas in confusion, and was met with a blank face that said *Remember your instructions.* Carlton sat back and replaced his expression with one of calm.

Rudolph turned to find Smith in the crowd, and was shocked to find the bright eyes of the hunched-over old man staring straight into his own. The eyes of the two men devoured each other silently, and Rudolph knew he was seeing his half brother, John Price Daniel, for the first time.

Laura sat with her eyes forward.

The clerk called the witness for the second time, before the man known to the residents of Hayley as Daniel J. Smith stood up and hobbled to the stand. Carlton watched as he passed, and threw Rudolph a glance. Rudolph's stricken look told Carlton the truth, and Carlton turned back with wrenching control to stare at the man being sworn in.

Thomas put a gentle hand on Carlton's shoulder, warning him to be silent, then walked slowly to the witness stand. The witness's bright eyes watched him carefully. Thomas looked at John Price Daniel with kindness, with recognition, as if he had known him for a long time. John knew the soft-spoken lawyer had won the battle. But the war was far from over. The ghost of County Pa was ready for the skirmish ahead.

"What is your name, sir?" asked Thomas.

"Daniel J. Smith," came the high, crackly reply,

"And your age?"

"Oh, I must be nigh-on to sixty by now."

"You look it, too," said Thomas, smiling.

The gallery chuckled.

"Order," said Judge Cunningham, and the spectators quieted.

"Where do you live, sir?"

"Hayley, down the road a piece."

"And how long have you lived there?"

"Came down about a year ago, I guess. Nice place, Hayley."

"Do you remember the exact date?"

"No. It was sometime in July, I think."

"July" Thomas repeated. "A month or two before the burglaries began in Albany, correct?"

"Reckon so."

"Do you know the defendant in this case, Carlton Townsend?"

"Sure," replied the witness. "Talked to him lots of times. Sat on the porch of the General Store and chewed the fat with me, he did. He's a nice feller."

"And are you acquainted with the defendant's brother, Rudolph?"

"Nope. Never met him."

Thomas walked to the jury box and then turned to look back at the witness.

"Are you acquainted with the child who was kidnaped in this case, Victoria Tanner?"

Rudolph watched the witness carefully. He thought he saw a slight change come into the jovial manner of the man.

"Little Brown Eyes?" replied the witness. "A good girl, she is."

Thomas walked back to the witness. "And what is your relationship with the late Price Townsend?"

The witness smiled slightly and looked Thomas in the eye. His glance was unwavering and strong, like a tiger stalking its prey.

"Don't got none," he answered. "County Pa's dead, ain't he? Hard to have a relationship with a dead man."

Thomas stepped back. He looked at the floor and put his hands in his pockets. The spectators leaned forward in their seats. They, too, had learned much about the unassuming lawyer. This was Thomas Moore's attack stance. Something big was about to happen.

"I suggest that you do have a relationship with Price Townsend, sir," said Thomas. "A blood relationship. I suggest that your name is not Daniel J. Smith, but is, in fact, John Price Daniel. I suggest that you are not sixty years old, but are, in fact, exactly thirty years old."

The witness smiled and the gallery murmured again. This time the judge did nothing to quiet them. Judge Cunningham leaned toward the witness, unmindful of the crowd.

"I further suggest, sir, that you have donned an exceptionally professional disguise, and perpetrated a hoax on this town and this community. I suggest that you sought to revenge yourself for your father's rejection, to the point that you framed the defendant for burglary and kidnaping. I suggest that you are the illegitimate son of Price Townsend."

The witness chuckled softly, but did not answer. He looked at Carlton and saw the rage in his eyes. He looked at Rudolph and saw the despair. He looked at Laura Townsend and saw the sorrow.

"The witness will answer," said Judge Cunningham.

"Suggest what you like," he said. "Sounds like a lot of fool talk to me."

"Perhaps you are right," said Thomas. "The court is not interested in talk, is it? The court is interested in proof."

"Damn right," replied the gnarled man. "Proof. You got any?"

Judge Cunningham frowned and said, "The witness will refrain from speaking oaths in this court."

"Sorry, Your Honor," John squeaked.

Thomas walked back to the defense table. He picked up the envelope Forrest Neill had given him, then walked back to the witness and handed him the envelope.

"What's this?" asked the witness.

"You asked for proof," said Thomas. "Perhaps this will do."

John Price Daniel opened the envelope and withdrew the folded poster that bore both the image of Daniel J. Smith and the photo of himself. Thomas walked back to the defense table and sat down next to Carlton.

The witness unfolded the poster. His soft chuckle filled the quiet room as he slowly folded up the poster again, then dropped it to the floor. The crowd murmured, but fell deadly silent when the witness stared out at them. Suddenly the bent-over figure sat up straight and strong, and the crowd gasped. They saw a new man on the witness stand, a man who exuded strength and cunning and power. A man who suddenly seemed to dwarf them. Then he spoke, and his voice was different, still high and gravelly, but now false and mocking.

"My compliments, counselor," he said. "A brilliant job."

Then, to the amazement of the crowd, and to the horror of the Townsend family, John Price Daniel took off his disguise. Off came the wig, the beard and moustache, the bushy eyebrows, the false nose. Off came the hump from his back. Off came thirty years, and the state of Georgia came face to face with its native son, the image of County Pa.

Laura fainted. Rudolph caught his mother in his arms, but could not drag his eyes from the image of his dead father which stared back at him from the witness stand. Carlton was horrified and could not move. Bubba and Jock walked quickly up the aisles, their guns drawn. The crowd began to stand and clamor. Photographers rushed to the front rail and began snapping pictures. "It's the cat burglar!" yelled a man from the balcony. Women screamed and the judge pounded his gavel to no avail. Baxter Brooks slumped and put his head in his hands.

There was pandemonium. Through it all, only two men sat calmly, ignoring the rush and the roar. Thomas Moore and John Price Daniel sat in their places, staring silently at each other. Then Thomas stood.

"I move that the case against Carlton Townsend be dismissed," he called out above the noise.

Baxter raised his head, but not his eyes. He shook his head. The judge took this to mean that the prosecutor had no objection.

"Case dismissed!" he yelled. "Take that witness into custody!"

52

There was a lot for Tori to think about these days. Ever since the day she walked into the Townsend game preserve, it seemed she couldn't stop thinking. She thought about everything furiously, everything that was suddenly happening in her life: going to live with her father at last, leaving her friends, leaving Hayley. She would be leaving her tree house, leaving the very earth she loved, leaving every path and meadow that seemed so much a part of her, so much that meant home. She would be part of a new family, with a stepmother and a half-sister she did not even know. And worst of all, she would be leaving her grandmother. For years, going to live with her father was all she wanted, all she dreamed of, but now, she realized how hard it was going to be to go.

Tori didn't realize that the only thing she never thought about was the day she was imprisoned in the cellar. It was always there, like a living presence that stood a few paces behind her, silent and waiting. She dared not look back. She began to worry. Whenever she was alone, a frown furrowed her happy young face. But she showed this face to no one. She filled her mind with the future. There was so much to think about now, so many changes coming.

It was hot that afternoon. Tori lay on her back, on the floor of the tree house, looking up at the thick green canopy of leaves above her. She couldn't stay in the house with Doreen, whose bossy ways had only intensified since she had become a widow. Mrs. Cooper was in Albany for the trial, and would not be back until evening.

Tori was weary. It was a new feeling for her. She had always been so strong and full of energy. Now, she found she was often too tired to sleep, and when she did sleep, her rest was snatched away by dreams that exhausted her further, dreams that vanished the moment she awakened.

Tori closed her eyes and tried to go back to a better time.

She heard a car approach and pass by below her. The car rattled resolutely, with a familiar fatigue, and Tori sat up quickly. Her grandmother was back. Tori jumped up and peered over the side of the tree house in time to see the old sedan turn into the drive on the other side of the house. The motor stopped. Tori heard not one door shut, but two.

A shiver of apprehension ran through her. Tori did not know why, but her heart began to beat faster. She watched anxiously for her grandmother to appear from the other side of the house. Mrs. Cooper came around the corner and looked immediately to the tree house, as if she knew Tori would be there. She waved to Tori, then looked behind her and called something to someone else. Mrs. Cooper went on into the house.

A man came around the corner of the house, a tall man, dressed in a fine black three-piece suit. He had his hands in his pockets and walked slowly. He stopped and looked toward the tree house, finding Tori staring back at him. He smiled and started walking to her.

Tears flooded Tori's eyes as she recognized Will Fable. He had come back as he promised he would! Tori scrambled down the ladder and ran to him, her heart bursting with gladness and, strangely, relief. He held out his arms and caught her. Forrest Neill said nothing as he held Tori. For the first time since her kidnaping, Tori was crying. He hugged her and let her cry.

From the back door, Elizabeth Cooper watched gratefully as her granddaughter expressed her emotions at last. Why Tori could unburden herself only to Will she did not know, but it was not important now. She blinked back her own tears and smiled, as the little yellow puppy scratched at the screen and yapped in bewilderment, then yawned and plopped down on his stomach.

That evening there was a soft knock at the front door. Tori jumped up happily from her place at Forrest's feet and ran to answer the knock. Jake Potter stood on the porch. He could see the change in Tori at once, as she smiled and took him by the hand.

"Guess who's here, Jake," she said, trying to pull him into the house.

"Now, hold on there," said Jake, standing his ground. "No need tramplin' me t' death."

"Will's come back, Jake," said Tori, still trying to pull him in. "Come on and see him."

Jake leaned down and took the excited girl by the shoulders.

"Tori," he said soberly, "ask Mr. Neill to come to the door. Please."

Elizabeth Cooper heard the exchange as she appeared in the hallway, and smiled at Jake as she approached them.

"Tori," she said, "run and tell Will that he has a visitor."

Tori was mystified by this strange formality, but she did as she was told, and disappeared into the house.

Elizabeth looked at Jake fondly. He was clean and neat, and looked handsome in his store-bought clothes.

"I have some chocolate cake in the kitchen," she said softly. "Come in later, won't you?"

Jake nodded. He seemed a little nervous.

"Yes, Ma'am."

Elizabeth left him on the porch and walked back to the kitchen. Jake leaned down and scratched the yellow puppy's ears, then walked to the far end of the porch. He hardly recognized the tall, clean-shaven, well-dressed man who came through the screen door a few moments later.

Jake took a step toward him.

"It's Jake Potter. Mr. Neill," said Jake with difficulty. "I come t' thank you." He snatched his hat from his head, as if he had forgotten to remove it in church.

They stood about twenty feet apart, and Forrest made no move to shorten the distance. He did not reply, and waited until Jake recognized Will Fable, not Forrest Neill.

"I must look funnier in these clothes than I thought," said Forrest.

Jake knew the voice, the wise eyes, the gentle kidding. He knew he was facing the hero of the amazing book he had read, his elusive guardian angel, Will Fable. He owed so much to this man, and he hardly knew him. Yet Jake did know Will Fable, he had traveled with him through every page of his book, suffered every trial, leaned every lesson, overcome every obstacle. Like hundreds of thousands of others who had read the book, Jake loved the man, Will Fable.

Jake knew then why Forrest Neill waited at the door. It was the lesson of the book. No man, Will Fable had said, is better than his brother. Jake drew himself up and summoned all his pride. He walked to his benefactor and extended a steady hand.

"I'll shake your hand and call you friend," said Jake with hard-won courage.

Forrest took his hand.

"I'll do the same," he said. "I'm very proud of you, Jake Potter."

53

Twelve miles away, John Price Daniel stared back at the men who peered through the bars of his jail cell at the Albany police headquarters. A slight smile twisted the corner of his mouth. Inwardly, he laughed at the stream of disbelievers who came to see for themselves the face of County Pa. The eyes of the curious, sneaked in at cautious intervals by the ever-obliging Sergeant Hardy, were met with the cool, calculating, catlike eyes of the accused. They spoke to each other in whispers, some even joked openly. The place was filled with a strange excitement, irresistible danger, and a thrill of evil. Here was the cat burglar, with the face of the feared and powerful County Pa.

John enjoyed the show, enjoyed the power. As always, he was in control of everyone around him, his only weapons being his supreme confidence, patience, and silence. From the moment he had been discovered, he had not spoken a single word to any of them.

John Price Daniel had buried deep the old feelings of claustrophobia which had tortured him for years after his childhood imprisonment in the coat closet. The possibility that he might not escape these walls did not exist.

Nothing had gone as he had planned, but nevertheless, the outcome was to his liking. The sensationalism of his unmasking was more thrilling than his own plan to resume the burglaries if Carlton should be convicted. As he believed his imprisonment was temporary, the attention he now enjoyed was a pleasant diversion, the confinement a dangerous challenge.

The simple fools! They actually thought they could keep him there. The game had been fun at first, but when the girl became involved, he had foolishly let the thrill slip away. Now the excitement was back, heady and consuming in its addiction. It was like being on the stage again, dramatic and glorious, thousands of eyes following every move as he led them through a maze of intrigue, mesmerizing and controlling their every emotion, every breath. And now, again, the play was in full swing, and he was the star. The second act was drawing to a close. Shortly, he knew, his brothers would come. He waited with cunning patience to blackmail them into arranging his escape.

Late that night, when he heard footsteps and hushed voices in the hall, John sat bolt upright on his cot and strained to hear. He went to the bars of the cell and pressed his face to the cold iron. They were coming. John's eyes glowed with excitement, every nerve was taut with anticipation. He was ready.

The door at the end of the hall opened, filling the dark corridor with shafts of light. John returned to his cot to wait for his brothers, a cunning smile on his face. It was eleven o'clock. Lights in the jail had been extinguished for more than an hour. A man was coming down the half-lit corridor. Jock Morehouse paused in front of John's cell and unlocked the door.

"You have a visitor, boy," he said gruffly. "Come with me."

John rose and walked to the larger man.

"Put your hands out," said the sheriff, pulling a set of handcuffs from his belt.

John smiled and did as he was told. He had learned many things in the circus. The sheriff had no idea that John carried the pick necessary to open the cuffs easily. The same pick could trip the ancient lock of the door to his jail cell, but John was not ready to escape. He wanted this meeting first.

Sheriff Morehouse snapped the cuffs shut around the prisoner's wrist and growled, "Come on."

He led the way to the little conference room. It was empty. John went in, and the door slammed behind him. Smiling, he went to the table and sat down in one of the chairs to wait. The door opened and Thomas Moore entered the room with Jock Morehouse.

"You got twenty minutes, counselor," said Jock. "This ain't Atlanta."

'Round here we do things pretty much by the book. Don't set well with secret meetings in the middle of the night."

John's eyes hardened in disappointment as he realized the lawyer was alone. For a fleeting second the possibility ran through his mind that the Townsends would disappoint him, that they would not see him, that they would negotiate for the ledger through this man, their lawyer. Anger began to smoulder deep within him, but he smothered the feeling. Common sense dictated that he was wrong. The brothers would be drawn to him; they could not stay away, it was human nature. At the worst, he could conceive that Rudolph would resist, but Carlton, he knew, must come.

"Thank you, Sheriff," Thomas was saying. "I'm the last one to break rules, believe me, but I had no choice this time. I am in your debt, sir."

Jock turned and left the room, closing and locking the door behind him. Thomas turned and looked at John Price Daniel. He was as Thomas expected—relaxed, unthreatened, disinterested; he was a real actor. Thomas walked to the table and set down his briefcase. Neither man spoke as the lawyer seated himself opposite the prisoner.

John liked Thomas Moore. He was sharp, intelligent, thorough, and resourceful. He didn't fit John's system of human classification; he broke all the rules.

Their eyes met. John regarded the lawyer with caution, but could discern only compassion and a sense of purpose in his gentle eyes. Thomas had a sense of peace and tranquility about him that soothed the troubled soul. Carlton had drawn strength from it, Dixie Lee had sensed it, and now, so did John Price Daniel. There was no conscious decision, nor even full awareness when John let the barrier between them slip away.

Thomas knew instinctively when to speak. He took a deep breath and met John's gaze directly.

"I have much to say and little time to say it," he began earnestly. "You have used silence well to this point, and I ask only that you listen. First, I will answer the question you ask yourself. Your brothers did not send me."

John listened intently, a flicker of surprise in his expression.

"They do not know that I am here, in fact," Thomas continued. "I have come on my own. Rudolph and Carlton will be here in the morning."

John's brows arched slightly. The lawyer was perceptive. John's curiosity was stirred.

"I have come to tell you something I discovered in trying to track you down," said Thomas, as if he could hear John's unspoken question. "From the trial you know that I discovered much about you." He paused. "I may know more about your life than you do yourself."

John smiled skeptically. His eyes spoke for him.

"I know, for example," Thomas continued, "that you discovered the name of your benefactor by rifling the files of my father in Atlanta. You used the name John Margolin, I believe."

John was impressed. He nodded appreciatively.

"I also know that you could not understand why your father rejected you when you contacted him, in view of his kindness to you financially until you completed college. I believe I can explain that to you."

A subtle change came into John's eyes. The pain of his father's rejection. It was too close to home, too deep to speak of, especially with a stranger. John lost something of his confidence at that moment, and his heart began to thump slowly, loudly, in his ears. He was on dangerous ground, and he knew it, but his need to know about his father was beyond control. His instincts were for self-preservation, but strangely, he found he could not harden his heart against the man who sat before him. He did not realize that pain had come into his eyes for Thomas to see. Without knowing it, he had been drawn skillfully into the unassuming lawyer's web. Sitting very still and stiff, he found himself nodding his acquiescence. For the first time since his discovery, John spoke.

"Please do," he said. "Explain my father to me."

Thomas was visibly relieved that John had broken his silence, and he smiled slightly.

"Thank you," he said. "I hoped our conversation would not be one-sided."

He opened his briefcase and withdrew several thick file folders. He put them down in front of him. He held up the first one, labeled with the words "John Price Daniel."

"This is your file, the one you discovered in my office, the one which gave you the name of your secret benefactor." He put the file down and opened it, drawing out a contract. He handed the paper to John. "Your benefactor's name was P. L. Townsend. The address given was Townsend Plantation, Hayley, Georgia." Thomas paused, waiting for some reaction.

"Go on," said John. "You said you could explain."

"When you saw a photograph of Price Townsend, you knew he was without doubt your father." Thomas was fishing.

"Yes," said John expectantly.

"And yet, when you wrote to him, he denied you so violently that you came to hate him, and hate the fact that he was your father."

John stared at Thomas, his eyes warning him to take care. A muscle worked in his cheek as he gritted his teeth.

"And this hatred," continued Thomas, "of your father and all that he held dear, has brought you here. You sought to repay evil for evil. You sought to revenge yourself on him by ruining his family and destroying his name."

With hard-won patience John said, "Still, you have told me nothing. Why would he deny that he had been my benefactor when any fool could see we were father and son?"

"He did not know of the resemblance until Montgomery brought him word of it."

John frowned. "Surely he must have."

"No," said Thomas.

"But he supported me all those years."

"No," said Thomas. "He did not."

"No?" John said. "What do you mean, no? He was the benefactor. You showed me the contract yourself. His name was P. L. Townsend, wasn't it?"

Thomas handed him County Pa's file. John saw a subtle change in the lawyer's eyes, and he realized in a flash of insight that the lawyer had been guessing. Suddenly John knew that Thomas could not have known his father's thoughts. Thomas could not have known John's own motives. He knew that Thomas had been walking him step-by-step through his own theoretic reconstruction of what happened, and he had not missed a thing.

Before John had time to react, Thomas said, "Open it," pointing to the file.

Again John's curiosity dictated, and he opened his father's file. The first document was a deed. The title read "Price (NMI) Townsend." John understood the abbreviation, and looked up in confusion. Thomas handed him the last file, marked "Paulette Laura Townsend."

John read the name on the last file. The significance of Laura's full name hit him instantly. Her initials were P. L. His eyes widened in disbelief and he dropped the file on the table quickly, as if it burned in his hand. The color drained from his face as he stared at the name.

"No," he said, struggling to stop his voice from shaking. "It's not possible."

"It's true," said Thomas quietly. "Your father never knew. She never told him. She never told anyone."

"It can't be true. It's a mistake."

John struggled against believing. If it were true, he had no ground to walk on, no life to remember. If it were true, he must believe goodness and kindness existed, that he had managed to hurt and wound the one person in the world who had been kind to him. If it were true, even his hatred of his father had no basis.

"John." Thomas's voice was soft.

The younger man looked up and met the kind eyes of the lawyer, but he could not bear his kindness and looked away.

"Your father was a very complex man," said Thomas. "He was a scoundrel, and he was a genius at bending others to his will. I don't know his motives. Perhaps he suffered much, as you have, and he survived the pain the best he could, in spite of the hurt he did to others.

"We are sometimes a poor and fragile lot, we humans. We strike out at others when we are hurt. Your father was just as human as you are. Don't hate him, and don't hate yourself."

Without another word, Thomas gathered his papers and left the room.

After Sheriff Morehouse returned him to his cell and left him in the dark, John Price Daniel cried.

54

The ride from Hayley to Albany the next morning was a long one. The atmosphere inside the yellow and black Packard was strained as the Townsend brothers headed for their meeting with John Price Daniel at the Albany police headquarters. The previous evening's argument had extended into the night, and neither had slept. The morning found them exhausted, but no closer to consent.

Somewhere deep in Carlton's consciousness was the knowledge that his rage was a release, that his need for revenge was instinctive, a protective reaction against his true feelings. These feelings were the same for all the Townsends: hurt and anger, grief and guilt. The pain was bittersweet, for the face of the offender haunted Carlton. It was Price Townsend's face; how could he not be drawn to it? This man had tried to ruin his life, and yet, Carlton felt the bond between them. It was more than blood, it was spirit, for John and Carlton were much alike, bold, adventurous, rebellious, clever, emotional.

Rudolph was affected just as deeply. He did not fight his pain as Carlton did. Like Carlton, he felt deeply the bond of blood, for like John, he had lived with Price Townsend's rejection, and like John, he had learned to survive.

Rudolph was no stranger to the dark depths, for he had found and faced his own dragons. He had no illusions about himself or others, but he had hope in the capacity for good in everyone. Rudolph knew that if Laura Townsend had been John's mother, if Rudolph had been born the bastard, it would be he, not John Price, that waited behind bars. In Rudolph's view, only one element of difference existed between them, a mother's love.

The strain and sorrow their mother now suffered was crushing to both her sons. Their need to protect her from any further pain was

intense, and, for that reason, regaining their father's ledger was impera-
tive.

Rudolph gripped the steering wheel and stared at the road before
him. He could not blame Carlton for his anger, but he could not allow
it to interfere with regaining the ledger.

"All right," said Rudolph, breaking the silence. "I've had enough."
He slowed the car and pulled off the road, as Carlton watched in silence.

"Until we can do this right," said Rudolph, turning to his brother,
"we're not doing it at all."

Carlton looked away, to the open fields that surrounded them on all
sides.

Rudolph studied his brother, waiting for some response. Receiving
none, he got out of the car, walked to the other side of the road, leaned
against the fence, and waited.

Soon he heard the car door open, and Carlton joined him beside the
fence. The tension was broken.

"I'm tired," said Rudolph, looking straight ahead at the cows grazing
in the distance.

"Yeah. So am I."

"If I have to, I will see this man alone."

Carlton was not impressed.

"Still trying to pull rank on me, big brother?" he asked. "Those days
are over."

"I wish they were," Rudolph replied. "You're too big to throw back."

Rudolph was surprised when he heard a soft chuckle from his
brother. He turned to Carlton, who looked back with a weak lopsided
grin.

"Funny what comes to your mind," he said, shaking his head. I just
thought of the first time you took me fishing and I caught that little six-
inch bass."

Rudolph remembered, and a slow smile spread across his face, as he
pictured six-year-old Carlton's pout when he learned the fish was too
small to keep. Throw it back, Rudolph had ordered, and Carlton obeyed,
hurtling the fish like a baseball to the center of the pond.

"You did say *throw* it," Carlton said.

Rudolph nodded, "That I did."

Their smiles faded and the memory slipped away, leaving them to face again the present. But strangely enough, the years they had shared were with them now, almost tangible, strong and solid.

"I need your help," said Rudolph soberly. "As long as he has that ledger, he's too dangerous to alienate. We may only have this one chance to get it back. For mother's sake, you must not lose your temper and threaten him. He's still got the upper hand. If we have to swallow our pride and beg, then damn it, *we will!*"

Carlton stared hard at him. He knew Rudolph was right; he was always right.

"We're not children anymore," Rudolph continued. "I can't tell you what to do. But, by God, you're going in there with me, and I'm going to trust you to keep your head."

Carlton knew then that he could do whatever he had to do. For Laura, he could do anything.

JOHN PRICE Daniel was waiting patiently in his cell for the door to open. His brothers would be here in the morning, the lawyer had said. John had tried to sleep, but all night it had eluded him. His mind was too full. He had relived his whole life in those hours, from a new perspective. Somehow, John had found the capacity to see things from another's point of view.

Every incident seemed more logical, now that he knew the truth. The unanswered letters of his boyhood no longer tormented him. Laura Townsend's provision for an abandoned illegitimate child that had been sired by her husband was kindness almost beyond John's comprehension. Price Townsend had also claimed no knowledge of John's mother, Rosellen; John wondered if even this may have been the truth. It was thirty years ago. Could his father have honestly had no recollection of his mother's name?

When County Pa had been convinced that John was his son, he had offered money if he would stay away, but he had also offered an inheritance. Why the change in his will if he felt no responsibility, if he wanted no contact? Could it be that his father had been afraid of losing Laura? Perhaps when he died in the plane crash, his heart had indeed changed; perhaps he was anxious to meet this son he had never known.

John marveled at his capacity for dreams. County Pa was dead, and John would never know why he had ventured to Savannah with the lawyer. The man was no saint, and a poor father to his legal offspring. Yet each time John cursed his own folly, the words of Thomas Moore assailed him: he was as human as you are; don't hate him, or yourself.

The quiet lawyer had, in fact, given John Price Daniel a new life. In the midst of this violent self-recrimination, John clung to Thomas's words. He knew that the hatred he bore his father must be erased. If he could forgive his father, he could forgive himself.

What about his brothers? They had cause to hate him, to want him punished. But he had no intention of rotting in prison. For the first time in his life he had a reason for living. He needed their help to escape. He could handle the locks, but not the guards. If he must use the ledger to bargain for his freedom he would do it, though he would never use it against them. It was up to them now. If there was a way to make up for what he had done, he would find it, even if they never forgave him. But first, before anything else, he must be free.

"IF YOU were anyone else, I would not even consider something like this," said Sheriff Morehouse as he led Rudolph and Carlton down the hall to the conference room. "But, Rudolph, I owe you this." He nodded to Carlton, "I owe you, too, Carlton. But even so, I'd never let you in here alone."

"You have my word, Jock," Rudolph replied. "No harm will come to him."

Jock opened the door and admitted the brothers. With a glance at the prisoner, who sat with his back to the door, he said, "He ain't said a word to anybody yet, although I don't know what happened last—" He caught himself. He had promised Thomas his discretion. "Well, maybe you'll have better luck. Try and make it quick." He left the room and locked the door on the three sons of County Pa.

The prisoner made no move to acknowledge their presence, but sat waiting. Rudolph and Carlton walked slowly to the opposite end of the table and faced their half brother. The face was their father's face, the face they had known as children, the strong, vigorous, youthful face of Price Townsend. It was uncanny and frightening. Their minds saw John Price Daniel, but their emotions saw County Pa.

John returned their stares dispassionately. He saw no hint of the shivering electricity which jangled Carlton's every nerve, nor the waves of feeling which drained the strength of his taller brother.

Rudolph moved cautiously toward his half brother, pulling out a chair to John's left. His need to protect Laura pushed every emotion aside, and he sat down with what appeared to be perfect assurance next to the ghost of County Pa. Carlton turned away. He walked to the far end of the room and stared out the open window through the iron bars. Rudolph accepted Carlton's action, thinking it was probably for the best, then looked back to John. He was met with confident, strangely benevolent hazel eyes, the exact pale shade of his own.

"You know why we have come," said Rudolph. "You have our father's ledger."

The prisoner remained silent. He seemed to measure Rudolph, searching his face, his eyes, his words. Slowly, slightly, he nodded that he had the ledger.

"Obviously, we want it back."

John smiled as he again acknowledged Rudolph.

"What do you want from us?" asked Rudolph, a slight frown appearing as he felt the beginnings of frustration. Was the man without a tongue? Surely he would not continue this silence.

John remained silent.

"If you want money, name your price. Much of the estate is in my name. I can sell it if that is what it takes. We can get you the best lawyers, the best defense money can buy." He paused. It was like talking to a stone.

"My mother," Rudolph said slowly, a bead of perspiration forming on his brow, "has been hurt enough. What my father, what *our* father, has done is done. We cannot change the past or punish a dead man. If that ledger is made public, it will be my mother, not County Pa, who suffers."

Still the prisoner listened, saying nothing. Rudolph began to get a sinking feeling in the pit of his stomach. There must be some way to reach him.

"I don't care about myself, I don't care if the whole world knows the truth about my father. But I care about my mother. The scandal would break her heart. Please. Return the ledger to me. Tell me what you want. I'll do anything you ask."

The cool hazel eyes never wavered. Still they probed, they questioned, they waited for something more.

"Can you not answer me?" said Rudolph, his voice rising.

There was no response. Carlton stood his ground with great difficulty, and lit a cigarette. The heat was stifling. Outside the window a dove cooed softly. The world outside seemed suddenly unreal. Taking a deep breath, Rudolph continued, in a quieter voice, "I had hoped that you would be willing to listen to reason. Perhaps I was wrong."

Rudolph pushed his chair back from the table, turning it in John's direction, but placing distance between them. Carlton turned sharply at the sound, but Rudolph threw him a quick glance and put up his hand to warn him away. Rudolph leaned back against the chair in a relaxed fashion, his arms resting comfortably on the arms of the chair. It was Rudolph's turn to stare, and he contemplated John openly.

"You know something, John?" he asked in a voice filled with regret, as he addressed his half brother by name for the first time. "All of this energy and this anger, it is for nothing. It will not give you what you want. Life cursed you with the same father I had, and the irony of it is that he never loved either of us."

John's eyes narrowed a fraction, as if he questioned Rudolph's words. Rudolph's brow furrowed and he looked away. Finally he spoke.

"After he died in that plane crash, I just wish you had tried one more thing before you learned to hate the rest of us so. God, I wish you had given us a chance. We are your brothers. All you had to do was show your face and we would have known you. I can't say for certain what would have happened, but I know that even now, after all the pain you've caused us, I can't look at you without feeling that you're a part of me." He paused. "I'll always regret the way it has turned out."

John looked at Rudolph with the same intent, open gaze, but Rudolph knew that his mind was far away. There was suddenly a different feeling in the air. Rudolph looked at Carlton and found him leaning against the wall, his head bowed slightly. Then Rudolph knew that all three of them realized they could have been more than brothers. They could have been friends.

When he looked around again, Rudolph found that John was gazing intently at Carlton. John looked at Rudolph, and nodded in Carlton's direction. Rudolph got up and walked over to Carlton.

"He wants to talk to you," Rudolph said.

Carlton raised an eyebrow.

"To talk? Optimistic, aren't we?" he replied.

Carlton pulled Rudolph's chair to the opposite end of the table. He sat down facing John Price Daniel. As with Rudolph, John stared at Carlton silently, waiting, but there was something different in his eyes. Even from Rudolph's vantage point behind Carlton, Rudolph could see recognition, even a hint of affection, in those steady, probing eyes.

Suddenly the breath seemed to catch in Rudolph's throat and a shiver ran down his spine, as his mind acknowledged familiarity in the shape of the man's jaw. He is close to you, Thomas had said. It all came together, and Rudolph knew. Daniel J. Smith was not John's only disguise. Rudolph struggled to keep his face blank.

John's silence was unreasonable and irritating to Carlton. What Rudolph recognized as familiarity and affection in John's eyes seemed, to Carlton, a look of amusement which mocked him.

"Damn you!" he cried, pounding the table with his fists. "I can't put up with this!"

He glared at the man who had his father's face, but he could not call up the rage, the hatred, or even the simple energy to tear him apart. It was almost as if he knew him, had known him always. And the face. Above all, the face devastated him. It was a face he loved. Carlton's growing recognition of his own undeniable bond to this cunning rascal only served to puzzle and enrage the younger Townsend further.

"I'm no damn philosopher," he growled, "and I'm in no mood to play games. As far as I'm concerned this is the last chance you've got to deal for that ledger. If you're willing to bargain, speak up now, or forget it."

Carlton's voice was silenced by the iron grip of Rudolph's hand on his shoulder. Their eyes met and Carlton knew that more would be required of him. For Laura's sake, he would do it, even if it meant begging.

"No, Rudolph," came John's deep smooth voice, "let him talk. He's entitled. Although common brawling seems a bit uncivilized, I'd be happy to oblige him. But I suggest we settle this matter the easy way. I will give you the ledger gladly, and call it even—for a favor."

The voice. Carlton knew it instantly. His eyes widened in disbelief as John was speaking. Rudolph remained at Carlton's side, his hand resting with steady firmness on his brother's shoulder.

"It was you!" Carlton cried, struggling to rise, furious now in the realization of how he had been used, how completely he had been fooled.

Rudolph held him firmly down.

"Yes," said John calmly, "as your brother seems to have already realized. Woody Price at your service, sir."

"You bastard! I thought you were my friend!"

Carlton fought to free himself from Rudolph's viselike grip, but could not. John blinked appreciatively at the outburst and nodded in agreement, as Carlton slowed his struggle to escape Rudolph's grip.

"Accurate," he mused, "both statements quite accurate."

The shock over, Carlton abruptly ceased his struggle and shook Rudolph off. Rudolph stepped back.

"You were the best friend I've ever had," said Carlton accusingly, his voice trembling. "How could you do all this?"

John smiled, but regret and guilt were in his eyes. Rudolph read these feelings perfectly before John could erase them, but Carlton saw only the arrogant smile.

John's heart was close to breaking. His brothers had passed the test. After all he had put them through, they did not do as he had done—they did not hate, they did not seek vengeance.

"You saved my life," said a bewildered Carlton. "Why? Why save my life when your aim was to . . . ."

With a will of iron, John controlled his emotions. His escape was his only goal now, and he knew he must, for a little while longer, use the weapons available to him to effect his release. What he must ask these men to do was a crime, and extremely risky, and he could not trust them as he wished to. Not even for love was he willing to risk his life. He would have to bluff. John's face was carefully blank when he answered Carlton's question.

"The answer is simple enough. What better introduction could I have managed than to pull you from a wrecked automobile? I had no idea the vehicle would explode. But I'm glad I saved you. If you had died, it would have ruined all my plans."

Rudolph caught the strain in John's deep voice, and saw the thin, fleeting line which formed between his eyebrows. He knew he was acting. In spite of what John said, Rudolph knew he had not imagined John's affection for Carlton, nor the torment in his half brother's eyes.

Carlton began to rise, slowly, from his chair.

"You cold-blooded—"

Instantly, Rudolph was beside him, just as John put up a warning hand.

"We have, I believe, a bargain to settle," said John. His eyes dared Carlton to come further. "If you will do as I say, I will give you back the ledger and be gone from your lives forever."

Rudolph silenced Carlton with a fiery glance. Turning to John, Rudolph said, "What do you want us to do?"

55

It was just after nine the next morning when Rudolph entered the Albany police headquarters again. The front office was, as usual, manned only by Sergeant Hardy.

"Good Morning, Sergeant," said Rudolph.

"Why, Mr. Rudolph," Sergeant Hardy replied, hurriedly tucking away the magazine he had been reading. "I didn't know you planned on coming in this morning."

"I'd like to see Mr. Daniel again for a few minutes."

"Well, sir," the man frowned, "I wish I'da known you were coming. I can't let you see him at the moment. The conference room is in use. Carlton's in there now with Sheriff Morehouse and Mr. Brooks, giving his deposition."

"Was that for this morning? I'd forgotten."

"Yes, sir, they may be in there the best part of an hour."

"I see," said Rudolph. He looked at his watch and, scowling, went to the window.

"Is there a problem, Mr. Rudolph?" asked Sergeant Hardy.

Rudolph looked again at his watch.

"A friend of mine is on his way here. He had to delay his flight to accommodate me. He's leaving the country on business and won't be back for months. Woody Price—perhaps you know him."

"Sure, sure," said the sergeant. "I've seen him around. Where's he off to?"

"Australia. He inherited a factory there."

"Damn," replied Hardy. "Australia."

Rudolph turned and came back to the front desk.

"He's due here any minute. Would you mind if I just talked to this

man, Daniel, through the bars of the cell? Once Woody gets here it will
only take five minutes to wrap this fool lawsuit up."

Hardy's eyes lit up with the undaunted curiosity of an inveterate
snoop.

"Lawsuit?"

Rudolph lowered his voice and spoke confidentially, "I wouldn't
want this to get around, Sergeant, but there's no way to deny that this
man is an illegitimate son. He's got a big idea he can claim some part of
my father's estate."

"Whew!" said the sergeant. "Can he do that? In prison?"

Rudolph continued, ignoring his question. "You'd be doing me a
great favor if I could get this meeting over before Woody leaves the
country."

"Hey, that's no problem," said the sergeant with a smile. "For you,
Mr. Rudolph, anytime."

"I have some papers here," said Rudolph, setting the briefcase on the
desk. "The prisoner could be reading them while we wait for Woody."

Sergeant Hardy grabbed the keys, led Rudolph to the jailblock, and
opened the outer door. "Go right on," he said. "I'll keep an eye out for
Mr. Price for you and send him back."

"You're a good man," said Rudolph. "Thanks."

When Hardy turned the corner, Rudolph walked to John's cell and
handed the briefcase through the bars.

"It's all there," said Rudolph quietly. "How much time do you
need?"

John smiled. "For me? Five minutes."

Rudolph turned and headed back to the office, checking his watch.
He nodded to Sergeant Hardy and took a seat next to the coffee machine.

"No sign of him yet?" Rudolph asked.

"No, sir," Hardy answered. "Hell, you weren't in there a minute."

"I decided to come back here to wait for Woody," said Rudolph,
drumming his fingers on the arm of the chair. "I just left the door to the
jailblock open. I had to get out of there. That guy gives me the willies."

Sergeant Hardy's eyes narrowed.

"Plum creepy, ain't he? Just like seeing a ghost."

Rudolph picked up a magazine and leafed through it, checking his watch frequently. After five minutes, he got up and waited again by the window.

"At last," he said. "There he is. I thought he'd never get here."

Sergeant Hardy looked up and nodded absently.

"Oh, by the way," said Rudolph, walking back to the desk, "one last favor, Sergeant. Would you please go and let Carlton know I'm here? I hope I won't have to, but I may need to pull him out of that meeting when Woody arrives. I should have thought of it before, but my nerves are shot. This last month has been hell."

"I don't doubt it," said Sergeant Hardy sympathetically. "The whole world's gone crazy if you ask me. I don't even want to pick up a newspaper anymore, with all that mess going on overseas. Be right back."

He left the room. Rudolph waited for the sound of the conference room door opening, before he opened and closed the front door of the station, tripping the bells. He left the office and raced silently back to the jailblock. The prisoner was there, now outside the cell, leaning against the wall at the end of the half-lit corridor. He wore the somewhat rumpled shirt, tie, and slacks that Rudolph had stuffed into the briefcase along with the wig, glasses, and makeup kit.

Rudolph walked down to him. John Price Daniel was gone, the cell was empty, the door closed and locked. Rudolph looked at the familiar face of Woody Price and could not suppress a shudder. It was like a dream, a nightmare; there were too many faces suddenly, too many ghosts.

John pointed to the door, and Rudolph turned to see Sergeant Hardy poke his head through the opening.

"How y'all doing, Mr. Price?" called Hardy, opening the door. "I see you made it." Hardy started down the corridor.

Rudolph looked at John and started up the corridor to head him off. If he saw the empty cell, it was over.

"Sergeant," said Rudolph softly, taking Hardy by the arm, "if we might have a little privacy—"

His words were interrupted by a clear, quiet voice from inside the empty jail cell. "Get him out of here."

The voice was grim and chilling. It startled Rudolph and Hardy, who turned and stared toward the cell at the end of the corridor, as did Woody Price.

"Or just forget the whole damn thing," continued the calm voice from the prisoner's cell.

Woody glared at the cell's imaginary occupant, and replied in his deeper familiar voice, "You'd best remember your manners, son. You're in no position to demand anything from these people."

In the dim light, Sergeant Hardy did not notice that Rudolph had turned very pale.

"Well," Hardy muttered as he reluctantly turned to leave, "at least you got the son of a bitch to say something."

Hardy left, closing the door behind him. Rudolph turned back to John with a pounding heart. He took a deep breath and joined his half brother at the end of the corridor. He looked again at the empty cell, half believing he would see John Price Daniel within.

"You might have warned me," he said to the man he knew as Woody Price. "I may go nuts before this is over. You've got five faces, and now you're throwing voices all over the place."

"Sorry, old man." With the disguise, John had by habit adopted the posture, mannerisms, and lofty language of Woody Price.

"Is there anything they didn't teach you in the circus?" asked Rudolph, weak with relief that the crisis had passed, but still tense and strained with the risk of the escape.

Sergeant Hardy looked up as Rudolph and Woody Price walked into the office.

"All finished? That was quick."

"Yes, thanks," answered Rudolph. "Would you ask my brother to join us for a moment?"

"Sure," replied the sergeant. "Just let me lock up that jail block right quick."

Bless Sergeant Hardy, thought Rudolph. Always the quickest, easiest way. Anxiously, Rudolph waited as he heard him lock the door and return on his way to the conference room.

"Never mind, Sergeant," called Rudolph as Hardy passed. "Mr. Price's plane is waiting. We can't wait any longer. Thanks for your help."

They were out the door. Rudolph moved automatically, like a mindless robot, through the remaining steps of the simple plan. It was as if he had lit the fuse to a bomb behind him, and now he walked from it in slow motion, his feet leaden, knowing that at any moment the world would explode around him. They were almost to the car. Now, the car was moving. No one was running after them. If only they could make it out of town. If only no one checked John's cell for a few more minutes.

"I may never get over this," said Rudolph, as they left Albany behind them. "This is never going to work."

John smiled broadly.

"Of course it's going to work. It already has. Believe me, not a soul will check that cell for hours, not until lunch, and around here, lunch is two o'clock."

Rudolph groaned and kept driving to Hayley.

"Relax," John said. "It's over. You pulled it off like a pro." He paused and looked over at Rudolph, who gripped the steering wheel of the car with white knuckles. "But I can tell you're just not cut out for a life of crime."

IT WAS a long hour for Carlton. It took every ounce of his willpower to concentrate on the men before him in the small conference room, to focus on his deposition. What was happening? What if they were caught? So many things could go wrong. How in heaven's name did they agree to such a risky plan? Still, the sergeant had come, as planned, to inform him of his brother's presence. There had been no alarm.

And now it was close to ten o'clock, time for the unsuspecting Thomas Moore to arrive. That was another mistake. They needed him, John had insisted. His integrity was above reproach; if he were involved, there would be no questions. But John didn't know Tom; he didn't realize the man was a walking mindreader. Tom would figure the whole thing out and turn them all in for sure. The door of the conference room opened and Sergeant Hardy admitted Thomas Moore. With a puzzled frown, Thomas apologized as he came to the table and extended his hand to Sheriff Morehouse.

"I'm so sorry. My secretary said ten o'clock. I can usually count on her to keep my appointments straight." Thomas shook hands with Baxter Brooks. "Am I too late to be of some assistance?"

"I doubt that is ever the case, Tom," said Baxter. "Have a seat. We've just about wrapped this thing up."

Thomas greeted Carlton and drew up a chair beside him. Carlton's fears that Thomas was too perceptive to be fooled were valid, for Thomas sensed Carlton's tension immediately. When the papers were signed and the meeting over, Carlton lingered in his seat as the other men rose to leave and bid each other goodbye.

"Coming, Carlton?" asked Jock.

"I'd like a word with Tom, if it's okay," replied Carlton.

"Okay with me," said Jock, and he left the room, letting the door swing shut behind him.

Thomas sat down again. "We sat here before," he said to Carlton. It was the same now as it had been then. Part of the young man before him was closed to him. Again he was protecting another. Under the circumstances, it was not hard to figure out who.

"Yes," Carlton replied with a sharp intake of breath. "A long time ago."

He looked out the window. It was hard to be there suddenly, alone with this man to whom he owed so much.

"Your mother," asked Thomas, "she is well?"

Carlton nodded. Keeping his eyes on the sky he said, "There is no way I will ever be able to repay you for all that you've done for us."

Thomas smiled. His gaze joined Carlton's as he also contemplated the puffy white clouds. Thomas knew that the brothers were desperate to regain the ledger from the prisoner. What they had done to obtain it he did not know, but he knew that if he asked Carlton what was going on, at that particular moment, Carlton could not lie to him.

"Debts and obligations should be left between business partners," Thomas said. "They have no place in friendship."

Carlton understood his meaning, and nodded. He looked at the older man gratefully. Thomas kept his eyes on the clouds.

"My standard fee has been paid. Beyond that, you owe me nothing."

The door opened and Jock Morehouse burst into the room.

"Daniel's gone!" he cried angrily. "He picked the lock and escaped."

"No!" protested Carlton, jumping from his chair.

"I found this on the floor outside his cell," Jock continued harshly, throwing the slender pick on the table.

"Could he still be on the premises?" asked Thomas quickly.

"How did he get that?" demanded Carlton hotly, pointing to the pick. "Didn't you search the man when you brought him in? I can't believe this."

"Of course we did," replied the angry sheriff. "we stripped the silent bastard. He didn't have nothing on him. Somebody must have passed that pick to him."

"And just who the hell are you accusing?" stormed Carlton. "Me? My brother? We're the only ones who've seen him. You told me that yourself."

"Gentlemen," interrupted Thomas, stepping between them, "please! We're wasting time. He can't have gotten far."

"You'll answer to me for this," Carlton snarled at Jock, "if he's not found."

"You've got your own answers to worry about," snapped the sheriff menacingly.

"Did anyone think to search the man's mouth?" shouted Thomas in frustration.

Carlton and Jock were silenced by Thomas's outburst. Neither had ever heard him raise his voice before.

"In his mouth?" repeated Jock with a grimace.

"The man was a sword swallower in the circus. I imagine it's quite hard to talk with a sword down your throat. You did say he never said a word."

Jock looked at the three-inch pick on the table. "Good God," he groaned.

Carlton looked cautiously at Thomas. As far as he could remember, there was no mention of sword swallowing in the detective's report of John's circus days.

The lawyer didn't seem to notice Carlton's stare.

56

John had no need to fear discovery, for, as Woody Price, he could walk freely down any street in Albany. Rudolph and Carlton alone knew the truth. John had told Rudolph to drive back to Hayley, to the Townsend game preserve. The ledger was there. The ride was, for the most part, a silent one. Both men were deep in their own thoughts. Both were cautious. Both were taking a risk. Rudolph could not know for sure that John would give him the ledger. John could not be sure that once the ledger was returned, he would be free to go. Each man waited for the other to set conditions, demand guarantees, as they neared the preserve. Neither brother spoke, neither made demands, and neither failed to realize the chance that he was taking. It seemed that they had decided to trust one another.

When the cabin came into view, Rudolph slowed the car and pulled over, parking in the shade of a giant pecan tree near the cabin. It was ten o'clock, time for Thomas to arrive late for Carlton's deposition. If all went according to plan, Carlton would persuade Thomas to see the prisoner following the meeting, and the escape would be discovered.

"What will you do now?" asked Rudolph, keeping his eyes on the cabin.

"Change my name. Stay away from the theater, away from New York. Maybe I will go to Australia for a while. Woody Price is under no suspicion. He can do whatever he likes."

"John, I have something to tell you."

"I know. It can wait. I'll be back in a minute." John got out of the car and walked behind the cabin, disappearing from Rudolph's view. Rudolph sat alone in the car, staring at the place where John had slipped from view. He swallowed hard and tried to suppress a shiver of apprehension.

Five minutes passed before John emerged, carrying County Pa's ledger under his arm. He paused as he reached the car. Rudolph got out of the car and stood, waiting. John handed the book to Rudolph without a word.

"You already know about my mother, don't you?" Rudolph said. John nodded.

"A great lady," he said.

"Tom told you, then. But when?"

"Close to midnight the day they locked me up, the night before you two came."

Rudolph nodded thoughtfully.

"I wonder why he did that?" he mused aloud, as he stared at the slim volume he held.

"Thomas Moore is an unusual man," replied John. "He seemed to think I was worth saving."

"Aren't we all." Rudolph had never seen the ledger he held before. He did not open it; he never would. "But the next morning," he said, "when we met with you, you still played our enemy."

"Am I any less an enemy today?"

Rudolph did not look up, but continued to stare at the brown leather ledger in his hands.

"I would say so. Today you risked your future on me. For all you know I may have a gun in my pocket. I may have the law behind the bushes. They may be waiting for my signal once this ledger is in my hands." He looked at John. "Does an enemy hand over his only weapon and wait willingly for capture?"

"Is that what I have done?" asked John. "Or is it that I have only taken the same gamble you did when you let me walk away just now? What made you think I would come back?" Rudolph searched his brother's eyes.

"I just knew you would."

John did not reply. He could not speak, but he did not have to. John Price Daniel clasped the hand offered in friendship.

"Where can I drop you?" Rudolph asked, as he started the car.

"Woody's place, north of Albany. But first I must ask a favor."

Rudolph looked up expectantly.

"There is a great lady I would like to visit, with your permission," said John. "I owe her an apology."

Rudolph nodded.

"I think she needs to hear it."

Later, as the car turned into the driveway of the Townsend plantation, Rudolph said, "There's Carlton's car. Maybe this wasn't such a good idea. I assumed Jock would draft him for the search party."

"Pull around to the stable," said John.

With an uneasy glance at his half brother, Rudolph did as he asked, driving past the house to the old barn.

"Let me talk to Carlton first," Rudolph began.

"No," John interrupted, "just send him out here. He's got a right to make up his own mind. I owe him that."

"Okay," Rudolph replied. "It's your funeral."

"I think he'll settle for a few teeth."

Rudolph smiled. "You know, I can't speak for Carlton, but I think I'm actually going to miss Woody Price around here."

John shrugged. "Maybe he can come back for a visit some day. If Carlton doesn't kill him first."

Rudolph found Carlton inside, and sent him out as John had asked. Carlton was still in a fury, confused and frustrated by this man who had been his friend, this man who was so obviously his father's son, this man who had tried to ruin his life. He appeared at the back door and saw John Price Daniel in the distance, leaning against the yellow and black Packard. As he came closer, a sharp blow seemed to knock the breath out of him, as if someone had kicked him in the stomach. He recognized the face of his friend, Woody Price. He had not seen John disguised as Woody since he learned the truth, and his mental acceptance of the facts did little to shield him from the emotional shock of seeing Woody again.

Carlton's eyes hardened as he approached his half brother, and he slowed his pace. John took a few steps toward Carlton. They stared at each other as they circled around slowly, ready to strike.

"What do you think you're doing here?" hissed Carlton.

"I want to see your mother," replied John with grim determination.

"Like hell you will!" cried Carlton. "You've hurt her enough! The best thing for you to do, my so-called friend, is to get away from this house, and this town, and this state, as fast as you can."

"I intend to," said John with maddening control, "as soon as I speak to my father's widow."

The circle they traced was getting smaller.

"You will stay the hell away from my mother, you slimy bastard."

John took off Woody's thick glasses and tossed them aside as he circled his adversary like the graceful cat of Thomas's dream.

"I will speak to her."

Carlton watched in revulsion as John removed the rest of his disguise. He now faced the image of his father once again.

"You will die first," growled Carlton.

"I'm not leaving."

"Oh, yes you are!"

Carlton lunged at him, catching him by the arms, trying to knock him to the ground. They locked together, eyes raging, every muscle taut and straining, but try as he might, Carlton could not make him lose his feet. Carlton had new respect for his half brother when they came apart just long enough to trade crushing blows.

Carlton landed the first punch, but reeled back when John followed his own counterpunch with a diving slam to Carlton's belly. The two men landed hard on the earth and rolled violently about, like savage wrestlers in a battle to the death. There were no rules in this fierce struggle, and they used every dirty trick ever invented to get the upper hand.

In minutes they were both torn and bloody, struggling to find the strength for another blow. They hit each other in slow succession, as if they were taking turns, then stubbornly dragging themselves back to their feet for the next punch. When at last the brothers could not get up again, they lay bruised and bleeding in the red dirt, panting for breath. Carlton looked at John.

"Give up?" he gasped.

John didn't move from his faceup spread-eagle sprawl.

"Hell no," he whispered between breaths.

Both men struggled to rise, dreading the effort another round would demand.

"Wait a minute," John panted, and Carlton gladly fell back to the dirt.

"What?" Carlton asked.

"You give up," John suggested.

Carlton didn't expect bargaining at this point, and squinted his one open eye at John.

"Me?" he panted. If he could have laughed, he would have, but he could only grunt. "I can't give up, you fool. It has to be you."

"You're probably right," John muttered. Carlton waited.

"Well?" he demanded weakly.

"Well what?" panted John.

"Do you give up?"

"No."

A half-cough, half-chuckle sputtered from Carlton's dry throat.

"Damn it, boy," he choked. "You're a Townsend all right."

IT TOOK more than a week for the signs of battle to fade. John and Carlton had dragged themselves to the house after their fight, and Laura had treated their wounds. John was deeply impressed with Laura's kindness, and found that he was never better treated than he was during the week he spent under County Pa's roof. More than bruises were healed that week. There was time for understanding and regret. There was time enough for forgiveness. There was laughter, too, and friendship.

When John was well enough to travel, he donned the guise of Woody Price and walked out of their lives, but not forever. It was a strange situation for all of them, for John Price Daniel could never show his face there again. If he came back, it would have to be as Woody Price.

"I would not change what has happened," said Laura as she sat with her sons at supper after John had gone, "but no one must ever know. Who could understand such a thing?"

"Not the local authorities, surely," replied Rudolph.

"I don't even understand it," said Carlton.

"Well," said Rudolph, smiling at his mother, "what's one more family secret?"

"Where will he go?" asked Laura. "What will he do?'"

"I don't know," replied Rudolph, "but he'll be all right."

Carlton looked at the chicken on his dinner plate. "I do know," he said. "But it's better you don't."

Rudolph frowned. "Surely he's not crazy enough to stay around here?"

"Not really," said Carlton. "He's just got some unfinished business to take care of, that's all."

Rudolph tried to stare him into saying more.

"Oh, don't worry," Carlton smiled. "When it happens, you'll understand."

57

Everyone knew the police would never catch him. He was almost a magical creature, appearing and disappearing at will. He had a hundred faces and nine lives, this phantom, and he laughed at the law with many voices. He was a legend; he was truly the ghost of County Pa. They searched for him a week, scouring the county with dogs and eager volunteers. It was a strangely jovial posse that pursued the ghost, except for the fuming officials in charge. Chief among these was Jock Morehouse, who vowed to follow the escapee into Hades itself before he would give up. Their intensive search was to no avail, and soon the ruffled egos settled for a weary truce.

One victory for law and order resulted, however, from the exhaustive search touched off by the escape of the cat burglar. A load of moonshine was discovered, hidden in a coffin aboard a freight car at the Albany depot. The shipper of the coffin, Mr. Hurd Buford, said that he knew nothing about the coffin's illegal contents. He had supervised the loading of the empty coffin himself at the depot in Hayley, he insisted. Unfortunately, a search of the funeral parlor turned up a bottle Buford had kept for his own enjoyment, and the dour mortician was booked.

The day after the jailbreak, a hazel-eyed man calling himself Woody Price had chartered a private plane in Atlanta. The pilot took him to New York City, where he reportedly left to claim his inheritance in Australia. When the maid came to clean Woody's rented home on the outskirts of Albany, she found everything as usual. There was nothing to indicate that Mr. Price would not return.

Two weeks after the escape, a man who gave his name as John Margolin visited the office of Thomas Moore in downtown Atlanta. The name was vaguely familiar to Jeannie, the receptionist, but she dismissed the possibility of ever having seen this man before. If she had ever laid eyes on this handsome, dark-haired, well-built young man, she knew she would have remembered him. Not even the thick glasses he wore detracted from his good looks.

To her surprise, Thomas asked for Mr. Margolin at once, and she ushered him into her employer's office. She watched as Thomas rose from his seat behind his cluttered desk and extended his hand to the young man.

"John," said Thomas as he shook the younger man's hand, "sit down, won't you?" Thomas dismissed Jeannie.

"I'm surprised to see you again," said Thomas carefully. With Jeannie out of earshot, a noticeable change came into the lawyer's voice. An escaped felon sat before him, and he was understandably guarded.

But John Price Daniel was an old hand at seeing through his opponents. He knew he was in no danger from this man.

"Are you, sir?" he replied calmly, removing the thick glasses of Woody Price. His eyes were not at all questioning. "I would have thought you were expecting me."

"And why would I do that?" asked Thomas.

"Because we understand each other so well," replied John. "Surely, you did not expect to fool me as easily as you fooled the Albany police, and my brothers as well?"

"You refer to your escape," said Thomas frankly. "I assure you, I had absolutely nothing to do with that." His expression completed his meaning silently: *and my position will not allow me to admit otherwise.*

The two men understood each other perfectly. John accepted his position and said, "Of course not," dismissing the subject. "Still, I have come to thank you for my life."

"My dear young man," replied Thomas, "I'm sure I have no idea what you mean."

John leaned forward in his seat.

"Mr. Moore," he said respectfully, "I did not thank you for my freedom. I thanked you for my life."

They contemplated each other in silence. Then Thomas nodded

appreciatively. This he could accept. He relaxed and a gentle smile crossed his face.

"Please call me Tom. Everyone does."

John hesitated before he replied. "What everyone does is not always right." He sat back in the chair and smiled. "I shall call you Thomas."

There was a flash of respect in the eyes of the lawyer.

"Yes," he said slowly. "Yes, you're right. I believe we certainly do understand each other."

Later in the week, Thomas Moore was in Albany for a meeting with Judge Jacob G. Allen. Governor Brown Boden had shocked the leaders of the Democratic Party by announcing, late in the campaign, that he could not continue to seek re-election, due to his health. The party needed someone to defeat the judge's old enemy, Baxter Brooks, someone with name-recognition and a fresh outlook.

Judge Allen knew that Thomas Moore was incorruptible, and that he would bring to the office of governor a dedication to honesty and justice that would bedevil state politicians for the next four years. The judge was getting on in years, and age had mellowed him. He could see that if the blatant political corruption of the past twenty years continued unabated, the state treasury would collapse. The judge put out the word: the fat cats would have to live out the next four years of famine, if not the next eight, because Thomas Moore was the only one who could beat Baxter Brooks.

As the summer neared its end, the town thrilled to the announcement that there would be a double wedding in December. The marriages of Rudolph Townsend to Camilla Goodson, and Carlton Townsend to Dixie Lee James, were sure to be the highlight of the Christmas season. A favorite topic of conversation among the regulars at Radium Springs was the choice of possible members of the wedding party. Who would be lucky enough to be chosen a groomsman or bridesmaid?

Rudolph had honored a request from Camilla, they learned, that he ask her friend, Forrest Neill, to serve as a groomsman. Paul Tanner was another early choice. Rudolph had also picked Thomas Moore as his best man. The belles of Albany were thrilled at the possibility that, following the election in November, Rudolph might have the governor-elect for his best man. No one was surprised to learn that Carlton had chosen Woody Price as his best man.

The people of Albany and Hayley had seen a lot of life that summer, but even so, no one was prepared when Elizabeth Cooper found the money.

58

"This is a strange request, Señor," said the man behind the ornate desk.

John Price Daniel sat back in his chair. "But you can do it, can you not?" he asked the bank official.

"Yes, Señor," replied the man. "The Bank of Mexico City is at your service. It will take some time, of course, and there will be a small fee, of course."

"Of course," replied John. "How much?"

"What is the exact amount you wish exchanged, Señor?"

"Two hundred and three thousand dollars."

The man arched his eyebrows and smiled.

"For the small sum of five thousand dollars, Señor," he said, "I can deliver to you the bills you wish. That will be one hundred and ninety-eight thousand American dollars, all with dates of 1929 or earlier, as you request. This is agreeable to you?"

John smiled. "The price is too high," he replied.

"But, Señor Smith," said the banker, "you must pay for such a service. We ask no questions here. You are assured your privacy. But there is a price."

"I will give you three thousand," said John. "Take it or leave it. And I want the bills in three days. If you cannot accommodate me, I will go elsewhere."

The banker puffed his cigar and stared at the American. He was no fool. "You drive a hard bargain, Señor Smith," he said, extending his hand. "You have a deal. Two hundred thousand American dollars, within three days."

John shook the man's hand. "Agreed."

THE FIRST Sunday in August was a beautiful day in Hayley. Mrs. Cooper and Tori were walking home from the morning service at the Good Shepherd Church. Neither could take their eyes from the gorgeous deep blue sky. It was a rare day, the kind of day when the sky is so blue, the air so fresh, the colors so vivid, that the beauty of the world does not seem real. The trees in the square were full and green, the birds were singing, the flowers bloomed all around them with brilliant abandon. There were no sounds of city life, no hustle and bustle of automobiles or machines, only the singing of birds, and the rustle of leaves as a soft wind blew. It was a day for sitting on the front porch, for fishing, or for a walk in the woods. It was a day for dreaming. It would be a day to remember.

"What shall we do today, Meema?" asked Tori as they opened the gate of the white picket fence.

"Oh, I don't know," said Mrs. Cooper with a smile. "It's such a lovely day, we should take advantage of it. How would you like to go for a drive? Maybe we could have a picnic. Would you like that?"

It was to be a surprise for Tori. Rudolph Townsend had invited Mrs. Cooper and Tori to spend the day at Radium Springs. The picnic basket was already prepared, the fried chicken in the icebox.

"Oh, Meema," said Tori, "that would be so much fun. When can we go?"

Mrs. Cooper opened the front door and they entered the house.

"Why, right away, if you like," she replied. "It will only take a few minutes to make up the picnic basket—" She stopped in the hall when she saw the large framed picture of Jesus praying in the Garden of Gethsemane, lying facedown on the floor. Broken glass littered the hardwood floor around it.

"Meema," said Tori, "the picture fell down. It's broken."

"My goodness," said Mrs. Cooper.

Tori went in, her shoes crunching on the broken glass. She reached down to pick up the picture.

"Wait, honey," said Mrs. Cooper. "I'll do that. You get the broom and the dustpan from the kitchen for me."

"Okay."

Mrs. Cooper put down her handbag on the side table, reached down to the broken frame, stood it upright, and leaned it against the wall. The nail which held the picture was bent downward. She fingered the nail in wonder. It seemed strong enough, and the picture did not seem heavy enough to have bent it so.

"Here, Meema," said Tori, returning with the broom.

Mrs. Cooper began to sweep up the broken glass, and Tori brought in the wastebasket. When the glass was safely cleared away, Mrs. Cooper pulled the bent nail from the wall.

"Look, Meema," said Tori. "There's something white sticking out."

Mrs. Cooper saw the edge of a piece of white paper lodged under the cardboard mat which framed the print. She pulled on the paper, which came free easily.

"What is it, Meema?"

"I don't know."

She opened the folded paper. It was a drawing. Mrs. Cooper looked at the drawing carefully, wondering what it could mean, and who could have hidden it. She walked into the front room and sat down to examine the drawing in the light of the window. Tori stood beside her, looking at the drawing over her grandmother's shoulder.

Mrs. Cooper could make no sense of the lines on the paper. It was three-dimensional, and looked like a rectangular box with a recessed center portion, like a desk. On the back recessed wall, dotted lines were drawn parallel to the edges, along the top, and down the sides. Two small cylinders were drawn across the dotted lines near the top, and red arrows emerged from the cylinders, pointing downward.

"It's the piano, Meema." said Tori.

Mrs. Cooper looked at her granddaughter questioningly.

"You understand this?" she asked.

"Yes," replied Tori. "It was me and Granddaddy's secret place. He used to leave surprises there for me."

Mrs. Cooper smiled. It would be like William Cooper to delight his grandchild so. But why the drawing? Why was it hidden?

"Would you show me?" asked Mrs. Cooper.

"Sure. Come and look."

They walked over to the piano, and Mrs. Cooper pulled the bench aside. Tori knelt down and pointed to the small wooden pieces at the top of the recessed inner wall which held the panel in place.

"Look," she said, pointing. "Just pull those back and it opens."

Mrs. Cooper knelt on the floor with Tori and saw the small wooden plugs. She found a crevice in the wooden wall, which followed exactly the dotted lines in the drawing. She was amazed she had never noticed the crevice or the plugs before.

Mrs. Cooper ducked her head into the recess and reached up to pull the plugs down, as the arrows on the drawing indicated. The panel shifted when she moved the first one back. When she released the second, she reached up to catch the panel of the secret compartment, which fell open heavily, threatening to hit her on the head. She shifted back and lowered the panel slightly, enough to see what was hidden in the compartment. Her eyes widened in disbelief as she saw what the secret place contained—stacks and stack of dollar bills, bound into bundles. Mrs. Cooper slammed the panel closed again. She could not bring herself to believe what she had just seen. Her heart began to pound.

"What's the matter, Meema?" asked Tori. "Is there something in there?"

Mrs. Cooper closed her eyes for a moment. She felt swimmy-headed. She took a deep breath and opened her eyes. Slowly, she lowered the panel again, letting it down to the floor. The money tumbled out in a heap all around her. She sat back, out of the recess, and stared at the bundles of bills. Tori's mouth flew open in astonishment. Neither one of them could say a word.

"Is it real?" asked Tori at last.

Mrs. Cooper picked up one of the bundles of hundred-dollar bills. She looked at it in wonder. The bills were old and a bit wrinkled. There was a musty odor to them, as if they had lain undisturbed for along time in a confined space. She looked at the date of issue. It was 1928. Before the crash. My goodness, she thought. All this time.

"I can't believe it," she said.

"Where did it come from?" asked Tori. She reached down and picked up one of the bundles to examine for herself.

"Your Granddaddy must have put it here before he died," said Mrs. Cooper. She was speaking to herself. Her mind was far away, in another time, another place. "Oh, William," she said. "Was this what you were trying to tell me?"

Tori frowned.

"But, Meema," she said, "Granddaddy didn't—"

"I never understood," Mrs. Cooper continued. It was as if she did not hear Tori's words. "I couldn't believe he had made no provision for us, that he was left with nothing. He was too good a businessman. Oh, my dear William." She began to cry softly.

Tori knew. She had kept the secret place to herself after her grandfather died, as a last link to him. Many times since his death, she had played their game, leaving little gifts for him as he had done for her, always hoping that one day the gift would disappear, that he would come for it. Not a month ago, the compartment was empty, as it had been on the day William Cooper died. Someone had given them this money. Someone had broken the picture in the hall and left the drawing. Someone had wanted her grandmother to believe that it had been there all along. Tori stared at the money, and then looked at her grandmother, who was still sobbing softly, believing that the money was left for them by Mr. Cooper.

It was all the money in the world, more money than they could want, more money than they could ever spend. Tori's mind was filled suddenly with pictures in her mother's scrapbooks, the lovely dresses, the beautiful brownstone. The money was theirs now, no matter where it came from. They were rich! But who could have done it? And what would her grandmother think if she knew the truth? Would she give it back? Maybe it was Rudolph. Or Carlton; he had money. Maybe Carlton wanted to help them. Or Will. He had lots of money now. Could Will have done it?

One thing was certain. Her grandmother might not understand if she knew the truth. She would not accept the money from Carlton or from Will or from anybody. Whoever left the money must have known that. Tori decided it was better for her not to know.

"Meema," she said at last, "please don't cry."

Mrs. Cooper reached out for Tori and drew her close beside her. They sat together on the floor for a long time, surrounded by the wealth of the ghost of County Pa.

59

The auditorium of Albany High School was filling rapidly. Backstage, various contestants milled about: baton twirlers in sequined costumes, barber shop quartets with fake moustaches, girl singers in long evening dresses, guitar players, banjo pickers, and even a ventriloquist with a cloth dummy. The annual DAR talent show was about to begin. Jessie Potter peeked through the heavy red velvet curtains of the stage, as all around her the contestants busied themselves with last-minute costume adjustments, checked garish makeup, drank a last cup of coffee.

"I just can't," wailed Jessie as she looked at the crowd.

"You have to," said Tori impatiently. "Jessie Potter, if you back out now, I'll never speak to you again."

"I can't help it," said Jessie, bursting into tears. "I can't go in front of these people. I'm too scared."

Tori balled her fists and stomped her foot in frustration.

"But nobody's even going to see you, goose!" she said. "You're going to be inside the tree trunk, remember? I've got the hard part. I'm the one who has to walk out in front of everybody. You don't have to come out until the end! The whole thing will be over."

"Don't fuss so," said Boozie, who was backstage to serve as Tori and Jessie's helper. "You make it worse."

"I don't care," said Tori. "She's going to ruin everything. And Daddy's out there! And Will, too! I don't believe it. She's going to ruin it. After all the time we spent making the tree and rehearsing the song."

"Don't pay her no mind, Jessie," said Boozie, patting Jessie on the shoulder. "You be all right. I can help you."

"Oh, foot!" said Tori. "You can't do anything. If I can't get her to go out there, how can you?"

"Iffen you want to do this, you better hush yo fussin'," said Boozie. "They ain't nothin' wrong with Jessie, she jus' a mite nervous. She need a friend to steady her."

"What are you talking about?" asked Tori.

"Me," said Boozie, "I can get in the tree with her. Then she won' be so scared."

Tori frowned. Try as she might, she could think of nothing wrong with this idea. She threw Jessie a glance, and found that her friend was smiling now, through her tears. Tori rolled her eyes and sighed.

"What a chicken," she said.

Out in the now-packed audience, Elizabeth Cooper sat with Forrest Neill and Paul Tanner. They had come early and had gotten splendid seats, third row center. Forrest, who had promised Tori he would come for the show, scanned the aisles behind them. They had saved seats for Jake and Mabel Potter.

"There they are," said Forrest. He stood up and waved to Jake.

Jake and Mabel made their way down the aisle and squeezed their way past the folks in the end seats. Forrest welcomed his protégé with a hardy handshake.

"Good to see you, Will," said Jake. Forrest's real name was far too formal for Jake's taste. "Hello, Mr. Tanner," he said, nodding to Paul. Elizabeth gave him a warm smile. "Miz Cooper," Jake greeted her, taking his seat, and ushering Mabel beside him.

"Just get in, did you?" Jake asked Forrest.

"This afternoon," Forrest replied. "I'm really looking forward to seeing the girls. Elizabeth tells me you three worked for days on the costumes."

Jake chuckled.

"It's not a costume exactly, it's more like scenery."

"Don't say another word, Jake," said Mrs. Cooper. "You'll spoil the surprise."

"You won't be disappointed," replied Mrs. Cooper. "Jake is a master with chicken wire."

Everyone laughed, happy to be in each other's company.

"Oh," said Forrest, "I almost forgot." He withdrew an envelope from his breast pocket. "You made another sale." He handed the envelope to Jake.

Jake smiled and took the envelope.

"Thanks," he said. "Thanks for everything."

"You're the artist," Forrest replied. "I'm just the middleman."

"The middleman?" Jake echoed. "Yes, I reckon you are. You're the Master's middleman."

A few rows behind them, Rudolph Townsend sat with his family. On his right was Carlton's future mother-in-law, Hedda James, with Bubba next to her. Camilla was on his left, and Laura, with Dixie Lee and Carlton rounding out the party. Next to Carlton was a bespectacled middle-aged man with dark hair and hazel eyes. He was wearing the collar of an Episcopal minister.

"Honey, look," said Camilla, nudging Rudolph. "There's Forrest in the third row, next to Mrs. Cooper."

"You're right," replied Rudolph. "I didn't know he was in town."

"He just arrived," said Bubba. "I saw him get off the train late this afternoon."

"Camilla," said Rudolph, "you have to get him to come over for a drink while he's here this time, or to supper. I'd like to get to know him better."

"You will," said Camilla with a smile. "He'll be your house guest for the wedding. He's a wonderful man, honey. I owe him a lot." She took his hand. "I wish you could have joined us the day after your—the cat burglar escaped. Forrest came over for coffee and we had a lovely long visit. But that was the day you had to go to Atlanta, remember? Mother called and invited Carlton to come, but he said he couldn't."

"He was a wreck," replied Rudolph with a grin.

"What do you mean?"

"Didn't they tell you?" said Dixie Lee, leaning forward in her seat to look at her future sister-in-law.

"Tell me what?" asked Camilla.

Carlton's firm hand pulled Dixie Lee back against her seat.

"Nothing, Camilla dear," said Laura. "All of us were quite shattered by the trial and then the escape. It was a terrible time. We all needed a little time to recover."

Dixie Lee smiled and took Carlton's hand possessively, thinking she knew the answer that Camilla did not know.

"Common barroom brawling," she whispered to her fiancé. "Honestly, honey, celebrating your release is one thing, but getting in fights is another. I was surprised at you. Won't you ever change?"

Carlton raised a satisfied eyebrow and smiled, as he remembered his condition after his fight with John.

"Not unless you marry me." he replied. His hazel eyes twinkled. "Even if you do, I'm probably ruined for good. It's up to you to reform ol' Carlton." He took her by the chin and looked into her eyes. "But you'll come through for me. You love a challenge."

Carlton gave her a peck on the cheek and settled back into his seat. He stole a glance at the stranger sitting next to him. The man did not return his glance, but arched one eyebrow and coughed. Carlton looked back down the row at Chief Bubba James. Carlton smiled broadly and nodded once, as if affirming a thought.

Rudolph looked at his brother, sitting happily with his bride-to-be. He smiled as he observed Dixie Lee. He wondered if she would ever know the truth about his love for Camilla. Maybe when they were old and gray, secure and settled in their ways, coddling a slew of hazel-eyed grandchildren, maybe then she would understand. He tried to picture Dixie Lee as a mature woman of his mother's age, or as a frail dowager in her seventies. Somehow, he knew she would never want to know the truth.

Dixie Lee felt Rudolph's eyes on her, and turned to smile at him. He gave her an affectionate wink and turned away. Dixie Lee watched as he took Camilla's hand and spoke softly to her. Poor Rudolph, she thought. Having to settle for second best. Marrying Camilla on the rebound. Everyone knew it. Dixie Lee sighed.

"Excuse me, darlin'," said Carlton, getting up and making his way to the aisle. "I'll be right back."

Dixie Lee nodded and looked back to the stage. She was still thinking about Rudolph and Camilla. Rudolph seemed happy enough with her, but Dixie Lee knew what was in his heart, what would always be there. Maybe in time, Camilla would make him happy. Dixie Lee wanted him to be happy, didn't she? Then why did she always feel such tension when she was around Camilla, such a sense of competition? Maybe she just wanted Camilla to make Rudolph a good wife. Camilla had better make him happy. She had just better.

Dixie Lee wondered what happened to Carlton. She turned in her seat and saw him a few rows down, talking to a dazzling blonde. Dixie Lee's blue eyes turned a little green, and she turned around in her seat in a huff. When the lights of the auditorium began to lower, Carlton made his way back to his seat and gave Dixie Lee a smile as he sat down beside her. Dixie Lee looked straight ahead. Her mouth was drawn up into a pretty frown.

"Who was that?" she asked.

"Maryscott Miller," replied Carlton. "She's a Charleston girl. Wayne Miller's cousin."

"How do you know her?"

"Hell, Maryscott and I go way back," replied Carlton lazily. "We were quite an item once."

Dixie Lee stiffened.

"And now?"

Carlton looked at Dixie Lee. His eyes were cool and he contemplated his fiancée with amused patience. It would be fun outwitting this she-cat for the next forty or fifty years. When at last she turned to him, he answered, "I invited Maryscott and her parents to the wedding."

Dixie Lee's eyes softened a bit, but she turned away, still pouting.

Carlton smiled. Careful, kitten, he thought, your claws are showing. Better pull them in. I'll clip them off before I'll let you scratch me with them. He nuzzled her softly and felt her relax.

The curtain parted and the show began. For the next hour, the audience was treated to a number of delightful acts. Tori, Jessie, and Boozie readied their props backstage, making sure that the face of the magic singing tree worked, its eyes blinking, its mouth opening and closing. Tori was to play a little girl lost in a forest. She comes to rest at the foot of the tree and sings of her sorrow. She falls asleep and dreams that the tree awakens and encourages her with a song of hope, and then points the way home with its branches.

When the librarian, Marianne Pittman, began her recitation of an original poem in front of the curtain, a couple of men from the barbershop quartet helped the girls move the chicken-wire-and-cloth tree into position at center stage. Boozie and Jessie climbed inside and tested the string control of the tree's face one last time.

Tori paced nervously at the side of the stage. She could do nothing further. Jessie would have to do it own her own. Maybe with Boozie there, she could manage.

Mrs. Pittman was speaking into the microphone.

> Then I wondered about the quickness of a moment,
> And realized that like my footprints,
> I, too, would be washed away.
> Soon the tide will come in,
> And no one will even know
> That I have been here, and walked this way.
> For I occupied only a tiny space
> For a fleeting moment
> Alone on a beach
> Somewhere in time.

Mrs. Pittman closed her notebook and nodded to the audience. She was met with enthusiastic applause as she exited the stage. This is it, thought Tori, as the podium was removed. The orchestra began to play Tori's song, and the heavy curtain parted. Tori's stomach wrenched, and she remembered her grandmother's instructions. She closed her eyes as the introduction played, and pictured herself as a child of five or six, alone in a dense forest, lost and tired. It worked.

Right on cue, Tori walked out in front of the audience. She walked first one way, then another, pretending to find one wrong turn after another. She came at last to the foot of the silent tree at center stage, and slumped down in front of it, on the green felt material that served as the grass. Tori wiped her eyes and began to sing her lament. At last she lay down and closed her eyes, pretending to sleep.

This was Jessie's signal. Inside the trunk of the magic tree, Jessie pulled the string and opened the eyes of the friendly tree's face. When the orchestra reached her cue, Jessie closed her eyes and opened her mouth to sing the words, but nothing came out. Boozie looked at her and nodded.

"Hurry," whispered Boozie, "the music's playin'."

Still Jessie could make no sound. She threw Boozie a desperate glance.

Beneath them, Tori cringed and tried to think of a way out. She stayed as she was, in her guise of sleep, and prayed.

Dr. Zdanis, the bandleader, knew the girls were scared, and led the orchestra through the melody of the tree's part, then said softly, "Again, from the thirtieth bar."

The orchestra began the tree's part again, and this time a strong clear voice rang out, as the mouth of the magic tree opened and closed in perfect simulation. Tori's eyes flew open in surprise as she recognized the beautiful high voice of little Boozie Brown. With a sigh of relief, Tori closed her eyes again.

In the audience, Mabel Potter looked at her husband in surprise. Mrs. Cooper smiled, recognizing the trained voice of her star pupil. All around them, the audience was stunned into rapt attention by the exquisite voice they heard, and everywhere folks turned to each other with nods of appreciation and approval. Such a voice had never been heard in Albany before, and from a child!

On stage, Tori pretended to wake, and looked up at the face of the tree in wonder. She stood up as one of the branches of the tree moved to the left, indicating the way home. Tori began to sing the chorus with the tree, placing her arms around it and laying her head to the trunk in a thankful hug. Then the song was over, and Tori waved goodbye to the tree as the orchestra began the final bars of the melody. The tree raised its branch in farewell, the music ended, and the curtain closed.

The audience was on its feet instantly with thunderous applause. Tori was ushered back out to center stage next to the tree, and the curtain was raised again. Tori bowed as the applause continued, and called to Jessie and Boozie, "Come on, come out."

Hesitantly, Jessie climbed out of the tree and joined hands with Tori. A large tear welled up in her eye.

"I tried," she said softly as the crowd continued to applaud. "I just froze up. It was Boozie. She sang, not me. They're clapping for her. What are we going to do?"

Tori smiled as the curtain came down a second time.

"We're going to confess," she whispered.

The audience was still clapping when the men came out to remove the tree. Tori ran over to the man in the fake moustache and said, "Wait. Raise the curtain one more time, please. Listen to them clapping. They want to see us again."

"You're a hit, all right, Honeybunch," said the man. "I can't see no harm in it."

He waved the other men off the stage and went back to the curtain. When the curtain went up, Tori walked to the edge of stage. She stood silently until the audience became quiet.

"Thank you for your clapping," she said, and the audience chuckled. "Jessie and I didn't mean to trick you, but Jessie was too scared to sing her part. A friend of ours sang it instead."

She turned to Jessie and motioned to her. Jessie went behind the tree and tried to coax Boozie out. The audience began to buzz. When Boozie did not appear, Tori ran to the tree. In a moment, a wide-eyed Boozie was pulled out onto the stage. Tori took her firmly by the hand, Jessie taking the other, and the three girls walked to the edge of the stage to face the stunned audience.

There was silence in the huge auditorium. This was a white school After a moment, a man in the third row stood up. "She was wonderful," said Forrest Neill, and he began to applaud. The man in the clerical collar sitting next to Carlton also stood up and began to clap. Then Laura, Rudolph, and Carlton, followed quickly by the rest of the audience, clapping and nodding in wonder that this tiny child could have so dazzled them.

Boozie stood with her friends and looked at the sea of white faces, standing and applauding her. Tori let go of her hand and stepped back a few paces, then Jessie followed suit. Boozie was left alone, and suddenly began to smile.

For a few moments, there was no division between black and white in Albany, Georgia.

TORI AND Mrs. Cooper watched as Paul drove away.

"Are you sure you want to stay with me another year, Tori?" asked Mrs. Cooper.

"Oh, yes, Meema," Tori answered. "It's only for a year. Then I'll be braver. You know I love Daddy, and I do want to live with him, really I do. But not right now. I can't leave you now, Meema."

It's all right, Tori," said Mrs. Cooper. "I understand, and so does your father. You've been through a lot. You just need some time. Besides, I have some plans that you could help me with."

"What plans, Meema?"

"I'm not sure yet," replied Mrs. Cooper.

"Do you mean about the money?"

Mrs. Cooper turned and looked at her granddaughter.

"Tori," she said, "we have more money now than we need. I'd like to use some of it to do something to help other people who are not as fortunate as we are. What would you think about that?"

Tori smiled and nodded her approval.

"What can we do, Meema?"

"I don't know, honey. I'm still thinking about it. The only thing I'm sure of is that I want to do something to help children."

They walked slowly to the house, arm in arm.

"I know, Meema. How about a music school?"

"We'll think about it, dear."

"How about a playground, with lots of swings and things?"
Mrs. Cooper smiled.

"We'll think about it," she said.

About the Author

Marjorie Bradford was born in Albany, Georgia, and raised in Uniontown, Alabama, where she was Queen of the Turkey Carnival in 1938. She attended Alabama College for Women (now the University of Montevallo) and then nursing school and became a registered nurse. After World War II, she worked at the VA Hospital in Montgomery, where she met George Bradford, a young doctor, who chased her until she caught him. They raised four sons and a daughter, all of whom graduated from the University of Alabama. Dr. Bradford died in 1983, and *Under the Same Heaven* was written in the years soon after his death. It is her first and only book, although she has written a number of fairy tales, children's games, and bedtime stories for her grandchildren. Mrs. Bradford acknowledges with gratitude the editing and significant contributions to the novel of her daughter, Betty Bradford Davis.